Zoe's Eyes

F. A. Turner

Rapier
PUBLISHING COMPANY

Zoe's Eyes
(2nd Ed.)
F. A. Turner

ISBN 978-1-946683-15-1
Library of Congress Control Number 2018954890

Published by
Rapier Publishing Company
Dothan, Alabama
www.rapierpublishing.com
Facebook: www.rapierpublishing@gmail.com
Twitter: rapierpublishing@rapierpub

Dedication

I dedicate this book to my Lord and Savior, Jesus Christ, who in 2017, woke me up early one morning and gave me this story to write. Lord, may your Glory shine through this!

To my mother, Sylvia Turner, who taught me how to be a woman of faith, strength, character, integrity, and to always stand up for what is right, even if it meant I had to stand alone. Thank you, Mommy, for raising me to be the woman I am today. Thank you for believing in me when it was hard to believe in myself. I love you with all my heart!

To my two best friends, my BFFs, my sisters April Matthews and Lisa Linton. Your love, support, and encouragement made me know you both have my back. The laughter we share and the "Sister's Network" that we text on to share our deepest secrets are special to me. God not only gave me the best sisters but the best BFFs a girl could ever have. I love you both!

To all my nieces and great-nieces, never allow anyone to put you in a box, or say you can't. Always dream big, the impossible, and then let go and let God give you the possible, which will lead you to your destiny in Him. I love you all very much!

To the many women, young and old, who endured and survived, or knew someone who endured and survived human sex trafficking. Never forget what happened, but focus on how you survived and came out to tell your story. Hopefully, through your story, someone will be saved from the snares of human sex trafficking. May God's peace and strength keep you looking forward and never backward.

To my editing team, thank you for all your assistance and patience.

To all women: This is our story because if it happens to one, it happens to us ALL!

Thank You!

The book "Zoe's Eyes" is a work of fiction that deals with the subject of sex trafficking. It contains graphic depictions of the ugly and brutal world of sex trafficking that may be troubling for some readers. While it is written to ensure the subject matter is compassionate and respectful to all, it may cause some readers who were victims of sex trafficking to struggle with its contents. Although it is something we should be aware of, discretion is advised.

Prologue

In a small village on the outskirts of Nairobi, Kenya, men dressed in guerrilla attire with bandanas over their faces to conceal their identity forcefully push a group of children along a dirt road. The children, girls, and boys of various ethnicities, Asians, Africans, and Middle Easterners, are told by the men to keep moving. The men finally stop the children in front of a parked truck on the side of the road. They shove the frightened and cold children into the truck as though they were cattle ready to be slaughtered. Once inside, a man slams and locks the truck's door. The children hear the door click. They look at each other but don't say a word. The truck drives off. It takes a couple of hours to reach its destination. The children try to sleep, but the long, bumpy ride keeps them awake. Suddenly the truck stops and the men get out. The children hear the voices, yet they continue in their silence. The oldest of the children, a small-frame, fifteen-year-old African teenage girl, peeks through a little hole and sees the men talking with some other men. They are speaking in a dialect she can't understand. She continues watching them. She quickly goes back to her place when she sees two men approaching the truck. The door opens, causing the children to adjust to the light that invades the darkness. Once their eyes adjust, they see more men. The new men are armed. The armed men tell the children to get out of the truck. "Quickly!" they shout, pointing their weapons at them. Another truck is waiting for them. Once again, like cattle, they are hurdled into the awaiting truck. Money is exchanged, and laughter permeates the air among the men.

Understanding what is happening, the African girl places her fingers to her mouth and whispers to the children to be quiet. The youngest, a little girl, begins to cry. The African girl pulls her close and places the young child's head on her small bosom. The child cries softly as the older female cuddles her. "Shhhh," she says as she strokes the young girl's hair to keep her quiet. Although she is only fifteen, she is now the mother of the group. Cuddling the young girl, she whispers, "This is the last night you will be a child. For tomorrow your innocence will be taken away." The rest of the children not fully understanding her words or what is going on, stare at the African girl. Their faces are blank, but their eyes portray the utter hopelessness they feel.

Eventually, they all fall asleep except the teenage African girl.

After a long drive, the vehicle comes to an abrupt stop, jolting the children from their slumber. The door opens, and once again, the light invades the darkness. "Get out!" the men's voices pierce the air. The children, still dazed from their sudden awakening, stumble out of the truck. Once outside, the men shove the frightened children with their weapons. "Move! Stand over there!" they yell, pointing to a spot where a group of women are standing. The children, in fear, quickly obey.

As the children move closer to the women, they realize the women are not women but young girls wearing too much makeup and dressed in scantily-clad clothes. The scantily clad-dressed girls look at the new recruits with sadness; some turn away. The men push them to help the new arrivals. "Help them," one shouts, pointing his weapon at the girls. With fear in their eyes, they quickly help the newcomers. No one says a word. The African girl tries to say something to one of the girls. The girl gives her a stern look. She understands and immediately keeps quiet. They separate the boys from the group. One boy looks back and smiles. The girl never sees him or the rest of them again. The African girl looks around the compound and sees a bordered wall surrounded by a concertina wire fence. She looks up at the fence and sees men in full armor gear securing the area. She takes a deep sigh, looks up into the sky, and says under her breath, "I will not cry! I will not cry!"

A woman in her mid-twenties comes out of a building. She looks at the new girls and immediately starts to separate them. Two men grab the young girl. She starts to cry. When the African girl tries to intervene, the woman slaps her to the ground. The little girl continues to cry as the two men drag her away. Everyone stares as the men drag the little girl away, but no one says a word. The woman tells the girls to take the new arrivals into a building that looks like an abandoned apartment building. The girls grab the new arrivals and take them into the building. Once inside, they separate the new girls by assigned rooms and floors. The woman tells them to help the new girls get ready for work.

One of the girls takes the African girl and an Asian girl to a room with a separate bath and toilet. "This is your new home," she tells them. Both girls look around the room, but neither says a word. She tells the girls to clean up and use the toilet. She picks out some clothes for them and asks, "What sizes do you wear?" They don't answer. She looks at them and says, "In the room are three mattresses on the floor." Pointing to the mattress farthest from the door, she tells them, "That one over there is my bed. You two decide on which one you want." The African girl shrugs her shoulders and looks at the Asian girl, "You choose first," she tells her. The Asian girl chooses the one by the door. The girl shakes her head and says, "That was a bad choice. You will be the first one picked when it's dark." The African girl looks at her and asks, "What do you mean?" The other girl says, "Don't you know where you are?" The Asian girl shakes her head, "No." The girl looks at the African girl and asks, "What is your name, and how did you get here? Were you sold like me, or did someone kidnap you?" The African girl says, "My name is Demee. My mother sold me." She tells them her story.

I was walking in the street in our small village, begging for money to buy food and medicine for my mother and siblings. A well-dressed man, which was uncommon in our village, approached me and asked me where I lived. He asked if I had any parents. He stared at me and told me that I was very pretty despite being dirty. I felt ashamed when he called me dirty. I told him we lived in the area where the most poverty-stricken people lived, which didn't say much because everyone in my village was poor. He asked me about my parents again. I told him my father was gone and my mother was sick. "What's wrong with her?" he asked. "She has tuberculosis," I said. He then asked, "How old are you?" I told him I was fifteen. He said, "Fifteen and you are not married? Why are you not in school?" I looked down to the ground, ashamed of my appearance, and whispered, "I have nothing to wear." He said, "Take me to your mother." I didn't want to, but when he told me he could help my mother and give her the medicine she needed to get well, I changed my mind. Even though I didn't trust him, I took him to my mother. I wanted to help my mother get well. We lived, all five of us, my mother, two sisters, and my brother, in a man-made shanty house. When it rained, the tin roof leaked. My mother was very sick, and the state of the house only made her condition worse.

When we walked into the small shanty house, my mother was lying on a mattress on the floor. The man looked at my mother and told me to get out. He reached into his pocket and threw some coins on the floor. My brother and sisters scrambled to the floor to get the coins. My mother nodded her head. She understood why he was there. She told us to get out. I looked at my mother and said, "Mama, whatever he has, we don't need it!" My mother told me again to get out, yet her voice was harsher. As I walked out of the house, the man looked at me and smiled. Under his breath, I heard him say, "She is a fighter. She will do well." He turned to talk with my mother. After what seemed like a long time, he left. I was outside by the door when he left. He smiled at me again when he walked past me. A cold, evil feeling went through my body. I shook it off and walked back into the house. My mother, no longer laying on the mattress on the floor, was sitting in a chair grinning. She had money in her hands. When she saw me in the room, she looked at me and said, "Demee, I have done you a great honor. The man that came here wanted you. I sold you to him." Shocked that my mother could do such a thing, I cried, "Mama, how could you? You know what they say on the streets? You know who these men are; we have heard rumors." My mother didn't care. Her mind was made up, and the deed was done. "No, you don't understand! This man will help you!" she said. "He will help me. Look at what he gave me! There is enough for my medicine and to care for the little ones. You must not be selfish, Demee."

My mother showed me a handful of money. "You must think of us all," she cried. "But Mama, what could a man like that want from me? He is a well-off man. What is he doing in this village? This slum?" "Demee!" my mother screamed in a high-pitched voice, "Please do not backtalk me. I don't have all the answers. You must do this for me so I won't die. If I die, what would happen to your brother and sisters? They will become beggars, and most likely, their lives will be a shadow of great distress!" I tried reasoning with her, "But Mama!" I cried. "What about me? I know I can't go to school now, but I plan to attend someday." My mother said to me, "Demee, look at me! Look at me! You are poor! How will you go to school? Tell me how?' "But Mama, please do not make me go with the strange man. I don't trust him." She looked at me and said, "It will be all right. He promised me that he would take care of you. He will bring you back to me in six years. You will be older and wiser." "But Mama how could you ask this of me? How could you? Do you know what he wants?" "Do you know Demee?" she asked me. "I have an idea," I told her. "I have heard the people in the slum talk about men like this. I have seen other girls who one day disappear and never return." Getting weary from the conversation, my mother said, "Demee, you don't have to like it, but do this for me. Now go while I rest. I'm tired." Those were the last words she spoke to me.

With tears in her eyes, the African girl continued to tell her story. "Once my mother's mind was made up, I knew there was only one thing left to do. I said to myself, 'I will not do this. I will run away. I will not go with him.' I was waiting until the night to run away. Night came, and as I started to run someone grabbed me. Before I could scream for help, a hand covered my mouth. I bit the hand as I tried to yell out for my mother. The next thing I knew, I was on the ground. When I woke up I was in another place. They called it a holding place. I thought I saw my mother as the vehicle pulled out. It may have been my imagination because I wanted my mother to come and rescue me."

The girl assigned to help them get ready listened to the girl's story with sadness. Her story was similar. She told the African girl, "You will learn to love it here. If not, it will be dangerous for you. To them, you are nothing but a lay. Some will feel guilty and try to be nice to you, especially the Americans. The others, just go in there and get it over with. I am lucky. I have learned to hide my emotions; some are not so lucky." Realizing it was getting late, she said to them, "Come on, let's get you both washed up," She paused and then added, "Before you meet your fate." Looking at the Asian girl, she asked, "How old are you?

"I'm thirteen," the girl answered.

"What country are you from?"

"China," the Asian girl told her."

Shaking her head slowly, the girl sighed, "Yeah, they love Asian girls here. Right now, they're a hot commodity. Me and you," looking at the African girl, "We're a dime a dozen." Pointing to the Asian girl, she said, "But you, it's getting harder to sneak you in. Sadly, you will be busy."

Suddenly, there was a knock on the door. Entering the room was the woman from the yard. Staring at the three girls, she said, "Less talking, and you," pointing at the Asian girl, "Hurry up and get dressed. Someone wants to meet you." She looked at the girl assigned to them, "Kiara, hurry up and get her dressed, or you know what's going to happen to you." Turning to the other two, she said, "You must be special. Only the special girls get this room." With a heavy sigh and an almost gentle smile, she added, "The clients here are much better than some. You," she pointed to the African girl, "Get some rest. Some food will be brought up to you. I will come for you tomorrow. But you! Staring at the Asian girl, she said, "I will be back in twenty minutes to get you. Oh yes, Kiara, make sure she is clean! Check her for lice and her private area to see if she's clean. Hurry!" With that, she walked out of the room.

Frightened, Kiara told the Asian girl, "Come on, I must get you ready! She's not nice when kept waiting. I worked too hard to let you take this away from me." Looking around the room, she told her, "It's not much at all, but it's the closest thing to a normal life for me. I get the girls ready; in return, I am rarely touched. By the way, what is your name?" she asked the Asian girl. "Fei Hung," the girl told her. "Good! I see you speak English. You will need it because some of the things they want you to do to them, you will understand and that will help you. Now sit down and spread your legs."

Kiara checked Fei Hung to see if she was clean as a shocked Demee watched. Satisfied with the results, Kiara helped Fei Hung get dressed. She knew the woman was prompt and would be there within minutes to retrieve the girl. Checking her once more, with sadness, Kiara looked at the girl and said, "Well, Fei Hung, we will be great friends because, after this day, I'm all you'll have. That goes for you, too, Demee. All we have is each other." Hugging the young Asian girl, she said softly, "Try to be brave."

"Is she ready?" yelled the older woman, barging in, this time not bothering to knock. "Yes, ma'am," replied a nervous Kiara. "Good!" The woman taking the Asian girl roughly by the hand, "Come, we don't have time. Time is money." Frightened, Fei Hung ran over to Demee, crying in broken English, "Please don't let her take me! Please, I'm afraid!" Demee grabbed Fei Hung and held her tightly. The woman approached Demee, her eyes fixed on her. She warned, "Your strong will could be your downfall. Now, let her go!" Demee, meeting the woman's gaze with unwavering defiance, released Fei Hung. The woman swiftly took Fei Hung and they left the room. Overwhelmed by a sense of helplessness and despair, Demee collapsed on her mattress, her sobs echoing in the room as Kiara, equally powerless, watched in silence.

Dragging a frightened Fei Hung, the woman stops at a door on the opposite side of the building. She opens it and forcefully pushes the girl through the doorway, quickly shutting it behind her. At the sound of the door closing, Fei Hung spins around. In a desperate attempt, she tries to open the door, screaming, "Please! Please! Help me! Please!" Hearing the girl's pleas from the other side, the woman pulls the doorknob towards her, preventing the girl from opening it. She finally releases it and, with a heavy sigh, walks away. Finding no escape, Fei Hung, weeping, looks around the slightly lit room. She sees a bed and a nightstand in the corner of the room. A lamp on the nightstand emits a slight glow that lights the room. In the glow, she sees three men sitting at a table in a corner. They appear to be drinking; one looks drunk. The men look at Fei Hung with salivating lips, ready to devour her on the spot. One of the men takes a big gulp of his drink and moves towards her.

"How old are you?" he asks her. She nervously answers, "I'm thirteen."

Grinning, he says, "You are just the right age." He turns her around and strips her clothes off. Staring at her naked body, he pushes her towards one of the other men in the room. The other man grabs her and takes his clothes off. He lays her on the bed. You can't hear her screams because of the other screams throughout the building.

Chapter One

Further south of the western corridor of Nairobi, Kenya, fifty miles outside the city limits, far away from the mainstream of the city's everyday hustle and bustle, yet not too far from civilization, a small but modern village lies hidden away where only a few know of its existence. The dense vegetation surrounding the village acts as camouflage. The village is not part of the safari, nor is the area considered dangerous; however, because of its location, very few people travel that far out of the security of the city's boundaries for fear of a lone wild animal roaming looking for its next meal.

To get to the village, you must take one of the city's main roads for forty miles, make a left when you get to a fork in the road, and continue on the road for ten miles until you come to a camouflage path. The path leads into the village. Only those who know it's there will notice the camouflage path. Although the village is small, it has a medium-sized commissary to purchase food, toiletries, and other supplies. There is a small eatery next to the commissary where the workers eat and relax. In the rear of the village there are several smaller buildings where the staff and volunteers sleep. At the far end of the village is the largest building, an apartment complex, where the children sleep.

In the midst of the village, you can hear the laughter of children playing. Their ages range from ten to sixteen, males and females; most are females. Many of the children when they arrived at the village were barely clothed; they looked lifeless, like zombies. Their little bodies suffering from malnutrition gulped down their food like they hadn't eaten in weeks. Some were so battered and bruised they had trouble walking. Unfortunately, many of the females, especially the older ones, were physically, mentally, and sexually damaged. Their emotional and physical scars were so deep that it would take a miracle from God to heal all their internal and external wounds for them to live a full, productive life. But thanks to the excellent medical staff, counselors, and support team, the children look peaceful and safe, running, laughing, and playing like normal kids.

From a distance, a young, beautiful African woman watches the children laugh and play. The sounds of the children's laughter bring a serene joy to her ears. As she gazes at them, she ponders on the journey she is about to take. She is not alone. There are three other people with the African beauty: a woman in her early thirties wearing African attire, a young Caucasian woman with sandy-blonde hair from America, and an African male. The male is in his early thirties, too. He's handsome with an athletic build. The African beauty and the Caucasian girl are both twenty-four. Like the African beauty, the three frequently stare at the children as they laugh and play. Although their demeanors are more serious and focused, the children's laughter calms them.

The woman dressed in African attire speaks to the three about the mission. The African beauty listens intensely. Unlike the others, she is from Nairobi, so the mission has a deeper meaning. She glances at the children once again. Her eyes portray her inner sadness. Looking up towards the sky, she softly says under her breath, "Father, not my will, but Your will be done." She thinks no one heard her, but the African male observing her hears her. He looks at the children. He sees their sad faces, too. He understands that life is cruel to the poor.

The woman in the African attire continues to brief the three about the mission. While she is talking, the priest comes over to join them. He says a few words before he blesses and prays for them. His prayer is interrupted because a young child is having an episode. In the middle of the prayer, he is called to handle the upset child. He quickly says amen and Godspeed, kisses them each on the cheek and walks away to tend to the child.

Camille, the woman in the African attire, looks at the two women and softly tells them, "It's ok to back down, even at this hour. God will deliver the girl. You don't have to worry about it if you don't want to go." The African beauty quickly blurts out, "No, we're ok." The other girl nods in agreement. Camille tells them to follow the path. "This area that we are in is safe. We are surrounded by Kenya's military and other international agencies that are in the fight with us. Right before you get out into the open be careful because that part of the area is thick. Make sure your phone's GPS is on. You have the number to call if you get lost or take a turn off course. Once you start, you are on your own. Other people know you are out there, but they can't assist you. They can't blow their cover. It will be too big of a risk. Remember, more are with you than against you. It's a dangerous mission, but we would not send you if we thought the stakes were too high or we would fail." They nodded, understanding the implication of her words. Camille hugs the two young women and then tells them she has to go to see about the young boy.

The African beauty stares at the woman as she walks away while the other two continue to talk about the mission. Deep in thought, she listens but doesn't comment. The man watches her. She is unaware of his stares. The American girl notices but keeps it to herself. The African beauty, yawning, tells the two that she is tired and excuses herself. They watch her as she leaves to go into the small house they share. They know she is going to pray. Once inside her room, the African beauty begins to pray to God about the journey. Praying without ceasing, satisfied, she soon becomes sleepy. "I know the Lord has heard my prayers," she says. She closes her eyes and immediately falls asleep.

After a while, the man and the young woman quietly enter the house. They see that the African beauty's bedroom door is slightly ajar. Looking in her room, they see she is sound asleep. The American woman tells the man that she is going to get some rest. He watches as she goes to her room, then turns back to stare at the African beauty sleeping peacefully on her bed. After a few moments, he goes to his room to rest. He knows when nightfall comes, it will be time to go.

The African beauty, deep in sleep, starts to dream. In the dream she is rescuing a child, but in the attempt, she is captured, sold, and killed. She feels the impact, a sharp pain, and sees a light, then someone touches her. She wakes up in a sweat. Panting, she looks around and notices that the room is dark. She looks out of the small window and sees it's pitch dark outside. She needs to hurry. The others will be waiting for her. She knows the children at the compound are safe, but there are so many that are not. She gets up, goes to the bathroom and washes her hands and face. Staring at her reflection in the mirror, she realizes she never finished the dream. She quickly reaches for her backpack, making sure she has everything, including some small toiletries and a few undies. She says a quick prayer and forgets the dream and goes out into the dark night to search for the other two. She sees them waiting for her at the gate and runs over to them. "I'm sorry. I overslept," she tells them. The male nods his head, "It's ok, but it's time to go." The three glance back one last time at the serenity of the village. The children are safe. An orphanage will be coming to get them by the end of the week.

The African beauty softly says, "Let's go."

Chapter Two

In another part of Nairobi, the men dressed in guerrilla warfare uniforms are celebrating. They just got paid, and to celebrate their sudden increase in wealth, they fill their lips with heavy drink. One man takes a sip of liquor and says, "We are fortunate that the younger girls and boys bring in more money." Another man raises his glass to his mouth and says, "The younger, the better the price, especially if they are virgins." He then begins to laugh, bringing the other men into an uproar of laughter. Their laughter fills the room. Everyone appears to be having a good time except one man. The man looks around. Troubled by what just took place, he shakes his head and walks out the door, slamming it behind him as the laughter continues in the background.

Another man watches the man walk out the door. Concerned, he follows him out the door. He waits until they are not within earshot of the others and asks, "What is it, Laos, my friend? What's bothering you? That woman you left behind in the last city we were in?" Laughing, he slaps his friend on the back, "I told you she was too much for you to handle."

Pulling away, the other man says, "No, no, man. I'm fine. I just needed some space away from all the drinking and celebration."

The other man laughs heartily, "You, from drinking? Since when do you stay away from the drinking?" Slapping him on the back once more, he urges his friend to go back inside, "Come on, let's go back inside, man. The others want to celebrate the money we got from the kids we just hurled in and the money we will get from that little bundle. With all that money, we'll be set for at least a month."

Laos looks at his friend and frowns, "Kosi, are you sure she isn't touched? The little girl? Did you check her? Her uncle said she wasn't as he greedily took the money, but from the looks of him, he could have touched her. It's not uncommon for his kind to touch their family." Kosi, confused by his friend's questions and concern for one of the captives, replies, "No, she's good, Laos. I had one of the women check her out from head to toe. She's still a virgin. A very frightened virgin, I might add, but still untouched for now," he says, grinning, showing his missing side tooth.

Laos sat down on the steps and stared at the ground. His mind was troubled. He was tired of the lifestyle he lived. Remembering how he almost got killed on this last job, he asks, "How much is Seian getting for this job? We risked our lives, so he had better get enough for all of us. It's getting dangerous with the law always on us. We can't trust anyone. Everyone wants into the business!" Kosi sits down next to his friend. "What business? Sex-trafficking?" Taking a wad of money from his pocket, he shows it to Laos, shrugging his shoulders, and says, "Hey, it pays the bills. And anyway, I don't hear you complaining when you're getting paid."

"Yeah," says Laos, "but I don't do no little girls. Besides, if I want sex, I get it free or buy it from a woman. Why would I want a little girl when I could have a woman who knows what she's doing?"

"Are we getting emotional, or do you just need a drink?" Kosi asks.

"Man, you sound like a fool! A drink? Man! This was a heavy one! I never thought we would get this low or it would get this low. It's perverted. Did you see the look on that little girl's face when her uncle sold her to us? She didn't say a word. She trusted him. Can you imagine what he told her parents? And when we took her, she still didn't say a word, but her tears said it all. What did he say to her that made her not scream?"

"Nah, she didn't trust him," says Kosi. "She was scared of him. He probably told her he would kill her, her parents, and her siblings if she screamed or said a word."

Shaking his head, Laos cries out in frustration, "Sick, just plain sick! It's sick! I know virgins come with a higher price, but young girls, sheesh, man! What have we become? Savage animals? What is the reason behind this evil, this craziness?"

Getting tired of the conversation, Kosi gets up. He looks up at the dark sky and says, "Yeah, it is sick and crazy, my friend, eh? But in their rationale, these sick, perverted men want them tighter. The tighter, the better it is for them. They don't care about the girls. They want them younger because they can control them." Becoming annoyed by his friend's sudden caring demeanor, he says, "Laos, you knew what you were getting into when you started in this business years ago. You didn't say anything about the money, the booze, and all the women you could pay for. And now you get holier than thou on me! Sheesh! What gives? Why now?"

Laos puts his hand on his head and sighs heavily, "Yeah, I know, but I never thought it would get to buying young girls…." Kosi stops him, "So buying and selling girls are okay as long as they're not little girls. Since when did you get a conscience?" With a heavy heart, Laos whispers, "When I saw the look in the little girl's eyes. That look will haunt me for the rest of my life.

Gently putting his arms on Laos' shoulder, Kosi tenderly said, "Come on, Laos, you need a drink. You're thinking too much about this. It's just one girl. She's poor. You and I know people don't care about the poor. We got work to do. Besides, don't let Seian catch you talking crazy like this. He will stop trusting you or, worse, kill you. Too many cutthroats wanting to get into the business. You know he's fair with us, and he doesn't touch the girls. That's why his clients trust him. He has many wealthy patrons from all over Africa, the Middle East, and some parts of Russia and China who buy girls from him. These clients don't care! It's not their daughters. They say their wives are no longer desirable, so they want fresh meat. Their wives don't know or don't care either. They shop, dine, and look lovely. I bet they are happy they don't have to put up with their husbands. Besides," he fumed, "It's the poor, the underprivileged, so don't get uptight about them. Why should you care? They didn't care about us when we were poor! You knew this was happening in our village. It was a way of life for us…a sad, miserable way of life." With a deep sigh, he said, "But it was the life assigned to us."

Now becoming riled up, Kosi swore, "Man, Laos! Now you're getting me upset!" Pulling his friend by the shirt, he said, "Come on, Laos, let's go back inside and get a drink. The guys are probably looking for us. You know they can get uneasy if they see Seian's two most trusted men talking among themselves. Come," opening the door to the tavern, reaching for his friend's hand, "Stop letting this get you down. You and I know the sad truth. That young girl and many like her were already doomed when they were born in war, famine, poverty, drugs, and diseases. They were born castaways. You know the rich and the well-to-do don't look twice at them.

Laos stood up and brushed off his pants, apologizing, "Yeah, man," he stuttered, "I'm…I'm…sorry, my friend, eh! It was getting too heavy. Someone or something was messing with my mind. I'm straight now. I just had a moment of consciousness." Slapping Kosi on the back, grinning, he said, "Let's go inside and get that drink and maybe some loose women. My treat, eh?" Opening the door, Kosi grinned. He was glad his friend was back to rational thinking, "Now you're talking, my friend! Let's go wet our mouths; suddenly, it's dry as a desert."

"Yeah," Laos replied. However, as he walked through the door, he couldn't shake the feeling of the little girl's eyes. Looking up into the sky, he whispered under his breath as he and Kosi joined the other men still celebrating, "Lord, have mercy on my soul."

Chapter Three

Leaving the safety of the village behind them, the three walked into the still night. As they concentrated on the task before them, the eerie sounds of the darkness infused the air. Their silent thoughts only intensified the darkness that surrounded them. The African woman's thoughts were on the mission, the American's thoughts were on the mission and her friend, and the male's thoughts were on the African beauty. Pretending to recon the rear for any suspicious activity, particularly any lone animal looking for its next meal, he let the two women walk ahead of him. In his deceit, he slyly gazes at the African beauty. He watches her as she walks the sparsely vegetated path, moving her hands like a small machete, slashing the few tall plants in her way to make the path clearer. She moves like a tigress in the night hunting for its prey: smooth, unnerving, and full of courage. She is graceful, well-educated, and beautiful, he thinks to himself. What is she doing out here on the outskirts of Nairobi, Kenya? Far from the safety of the city. She should be somewhere else, but not here. She doesn't belong. She doesn't look like the female who would go about saving the world. Her nails are too manicured, and her speech is too articulate. He grins at the thought of her as a Marvel comic heroine. "No," he mutters, "She looks as if she should be on holiday with her family or perhaps her boyfriend." He shakes his head, "She definitely doesn't fit the norm." He continues to stare at her from a distance. They call her Zoe. Her name means life. He murmurs, "There is something about the Zoe girl."

Catching up with them, looking up at the stars, he says, "Seems like the weather is perfect for us." They agree, and once again, silence infuses the air. They walk for hours until they reach the road and see the car. They sigh simultaneously. The first task of the mission is completed. As if on cue, they look up into the sky. Daybreak had come. They had been walking in silence and didn't notice that the night had turned into dawn; the first rays of sunlight showed through the darkness. They head for the vehicle. The male gets into the car first to check for any traps. He gives them the okay as he reaches under the mat. He finds the key in the center like Camille said it would be. Retrieving the key, he shows it to them and says, "Ahh, the key. Well, ladies, everything is going as planned so far. Shall we go and finish the mission?" Both women nod their heads and get into the vehicle. Zoe gets in the front seat. The American settles in the back and closes her eyes. She needs to rest. Zoe, determined to stay awake, keeps her eyes open and alert, watching her surroundings. This was unfamiliar territory to her. She wanted to know where she was at all times. The male watches her from his peripheral view but doesn't say a word.

It was only a three-hour drive, but it seemed like an eternity for Zoe as they drove in silence the entire drive. Finally, arriving at their destination, a small yet modernized town just over one hundred miles from the village, Zoe tapped the American on the shoulder, calling out her name. "Patty, we're here. It's time to get up." Waking up from her slumber, Patty yawned loudly, smacking her lips, "I have to get used to this time zone." Yawning again, she said, "Anyway, I needed the rest." Zoe smiled and assured her that it was ok. "Don't worry, my friend, we all do. I wished I could, but I found myself wide awake." She knew why she couldn't sleep but kept it to herself. She kept thinking about the dream. She didn't dare tell the others, especially the male. She knew Patty would be full of questions and concerns. The male, she thought, would probably ridicule her, calling her foolish, or, worse, a child for being so paranoid. For some reason, she didn't want him to think of her as a child out of her league. She didn't know why she felt this way, so she kept the dream to herself.

Parking the car at the edge of the town, they grabbed their belongings and started walking, searching for the first location to meet up with the first point of contact. Zoe noticed that the town had a few mid-rise buildings. It's a very quaint town, she thought to herself. Although the roads were primarily composed of hard gravel and dirt, they were surprisingly leveled, making walking and driving on them easy. After walking for thirty minutes, tired and hungry, they were about to sit down for a quick rest when the man pointed to a building, a small, charming store that specialized in exotic fruits from China and other parts of Asia. Brushing the sand from his pants, the man takes one last look around him and says, "Well, we are here. It's now or never. You can still back out if you want to. No one will look at you differently." Ignoring his words, the two young women walked past him. Opening the store door, Patty turns to Zoe, laughing, and says, "It's ride or die chick!" Zoe laughs, "So American!" The laughter was what they needed to calm their fears.

Entering the store, still laughing like two best friends, they looked like tourists. The male watches them as he enters the store after them. He hesitates and looks around. He is looking for the first point of contact. Inconspicuously, he shifts his eyes toward a middle-aged man assisting customers. He walks over to Zoe and discreetly shares the news with her. They browse around pretending to buy something as the man waits on the customers. They approach the man when the last customer leaves the store. "May I have a Fanta orange soda?" asks Zoe. He stares at them and replies, "How about a Coke instead." He knows who they are. He was informed that they would come today. As he is about to speak, a customer walks in. He puts his hands to his lips, signaling for them to be quiet, as he watches the customer browse the aisles. They pretend to hang out, browsing through the store, picking up items, laughing and joking. So they don't appear suspicious, they talk about school, social media, and current world events. When the customer leaves, they go to the cash register to pay for their drinks and snacks. The man looks down as he takes their money. He looks around to make sure no one else comes into the store. Once he is satisfied, he begins to speak softly. He tells them how sex trafficking is getting worse in the town. "They are going after girls between the ages of twelve and fourteen, sometimes even younger." The three listened intensively, nodding their heads as they watched the door for incoming customers.

He tells them about the young girl abducted a few days ago. "The girl is around eight or nine. So far, the word is she hasn't been touched. Her price is high because these sick people want them at this age now." He shakes his head. "They are getting them younger, ruining their precious lives. I don't know why, nor can I understand this cruel world where kids are exploited in this manner. They are so innocent, so precious. It's not fair because of their poverty or class structure. I want to kill them all, but I am doing what I can to stop it the best way I know how."

The man asks him, "Why are you suddenly getting involved? Why the change of heart now? You know if they find out about you helping, they will kill you...no questions asked." The storekeeper looks solemnly at Zoe and Patty and says, "For them." Zoe, feeling the urge to cry, holds back the tears. He continues, "Like so many in this town, I am tired of what I see. We may not have much money, but we are good people. We leave others alone and care for our own with what we have. Our town is very charming, very hospitable. We get tourists from all over Kenya and other parts of the continent and the world. The climate is always pleasant, particularly during the warm season. It's a lovely place to visit and live. Unfortunately, with all its beauty and charm, there is a dark side to our town: human and drug trafficking. We see too many young girls and boys from all ethnicities come and go. It finally got to me! It just got to me! It got too much for me to see and not do anything. Yes, it's dangerous, but what does one do? Die a man of valor and courage, or live as a coward?"

Zoe, touched by his sincere honesty, reaches out to him, "You are kind and good, sir. God will surely bless you."

Gazes at Zoe and Patty, he says, "Please be careful little ones. They are saying someone is in the loop, a mole, but they don't know who the person is. Just be careful. Here, take this." He gives them a couple of candy bars. "It's not much, but it will come in handy, especially if you are in a place where nothing is available. There is one thing I must tell you. It's ugly, but I must tell you the truth, even if it's ugly…." He pauses, tightly shutting his eyes; they can see the tiredness in his eyes. He opens his eyes, and in a whispering tone, he tells them, "Some of the men when they are drunk, they rape the girls before they are sold. Even though it's a good possibility that they have not touched the young girl, please pray that she will stay that way. If she is not rescued, the inevitable will come…but" stammering, "I pray that she has at least a couple more days of innocence." Pointing to Zoe and Patty, he asked, "By the way, I wonder why they are sending you two?" With an air of defiance, Patty boldly tells him, "They are not expecting women to take on, as you say, a billion-dollar business." The storekeeper, troubled by Patty's comment, gravely tells her, "Do you know how serious this is? Regardless of why they selected you, the men in this business do not care that you are women! You can all get killed, and no one will ever find your bodies."

Zoe, trying not to be alarmed by the man's words about the possibility of being killed, quickly tells him, "God will take care of us! He called me to do this, so I know He has us." The storekeeper unfliched by Zoe's words, calmly says, "I know your God will take care of you. He is my God, too. It's still dangerous! The people you are dealing with have no God! They don't care about you!" The man seeing the women getting upset over the storekeeper's words, sharply tells him, "Sir, no need to frighten them! They have already counted up the cost and made up their minds. Now, please tell us where we are to go next!" The older man glared at him with an odd stare. He was about to say something, but Zoe intervened, taking control of the conversation. She didn't want the two men to get into a confrontation. Remembering Camille's words about the mission being too vital, she knew they couldn't afford to be compromised by a little disagreement.

"Sir, please excuse my friend's lack of tact. You have been kind. We appreciate your concern. But it's getting late. I know you are looking out for us, but we must get to our next destination. There is a child who needs rescuing." He smiled at Zoe, and with fatherly eyes full of concern, he said, "The diner is a couple of blocks from here. Someone at the diner will give you more information. You must ask for the ham sandwich and coke. Don't ask me why, but the ham sandwich is their specialty. It's not an ordinary ham sandwich. It's like an American ham sandwich, cascade with three different kinds of cheese. The tourists go crazy for it. And since you are considered tourists, you must act like them so no one will presume otherwise.

"Ugh!" Zoe cried, shaking her head in disgust, "Ham sandwiches! I don't like ham."

"Regardless, you must ask for this," said the storekeeper. "You are college students on holiday. Don't forget this!" he warned them, his eyes reflecting his worry. Just then, customers entered the store. He rang up their purchase as they laughed, pretending he said something funny. Putting the receipt in the bag, the storekeeper gazed at the man as he handed the bag to him. The man nodded his head in thanks as he took the bag. As they were about to leave, the storekeeper gently grabbed Zoe's and Patty's hands, "You are both beautiful. It's a dangerous thing you do. Please be careful." In unison, the two women thanked him. "We will," they assured him. He was about to say something else but decided against it and let go of their hands. The male didn't say anything but watched the interaction among them. Saying their last goodbyes, the storekeeper watched them as they walked out the door.

Once outside the store, they heard someone calling Zoe's name.

"Zoe! Zoe! Zoe! At last, I have found you!"

Chapter Four

Zoe turned around at the sound of her name to see her handsome and only older brother Jaheem running towards her. "Jaheem, what are you doing here? How did you find me?" she screamed. Both relieved and happy to see him, she gave him a big sisterly hug. Jaheem, recovering from the shock that he found his sister, welcomed her hug with equal affection. Breathing a sigh of relief at seeing her, he suddenly became overwhelmed. Forgetting where he was, he pulled away from her embrace and started yelling, "You crazy fool! How did I find you? You forget I work for the government and I...." He stopped in mid-sentence as his eyes darted to the two people standing a few feet away. Dropping his voice to a whisper, filled with a mix of worry and suspicion, not wanting to talk in front of them, he took her by the arm and gently pulled her away. "Zoe, we need to talk!" Reluctant to tell them Jaheem was her brother, Zoe mumbled, "Please forgive me, this is my...uh...uh, my friend." She then introduced Jaheem to them, not revealing their names, "These are my friends. We are on holiday." Seeing her brother becoming impatient and hoping they would understand, she apologized, "Ummm, excuse me, but I need to talk with my friend. The man gave her a strange look. Apologizing again, she looked pleadingly into their eyes, "It will be brief. I promise." Before they could comment, Jaheem forcefully took her by the arm and walked away. Embarrassed by her brother's roughness, Zoe tried to hide it by smiling at the two as he pulled away. She didn't want to cause a scene, but inside, she was seething. Gritting her teeth, she softly yelled, "Jaheem, what are you doing here? Are you trying to blow our cover!"

Struggling to keep his anger under control as well, Jaheem lashed out at his little sister. "Don't be foolish! You have no cover! Zoe, what are you doing? Mother and Father have told me of your crazy antics. Quitting medical school! Are you mad?" Offended by his choice of words, Zoe angrily replied, "First of all, I'm not a crazy fool and I'm not mad! Only dogs get mad! And what I'm doing is not crazy!" Jaheem, seeing his sister getting upset, mentally took a step back to regain his composure. After all, she was his little sister, his only sibling. He didn't want her to get upset. Affectionately pulling her close, he said, "Zoe, please forgive me. I'm only concerned. I love you! I don't want anything to happen to you. It took a lot of pulling and scheming to find you. I had to go through some serious red tape! You must stop this and go back home at once! Go back to medical school!" Feeling her anger rising again, Zoe pulled away from her brother. "Jaheem! Don't you see I can't! God called me to do this. I can't explain!"

Controlling his temper, a method he learned in interrogation school, Jaheem said in a calm voice, although he was anything but calm, "Called by God, you say? What is this foolishness you are talking about? God didn't call you to die! Are you willing to die? Because if you continue this mad journey, you will!" Zoe," he begged her, "It's too dangerous for you. Listen to me! Go back home!" Zoe, deeply upset with what he said, pretended it didn't upset her. Courageously, she replied, "Then I will die knowing the Lord is pleased with me. Jaheem, courage without fear is not courage. Everyone God calls is afraid, but we answer the call, even though we are afraid. With tears in her eyes, she cried, "Jaheem, I didn't ask for this. I didn't choose this! He chose me. Many are called, but few are chosen. I didn't ask to be chosen."

Trying not to make a scene or get his little sister further agitated, Jaheem took a deep inhale, then exhaled slowly. He had to maintain his composure. He knew when his little sister quoted the Bible, she blocked out everything and everyone. He wanted to make sure she understood this wasn't church or Sunday school. The people she was going up against didn't read the Bible. Their faith was in the almighty dollar, and they would kill if someone came against them and their god. He gently whispered, "Zoe, please listen to me. Please! I know you have faith. We all do. You come from an affluent family. You are beautiful, educated, and enrolled in medical school, one of the finest in the world. You have traveled the world. Don't you see that you are wasting your life doing this?"

Zoe knew he could never understand. How could he? She didn't understand. "Jaheem, please try to understand!"

"How can I understand?" he replied, his voice filled with frustration. "You are wasting your life. You want to help others? Then finish medical school. Become a doctor and go to the impoverished places in the world. They need doctors. You can help this way! You will still be making an impact, and you will be safe!"

"Yes, but that is not what I'm called to do! Don't you understand? Anyway, it doesn't matter what you say. My convictions are strong, and you can't sway me. You know me! You know how I am! You and Father always say I'm my mother's daughter." Smiling at the thought of her words, she realized she was no longer upset. They both knew that she was going to go through with it, regardless of how hard he tried to talk her out of it.

Shaking his head, he looked at her soberly, "Yes, I know how strong your faith in God is. I also know how strong your beliefs and convictions are. You forget I've watched you growing up. I know what you believe is true, and that's what matters. Yes, you are our mother's daughter, but you are more than that, Zoe. I'm afraid for you, my dear, sweet, beautiful sister. I don't want you to die!" Getting choked up, he said, "I love you and need you, my 'little pumpkin girl.'"

Zoe smiled upon hearing him call her by his pet name for her. Hoping to sound brave for her big brother, she said, "If I die, I die, but just think of my crown." She then gave him one of her biggest smiles that always won him over. It worked. Embracing each other tightly, neither wanting to let the other go, Jaheem, breaking the silence, whispered in her ear, "Zoe, please consider stopping this madness. Upon hearing his words, Zoe pulled away from his embrace, and in a mellifluous voice, she said, "Jaheem, I'm going to be okay. Now please say hello to Mother and Father when you see them. Mother was in full rage when I told her. Dad, on the other hand, tried his best to understand. I don't think he truly does, but he trusts me, and more importantly, he trusts God. I believe he has made his peace. However, it … ummm," she paused, "Tell them I'm safe." She decided not to tell him about her dream.

Staring at the two people patiently waiting for her, "Zoe," Jaheem asked, "Who are they? Do you know them very well? Do you trust them?" Zoe looked at the two individuals and answered him. "The girl's name is Patty. She is from America. The man's name is Kato. He is a refugee from Sudan. He is on our side. And yes, Jaheem, I trust them. Now, I have to go. I love you!" she said, growing impatient with the conversation. Jaheem, understanding her words, sighed. He knew there was nothing else to say. They embraced one last time, affectionately kissing each other on the cheek before letting go. "Here, Zoe," said Jaheem, pulling money out of his pocket, "Take this. It's enough to get you some decent food and to get you back home if you change your mind." He choked at the last words. He knew she wouldn't. "Don't forget that I love you!" he said, his voice breaking, as he handed her the money. She took the money and gave him one last hug, "I love you more!" she said as she walked away. Halfway, she turned around, taking another look at her brother, she blew him a kiss, "I'll see you again." "Yes, in heaven," he said with a heavy sigh. Tearing up, he saluted her with the salute they shared as children. She returned his salute, "Yes, definitely in heaven, but before then. I will see you on this side of glory. I love you," she called out as she walked toward the two people waiting for her. Jaheem stood watching her and whispered, "I love you too, my beautiful, sweet, stubborn sister," but it was on deaf ears; she was already with the two people named Kato and Patty. He looked at her one last time before walking away.

Patty watched as Zoe and the strange man interacted with each other.

Although she couldn't hear what they were saying, she knew from their body language and facial expressions they cared for each other deeply and that the man was greatly concerned for her friend. The male watched too. However, his primary focus was on the surroundings. He wanted to make sure nothing was out of the ordinary. Zoe was thankful that they were patient while she spoke to Jaheem. She walked up to them, trying to forget about her brother's remarks about seeing her in heaven. She looked back and saw that Jaheem was nowhere in sight and became a little scared. She asked the man, "Kato, are you afraid?"

"Every day, but it still doesn't stop you. You get used to it and do it afraid." Then, gazing into her eyes, watching for anything that would cause alarm, he said, "You know you can turn back now. No one will think less of you. We will understand."

She turned away, glancing around one last time, hoping to see her brother. He was nowhere in sight. Disappointed, she sighed, "No, I'm in this too deep. I can't. I counted up the cost and came to this... if I go back and live, I will be just living because I didn't trust God enough to believe Him. I didn't try. I don't know why I am here, but I'm here. My courage is not as strong as yours, Kato. Honestly, I'm a little scared, but as you say, do it afraid."

"Then why don't you…" Patty asked.

Before Patty could finish her sentence, Zoe interrupted her, "I can't. I wish I could, but I can't. How about you, Patty? Aren't you afraid? You can quit right now, too. Why don't you?" With a sober stare, Patty replied, "I can't. Like you, I have my reasons. I just believe with your faith, my reasons and his," pointing to Kato, "courage, knowledge, and wisdom, I believe we will be okay. That's what keeps me going day by day!" "Me too," echoed Zoe. Relieved they could openly talk about their fears with each other, Zoe suddenly became courageous. "Come on!" she cried, "I'm hungry and dirty, and the need to shop is in me, even if it's only to get some new undies, which is the most important thing for me at this moment. A shower, new undies, oh yeah, and a latte from Starbucks." She laughed at the last remark about a latte from Starbucks."

Happy they changed the gloomy conversation, Patty laughed, too. "Oh, no!" said Patty, "Not just any latte, but a double pumpkin spice latte with extra foam, and I dare not forget a large American pizza with the works and with extra mozzarella cheese! Oh, and, of course, some underwear!" She winked at Zoe, and like schoolgirls, they started giggling. For a brief moment, it felt like they were actually on holiday without a care. Kato looked at them and said out loud, "Silly girls." He didn't care if they heard him. He was agitated at the two. "Didn't you know what you were getting into?"

Zoe paused, ignoring his condescending tone. "No. If I had, I wouldn't have said yes. I wouldn't have done it. That's faith," said Zoe.

"Uh-huh, that's the same way with me," said Patty, still daydreaming about a pizza.

Kato, genuinely concerned for them, said, "Alright. Come on. Let's get something to eat. I know the place where we need to go. The storekeeper put a note in my hand as he gave me the change from our purchases. It's only a little ways from here." Pointing in the direction they needed to go, he said, "It's a couple of blocks in that direction. We should get there by lunchtime, which is a great time. There will be many people there from all walks of life." Looking at Patty, he continued, "We won't look too conspicuous. This is a tourist town, especially during this time of the year." Taking one last look around, searching for anything suspicious or out of the ordinary, with a sense of urgency, he said, "The journey ahead is long. We have a child to rescue and every minute counts. We have to get going!" Zoe and Patty turned in the direction he pointed. The three, pretending to be college students on holiday, walked toward the direction of the restaurant that would provide them with the information they needed. From afar, the storekeeper watched them through the store's window. Unbeknownst to all of them, another set of eyes was watching in the distance.

Chapter Five

"Jaheem, did you see her?" Anna asked impatiently, her voice filled with concern as she anxiously awaited her son's response.

"Yes, Mother," he said wearily, "I not only saw her but also spoke with her. She was with two others, a young woman about the same age as Zoe from America and a male, most likely from the continent. Zoe said he was from Sudan, but I seriously doubt that."

Feeling somewhat relieved that he was able to find and speak to Zoe, Anna bombarded him with questions. "How is she doing? How did she look? Is she okay?"

Well, from what I could see, she's okay. She looks okay! Like she had no cares in the world…like Zoe," he said sarcastically. He was still upset at his sister but more upset that he couldn't talk her out of her madness.

Anna, frustrated, angry, and tired, ranted at her only son as if it were his fault. "What is she doing wasting her life? She had it made here!" Throwing her hands in the air in exasperation, she shrieked, "Look around! A big, beautiful home, servants, the finest clothes, and the finest dining. She doesn't need or want anything. Whatever she wanted, it was at her beck and call. Her father and I are successful, well-renowned surgeons sought after all over the continent and Europe. We paid good money for her to study in America at the prestigious Johns Hopkins University. She was to become a doctor and be part of the family business." Tearing into her son, blaming him, "What is wrong with the two of you? Where did your father and I go wrong? First, you dropped out of law school to become a government servant, and now my only daughter is lollygagging around who knows where with people we don't know, trying to save the world!"

Jaheem, deeply hurt and blindsided that his mother was somewhat blaming him, quickly reverted to his training on maintaining calmness in hostile environments. "But mother," he scowled, glaring at his mother, wondering how she turned this against him, "Isn't she in the family business? She is not actually helping the sick get well as far as medical, but she is helping the sick. Isn't that what you wanted?" He knew he was being cynical, but it wasn't his fault. He was as frustrated and upset as his mother. Since he last saw Zoe, he rarely had any sleep.

Rolling her eyes at her son, Anna shouted, "You know very well what I am talking about! Don't be condescending, Jaheem!"

Grinning, she knew him too well, he thought. His voice now softened with empathy as he spoke. "Mother, I'm not being condescending. I was being cynical. But regardless, I'm just as scared or frightened for her life as you and Father. I know my sister. I know her faith is strong. Very strong! It's stronger than all three of us. I have to believe God has her. Right now, we must stay focused and believe." Jaheem wanted to believe that Zoe would be okay. He wanted to believe that they would see her again. He wanted to, and yet he knew there was a possibility they wouldn't. The world of drug and human trafficking was brutal. Innocent people were killed every day. So, for his mother's sake, he didn't want to upset her any further with the grim reality of Zoe's future. Turning off his thoughts, he continued to listen to his mother ranting. He can see the tiredness on her face. He could see that she hadn't slept for days. Her eyes were tired and worn from the lack of sleep. He knew his mother as well and was familiar with her moods. And this was one of the worst. The entire house got out of her way when she went on a rant or tirade. They were rare, but when they came, they came in a strong force. However, in her defense, her emotions or moods were justifiable. Her only daughter was out there trying to fight against a billion-dollar business with a three-man army. She was in danger; worse, there was a possibility that they would never see her again. Of course, his mother was worried and concerned about her only daughter. Realizing what his mother was going through, he took off his business face and put on his son's face. He felt her fear and uncertainty but, more importantly, her pain.

Anna realized the mood had changed. No longer raising her voice, she calmly said, "I know what you are saying is true; however, she is my daughter—my only daughter! Our friends ask about her. I dare not tell them what she is doing."

"No, Mother, you can't! They will kill her for sure!" he warned her. Anna, irritated with her son's response, started to raise her voice again, "Oh, don't be foolish! I'm no fool! I won't say anything! Anyway, I'm too embarrassed to tell them she is wandering around in the jungle playing savior." Jaheem smiled. The war was back on. "But Mother, she is saving, well, not literally, but she is saving children from the sex trade, from human trafficking, which is noble, don't you agree?"

"Ughhh! Jaheem, don't start with that again!" shrieked Anna.

At that moment, Anna's husband, JaMar, entered the room. He could see the strained look on his wife's and son's faces. Attempting to calm the room's atmosphere, he hugged his wife and kissed her on the cheek. Looking at his son's wearied face, he knew he had no luck with Zoe. "Son, I take it that you have seen your sister, and from the likes of your mother's stance, she is not happy with the results." Jaheem wearily looks at his father. Slumping in the chair, he shakes his head, confirming his father's words. JaMar lets out a small sigh, "I take it Zoe is not coming back no matter how hard you tried to persuade her, eh?" Jaheem, with a sense of resignation, solemnly answers his father. "No, Father, she isn't." "Ah yes, that is my Zoe," said JaMar. "Is she well?" asked JaMar. Relieved his father came to his rescue, he replied,

"Yes, Father, she is well. And yes, Zoe is still Zoe. Stubborn as, what do you always say? Ah yes, a mule."

Irritated at her husband for being so calm, Anna asked, "JaMar, aren't you at least concerned? Here I am ranting and raving, and you are calm as the morning sun! Really JaMar!" she said bursting into tears. JaMar gently reaches for his wife and pulls her into his arms, "Every day, Anna! Every day! I won't stop until I see my Zoe's beautiful face walk through the door. I pray and ask the Lord to keep and protect her and have His guardian angels to watch over her until she is safely back in our care…and," he said looking at his wife… "and if something should happen to her, to give me the strength." Burying her face deep in his chest, Anna let out a gentle sob, "Don't talk like that, JaMar! Please don't! I cannot bear to hear that kind of talk!" Turning to her son, she said, "Like you, Jaheem, I tried talking sense to her; it was useless. Your sister, when she believes in something, is like a steel wall, and nothing can penetrate that wall. When she makes up her mind, it's made up."

"Mmmm," JaMar grinned, looking down at his wife, whose head was still resting on his chest, "My dear, I wonder where she gets that from?" Anna looked up at him. "Ahhh," he winked at her. "She is just like you, isn't she, Jaheem?" They both laughed, but Anna didn't find it amusing. "No! This is different. In this case, she is not like me. I would have the sense not to do something as foolish as this, something so insane, or something that could get me killed. I know she is not like me. No, in this case, she is not mine. She belongs to God. God has her. She belongs to Him. She believes He is telling her to do this!"

With that revelation, JaMar quietly said, "Then, my dear wife and son, if God has her, we must trust Him. After all, before she was ours, she was His. I remember when Zoe came home and told us about wanting to help in the fight against sex trafficking. And now she is doing something about it. Regardless of what happens, she is making a difference. My dear, isn't that what we raised our children to do? To make a difference." Frustrated at the two men, Anna replied, "I know what both of you say is true. It all makes sense, but common sense is thrown out the door when it comes to my Zoe. I miss her. My heart aches for her. You both will never understand the love a mother has for her children." Weary of the conversation and at the two men, Anna walked out of the room, murmuring aloud, "I must go wash my face. I need a breath of fresh air."

Jaheem breathed a sigh of relief as he watched her leave the room. Now was a good time to share his concerns about Zoe with his father. "Father, I didn't want to share this with Mother, but I'm concerned about Zoe. That world is brutal, and Zoe is a mere child. She has been sheltered from that side of humanity."

JaMar nodded. He understood Jaheem's underlying words. "Son, we must stay strong despite how we feel." JaMar remembered the day Zoe told them that she was quitting medical school.

Chapter Six

"What do you mean you are quitting medical school in America to do something so ludicrous and downright insane? You don't know anything about that kind of life! You were brought up without any needs or wants. And now you're leaving a prominent school like Johns Hopkins University School of Medicine to do some hair-brain idea like this?" You're talking foolish, Zoe!"

"But Mother, you don't understand. It's not a decision I'm making lightly. I truly believe God has called me to do this," her voice filled with unwavering determination as she tried to reason with her mother about her decision to leave medical school. But her mother wasn't listening to her reasons.

Furious with Zoe and her decision to quit medical school, Anna shouted, "God didn't call you to do this, Zoe! He doesn't call you to do foolish things! He would not lead you down this path. I can't believe you're even considering this, Zoe!"

"Mother, you always taught me to pray and ask God for His will for my life. It's not like I won't finish medical school. I'm just taking a break, that's all. I promise I will go back," Zoe reassured her.

Anna, throwing up her hands in exasperation, asked, "When? When, Zoe, pray tell me when?"

"When it's finished," said Zoe, looking away from her mother's angry glares. She took a deep breath and tried to calm herself; she didn't want to upset her mother any more than she already was. "Mother, please try to understand. It's not like I woke up one morning and believed I was superwoman. I never imagined that I would one day fight the evil men who abduct young girls and boys and use them as sex slaves. I didn't. I didn't know anything about sex trafficking until I attended the meeting. I tried to get it out of my mind, but a week later, after I attended the second meeting, I felt the Lord leading me to do this."

"Humph! So now the Lord speaks to you, Zoe? You expect me to believe He only spoke to you out of all the people who attended the meeting! Now you are delirious! God doesn't speak like that—like a mad person! Zoe, you are wasting your life!"

Trying to remain calm and not get upset with her mother's choice of words, Zoe boldly challenged her mother, "Am I wasting my life to try to help another person live? Am I to stand back in my lap of luxury and do nothing, especially with what I know now? You and Father didn't raise me to be like that. You always told me to be a doer, not a talker. Well, Mother, I am doing!" Pleading with her mother, hoping she would understand, "Mother, they are helpless children. Surely, you have heard or read about this in your circle?"

Insensitive to Zoe's words, Anna looked at her daughter and slammed her fist on the table, "Do not use my words against me! This is not what I meant when I told you and your brother to follow your hearts! All I know is that my daughter, who has less than two years to finish medical school before she starts her internship, wants to parade around in the jungle playing some American GI Jane with who knows who, doing who knows what to try to save the world. Zoe, this is not Hollywood, where they yell cut when the scene is not going well. No, my dear, this is real. You don't get second chances!"

"I know, Mother. I know this is real. And I won't be in the jungle. We don't have jungles in this part of the land."

"Don't get smart with me, Zoe!" screamed Anna. What will I tell my friends? What will I tell your family when they ask of you? You know I can't lie. What do I say? She is off saving mankind. Or how about this? She has been looking at too many Marvel superhero movies since she moved to America, and now she believes she is one of them. The only difference is she has no power!" Shaking her head in frustration, Anna walks out of the room, speaking in her native language.

Watching her mother leave, Zoe whispered under her breath, "You are wrong, Mother. I don't need superpowers. I have the greatest power. The Lord is with me." Looking up at the ceiling, she said out loud, "Lord, how can I make her understand when I don't understand? Are you sure this is what you have called me to do? I don't know the first thing about what you are calling me to do."

"Who are you talking to child?"

Zoe turns around and sees her father. Relieved, she goes to him and hugs him. Smiling, she says, "Father, I guess you heard. I am officially crazy. Or that is at least what Mother thinks."

JaMar smiles and hugs his daughter. "Do you think you're crazy?" he asks her.

"No…but I must admit I'm terrified."

"Why?"

"I don't know. What's really crazy is that I am more terrified of not doing this than doing this. If you can possibly understand what I am trying to say."

He sits down, puzzled by her words, "Explain yourself, child."

Sitting beside her father, Zoe tells him, "I don't know if I can."

"Try."

"Well, Father, I'm scared. Petrified! But deep down inside of me, really deep, if I don't do this, I feel like I will never experience my true life's purpose. Father, everything was planned out for me since the day I was born. You and Mother have made a good life for Jaheem and me. I should be satisfied. I should feel happy and blessed. In my mind, I want to finish medical school and become a doctor. That is what I always assumed I would be: a doctor. My life would be full, no cares or worries." JaMar raised his eyebrows as she mentioned no cares or worries. Zoe gave her father a big smile, "Okay, okay, you know what I mean. I mean, I know what I would be doing. I will be traveling with you and Mother in the family's business. Money wouldn't be an issue, which means fewer worries or concerns. It would be easy to do, yet I can't, not now anyway. Maybe later. For now, it's a voice within leading me. I wish I could shake this feeling, but I can't. It's too strong."

As Zoe spilled her heart to him, JaMar was conflicted between being a proud parent and letting her go or being her father and telling her she could not go. He knew if he told her she couldn't go, she wouldn't. But what would be the cost? He would win initially, but eventually, he knew he would lose, and worse, he would lose Zoe. He pondered in his heart and finally told her, "My dear, the reason why you can't shake this is because God never operates in feelings. When God calls you, your feelings go out the door along with your will. It's in your eyes. Your eyes will always have the answer."

Knowing her father was blessing her, Zoe breathed a sigh of relief, "But Father, I'm so frightened and afraid. I don't know how to do this."

JaMar took her hands, "Zoe, I taught you always to pray and let God lead you. I never thought in my wildest dreams that He would lead you this way. I've always known you were special, so full of life and courage. You were always lively and strong-willed," he grinned.

"Don't forget opinionated," she laughed.

"Ah, yes, opinionated, but you get that from your mother, eh? Speaking of your mother, Zoe, give her time. It's hard for her to fight the will of God. Believe me, she will try, but in the end, we know, and she knows that she will lose. I guess all those attributes I just said were for such a time as this."

"Do you think she will finally see the big picture?" Zoe asked, hoping her mother would be okay.

JaMar gazed into her eyes and softly said, "To be frank, no. She will never see or believe what you see or believe. You are her daughter, her child. Her job, or sacred mission is to nurture and protect you and fight against anyone who tries to hurt or harm you. Even God. She has done well in the past, but this time, she is fighting a losing battle. You can never win against God."

Understanding what he said about fighting against the will of God but not about her eyes, Zoe asked, "What do you mean there is something about my eyes? I don't understand."

"You will, my dear. You can't see clearly now, but soon your eyes will be the gateway to the path you must take."

Not understanding everything he said, she asked him, "Father, what do you see and believe? Do you see what I see and believe what I believe?"

"No, Zoe. Everyone on this earth must carry their own cross. Anyway, does it matter if I can't see what you see?"

Shaking her head, "No, it doesn't. In the end, I have to obey Him."

Yes, I know," he said, his voice mixed with pride and sorrow. With a heavy heart, he told her, "Zoe, as your father, I am extremely proud of your decision, yet also filled with concern. I know, daughter, that God has you, and that will give me the peace I need until I see you again. Whether it will be on this side of heaven or the other side."

Zoe, overwhelmed with tears of her father's blessings, hugged him. "Father, I love you! And it will be on this side of heaven! I promise! I'm still scared, but knowing I have your blessings makes it easier for me." Giving him a peck on the cheek, she said, "Thank you, Father!"

JaMar, overcome with emotions, cleared his voice. "I know. Come on, let's get something to eat. What would you like?"

"A peanut butter and jelly sandwich!"

JaMar looked at her strangely, "Peanut butter and jelly? What gives?"

Shrugging her shoulders, she told him, "I don't know. I had my first PB&J sandwich in America. I have been craving it since. Don't ask me why?" she laughed.

Shaking his head at her innocence, he said, "Hmmmm, PB&J! Really?" Cocking his head, "Of all the delicacies you could choose from, you choose peanut butter and jelly…only in America." JaMar started laughing.

With a sad look, Zoe said, "Father, I have to leave tomorrow."

"I know, Zoe, I know," sighed JaMar as he tried to hold back the tears. He reached for the bread to make his daughter a PB&J sandwich, silently praying it wouldn't be her last.

Chapter Seven

The three walked toward the restaurant in silence. Patty, getting a little anxious, pulled out the chocolate candy bar the storekeeper had given her from her pocket. Grateful for the delicacy, she asked if they wanted a piece. Kato and Zoe shook their heads no. Shrugging her shoulders when they refused, she took a bite of the chocolate candy. In awe of how much the young woman liked to eat, Kato asked, "Patty, how could you eat that now when we're on our way to the restaurant?" "Hey," she cried, "I like to eat something sweet when I'm nervous, and chocolate has always appeased or calmed my nerves." She popped another piece in her mouth. Seeing his disapproval stare, she said, "Dude, don't judge me; just let me eat this in peace! Besides, who knows when I'll eat another piece of chocolate, so I'm enjoying the moment."

Focused on getting to the restaurant and what her brother said, Zoe wasn't paying attention to their conversation until she heard Patty's last remark about enjoying the moment. Patty is right, she thought. They didn't know when they would get to eat again. Hopefully, this would be a piece of cake, and soon, she would be back home with her parents eating all the ice cream she wanted. She smiled because ice cream was her weakness.

"Patty," Kato said firmly, "I am not judging you. Just be careful." Sighing, he wished he'd never agreed to this mission. "Two foolish young girls," he said under his breath. Observing his posture, Zoe remembered what her brother had said about the dangerous territory they were treading. She prayed that they didn't get too careless as Kato tactfully implied. Deep in thought, she didn't hear Patty's question about the man she was talking to outside the store.

Finishing up the candy bar and licking her hands, Patty repeated the question. "Yoo-hoo, Zoe, can you hear? This is the second time I asked you who was that handsome, hottie of a fine man you were talking to? By the looks of you two, you are more than friends."

Coming out of her trace, Zoe sheepishly looked at the other girl, "Huh? Oh, I'm sorry, Patty," she apologized. "I was deep in thought. What was your question again?" "Yeah, I could see," said Patty, wiping her hands on her khaki cargo pants. "Again, for the third time, who was that handsome man you were talking to outside the store? I wasn't going to ask, but hey, what we're doing, we can't have any secrets between us." Zoe smiled at her friend, "Oh, yeah, as you say in America, 'My Bad'. And that hottie, as you put it, is my older and only brother." As always, he was being very protective of me. Can you believe he came to take me home as if I was a child? How insane is that? Me, almost twenty-five!" Humph!"

Kato also noticed the two but didn't say anything until now. "Well, at least you have someone who loves you enough to try to talk some sense into you," he said dryly. His words reminded Zoe of her brother's, causing a touch of annoyance in her. "Kato you sound like my brother! Just so you know, Msee, Patty and I are not children!" she snapped.

"Touché," Kato replied in a child-like voice, mocking her. Then, in a more serious tone, he said, "Listen, you two, I didn't mean any harm. We have to be together if we're to accomplish this mission. Agreed?" They both shook their heads, "Yes." "Look, Zoe," said Kato, this time more affectionly, "Your brother was probably telling you how dangerous it is. He was only being a big brother trying to protect you. I know I would if you were my sister." Looking at the two young women, with compassion in his voice, he gently said, "It is, you know. It's very dangerous!" He was genuinely concerned for their safety. He understood how dangerous the mission was. He wanted to make sure they knew what they were getting involved in. It was still time to turn back. Grateful for his sincerity and half-cocked apology, Zoe smiled at him. "Thanks, Kato. It's nice to know you care about us. Sorry, I kinda snapped. And yes, my brother informed me that it's dangerous. He also said that there was a possibility…." She couldn't continue, yet they knew what she was going to say next.

Curious about Zoe's parent's stance on what she was doing, Patty asked, "Zoe, how do your parents feel about you doing this? Mine don't know the seriousness of what I'm doing. I told them, but I kept it on the low so that they wouldn't get too uptight. If anything happens to me, my grandmother knows all the details of the mission. She will inform them. My parents wouldn't understand. Besides, I don't think they would care per se. Don't get me wrong. They love me very much. They would be terribly hurt if something should happen to me. It's just their way. When you are a blue-collar family, you look at life in reality and not through rose-colored glasses."

"My father is with me," Zoe told her. "He doesn't understand, but he supports me. He knows that I don't have a choice. He said it was something about my eyes." Shrugging her shoulders, "Whatever that means!"

"What about your mother?" asked Patty.

"My mother," Zoe cringed, remembering the last conversation with her mother, "That's another matter. To put it mildly, she was extremely upset. I think she's more upset that I didn't finish medical school so she can brag to her friends about me. She wanted me to go into the family business. My parents are renowned surgeons and expect me to follow in their footsteps."

Kato sneered, "Yes, it's nothing like upsetting your parents and not going into the family's business. Class structure at its best."

Zoe was about to respond, but Patty seeing another confrontation on the horizon, quickly changed the subject. "Kato, tell us what you know about the little girl. I know we've been briefed, but there must be more to the story you are not telling us." Zoe, relieved Patty had sensed a storm brewing between her and Kato and changed the subject, joined in the conversation, "Yeah, Kato. Do you know where she is? Or are we just searching for a needle in a haystack?" Kato, also happy to change the subject, answered Patty's question. "No. They abducted her last week. She is with the traders from the Niobium village. They are very skillful but not so bright."

"What do we know about the young girl other than her age?" asked Patty. She and Zoe were horrified when the storekeeper told them the young girl was eight or nine. When Zoe heard the girl's age, she gasped loudly. "My God! What have we become? What can a man do with a child that young? She's just a baby! They will kill her or emotionally scar her for life. Either way, she is dead!"

With a frown, Kato replied, "Unfortunately, there is a high ransom for her. She is considered new and fresh. Besides, they don't look at the age. The person who is paying for her will probably keep her until he is ready for her and then sexually molest her until she is no good for anyone."

"How do you know they will not touch her?" Zoe asked. She wanted to be sure.

"The rumor on the underground is that the person who purchased her paid a hefty price. The money is so good they won't touch her. Again, they're not the smartest, but they're not stupid. I guarantee that if they harm the young girl, they will end up dead."

"Why are these men doing this?" Zoe asked him. She wanted to know.

Kato knew Zoe wouldn't be able to comprehend the harsh realities of the world of sex trafficking. Maybe later, but not right now. To satisfy her questions, and for the sake of them both, he gave them a general perspective they could understand. "Many cultures feel women are inferior and they are only here in this world for sex, to have children, or whatever the needs are in that culture. In some cultures, women have no voice. If they speak out, their family can beat or kill them without repercussion. Unfortunately, sometimes men who molest young girls do it so they won't molest their own children or family members. It's perverted, I know. It's about the class structure and the need to feel powerful. The victims, the innocent children, or poverty-stricken adults are powerless." Kato paused briefly. Looking into Zoe's eyes, he continued, "That's what I meant about class structure. I didn't mean to offend you. If I did, please accept my apology again."

Seeing his apology was genuine, Zoe gave him a small smile that said, I forgive you, no worries. Kato smiled back at her. However, she was still not satisfied with his response, "Regardless of how they consider women inferior, how can they justify their actions?" she asked.

"I have news for you, Zoe," he said, "It's been happening for a very long time. This battle is old. The sex trafficking trade is a billion-dollar business. Every day, young girls and boys from all over the world, even in America, are forced into sexual slavery.

Disgusted, Patty cried out, "I just can't understand how people could do this! What kind of monsters would harm innocent little children?"

Kato frowned, "You would be surprised by the who. People you would never imagine, all types: Caucasians, Blacks, Latinos, Mexicans, Africans, Asians, professionals, athletes, doctors, lawyers, politicians, entertainers, and I am sad to say, even the clergy. Some less developed countries don't have money to help their people. Where do you think the money is coming from? Many of the girls are from countries in Asia, Africa, the Middle East, Europe, and also South America. The runaways you never hear from again, most likely, were sold into sex trafficking. There is no eloquent way of telling you the harsh realities of this world. For many, like the little girl, it is their life."

"But Kato, why do they want the young girls?" asked Zoe, still deteremined to pull out the truth from him. Kato's gaze met hers. He understood her innocence. She was not ready to hear what she wanted to know. "Zoe, you don't want to know the truth. Not yet, anyway."

"But I do! " she pleaded.

Kato quickly diverted the subject, "Come on! We must get going. It's quite a journey ahead, and we have to get to the restaurant to meet our next point of contact." Seeing the restaurant up ahead, scanning the area, in a low voice he said, "I feel something in the air."

Patty looked around. Suddenly anxious again, she asked, "What do you see? Did you hear anything? Do you think the police know anything? Do you think they have informants?"

"No," Kato replied to her questions. "As you Americans say, all is quiet on the Western front. But something is definitely happening. I can feel it. It's too quiet. As for the police, most likely they know something, but money pays, and when money is involved in this business, so is corruption." Realizing he was causing them to be a little frightened, trying to sound cheerful, he said, "Don't worry, God always has a ram in the bush. Besides, we are students home from school on holiday. No one will know the difference. See, we are here!" Pointing to the restaurant ahead, he smiled, showing his beautiful white teeth, "There's the place."

"Zoe," whispered Patty so softly that only Zoe could hear, "Aren't you a little nervous?" "Petrified," Zoe whispered back. Attempting to calm her friend's fears, even though her fears needed calming, Zoe reassured her, "Don't worry, Patty. God has us both. When I get scared, I scream under my breath, Jesus, Jesus, Jesus! And then a peace comes over me. Maybe that's what you need to do, or find out what calms you. Patty closed her eyes and silently whispered, Jesus! Jesus! Jesus! under her breath. Zoe, touched by the moment, let out a small sigh. Suddenly, her fears went away. She had a peace. She knew what she was doing was the right thing to do. They walked in silence the rest of the way.

Reaching the restaurant, tired and relieved, Zoe let out a small shout. "We are here! Now we can eat some real food and chill a bit. I don't know who we are to meet, but for now, I just want to sit down, eat, and rest my mind." Pulling out the money Jaheem gave her from her pocket, she announced excitedly, "My treat! My brother gave me money for food. I hope it's good!"

"Your brother! Well, good for him!" Kato said mockingly.

Zoe ignored his mockery, "Yes, my brother. So it's my treat. And suddenly, I'm famished.

"Me too," echoed Patty.

Zoe laughed at her friend. "Patty, you just finished a candy bar. How can you be hungry?"

"Hey, I told you when I get upset or need to calm my nerves, food is my comfort."

Zoe nodded. She understood perfectly. "Ice cream is mine," she told her.

Grinning, Patty replied, "That's why I knew I liked you the first time I met you." She put her hand up and shouted, "High-five!" They gave each other a high-five. "I love me some ice cream, too," said Patty. "My favorite is Blue Bell Cookies and Cream. It's hard to get in Baltimore, but I get it where my grandmother lives. That's the only store I know that sells that particular brand."

Kato was amazed at how they always talked about food. Shaking his head, he asked, "Do you two talk about anything besides food?"

Smiling, Zoe answered, "Yes, but right now, food is the most important thing to us." Patty shook her head, "Yup!" He smiled at them as he opened the restaurant's door, "Ladies, shall we go in?"

Zoe and Patty, in unison, said, "We shall."

Chapter Eight

Several days had passed since Zoe announced she was leaving medical school to pursue a life living in the jungle, as Anna called it. JaMar wished she were only living in the jungle. He trusted the jungle animals more than humans. Animals only kill when they are hungry; death would be instant. In the world his daughter was involved in, death would be followed only after torture, and for his beautiful Zoe, the thought of what could happen to her if she found herself in the wrong place or with the wrong people worried him. His conversation with his son Jaheem about the underworld of sex and drug trafficking didn't ease his mind. It only caused him to worry more. He didn't let his wife know how concerned he was about their daughter. He had to be strong for her, as he was for Zoe when she told them the news.

Marveling at the beautiful home he and his wife labored to build, he couldn't help but wonder what Zoe could possibly want, desire, or need. "Everything she needs is right here," he said out loud. Their professions made it comfortable for both of their children. They didn't spoil them, but rarely did they go without. Such wealth in his country was not rare but not as common as it should be for the true natives of the land. Many of his peers were servants, manufacturing laborers, or worked on the big farms for mere pennies compared to their bosses, even though Kenya had vast wealth in natural resources.

Growing up borderline poor, his mother, a teacher, and his father, a carpenter, instilled in him a mindset that he could be anything he wanted to be. The only limitation was in him. His parents saved and sacrificed to send him and his only sister to medical school. His sister Dalia, an obstetrics-gynecology physician, practiced in America. She visited them at least once a year. He frowned thinking about his sister. Zoe was to stay the summer with her in Colorado.

He knew he wasn't supposed to question God, yet looking around at the empty house, he couldn't help it. He knew no matter what, he raised Zoe with a God's conscience. From the moment she could talk, they taught her about Jesus. Unlike her brother, Zoe was captivated by the stories in the Bible. She prayed all the time. Even as a little girl, she prayed for others. Yes, she was different. He couldn't help smiling. She was just like Anna, her mother.

JaMar was instantly attracted to Anna. He remembered the first time he laid eyes on her. Watching her from afar, his first impression of her was a beautiful firecracker. She was well-learned, articulate, witty, and passionate about their country's politics, and more importantly, she was all business. He knew from the moment his eyes glanced in her direction he wanted to get to know the five-foot, three-inches firecracker. As luck would have it, she attended the same medical school as his sister, Dalia. He had promised Dalia he would attend a lecture with her that day, so he trotted off to the campus searching for her. Unable to locate Dalia, he checked the lecture hall to see if she was already there. That's when he saw her. She was talking to her colleagues. Forgetting about his sister, he watched the woman he called Firecracker take her seat in the front of the classroom. Finding a vacant seat in the back of the hall, he continued to watch her engrossed in her books, taking notes. Every few minutes, she would look up from her notes, ask a question, or comment about the topic the professor was speaking on. She was like a bullet charged from a gun penetrating its target. The professor appeared as if he was sweating when she asked a question or when he called on her to speak. JaMar, not one to stare or stalk, couldn't take his eyes off the beautiful woman. Oblivious to the lecture, he heard someone call out his name. It was Dalia. She had come in late and also found a seat in the back. After the lecture, greeting his sister with a warm embrace, he asked her, "Who is the beautiful firecracker that had the professor sweating bullets?" Dalia laughed, "Oh, you mean Anna. Yes, she's a pit bull. That's the name we call her." Seeing him frown, Delia let out a hearty laugh. He loved it when his sister laughed. It was jolly like Santa Claus. "Don't be shocked, JaMar. She likes the name. She knows she is a pit bull." "Well, she is more like a firecracker to me," he said. "Hmmm," laughed Dalia, teasing her brother, "I see your interest is piqued. Would you care to meet the …uhhh…firecracker?" "Yes, I would," he replied. Dalia took him over to meet Anna, who he discovered was practicing to be an OB/GYN like his sister.

As Anna and Dalia discussed the lecture JaMar stood quietly listening. He hadn't heard any of the lecture. His mind was on the firecracker. Anna informed Dalia that she had to get to class, reminding her of another lecture later that night. Disregarding his sister's snickers, he turned to the beauty and politely asked if he could escort her to her next class. She hesitated initially, but seeing Dalia's wink, she smiled and accepted his invitation. As they approached the building where her class was located, he got up the nerve and asked if she wanted to get a quick bite later that night. Anna smiled but politely refused. Not accepting her refusal, with persistence, he asked her again. This time her smile turned to a yes. She informed him that she usually refused dates; she was focused on her schoolwork and becoming a doctor. "My parents sacrificed a lot for me to attend this university." Grinning, he told her that his parents had also sacrificed much for him and his sister to attend medical school. She smiled at him and walked to her class.

He waited for her class to end and afterward, they walked over to the campus cafeteria to get something to eat. Engulfed in conversation, they found out they had a lot in common. Both were inspired to be professional physicians with their own practices. As far as social status, they both came from poor villages. His family worked as local workers, whereas her father was the local constable. Money was still tight for Anna's family, but her father's position brought many perks around town. It took a lot for her parents to send her to school. She didn't want to disappoint them. She was the first in the family to attend college. The rest of her siblings attended trade school. She made that very clear to JaMar.

They continued meeting weekly, attending lectures and dinner afterward. After a few dates, JaMar realized he was falling in love with the beauty. Although Anna also loved him, she wasn't interested in a long-standing relationship. However, the more they got to know each other, the more persistent JaMar became. She finally said yes when he proposed to her the third time. Anna made him promise that they would finish their internship and start their practices before they would have kids. Overjoyed that she said yes, JaMar agreed to her requests. He would promise her anything as long as she said yes to be his wife. They wed in a simple yet elegant ceremony after medical school with only close family and friends in attendance. His sister Dalia was his best man. "After all," JaMar said, "She was the one who introduced me to Anna." Now, they both were successful surgeons with flourishing practices, a beautiful home, two beautiful children, and not a care in the world, that is, until now. With a heavy sigh, he closed his eyes, reminiscing how pleasant and calm their world was only days ago. Deep in thought, he didn't hear his wife enter the room.

Still grieving over Zoe, Anna, looking tired, found her husband in the same state she was in. "Ahhh, there you are, JaMar. I see that your eyes are closed. You must be thinking or praying, or both." With a lopsided grin, he said, "No, my dear, just thinking." It was all he had done since Zoe left. "Where have you been?" he asked. Although some lines on her face weren't there a few days ago, she was even more beautiful since the day they met. He could tell she had been crying because of the wetness around her eyes.

"You sleep and think. As for me, I go into the garden to sit and look up into the sky. Sometimes I watch it from dawn to dusk to dawn again. I find myself doing this as of late. It calms me."

"Yes, I know all too well," he replied. "Thinking calms me."

Knowing they had the same conversation many times every day since Zoe left, Anna, still trying to grasp Zoe's decision about quitting medical school, asked, "JaMar, what does she know about living in that world? Zoe never lacked anything in her life. Why didn't you stop her?"

"How?" He was tired of the same conversation, yet for the sake of his wife, he went along with the flow, even though he knew where it would lead.

"You are her father. She would listen to you."

"Listen to me?" he laughed. Looking affectionately at his wife, he said, "Do you listen to me? She is just like you, stubborn as a mule, as Jaheem said."

"Be serious, JaMar. This is no laughing matter. We are talking about our daughter."

"Yes, but you remember, before she was our daughter, she was His daughter. Our responsibility was to raise her to follow her heavenly Father."

"JaMar, don't get deep on me. I believe in God. I go to church. I pray! You still should have stopped her!" Her voice cracked as she was on the verge of crying again. Blowing her nose with the tissue in her hand, she cried, "It seems like all I do is cry since Zoe left."

JaMar with a blank stare on his face, said, "I couldn't stop her. She had that look in her eyes."

Anna stared at him as though he was mad, "Look? What look?"

"You know the look she gets when she knows she is right. I'm talking about that strong conviction she gets about something before she gets that look. When she gets that look, you can't stop her. She is like a herd of elephants. When she was little, we thought she was stubborn. Remember when she was adamant about something, and nothing we said or did would change her mind?"

"Ah, yes," Anna recalled. "Like the time Getty got sick. She looked at Getty and right away said Getty was sick and that he needed to go to the vet immediately."

"We didn't believe her, but she was persistent."

"She started crying. Then she got her jacket, swooped Getty in her arms and started towards the door. When she opened the door, I asked her where she was going. She said she is taking Getty to see the vet, Dr. Okoye. I told her the vet was ten miles into town. She looked at me and said, 'Well, I should pack me and Getty a lunch.'"

JaMar grinned, remembering the incident, "Yes, she finally wore you down."

"Yes, I was very exhausted that day." Anna remembered the day as if it was yesterday. "It was a busy day at the practice. We went to see Dr. Okoye, and she was right. The doctor said our cat would have died if we had waited another day. He had a virus and had to take antibiotics for three weeks in his food."

"Well," JaMar said. "That's the look I am referring to. Not stubborn but determined. Her eyes say, please believe me. I know what I am saying. I know what I'm doing."

"Well, I still don't like it! I still don't understand!" Anna fumed. "You and Jaheem should have stopped her foolishness!"

Seeing his wife becoming agitated again, JaMar calmly said, "Sometimes, Anna, my dear, we don't have to understand. Sometimes we just have to trust and believe." "Humphhh! Well, I still don't like it," muttered Anna walking out the room." JaMar watched her leave. Shaking his head, he whispered softly, "Yes, Anna, Zoe gets it from you. You are both firecrackers!"

Chapter Nine

Zoe, Kato, and Patty entered the crowded restaurant. As Kato predicted, it was bustling with locals and tourists. Observing the surroundings, with a smirk, he laughed inwardly. You could quickly tell the tourists. They studied the menu as if they were searching for something exotic to order. They often asked for exotic game meat, such as ostrich, crocodile, zebra, giraffe, or gazelle, and were disappointed when they were not on the menu. They were surprised by the food selection. Other than the different cultural foods and spices, the locals ate the same food as everyone else. "Of course, our food is healthier," he snorted. Tourists often amused him, especially tourists from Western countries. He found it amusing that some people still view Africa as one vast Third World country with backward plumbing and primitive living conditions, even in this day and time. Although some countries struggled and were considered primitive by Western standards, Africa is a continent of many prosperous and thriving nations. It was unfortunate for them they couldn't see the continent's majestic beauty. Shrugging his shoulders at their ignorance, he searched for a table close to a window.

Zoe scanned the restaurant. Seeing people from all over the world relaxing and enjoying each other's camaraderie made her smile. She was proud of her country and its beauty and history. She loved America, but her identity came from Kenya. Looking around, sensing a calmness in the air, everyone appeared on holiday. They were sipping fresh pineapple juice and Cokes, leisurely eating their meals while relaxing in the coolness and charm of the restaurant; they seemed to have no care in the world. Although it wasn't an upscale restaurant she'd occasionally dined in with her parents, its ambiance was perfect, inviting, and modern, with images of the local culture strategically placed on the walls. It was a place she would have visited if she were on an actual holiday. It was calm and serene, and the weather only intensified the restaurant's warm and inviting atmosphere. It was a beautiful time of year. The temperature was in the low eighties, with very little cloud coverage. "It's perfect," she said under her breath. Taking everything in, she sighed as she realized she wasn't here on holiday. She was here on business and very important business. This realization snapped her back into reality.

Finding a booth near a window, Kato summoned them to follow him. He was in luck because it was the only booth left in the crowded restaurant with a window view. He preferred tables with window views. Always observant, he wanted to watch who came and went. "In this business," he thought, "You must always be careful. You never know who you can trust." Stopping in front of the booth, he asked them, "Is this ok?" Zoe nodded yes. Patty, looking around before commenting, satisfied, said, "It's good," and sat down next to the window. Kato sat beside her. "This is charming," said Patty, admiring the surroundings. "I can see why this is a great place to visit for a holiday or vacation, as we say in my country. It reminds me of the Florida Keys without the ocean view: calm, serene, and very relaxing. If we weren't here for business, I would get a few margaritas and chill."

"Ummm…hmm! It is nice," said Zoe, sitting across from the two. Mesmerized by the restaurant's ambiance, she smiled, "But for me, I could go for a citrus wine." She wasn't a drinker but occasionally had a glass of citrus wine. "Ok," joked Kato, "Are we going to talk about food again? Just sit and relax. Someone will be coming to take our orders." "My bad," said Zoe as she grinned at Patty. "Yeah," said Patty, winking at Zoe, "We do talk about food a lot." "What else is there to talk about?" laughed Zoe. They all laughed as they picked up the menus on the table and browsed the selections, enjoying the camaraderie.

Still browsing their menus, Kato, without warning, looked up from his menu and sarcastically said, "Patty, don't ask for anything exotic. Don't embarrass yourself or us!" Hurt by his unexpected attack on her, Patty retorted, "Kato, FYI, this is not my first rodeo." "Point taken," he replied haughtily. Stunned by his sudden change of character and outburst, Zoe gazed angrily into his eyes. She quickly changed her demeanor when a beautiful African woman in her early thirties approached the table. With a smile, she asked for their order in their nation's greeting, "Jambo! May I take your orders?" "Jambo," replied Zoe, her voice strained as she tried to regain her composure, "I'm still looking over everything." Patty didn't say anything but continued looking down at her menu. She was still hurt over Kato's comment. The woman stared at them as they looked over their menus. She quickly gazed at Kato. Kato stared back before looking at his menu. He knew she was the one but didn't say anything.

Looking up from the menu, Zoe said, "Ummm, I will have a Coke and an order of fries."

The woman blinked, "Ok, do you mean a ham sandwich?"

Shaking her head, Zoe replied, "No, I'll have a Coke and an order of fries. Thank you."

The woman, slightly frowning, asked again, "Miss, you sure you don't want a ham sandwich on rye bread with a side of pickled scallions?"

"Huh?" Zoe looked at her like she couldn't hear, "No, I said I want...."

Getting annoyed, Kato clapped his hands in frustration, "You know, a ham sandwich with a side order of pickled scallions and fries would be great. So yes, bring me a ham on rye, please." He pointed to Zoe, "Bring the young lady the same." Understanding who the woman was, Zoe quickly said, "Yes, that would be great! Also, please bring me a Coke with the order. I'm thirsty." The woman inhaled impatiently, nodding her head, moved on to take Patty's order. "What would you have, Miss?" she asked Patty. Sensing the waitress was the point of contact, Patty suddenly wasn't hungry. Her instinct told her not to trust her. "I only want a bottled water. Licking her lips, she said, "My mouth is parched, and only water will do the trick." Kato gave her a stern glare. He turned to the woman and apologized. "She's an American visiting our country for the first time. Bring her some American French fries, a burger, Coke, and a bottled water. Add a burger for me too. I can eat a ham sandwich and a burger. I'm hungry!" He winked at the woman. She smiled back at him. Neither Zoe nor Patty saw the interaction between the two. The waitress finished taking their order and walked away. Sulking, Patty watched her as she went to wait on another table. Then, turning to Kato, she seethed, "Kato, why did you order for me? I told you I didn't want anything! She may put something in my food! Kato angrily whispered, "Patty, don't be so paranoid. Trust me! You're going to need to get something in your stomach."

Fed up with how he spoke to her, Patty angrily asked. "Kato, dude, what's up with you all of a sudden? I'm not some imbecile! I'm a grown, intelligent person! Not your child!" "Then act like it," he snapped at her. "Trust me, okay! And stop making a scene. We're supposed to act like we are college students on holiday." Looking out the window, acting inconspicuous, he calmly said, "You know that's the contact, don't you?" "I figured that, but to what degree? I wonder...," said Zoe. "I don't trust her!" blurted out Patty, her voice filled with concern. "I don't know, but I know whoever she is, she knows something. I can sense it. Just be careful," Patty warned them.

"We will," replied Zoe, then looking at Kato, gritting her teeth, pretending to smile; her voice rising, she asked, "Kato, have you lost your mind? What were you doing? She was supposed to ask me twice. I was supposed to say French fries twice and then wait for her response. I knew what I was doing. Camille gave me explicit instructions on what to do and say. I was seeing if she was the contact. What is wrong with you? All of a sudden, you're acting strange!"

Kato could see she was getting upset. "Zoe, I'm sorry," he apologized. "I thought you forgot everything. You had a far-away look in your eyes."

Turning to Patty, he apologized, "I'm sorry to you too, Patty. We are in this together. I didn't mean to hurt you." He didn't want them to get any more upset than they were. They had to stay focused. Zoe, still upset about how he treated Patty and his sudden change of character, said sharply, "Well, act like we are! If Patty only wanted water, she's grown enough to know what she wants!"

"Zoe!" screeched Kato, now angry from her rebuke, "Look, I said I was sorry! You had that blank stare on your face! And Patty, you were acting like a dumb blond...." "Don't say it, Kato!" warned Zoe. She took a deep breath to regain her composure. She didn't want them to forget why they were there. "Look," she calmly said, "Now that we know the woman is our contact, I'll wait a few moments before I go to the restroom as planned. That way it won't look suspicious." Still upset about Kato ordering her food, Patty nodded her head. Suddenly overcome with the heat, she cried out, "Whew! Is it hot in here or what?" She took off her jacket and began to fan herself. "Where is my bottled water?" She said it loud enough for the table next to them to hear. "Get it together, Patty!" Kato said, losing his calm, "We're not in America! We are in...." Forgetting where she was, "Zoe screamed, "Kato, leave her alone! What has come over you?"

"Shhh!" he whispered, "Here comes our food." "That was quick," said Patty as a different waitress brought their food to the table. "It's just burgers, fries, and ham sandwiches, Kato said mockingly. "Nothing fancy." Patty was about to say something but decided against it when she saw the waitress watching her. Relieved by the interruption, they sat in silence as the waitress served them their food. Taking her cue, Zoe excused herself to go to the restroom. With authority in her voice, she said, "Bless the food, Kato!" "You know," said Patty, watching Zoe walk away, "I was only doing what you perceived. I was acting like an uncouth Westerner. I guess we all have stereotypes, don't we?" Kato remained quiet as the waitress finished serving them their food. "Where is the woman who took our order?" asked Patty. The waitress pointed to the other woman, "She's waiting on another table. She only takes orders. She doesn't serve the food." "Oh," said Patty. Satisfied with the answer, she bowed her head as Kato blessed the food like Zoe told him to.

Chapter Ten

"Excuse me, where is the restroom?"

Annoyed that the young woman interrupted him, the grumpy middle-aged busboy scowled as he pointed to the back. "In the back, straight ahead around the bend, the second door down. By the way, you have to close the door tight to keep it shut. Close it with your foot. That way it won't open. Don't lock it. Just close it with your foot." Then he went back to clearing tables from the afternoon lunch crowd.

Walking to the back as directed by the grumpy man, Zoe saw two doors—pausing, she said, "Ok, which way did he say? I'm not good with directions, and he didn't say left or right. Confused, she finally asked the cook. "Excuse me, sir, which door is the restroom?"

"It's back there! Second door on the right," he shouted. Shaking his head, grumbling, "Humph! You college students think you are better than the rest of us working class but can't figure out which door leads to the bathroom." Laughing at her, he went back to work.

Embarrassed by his hurtful comments, Zoe meekly said, "Thank you, kind sir." Wondering what she did to make them upset, she decided to ignore them. After all, she couldn't let their actions affect her. She had other things to think about. Trying not to get upset by the two rude men, she said out loud, "Dang! They sure have some attitudes here. What gives? All I asked was which door to the restroom. I won't bother them again. I hate when people prejudge others." They did that when she was in America— prejudged her. There were times, unfortunately, more often than she cared to admit, when she had to deposit checks from her parents into her account, and because of the sum, the bank would put a hold on them for ten days. She would get stares from the Caucasian tellers. They didn't say anything, but their eyes said, "What are you doing with this kind of money?" It was eventually resolved when she complained to the bank manager. She never had the problem again; however, the stares continued. She finally opened an account at a different bank and set up direct deposit. People prejudge you for anything and everything, she thought. Sighing, "Oh well, that's their issue," she said opening the door to the clean but small bathroom. Hurrying, she attempted to close the door. "Whew! I didn't know I had to go. Now, what did the first grumpy man say? Oh yeah, shut it with your foot…." As she was closing the door, someone tried to come in. Alarmed, she cried out, "Excuse me! I'm in here!"

"Relax, it's me," cried a woman's voice. "Besides, it's not like I haven't seen what you have. What took you so long? I have to get back to my shift." It was the waitress who took their order. The woman stared at the young woman, wondering what she was doing there. She didn't look like the rest. "What's your name?" she asked.

Stumbling over her words, Zoe stuttered, "Z-o-e," then she apologized, "Sorry, I…."

"Zoe, eh? Nice name. By the way, don't apologize," said the woman, "But you must be careful. Who are those two with you?" Without waiting for a response, she continued, "The girl, she's American, isn't she?"

"Yes," answered Zoe.

"I can tell by her mannerisms. That man, is he your boyfriend or the

American's boyfriend?"

"Neither. I met the girl at a meeting in America. The man's name is Kato. I met him a few days ago. He has been with the organization...." The woman abruptly cut her off. "You talk too much! Don't talk too much! Those two, are they ok? Do you trust them?" Zoe stumbling over her words again, answered the woman, "Yes! Yes! I trust both of them. They're safe. The girl is looking for her friend, who was abducted and possibly sold on the sex trafficking market. She is here with us to help and hopefully get some leads to her friend's whereabouts." Zoe, a little leery of all the questions, stopped talking. The woman was about to say something but decided not to. There was no need to inform the young woman that the possibility of finding the girl's friend was one in millions. It was like finding a needle in a haystack. Impossible. "Ok, ok!" Satisfied with Zoe's answers, she asked, "You look scared. Are you scared?"

Zoe shook her head no.

"Good," said the woman. "You can't afford to be scared. This is not Disney World. The people here will kill you, and no one will ever see your pretty face or body again." Rushing, she looked at her watch and said, "I have to get back out there. The men who abducted the little girl are coming into the restaurant soon. Come every day, five days straight, at the same time. They order the same thing. Not too bright, but again, they are not being paid for their intelligence. They are paid for their brutality and carrying out orders." Suddenly changing the subject, she asked Zoe, "Have you ever fired a weapon?" Zoe shook her head no. Everything was happening too fast, and she had to admit she was a little shaken by the woman's words about getting killed. It was the second time today she heard the word 'killed.' The first time was earlier from her brother Jaheem. "No, my weapons are prayer and Jesus," she answered.

The woman pulled out a small handgun from inside her blouse. "Well, meet Jesus. And when you fire the gun, that's praying. This is what you call this weapon because it, or He, will keep you from getting hurt."

"I don't need a weapon," Zoe said indignantly.

Impatiently, the woman told her, "Yes, you do! Trust me! I'm on your side." Taking the small gun from the woman, Zoe looked it over. "How did you know? I mean, how did you know we were the ones? Many people come in here."

"They said three college students were coming: a male and female from our land, and a female from another country. They didn't tell us where she was from. They only said she was Caucasian. But you asked how did I know? I knew it was you the first time when you walked through the door. Your eyes said it all. When I saw you and looked into your eyes, I knew. There was a prompting, a gut feeling."

"Oh," said Zoe, "like Elizabeth with Mary when she was pregnant with Jesus. Mary came to visit her and the baby inside Elizabeth's womb leaped." Zoe knew she was rambling. She often did when she was excited or nervous. She was both.

Staring at the foolish girl, the woman laughed, "No, like a prompting in my gut. You ain't carrying the Messiah." She continued to laugh. "You are strange." Slightly hurt by the woman's laughter, Zoe apologized again. "I'm sorry. Sometimes I overthink." Realizing she had hurt the young woman's feelings, the woman quickly stopped laughing. "It's ok, sometimes, I'm just plain ol' mean. I take it you've never fired a weapon?" "No," said Zoe, relieved the woman was no longer laughing at her.

Taking the weapon, the woman demonstrated how to fire it. "Ok, when you are in danger, all you have to do is point and shoot. Do you understand?" Zoe nodded. "Good, just trust Jesus and point and shoot. Here, you need some extra stuff around your waist. That's why they told you to wear loose-fitted clothes. Here are some nuts and dried fruit packets to put in your pockets if you get hungry. It's enough for all three of you. The location is out of the town's lighted area. It will be dark, so no one will see you. The night can get a little cool. Wear a light jacket or sweater. We don't know how long you have to wait for them to bring the girl out. Just in case it rains, here are two rain parkas. Make sure you give it to the American. Americans are soft," she said with a chuckle. "Here's a pair of infrared night-vision goggles and a cell phone. I know you already have a phone, but they can't trace you from this phone. If you get in trouble, dial this number as soon as possible." She showed Zoe the number. "Make sure you keep it on vibrate.

Studying the beautiful young woman, she said, "Don't worry, they won't bother you. You are too educated. They can tell you are from a higher class structure. Also, many young people and foreigners are here. You and your friends will fit in. Remember, you are college students on holiday! Act like it! Don't ask questions, but be very observant. And please don't talk about any Bible stories anymore," she chuckled. "Laugh and joke when you are walking about town. I told you the men who abducted the young girl are not very bright, but they are very brutal," she emphasized the word brutal. "Our laws of the land are different than America's and where you come from." Then she handed Zoe a case of ammo and a small knife.

"What's with all this ammo? I don't need all this ammo and a knife. Where am I going to put the knife?" The woman's patience was wearing thin, "Don't be foolish! You need this! I doubt if you use any, but just in case, you will have to protect yourself and your friends." She pulled some tape from her blouse. Zoe was amazed at how much she pulled out from her blouse. She wondered if the woman had any breasts or just items. "Lift up your blouse," the woman commanded. Zoe quickly lifted up her blouse, exposing her bra. "I'm going to tape this knife and gun to your side. The gun is on the right and the knife is on the left. Remember this," she warned. The woman taped the knife and small handgun to Zoe's sides, making sure they were snugly fit but not bulky so you could see them through Zoe's clothes. Satisfied, she said, "See, they are easy to retrieve if needed. I know it's a little uncomfortable, but if need be, they will save your life." She sighed and shook her head. "I don't know why they sent you, but it's my job to protect you, and it's your job to find that little girl. I pray it's not too late. The word in the underground is she's still safe. The person who purchased her paid a high price, so everyone knows not to touch her."

Zoe, trying to grasp she was carrying weapons on her body, finally heard what the woman was saying, "Are you telling me that people in this town know what's happening and they are not saying anything?" Looking into Zoe's eyes, the woman replied condescendingly, "I told you this is not the world you are used to. This is their world. What can they do? Who can they turn to? They are scared. The few who are willing to speak out, if they are caught it would be devastating to them and their families. That's why, my dear child, one must be careful, including you."

"Why are these men doing this?" She asked hoping the woman would answer the question that Kato kept avoiding.

"Who knows? Am I a man? No! I'm a woman. I can't understand. I don't see the rationality behind a grown man wanting a child! If it was a prostitute, that's different! I can understand. They are paying for a service." Zoe couldn't believe that the woman said prostitution was okay. The woman, ignoring Zoe's stares, continued. "These men are sick and perverted. Unfortunately, these people don't see what they are doing to these children. They only see that their needs are being satisfied. Selfish, aren't they? They can justify their actions; they are without remorse. It's all about, as Americans say, the 'Benjamins' or the 'Booty.'"

"Oh, it's like when Jesus was on the cross. He said, 'Father, forgive them because they don't know what they are doing….'"

The woman shook her head, "You can tell you read your Bible, but it's not that deep."

Zoe apologized for her Bible knowledge again, "I'm sorry," she said.

The woman smiled at the young woman's innocence. "You are young, fresh, and beautiful. Don't let your youth get the best of you. Focus on getting the little girl. Keep your eyes open and your mouth shut." She hesitates. And Zoe," she pauses, "Don't trust no one. I mean, no one!"

"No one. Not even you?"

"No one! Not even me! You are talking about a billion-dollar business. Money makes people kill. She looked at Zoe and said with compassion, "Don't worry. God has you." Zoe tapped her right side, feeling the gun. She smiled and said, "And Jesus," The woman smiled back at her. "Yes, and Jesus.

Touching the woman softly on the arm, Zoe told her, "They sent me or us because they would never expect a woman to take such a risk and endanger her life. They don't think much of us, do they, these people you refer to?" With a haunting look in her eyes, the woman turned away and, in a whisper, said, "Sadly, no."

There is another reason why they sent me. I am called to do this, Zoe told her."

"Called or not," the woman said as she held Zoe's hands in hers, "Just be careful. By the way, I don't know about the call as you say," she said releasing Zoe's hands, opening the door to leave out, "But I can see something in your eyes. God's grace be with you. You don't have much time. You better go, eat, and leave." She reached into her bra again, pulled out a small piece of paper and handed it to Zoe. "I almost forgot. Here is a note with instructions. Read it when you can. Make sure you follow the instructions." Staring at the young woman one last time, she closed the door behind her.

"Wow! What a day!" said Zoe out loud. Remembering to shut the door with her foot, she used the bathroom. Washing her hands afterward, looking into the mirror, she saw her reflection: strong, tall, and courageous. That's what she saw on the outside, but inside, she was scared. Tapping the gun, Jesus, she took a deep breath and looked up at the ceiling, "As long as I have you, Jesus, I'm safe." She opened the note the woman gave her and began to read it. "Oh no!" she cried out in horror. "The little girl is only eight!" Putting the note in her pocket, she took one last look in the bathroom mirror, moaning; she said a quick prayer and left. Walking back to her seat, avoiding the two grumpy men, she didn't see the man walking towards her.

Chapter Eleven

"Man! I didn't know I was hungry!" said Patty as she ate the last fry on her plate. "Those fries were so good! Some of the best I've ever eaten!" Kato shook his head, "Seriously, Patty, you're so basic. Stop acting uncouth. You know they're not American fries. We're not in America. They are just fries." Tired of his sudden constant picking on her, Patty slammed her fork on the table, "Would you stop treating me like I'm a child or worse, some airhead! I'm getting tired of your crap! Sensing she was upset, Kato started laughing at her. His laughter made her angrier. "It's not funny! I'm not…," she said, carefully choosing her next words. Trying not to cry, she let out a small scream, "Ugh! It's not a joke. You're so annoying. You're are nothing but an… !" She stopped before saying something she'd regret.

Kato stopped laughing, "Good! You almost cursed!" He saw she was on the verge of tears, "Don't cry!" he said. "Stop the watery eyes. You need to get serious and not act like some wide-eyed doe. I can't watch this and watch you too. We are about to take on dangerous territory. I need you to be focused." Frustrated, he looked at her, "I wish you would've cursed." "I'm sorry," she said wiping her eyes. "I don't curse. And if I do, I only curse when I'm extremely upset or mad; even then, it takes a lot for me to curse. It's just that I hate it when someone takes me to that place, and since we got to the restaurant, you've been trying to take me there."

"Those words," said Kato, touching his belly, "Came from here, your inner fear. And it's all good! You need to be afraid because your fear will keep you alive." At that moment, two men walked into the restaurant. Kato eyeing them, immediately grabbed Patty. Whispering into her ear, he said, "Shut up and kiss me passionately like you are enjoying it." As Patty was about to protest, he forcibly told her, "Don't say anything and don't protest. Don't look, but the two men who just came into the restaurant, watching everyone are the ones." Patty's instinct took over. She tried to look towards the door. Kato grabbed her before she had a chance, "Don't! Now, act like you enjoy kissing me." Patty, seeing the men from her peripheral view started kissing Kato. Kato mockingly said, "If we are going to kiss, then my dear girl, I need some tongue." With that, he thrust his tongue into her mouth, causing Patty to almost choke as his tongue invaded her mouth. Keep kissing me," Kato commanded. She continued kissing him but did not enjoy any minute of it.

Kosi and Laos sat down at the table where the waitress said they usually sit. Looking over the menu like they did every time, knowing it by heart, they glanced at the selections. Kosi put his menu down and scanned the restaurant. He saw a couple of tables filled with locals and some visiting foreigners. Noticing a couple kissing, he nudges the other man, "Eh, Laos, that one over there, look! He's really giving it to her, eh? She looks happy." He grins and jokes. "She's happy because she knows what she's going to get tonight, eh, my friend?" The two men stare at the couple kissing.

Getting bored, Laos said, "Come on! Stop watching them. We need to concentrate. We must get the young girl to the pickup point tonight at ten sharp. I swear I would let her go if the money wasn't good. She's a baby," He swore out loud, "Sick bastards!" Kosi, not wanting to hear the man's complaints again, swore, "Laos, man, are we bringing this up again? I thought you got over this. Look, once this job is finished, why don't you and I go on a small holiday. You know, go down to the coast, get some women, some booze, and relax, eh?" Laos looked at him as if he lost his mind. Kosi ignored his friend's look. He gently shoved him and said, "Hey, we've been in this business for twenty years? Surely we can take a break." "Yeah," Laos nodded, "But I will still be glad when this job is over." Kosi grinned, showing his missing side tooth, "I promise we will celebrate when this job is completed. We're going to get paid big for this job. I can taste the booze now. Heck, I can taste the women," he laughed. His laughter caused the other patrons in the restaurant to look in their direction. Not concerned by the stares, he said. "Order for me, will ya, Laos! You know what I want. Heck, they all know what I want. As much as we come here, our food should be ready. Anyway, I got to take care of some business," winking at his friend, he got up from the table. Knowing he meant the bathroom, Laos nodded and watched the man walk towards the back. Now alone, he thought about the mission. Not happy about the situation, he closed his eyes tightly, tilting his head back, he let out a small sigh. He was tired of the business. He was tired of his life. The little girl's face continued to haunt him at night. He opened his eyes just in time to see his friend bumping into a beautiful young African woman. Grinning, he said, "Now, that is my kind of woman!" After all, he was a virile man.

Zoe, deep in thought about the note and the weapons strapped to her sides, walking back to her seat, didn't see the man heading towards her and bumped into him. "Excuse you," he said with a slight growl. "You need to watch where you're going, Missy." "Oh, excuse me. I'm sorry. I didn't see you," she murmured. She had her share of grumpy men for the day. "My, aren't you a pretty, healthy thing," he sneered. "Too bad you're not what the doctor ordered. A little too old, but still pretty. I bet you're no virgin either, eh? You have a boyfriend? I can just bet he loves giving it to you, doesn't he?" Grabbing her arm, with lust in his eyes, he said, "Shame I'm on business. I would love to...."

Zoe angrily lashed out at him, "Sir, please get your hands off me. My parents are well-renowned surgeons in this country. They will have your head if you ever touch me again!" Kosi, taken aback by the sting of her words, scoffed, "I don't care who you are or who your parents are, girlie! You are no better than the rest of us! Don't ever forget you and me; we are the same!" He grabbed her by the waist and tightly squeezed her. Releasing her, he laughed all the way to the bathroom. Shocked at his blatant display of vulgarity in public, Zoe regained her composure and walked back to the table. "Lord, please help me. Please keep me safe. I'm here, aren't I?" She was unaware of the people who had witnessed the entire scene but didn't do anything. Troubled by the man's words and actions, arriving back at the table, she saw the ham sandwich and let out a small scream. "Ughhhh!"

Kato observed the interaction between Zoe and the man but said nothing when she came to the table. Acting oblivious, he asked, "What took you so long? You were gone too long. You must be careful in the future." Not paying attention to his remarks, Zoe turned to Patty, "I see you liked the fries." Patty coolly replied, "Yeah, they were good. I didn't know I was hungry." She was still fuming about the kiss. Not understanding Patty's tone, Zoe brushed it off and asked Kato, "Did you see that man touch me?" "Yes, I saw him. I believe he is one of the ones. But don't worry. He's not the mastermind behind the operation. The other one is," said Kato pointing to the other man sitting at the table. Still infuriated about the incident, Zoe said, "I believe he felt my weapon when he hugged me. He surely must have felt that my pockets were full of stuff. What are you talking about, Zoe?" asked a bewildered Kato. And what do you have in your pockets? What weapon and what stuff?" Agitated about the man and the thought of eating the ham sandwich, Zoe became annoyed with his questions, "Ughh! Just let me rest my thoughts. I will tell you everything. Let me eat or try to enjoy my ham sandwich." She shook her head in disgust as she stared at the sandwich. Grumbling, she cried, "I don't even like ham!" Thankful for the plate of fries, "Well, at least I have some fries," she said, stuffing a handful into her mouth.

Not waiting for Zoe to swallow the fries in her mouth, Patty asked, "Did you meet her? Was she the one? The woman who waited on us?" Sensing the urgency in Patty's tone, Zoe, covering her mouth, answered the woman's questions. "Yes, Patty, to all three questions." The woman or waitress is the contact." "Did you get a strange feeling about her?" Patty inquired. "No," said Zoe. "Everything happened so fast. But she told me not to trust anyone, not even her. I did discover the young girl is eight."

"OMG! That's a baby!" cried Patty. "The sick perverts!"

"I know," said Zoe. "I can't cry now, but when this is over, I will cry for the little girl and for the ones we can't help. Anyway, she doesn't believe the young girl has been touched. The girl's location is around the way. It's the house at the bend. It's known as a smuggling or a movement house, moving girls from one location to another." "Are there many?" asked Patty. "Probably!" said Kato, "but our focus is on the girl." Patty, no longer upset with him, asked, "I wonder why this particular girl is special? I always wanted to know." Zoe felt the same way.

"Who knows?" Kato replied. "If they can get away with this, they may start smuggling and raping them younger. They will keep her locked up and fed. I guarantee she's too frightened to eat. Even at her young age, she understands fear. Human nature is awesome!" The women nodded. "I guess whoever is buying her likes them well-fed. The irony of it is…." he stopped in mid-sentence. Glancing at his watch, he impatiently said, "Come on! Let's pay the tab so we can go. He looked at the barely eaten sandwich on Zoe's plate, "You better eat at least half your sandwich so it doesn't look suspicious." Zoe took another bite. Teasingly, he said, "That's a good girl. Eat it up and smile like you are enjoying it."

Taking one last bite of the half-eaten sandwich with her mouth full, Zoe said, "OK, finish! I just need a sip of Coke to wash it down." Kato looked for the waitress. He saw her at another table and yelled, "Waitress, we're ready for the tab." The waitress turned around and saw that it was them and swiftly walked over to the table. "I see that you enjoyed your sandwich," she said to Zoe, "and your fries," to Patty, as she put the check on the table. Kato pulled out some money and paid the bill, leaving a generous tip. "Thank you, sir." She took the money and walked away. Zoe swallowed the remaining food in her mouth. "Hey," she cried, "I was going to pay the bill! I got money from my brother, remember." Winking at her, Kato grinned and said, "Well, don't ever say chivalry is dead. He looked at them and asked, "Where to next, ladies?" Taking one last sip of Coke, Zoe wiped her face, tongue, and mouth with her napkin, "Camille said we have to find the hotel for further information." "Well, let's get going," replied Kato. They got up and walked to the door.

The woman watched as the trio walked out the door. She walked over to the table where the two men sat. "Where is the other one?" she asked the man. He pointed to the back of the restaurant and said, "He went to the bathroom." Scanning the restaurant, he asked her, "Where are the ones who are to liberate the girl?" Pointing to the door, the woman replied, "The three that just left. The two from the continent and the girl with the sandy-blond hair from America." Pretending she was waiting on the table, she asked for his order. Laos pretended to make small talk as he looked over the menu, "Oh, so the two kissing. I thought the kisses were not genuine; rather sloppy on his part, if I must say so myself." Shaking his head, he frowned, "That's their army! Those three stupid young fools! Who do they think they are? What makes those fools believe they can come against a billion-dollar industry and no one will know? That no one would suspect them or no one would talk. In this world, nothing is sacred but the dollar, not even a man's word." Wearily, he said, "The young women are both beautiful…ebony and ivory. Shame we have to kill them both, that is before they are used up. Oh well, instead of one girl, we have three. Seian will be pleased." His tone became more solemn, "This business is getting too dangerous. There's rumor going around that there is a mole. Did you hear anything about this?" he asked her. The woman shook her head no.

Sitting back in his chair, Laos pondered, "I can smell a different type of fear. It's different. Can you feel or sense it?" "No," she answered, "But the locals are scared. I believe they know about the girl and are afraid of a blood war right in the heart of their beautiful town. Everyone seems nervous. They fear for their lives and the lives of their families." Staring at him, she noticed his countenance had changed. "What's wrong, Laos? I sense something heavy on you." Sensing her looks, Laos quickly straightened up, "Nothing. I'm good! I pray that there is no blood war. The young girl's parents are poor, but they know some very prominent people." "The little girl is safe, isn't she?" the woman asked. "Yes! I'm no fool! I don't cross Seian!" he growled. "I know what would happen to me if I did. Besides, even I know that she is too young. If the money wasn't good, I wouldn't be here. I'm getting too old for this world." With compassion, the woman said, "Yes, I know it's a dangerous world we live in. I also know that you and Seian have been together for twenty years. I know he can trust you." Changing the subject to get him back focused she said, "By the way, I gave the young woman some supplies, including a knife and a small gun. She will probably need them, but knowing her, she won't use the weapons." Laos didn't say anything.

"Laos," the woman still concerned about him, asked again, "Are you sure you're okay? You're not getting a conscience, are you?" "Shut up! There is no conscience in my soul," he snarled. Looking across the room, he sees the other man approaching the table. "Be quiet! Here comes Kosi! I don't want to talk about this anymore. Don't tell him what we talked about." The woman agreed. Then she said, "Laos, promise me this. If she is to die, the young African beauty, kill her gently. There is something about her I can't explain. She's an innocent soul. She truly believes she is called by God, whatever that means," said the woman. "Well, she is to meet her Maker soon," Laos said as Kosi sat down at the table.

"Who will meet their Maker soon?" Kosi asked, wondering who was going to die. "Kosi!" Laos turned to his friend, "The couple that was kissing are the ones we are looking for. It's a three-man army, my friend, trying to take down a billion-dollar industry. And the girl that you bumped into makes up the three. Laos tilted his head back and laughed so loud that the other patrons stopped eating and looked at the table. "Laos," the woman hissed, "You are making a scene!" She was getting tired of them and the conversation.

"You know that girl who bumped into me?" said Kosi, "She's beautiful, but she thinks she is better than the rest of us. Just give me one night with her, and I will show her! She won't be snobby then. He laughed. "Kosi, Laos said, "Just leave her be. We have other fish to fry. Besides, when this is over, we are going down by the coast?" Grinning, Kosi nodded his head. "Alana!" the cook yelled at her from across the restaurant, "You have other customers." "I gotta go," she told them. Fortunately for me, I know what you both want. Same thing as always." She wrote something on her pad and walked away.

"Now there goes a good woman," Kosi said to Laos. Laos didn't say a word. He knew better.

Chapter Twelve

The three walked out into the warm sun, each in their own thoughts. Zoe, aware that she was carrying a knife and a small gun, started to feel the pressure of the mission. To make matters worse, she began to feel nauseous as the pork bubbled in her stomach. The sun's heat only intensified her nauseousness. She could feel the need to vomit was on the horizon. Going around the rear of a nearby building where no one could see her, she started throwing up everything she had consumed. "Ughh, I hate pork," she cried in between vomiting. Patty, concerned for her friend, went with her and watched her vomit. "Are you ok?" she asked. Bending over, clutching her stomach, Zoe shook her head, "Yes!" Patty reached into her bag, pulled out a bottle of water, and handed it to Zoe. "Here, have some water," she said. "You are heaving out a lot of stuff. I've seen people who drank more than you heave less." Zoe, wiping her mouth with her sleeve took a sip of water, said, "Thanks. I'm fine, just a little tired, but I'm ok." She took another sip of water. Wincing from the foul taste in her mouth, she cried, "Ughh, vomit and water don't mix!" Looking up at the sky, sighing, she said, "I wish I could take a quick nap to get my mind straight, but now is not the time to sleep. The woman told me they were going to take the girl later this evening, so we have to get moving." Wiping her mouth again with her sleeve, she screeched, "Ugh! I hate pork. It seems like a joke that ham would be the one thing to ask for."

Kato, watching the entire scene, walked over to the two women. "Here, have a lifesaver," he said, taking a piece of candy from his pocket and handing it to Zoe.

"Really?" shrieked Zoe.

"No, I just wanted to see you smile. Dirty breath? Try Mentos." He began to laugh. Even Patty had to smile at his joke.

"Too, too funny, Kato! Not!" Annoyed at him and his jokes, Zoe could no longer hide her displeasure for the man's sudden tauntiness, "You've been watching too many American commercials. Pork has always done this to me. You know Kato, as the oldest of the three, you sure can be petty at times." Not wanting them to see her frustration, she angrily walked away. With tears in her eyes, she cried, "This is crazy! In my wildest dreams, I never thought I would be carrying around a gun or knife." She didn't want to think about the possibility of using either. Hopefully, they get the girl, leave, and her life will return to normal. "That Kato makes me so upset. I could punch him in the mouth!" she fumed. She walked a great distance before she realized she left them behind. Turning around, she stopped and waited for them.

"Zoe!" Kato screamed when they caught up with her. "What's the matter with you? We must stay together. It's not time to get sensitive! For goodness sake, it was a joke!" he growled.

"It was sort of funny, Zoe," agreed Patty. You have to admit it was classic." She tried not to crack a smile.

Calming down, Zoe looked at both of them and began to chuckle. "I know, and now that I had a chance to calm down, it was funny. I'm sorry for walking away and losing my cool, but Kato sometimes it seems you like to irk us for your own pleasure. At times, you're a bully!"

"No," he said jokingly, "I am Kato. I'm a man on a mission. I'm Batman."

"Really!" both Patty and Zoe laughed.

"Batman," shrieked Patty. "You are more like The Incredible Hulk."

"No," laughed Zoe, "The Incredible Hulk is my guy. And besides, The Incredible Hulk is derived from Bruce Banner, who is brilliant. Therefore, this shuts out Kato." Both girls shrieked with laughter once more. Even Kato had to smile. For some reason, he liked it when Zoe smiled. It was as if harmony was restored. They continued walking down the street talking, laughing, and joking as if they didn't have a care in the world. Zoe, glad they were getting along, told them about her adventures in America and medical school. In the middle of one of her stories, she screamed in a high-pitched voice, "There's the hotel! There it is! That's the hotel!"

"Zoe!" Kato, trying not to sound stern, "Shhh," he whispered. "Do you want everyone to know? Woman, you do get excited, don't you?" He noticed that trait in her right away. It made him smile when she got excited about things. He didn't know why. "She's a firecracker," he said under his breath.

"Oh yes, my bad," she grinned. "I can get excited."

"Yeah! We've noticed," said Patty with a glint in her eyes.

Now speaking in a hushed tone, Zoe pointed to the hotel and squealed, "There's the hotel where we are staying in and meet our next point of contact. The woman at the restaurant gave me a phone." She pulled out a small phone from one of her cargo pockets. "She gave me a number to call in case something happens." Looking at the two of them, "I don't think we need to call anyone. I believe everyone is scared." "I agree," said Kato. "We will only use the phone in case of emergency. We don't know who else can access the number or is listening. Zoe put it in your backpack for safekeeping. It's lucky for us that there are enough people around town. It's as if everyone is on holiday here in this quaint little town, especially the men."

Observing for the first time, Zoe noticed the many men in the town. Many were foreigners. Turning to Kato, she asked, "There are many men here, aren't there?" Before Kato could respond, Patty said, "I was thinking the same thing. I'd also noticed the men were here by themselves. I wondered why. Where are the women or their wives?" Kato didn't want to tell either of them the truth, but the look on their faces made him tell them the realities of the quaint little town. "Unfortunately, in this dark, ugly world we are about to journey through, this beautiful, charming little town is known for sex trafficking. Men don't come here for the town's beauty or serenity, but as blunt as I can say, they come here for an easy lay. They come here to sleep with underage girls and boys. They can get away with it here. It's a pedophile's dream." He shrugged and continued, "Not to mention, it's usually warm, particularly this time of the year."

"What about the locals? Are they a part of this?" asked Patty.

"Someone is getting paid. But I doubt it's the locals. Maybe a few. It's high up. Most of the locals know what's happening, but they are afraid. They live in fear. The unspoken rule is that if they don't say anything, their families will not be harmed, and peace will be in the land. Human sex trafficking is a billion-dollar business. In the next couple of years, statistically speaking, it is believed it will surpass the drug trafficking business." Both women looked away.

"Such beauty and tranquility," whispered Patty, "while evil lurks through it. I hate to think about what really goes on at night. I can't imagine the horror stories. I hope my friend is not tangled up in this." "It's the harsh realities of this world, Patty. It is what it is," Kato said nonchalantly.

Not wanting to think or talk about the town's secrets any longer, Zoe said, "Come on, we need to get a room." Attempting to find the humor in all the darkness, she jokingly said to them, "Anyway, I need to brush my teeth. I can still smell the ham strong in my nostrils." They all smiled. "By the way, Kato, I'm Batman!" she said, wanting to vex him for pulling the lifesaver joke on her. Knowing what she was doing, Kato winked at her, "No, I'm Batman. You're Robin." Like a little kid, Zoe laughed, "No, I'm Batman!" She didn't know why his wink bothered her. "Well," said Patty with a naughty smile, "You two can be Batman! I'm Captain America!" Kato and Zoe turned to each other and laughed. "Really! said Zoe, "Typical American!" The three of them burst into laughter.

Still laughing as they walked through the door leading into the lobby, they stopped in awe, admiring the beautifully decorated and spacious interior. With various color palettes of mauve, pink, sage, and yellow throughout, it was nothing like the dreary, gray building they had lived in for the past couple of weeks. Although small compared to the larger Western hotels, it was large enough to accommodate the many travelers who came and went. Known for its hospitality, charm, and beautiful décor, the owner, an African businessman who specializes in Internet marketing sales, decorated it based on his frequent travels abroad to China and parts of Europe. It showed in the decor from the various items, antiques, and souvenirs. Although it was beautiful and spacious, one could feel the comforts of home. It had the ambiance of a home away from home, something Zoe was used to when she traveled with her parents. For a brief moment, she forgot why she was there. She felt like she was on holiday with her parents and brother. Patty's sudden burst of excitement brought her back to reality.

"Wow! This place is amazing," she exclaimed.

"Yes, it is!" said Zoe in a whispering voice. "It's beautiful!"

"You know," said Patty, looking around, "I could really stay here and just chill out, just unwind, if you know what I mean." In a solemn voice, she turned to Zoe and said, "I wish we were on a real vacation instead of what we are here for." Zoe understood. She felt the same way. "Wow! I didn't know Kenya was so beautiful and modern!" uttered Patty in amazement. Zoe decided not to comment. She didn't want to focus on her friend's ignorance or tell her that many places in Kenya and Africa were breathtakingly beautiful. She knew her friend like many people, assumed Africa was a big poverty-stricken land filled with savages dressed in grass attire. She chuckled at the thought of seeing her mother dressed in a grass skirt.

Feeling homesick, she said, "Yes, it's quite charming and very serene. It makes me miss my home very much." Looking around the lobby, wishing she could turn back time, Zoe said softly, "I agree with you, Patty. Any other time, we could relax and enjoy the charm of the hotel and the city." With a deep sigh, she said, "But we can't, can we?" A sad look came over her. Seeing Zoe sad bothered Kato. He understood how some foreigners misconstrued their culture and their land. It was their ignorance and, quite frankly, their loss. People were the same, just different cultures and ethnicities, but their needs were the same. Maybe someday we will get this, he thought. "Oh well," he said, shrugging his shoulders. He then did a quick recon of the area while the women remained mesmerized by the beauty of the place. He wanted to make sure nothing appeared out of the ordinary or unfamiliar. He looked for anyone or anything that seemed out of place. Satisfied, he said, "Let's check in."

Zoe spotted an older gentleman emerging from one of the office doors behind the front desk. He must be the clerk, thought Zoe. His uniform was immaculate and very Westernized. She saw similar ones on the hotel clerks when she had traveled abroad with her parents to Europe and the more prestigious downtown Baltimore hotels. She knew he was from another part of the continent by his facial structure and mannerisms. He didn't look like a local. He caught her staring at him and winked. As he neared the computer workstation, he asked, "May I assist you?" Moving towards the man, Kato replied, "Yes, sir, we need a room."

The gentleman looked at the computer screen, "Do you have reservations? We're pretty booked. Carefully observing them, he asked, "What brings you to this part of Kenya? College students on holiday never stay here. I see many people come and go, but you three don't look like the usual guests, especially you," he said pointing to Patty. "It's okay, my friend," said Kato. "We wanted to visit somewhere different. We are showing our American friend our beautiful country. We're tired and decided to stop here and get a room. If that's fine with you," he added, "kind, sir?" Taking her cue, Patty said, "Yes, it's beautiful. I didn't know how lovely your country is. The books don't portray its breathtaking beauty." The gentleman smiled at her, "No, they don't. To some parts of the world we still live in huts with no modern conveniences." He grinned as he typed something on the computer, "Ahhhh, yes! I see I have a room available." He knew they were the ones he was waiting for. "What is the cost, my good sir?" Kato inquired. "It's free," the man replied. "It's something about her eyes," Nodding his head towards Zoe. "Besides, it would be a shame to have you pay for the last room in the house if you want to call it a room, especially if you are only staying for one night. You are, I assume, only staying for one night?" Blushing at his compliment, Zoe rushed to speak, "Yes! Thank you, sir." She was used to people she knew commenting about her eyes, but not strangers, not to her face anyway. Stammering over her words and full of gratitude, she continued to thank the older man. "It's lovely. I must tell my parents about this place when I get home."

He smiled at her, "You are welcome. By the way, there are some mints over there," he said pointing to the bowl of mints on the counter. Embarrassed, Zoe said, "Oh my, please forgive me!" Blowing her breath in her hands, she could still smell the stench of the sandwich and now vomit. "I had something that didn't agree with my stomach. I threw it up and the smell is still in my mouth." "That's okay," he winked. "I did a lot of partying and drinking in my day too as a youth, but still take a mint." He smiled at her as he finished checking them in.

"Do you need help with your bags?" he asked. He knew they didn't have any bags. By the look on the man's face, Kato sensed the man knew something. He shook his head no. He handed a key to Kato. Kato thanked the man and grabbed Zoe's backpack. He and Patty walked toward the elevator. Zoe grabbed some mints and smiled at the gentleman. She saluted him as she popped a mint in her mouth. He returned her salute. Running to catch the two as they were about to get on the elevator, she turned one last time and waved at him. Watching them get on the elevator, the man waved back as the door closed. He went into the back office, picked up the phone and dialed a number. Waiting for someone to pick up, under his breath, he said, "Lord, please be with them. They have no idea what they are getting involved in."

Chapter Thirteen

Opening the door with the key, Kato scanned the room from the dooway. "Well, he told the truth. It's small, but it looks safe," he said, entering the room. "Yeah," said Patty, entering after him, "But it's nice, clean, and neat!" Zoe, the last one to enter, looked at the only bed in the room and cried, "But it has only one bed and it's small!" They all stared at the one queen bed. "That's okay," said Kato. "It looks sturdy enough to accommodate all three of us." Patty went over to the bed and sat on it, rocking up and down to test the mattress. "Hey, the mattress isn't bad. It's top quality, too! It has an innerspring like some of the beds in our hotel chains in America use." Then, noticing the view from the window, in a loud-pitched voice, she cried out, "Whoa! Check out the view!" She went over to the window to admire the breathtaking view. "The land is so lush. And how cool you can see the mountains in the background!" Zoe went over to Patty's side. Together, they marveled at the view. Patty turned around, gazing over the room. Optimistically, she said, "If this is the only room left in the house, it's not that bad. Besides, the view is awesome. It makes up for the room size."

"Yes, I keep forgetting how beautiful my country is," said Zoe. "It's rich in culture and natural resources. It is a leading producer of tea and coffee and the third-leading exporter of cabbage, onions, and mangoes."

"What?" said Patty, raising her eyebrows, impressed with Zoe's knowledge of her country.

Zoe grinned. "What? I googled it!"

Realizing the other woman was making fun of her, Patty rolled her eyes, "Give me a break! I know Kenya is a prosperous and vibrant country. You know, I did have some college, and I was a good student in high school. Laughing, Zoe reached out her hand to Patty's. "Just kidding, my friend! Truce?" "Truce," grinned Patty. They were becoming great friends. "I was only messing with you," teased Zoe. "But it does make me laugh that some foreigners think Africa is one big country instead of a continent of many countries. Or that we are primitive compared to Western standards."

"No, it isn't like that!" exclaimed Patty, defending herself and others. "We just don't see all of this." "Ahhh, yes, the media," Kato said dryly, joining the conversation. "It only portrays what they want you to see or believe. Always know, my dear, what you see is not always real. We are very modern, as you can see. We are up to date with technology. We have the Internet and smartphones, and we even have McDonald's. We are far from uncivilized," he sneered.

Breaking the spell of camaraderie between her and Zoe, Patty, fed up with Kato's snide remarks, no longer able to control her temper, screamed, "Kato shut up! Just shut up! Dude, what's your problem? Look, I'm not from here! OK! So let up on me!" Kato, unfazed by her outburst, with a smirk, said! "Impressive. I like the way you melt down. It's easy to make you upset. But you still don't curse, do you? I want to hear you curse." Frustrated at their constant bickering, Zoe yelled at the two, "You two stop arguing and try to get along! We are here to complete a mission, not ride each other. I'm going to brush my teeth and freshen up. I need to relax my mind and, for a few short hours, act like I don't have a care in the world. Sheesh! Get it together, will you!" Leaving them speechless, she went into the bathroom, slamming the door behind her.

Hearing the door slam and upset by Kato's constant bullying, Patty scowled at the man who caused all the trouble, "Kato, what's up with you? You think you're so smart, but you're nothing but a dumb…!" She stopped before she said the word. "No, you're not worth it! I won't allow you to make me so upset I do something out of character. I won't give you the satisfaction." With a mischievous smile, she said, "But you are a butt hole!"

"Oh, so you are a good Christian girl," he teased.

"No, I just don't curse. My grandmother always told me that young ladies don't say bad words or curse. It's now ingrained in me."

"Good for her!" He replied.

"Yes, but she cursed like a sailor all the while." They both laughed. Their laughter broke the tension in the room. "Look, Kato," said Patty. "I'm not as privileged as you like to believe. My family had to work hard to get where we are today. Just like you believe, we think you are all poor in your country; everyone believes everyone in America is rich. We are all living the American Dream! We're not! We work hard to make ends meet just like the people in your country. So, I refuse to allow you to think I'm a privileged, rich, white girl from America who never experienced hard times."

"No," he replied sarcastically.

"No!" she snapped back, ignoring his sarcasm. "My parents are hard-working people who work factory jobs and make an okay living to keep our family together. My father had a drinking problem, but he eventually got himself sober, so you see, I can say the same things about you."

"About me? What do you mean?" he asked.

"Just like you believe or assume we prejudge all Africans. You prejudge Americans. You can't believe everything you hear about our country either. We have many people that are poor in America."

"Yeah, but American poor is not really poor."

"That's a stupid thing to say for someone who appears to be intelligent! Poor is poor!"

"Okay, okay! Don't be so touchy! I didn't mean any harm. I was only messing with you. I have a funny way of dealing with things when a lot is on my mind. As you may have noticed, I'm a little cynical." "Yea, I've noticed, although I wouldn't call it cynical, more like a butt hole, or as Zoe called you, a bully!" "I deserve that," he said. Now remorseful, Kato humbly said, "Hey Patty, I apologize for getting you riled up." "No worries," said Patty accepting his apology. "Besides, it's getting down to the wire, so it's normal for us to start getting on each other nerves. But just stop riding me, dude!" Kato nodded his head. "Okay," he said. Changing the subject, Kato asked, "So what happened? How did you end up all the way here from America? How did you and Zoe meet? I have always been curious about your story." "It's a long story," she told him. "I have nothing but time," he replied. Patty sat down in the only chair in the room and began to tell her story.

"My best friend Elizabeth, Lizzie for short, was snatched, or that's what I believe. I'm sure she was snatched and is or was a victim of sex trafficking. But regardless, she is gone and most likely dead. We've known each other since third grade. We liked the same boy, Joshua Kingsley. One day in class Liz tripped me and said that Joshua was her boyfriend and that I should stay away from him. I hit her in the stomach and she started crying. Our teacher, Ms. Courtney, was watching. She came over and asked us what was wrong. We didn't tell her, but she saw the entire thing. She pointed to Joshua, saying to the both of us, 'You are fighting over Joshua, and he is playing with Lauren.' We went over to Joshua and pushed him to the ground. We've been best friends since. We got into trouble for pushing Joshua, but we did notice as Ms. Courtney was scolding us she was smiling. From that day, we never let a boy come between us, that is until the day I saw her last. That was about a year and a half ago. We met him. He said his name was Dave. We were at a trendy bar in a college hang out area. All the college and hip twenty-somethings hung out at this place to talk politics, world events, the economy, sports, and sometimes hook up or get on the free WiFi. There was always something going on. Always a debate about something or another. You know we were letting our voices be heard, but the funny thing was no one was listening to each other.

One day just hanging out, this guy, Dave, walked in wearing black designer jeans, a cobalt blue cashmere sweater, and a scarf around his neck. He was very chic, very cool, and very attractive. He had dark features. I could tell he wasn't from the U.S. from his accent and mannerisms; he looked foreign. He looked older, in his late twenties, so I assumed he was a graduate student. He saw a couple of girls and spoke to them. They gave him the brush off, so he came over to Lizzie and me. He introduced himself and ordered us two apple martinis, which was unusual because almost everyone drank beer. I declined the drink, but he was smooth and charismatic. He eventually started ignoring me, talking directly to Liz. Liz drank both drinks. As he kept talking, something in my gut told me to get Liz and go. The more he spoke, the more I noticed him sweating and acting weird. Not the cool, smooth person when he first approached us. I believe he slipped something in the drinks because Liz started acting strange. Two martinis didn't get Liz drunk. She could handle her booze. She was an all-around "fun girl," if you know what I mean." Kato nodded his head, fully understanding what she meant.

"We were best friends, but we were different when it came to certain things. I didn't judge her; she was my girl!" "Oh, like her guardian angel," he smirked."No, like her friend!" said Patty rolling her eyes at him. "Believe me, I wasn't perfect. She would hook up for one-night stands with guys she just met. I hated when she did that, and I could see this was headed in that direction. I told her to come on, let's go, but she said no. David was smooth with his foreign accent. He said that he would take her home. He was cute, but at that moment, I was pissed off. He was starting to get on my nerves. It was something about him. I told her one last time to let's go. He told me to leave her alone, 'she's a big girl.' Liz nodded her head, agreeing with him; slurring her words, she said, 'Yes, I'm a big girl.' I got mad, got my coat, and walked to the door. Looking back before walking out the door, I said, 'Liz, let's go! Are you coming or not?' She said no. That was the last time I saw my best friend." Tears filled her eyes, and in a whispering tone, she told him, "You see, if I were her guardian angel, she would still be here, safe and secured. I would have protected her from the big bad wolf."

Kato, sensitive to the moment, comforted her, "It wasn't your fault. You can't take the guilt. You tried to help her. She made her decision." "Yes, I know," Patty replied. Looking at the view of the mountains, no longer holding back the tears, she moaned softly, "It took me a long time to come to grips with that truth. But I knew something wasn't right. I should have dragged her butt out of there, letting her kick and scream, but at least she would still be here with me today. That's my regret.

I called her the next day. Her phone immediately went to voicemail. I knew something was wrong because no matter what, Liz would instantly text you if she didn't pick up her phone. She was avid about texting. I tried texting her several times with no response. I got worried and called her mom. Her mom told me that she didn't come home, which was nothing strange. Two days later, when we still didn't hear from her, Liz's parents finally called the police. I described David, the name he gave us to the police. They looked at us and said that if we were a praying family, we needed to pray because from the description I gave them, they said they believed this was the same man who preys on young girls. His "MO," you know, "Method of Operation," was to go to places like the one where we were hanging out and be low key, watching who was vulnerable so he could approach them and possibly pick them up. The police said they had complaints from other girls about him harassing them. They did a check on him and found out that he would buy the girls a colored drink and put a pill in the drink. The drink doesn't show the pill. He sells the girls to visiting foreigners who prefer American girls, particularly those with blond hair and blue eyes, like Liz. The police eventually found her phone in an old, run down hotel using a nearby signal tower to locate her last phone message. They told us that she probably was no longer in the country. That's when her mother lost it. Her father became numb and hasn't been right since. I looked everywhere. I called all our friends and put messages on social media, but nothing came up. The man named David never did show up again at the hangout. I did some research and found out that this type of thing happens all the time, even in America. I lost my best friend, so I decided to be a one-woman crusade. If I can help one person, a child, or a young girl, I did my part. So you see, I'm not soft. I'm hard when I need to be. "I know. You're Captain America," he grinned. "Yes, I'm Captain America!" she said smugly.

Chapter Fourteen

Hoping to get some peace before the night's journey, Zoe went into the small yet pleasantly decorated bathroom for some alone time. For as long as she could remember, she had to use the bathroom when she became nervous. Very little came out, but it was still a relief. Some people experienced butterflies when anxious; she had a weak bladder. After washing her hands, she took her toothbrush and toothpaste from her backpack and brushed her teeth. She smiled thinking about Kato's crack about her dirty breath, mimicking the popular American commercial. It wasn't funny then, but now it brought a smile to her face, somewhat easing her mind. Putting the toothbrush and toothpaste back in the bag, she bumped against her stomach. Feeling the small gun the woman called Jesus, anxiety came over her. She attempted to go to the bathroom again. Nothing came out. Rewashing her hands and grabbing the towel, she saw her reflection in the mirror. Taking the cloth she had used to wipe her hands, she ran cold water on it and wiped her face. The water felt cool on her brown cocoa face. Staring in the mirror at the image looking back at her, she began to think about her first introduction into the world of human sex trafficking. She remembered the day as it was yesterday.

A couple of female students at the university were talking about a meeting off campus at a local hangout where students would go to unwind after a long, grueling day of studying medicine and cutting up cadavers. Zoe was adamant about her studies and rarely took time out to socialize. She was well-liked and sought out for her engaging conversations. She was the young woman with the beautiful yet compelling eyes, as many associated her with, particularly the guys. Her face portrayed a smile that could brighten anyone's day. So, it wasn't a coincidence when one of the ladies approached her about going to the meeting held at the local hangout she would sometimes go to.

Gnawing on her pen, which she often did when she concentrated on something, she thought about the invitation. After pondering for a moment, she said yes, even though she didn't know what the meeting was about. She knew the circle of young women who were going. They were studious and focused like her, so she knew the meeting was business. After all, one couldn't get into the prestigious Johns Hopkins School of Medicine without exemplary study habits. One wouldn't be able to survive the first three weeks alone. The professors were some of the best, if not the best, in the world.

As the women entered the café, they saw the place crowded with women from various backgrounds and ethnicities. Some seemed a little edgy. Zoe sensed this was not a meeting about school or medicine but something equally important. Although cold outside, the cold didn't stop the women from showing up in numbers. Zoe and one of the ladies she came with sat at a table where two other girls sat. Sitting next to a sandy, blond-haired girl around her age, Zoe asked the girl what the meeting was about. Annoyed by the question, the girl stared at her and was about to say something biting, but seeing Zoe's face changed her demeanor.

"It's a meeting on sex trafficking," she told her.

"What?" cried Zoe in astonishment. She had heard about sex trafficking briefly around town and in her own country, but that was the extent of her knowledge. Her parents, prominent surgeons in Nairobi, were not troubled with many things outside their privileged world. They were not snobbish; however, their circle of friends concerned themselves with their practices and other social issues, such as the country's political state, the economy, and fighting for better healthcare for the underserved.

The girl whispered, "Several young girls are missing in this area. The police think it's a sex trafficking ring operating in the city, preying on young girls and women. They are here to warn and educate the women in our community. Sex trafficking is big in Atlanta. Now it's moving up north." Shocked at what the meeting was about, Zoe exclaimed, "I never knew it was here in America. I knew there were cases in my country and other parts of the world, specifically in other countries in Africa, Asia, and Russia, mainly the lower class. I never knew it was a concern in America."

Listening to the conversation, the other girl at the table interrupted and said, "It's here just like it's in every part of this world. America is no exception. We like to think it doesn't happen in our country, but it happens more often than we know." In a low whisper, the sandy, blond-haired girl said, "It happened to my friend, Lizzy." Fighting back the tears, she said, "It happened right here in this place." The other three girls listened intensively as the sandy blond-haired female told them about her friend Lizzy. "My only prayer is that she's still alive. Although the chances are slim, and if she is alive, she's probably somewhere in another country. But it's my only hope. It's a slim hope, but that's all I got." Zoe was about to say something, but before she could, the local police started the meeting. A hush filled the room, and all eyes were on the policewoman in the front who began to speak. As Zoe listened to the speaker, thoughts filled her mind about what the young, sandy blond-haired woman had told them about her friend.

"Ladies," the policewoman began in a serious tone, "First, I want to thank you all for coming out on this cold, brisk day. For many of you, it's a day to stay in and do nothing. As for me, I could be watching 'The Bachelor' to see who is going home today." There was a slight snicker from the women. She continued, "I'm glad it's a diverse group. We have college students, high school students, working women, single mothers, and women from different ethnicities, but you all have one thing in common: you are all females."

Someone laughed and yelled out, "No fooling!"

The officer laughed, too. "But seriously, ladies," she continued, "What we are here for is no laughing matter. Unfortunately, it's real, and it's happening in our country. It's happening in our city. And that is drug and sex trafficking. Over twenty young girls and young women have gone missing in the past several months. Their ages range from fifteen to twenty-six. Black, Caucasian, Latino, Mexican, and Asian; there is no discrimination. I'm here to warn you that the threat is real, and we are doing our best to find the culprits. The ringleader! But we need your help. Please let me inform you that we are not here to frighten you but to help you as you assist us." A hand in the back went up. "I thought this was a third-world problem and only existed in the more impoverished countries, such as Asia and Africa?" Zoe cringed at the mention of Africa. Silently fuming, she said under her breath, "Africa is a continent of many countries, many of which are wealthy."

The policewoman replied, "Sex trafficking is a billion-dollar business. As I stated before, it has no boundaries as far as countries are concerned, nor does it discriminate. Sex trafficking affects the poor and the rich. As the money and demand get more enticing, we have seen an increase in this country. And this is where you can help us. Back in the day, we had something called the "Buddy System." Well, that's what we are asking you to do. Establish a 'Buddy' or accountability partner. Places like this café are hangouts where traffickers thrive on victims. They look for the vulnerable, pardon my language, the homely, the insecure, and the drunk or drugged girl. If you are out with the girls, walk in threes. Don't leave the other behind. Do not hook up with strangers, and don't let your friends hook up with strangers. If you have to, drag their butts home. They may hate you at the moment, but believe me, they will thank you in the morning. If someone wants to buy you a drink, go with them to the bar, watch the bartender make your drink and hand it to you. Watch out for colorful drinks. Someone could easily slip a pill or something in it. You won't know until it's too late. If you are out partying, have a designated driver or call an Uber. Do not leave your friend to go home alone. Also, make sure you have your tracker active on your phone if you are by yourself or become suspicious of someone."

Another hand in the front went up, "This all sounds basic and juvenile as if we are in kindergarten." A couple of murmurs went around the room. "It does, doesn't it?" said the policewoman. "But what did we learn in kindergarten? We learned the buddy system. The problem is you don't think this will ever happen to you, and we pray it doesn't. That's why we are here to inform you and make you aware that it does happen. The good news, if you want to call it good news, is that it's not as prevalent in America as in some other countries. However, sex trafficking is growing at an alarming rate in our country. Each year, the statistics of people trafficked are on the rise. Atlanta is a major hub. As we crackdown in that city, it's moving up north."

"Why haven't we heard about this until now?" a woman asked. A woman shouted from the back of the room, "Well, you are hearing about it now!"

A policeman stepped in. "Listen, ladies, there is a threat, and the danger of the threat is real. Again, we are not here to frighten you. Hopefully, you take this seriously enough to take it to heart. We don't want to hear about another young girl missing. As a father, I can't fathom the thought of my daughter missing, yet some fathers are dealing with this today. And as for informing the public, we have been talking about it. Unfortunately, politics and other world events have been the main focal point in our country. Our voice gets very little air time with the media. That's why we are going throughout the communities to talk to women. We are going to all the middle and high schools to speak with parents, teachers, administrators, children, and teenagers. How many here are in high school?" Several girls raised their hands. "Good," he said. "I'm glad you are here. You need to hear this because you are the most rebellious about going off alone and not obeying your parents. Remember, for every action, there is a reaction. We are not preaching to you; we want you to be safe. Please take what we are saying seriously." He looked at his watch and said, "We are almost out of time. Before we wrap things up, I would like you to meet Camille. Camille is part of an agency that helps rescue young girls and boys from sex trafficking. She is from South Africa and travels globally speaking on sex trafficking."

A beautiful woman stood up and began to speak. "Hi, my name is Camille, and as the detective said, I am from South Africa. I believe my purpose on this earth is to help with the crusade or fight against sex trafficking. Not to prolong the time and get you out of here, there will be another meeting here next week at the same time to discuss this further. If you have questions, please speak to me after this meeting. I want to answer your questions and help you understand more. I also have some literature on sex trafficking. As you leave, please pick up the literature to read and give to your family and friends. Become well-informed. The statistics are alarming. For some of you, your purpose may be to assist in the fight to end human sex trafficking. She looked at the two officers and said, "That's all I have." The female officer closed the meeting. She told the women that a police escort would be available for anyone needing a ride home.

Pondering over everything she heard, Zoe didn't hear the females she came with ask if she was ready to go. "Huh? Oh, sure. Give me a minute," she replied. "I want to say hello to Camille. After all, she is from my continent." They nodded and said they would wait for her at the door.

"That was something else, wasn't it?" The sandy, blond-haired girl at the table said. "By the way, my name is Patty."

"Hi! I'm Zoe."

"Zoe, huh? Pretty name. Where are you from?

"I'm from Nairobi, Kenya. And you?"

"Here."

Not wanting to appear rude and feeling awkward, Zoe said nothing.

"Hey Zoe, I'm coming back next week. I'm really thinking about helping with the crusade. I don't think it's my calling or purpose, but I feel I need to do it, if you get my drift." Zoe nodded, not understanding what the girl was talking about. "Uhmm, I'm going to meet Camille and get some literature. My friends are waiting for me at the door." "Okay, and hey, it was nice meeting you! Will you be here next week?" "I will give it some thought. This information caught me off guard. But it's something to think about," Zoe told her. "Well, if you are here, I'll see you." Leaving to speak with Camille, Patty looked at Zoe, "I hope you come back. It's something about you! Your energy says this is you, but oh well," Looking over at Zoe's friends, she said, "You'd better go. I see the students are getting restless." "How did you know we are…that I'm a student?" Zoe asked her. Grinning, Patty responded, "I told you, it's your energy. Besides, you look like a student. See ya!" She left Zoe standing with her mouth wide open as she went to speak to Camille. Zoe wanted to talk with Camille, but when she glanced at the women waiting for her at the door, she could tell they were becoming restless. Torn between wanting to speak with Camille about sex trafficking and having them wait for her or leaving with them, reluctantly choosing the latter, with a heavy sigh, she walked over to join the group waiting for her.

For the next couple of days, Zoe could barely study. Her mind was constantly on the meeting and what the policewoman talked about. She decided to go to the next meeting alone. It was still light outside. If the meeting lasted long, she could get a police escort. She was one of the first to arrive at the next meeting. This time, she took a seat near the front. She didn't want any distractions. As she pulled her chair out to sit down, the sandy, blond-haired girl named Patty approached the table and pulled the seat next to hers out. She smiled. "I knew you would be here, she said." "How did you know?" Zoe inquired. "Your eyes." The girls smiled at each other and began small talk while waiting for the meeting to start.

Zoe never forgot that day. It changed her entire life. She and Patty have been together since. Still looking in the mirror, smiling back at the reflection, she knew it wasn't a mistake. It was the right decision. All her anxiety was gone. She didn't have to go to the bathroom anymore. Wiping her face again with the cold washcloth, taking one last look into the mirror, she turned off the light and walked out into the room. Seeing the other two engage in what appeared to be a peaceful conversation, she smiled. "Good! You guys are finally getting along! It's about time!"

Chapter Fifteen

Hearing her stomach growl, Zoe realized she was still hungry. Except for what she had at the restaurant, which she threw up, she hadn't eaten in almost twenty-four hours. Missing her cook's delectable dishes, she let out a small groan, "I'm hungry!" she cried, touching her stomach. "I can go for some real Nairobi food and not ham sandwiches!" Curling up her lips in disgust, remembering the taste of the ham, she reached for the phone to call room service. "I have a craving for some Jollof rice. Do you want some?" she asked Kato and Patty.

"Never heard of it. What is it?" Patty asked.

"It's rice with TPO."

"TPO?" Patty smirked.

Ignoring her friend's smirk, she explained, "It's rice with tomatoes, peppers, and onions. Don't knock it until you try it; it's good. My cook makes it for me all the time."

"Your cook?" Oh, my! Well, la de da," mocked Patty.

"Yes, my cook," replied Zoe, ignoring her friend's mockery.

Kato butted in, "Yes, our little Zoe is wealthy. She has a maid, a cook, and a gardener." Zoe rolled her eyes at them as she ordered the food. Even though they were giving her a hard time, she ordered enough for all three in case they were hungry. Hanging up the phone, gazing at Kato, trying to keep her calm, she said, "By the way, Kato, I'm not wealthy. My parents are well off, but that doesn't make us rich." For some reason, she thought he was trying to pick an argument with them. Kato didn't say anything. He didn't want to get the women riled up again. The mission was too dangerous for them not to be on one accord. Too much was at stake. He decided to call a truce. "My apologies, ladies. It does appear that I have become a monster, or as you called me Patty, a butt-hole. I guess we are all getting a little edgy." Just then, someone knocked on the door. "Room service," cried a voice on the other side of the door.

"That was quick," said Patty. "They sure bring your food fast here!"

Zoe opened the door to allow the waitress access into the room. A young woman entered with a small table with enough food to feed them and more. "I have brought you enough rice to eat as much as you like," the young woman told them as she put the food on the terrace's patio table. "I also bought you a bowl of fruit, some Shuku Shuku for your long journey, and a pitcher of ice-cold, fresh pineapple juice." She gestured for them to come out on the terrace. "Come, Come! You must eat on the terrace and act like you are on holiday like the many people do when they come here." She pointed at the other people eating on the terraces. "See, eh," she said in broken English.

Feeling a little uneasy by the woman's knowledge of them, Zoe asked her, "What are you talking about?" The young woman continued talking as she prepared the food on the terrace. Concentrating on placing the silverware, in a whispering voice, she told them, "I know why you are here. The car will move tonight. You can see it from the terrace with your night-infrared vision goggles when it's dark. It will be the second to the last car parked on the other side of the street. She will be there. Her fee is high, so please be careful. If you are not, you will meet your Maker tonight." She paused and looked at Zoe, "Let God lead you and do not trust anyone. There is a message on the napkin, see." She showed them the napkin. "Take care! May God be with you." She bowed, letting them know the food was ready for them to eat. Without waiting for a reply, she kissed Zoe on the cheek. Taking one last glance at the three of them, she bowed again and left the room.

Unfazed, Kato sneered, "Now, that was a theatrical performance, if I may say so myself." He put some rice on a plate, "Yum! It looks pretty good." Shaken up by the young woman's words and kiss, Zoe touched her cheek. She looked as if she was about to cry. Seeing Zoe becoming unglued and about to cry, Patty went over to her. Breaking the tension, she touched Zoe's shoulder, "Girl! Thanks for ordering us some food! Lord, I didn't realize I was still hungry. It's not too long ago I had fries and a burger and now I am hungry again. What in the world is Shanka Shanka?" she laughed at her mispronunciation of the food.

"Huh?" said Zoe. She was grateful that Patty had stepped in. It snapped her out of her trance. Regaining her composure, she answered, "Oh yes! It's Shuku Shuku." Laughing at her friend's pronunciation of the dish. Zoe repeated it, but slower so Patty could understand. "It's Shuku Shuku. They are coconut balls, and they are quite good. The ingredients are coconut, egg yolks, and sugar. Here, taste one." She handed one to Patty. Patty took it and put it in her mouth. Chewing it slowly, savoring the flavor, she said, "Mmmm! It's good! Not too sweet, but sweet enough."

Kato noticed how Zoe, the usually calm one, almost lost it when the young girl kissed her cheek and how Patty, usually the easily agitated one, came to her rescue. These girls are good friends, he thought. Filling his plate with fresh fruit and Shuku Shuku, he wondered how everything would pan out in the end. How could they follow the plan if he had to watch both of them? The price was too high if they failed, or worse, if he lost them. Not wanting them to know what he was thinking and to change the atmosphere in the room, he gently nudged them to sit on the terrace. "We need to do as we are told and sit and eat on the terrace."

Mocking the young servant woman, "Let us be merry and happy as if we haven't a care in the world. We are on holiday. Zoe, sit." He pointed to a chair for Zoe. "Patty, sit." He pointed to a chair for Patty to sit. Now eat and watch the people." Laughing at his expression of the girl, both women sat down as they were told and filled their plates with the delicious food. "She was right," Zoe said, "There is enough to feed several people, and I'm hungry. I hadn't had anything since the ham sandwich, and we know what happened with that." Taking a forkful of rice, she waited until she swallowed her food before she spoke, "Listen, I know I almost became unglued when the girl kissed my cheek. I'm sorry. It's so much to take in! How does everyone know who we are and why we are here? It's insane, right!"

"Don't worry," Patty said, comforting her friend. "We are in this together. There were many times you had to pull me together. But it does seem crazy, like a B-rated spy movie. Zoe laughed, "It's more like a C-rated movie." They all laughed. In a solemn tone, Zoe asked, "Kato, are you getting scared? Or is it a man's thing not to show emotions in the face of danger?" With a mouth full of rice, Kato told her, "Zoe, men get scared too. I'm not scared, but I am concerned. I have to make sure you two are safe. I promised Camille I would look after you both. What keeps me focused is the little girl. That's our mission. I keep focused on the mission."

"Kato, how many girls have you rescued?" asked Patty.

"Girls and a few young boys, too," he noted.

"How many?" Zoe was now curious about him.

He stared briefly at her before answering the question. With a heavy sigh, he said, "Maybe twenty. We get them out of the hands of the traffickers. Then we take them to an orphanage like the one we left. They don't touch the orphanages! They are safe zones. These men are very superstitious. They fear the nuns," he grinned.

"Wow! Twenty, that's impressive," cried Zoe. "How did you get involved in this life?"

He popped another coconut ball into his mouth. Between bites, he told them his story. "Like Patty, I lost a loved one. I lost my sister, Elan. My family is from Sudan. We fled because it was a war-torn country. Even at a young age, my sister was brilliant. Some local men from the village we were living in at the time, resting from our flight, approached my father. My father couldn't find work to feed his family. They told him to sell my sister. She wouldn't be in any harm. She would be working in a clerical position in the city. This way, he can get back on his feet and over time go back and get my sister. My mother pleaded for him not to do it. He didn't at first. Eventually, he did as food and money became scarce. He never hugged my sister. He just took the money and gave her to the man. My mother screamed, punching him on the back. He pushed her onto the ground and walked away. My mother wept for my sister for days; she never got over it. In my young mind, I didn't understand what was happening. I often wondered if my father or mother knew. They both said nothing. A few weeks after that, my father left. I never saw him again. I hated my father for a very long time. I hated him for what he did to our family, to my mother, and my sister. Soon, my hate turned into a crusade.

"Ah, now I see, Batman!" said Zoe.

"Yes, Batman!" winked Kato. "Eventually, I had to learn how to forgive my father because it was eating up the inside of me. I'm not fully there, but I am much better than I was. It's a cruel world we live in if you are poor and people see you as of no value. Many young children, girls, and boys are sold as human or sex slaves every day. They have no voice. They are promised employment or a better life, looking for a way out of their misery- their stink- only to discover it will worsen. They don't realize they will be sold for sex, then used, abused, mistreated, and eventually thrown out like yesterday's garbage. The irony is that the men who do this to these girls come from all over the world, even America. They are rich, middle class, and upper class: doctors, lawyers, professors, politicians, engineers, and even the clergy. These men fool themselves into believing that the young girls enjoy being touched."

Shocked by what he said, Patty said, "My God, how can a twelve-year-old enjoy being brutally raped?"

With venom in his voice, Kato looked at her and said, "This is what these men want to believe. I believe this is to ease their conscience. The clergy are the worst. They use scriptures to justify their actions. 'It is better to burn.' Then they return to their nice homes and families and preach hell and damnation to anyone who doesn't believe in God or live according to their values or morals. They are full of self-righteousness, while the young girls they abuse must deal with the emotional trauma for the rest of their lives. They drug the girls up so much that they become numb to the pain and the sex. Some girls can see up to ten or more men in a day. Sounds surreal, doesn't it? Like I'm making it up? I'm not. But I am proud of the countries that are fighting this war. They are taking great strides in making laws to stop all forms of human and sex trafficking. Unfortunately, even with the laws, it's still hard to stop. The money is crazy, and bribes are the norm."

"Did you ever find your sister?" asked Zoe. Her heart ached for all the sadness he endured in his life. "Yes and no," he answered. "I searched for years looking for my sister. After my mother died, I left and went to where she was last seen. Miraculously, many years later, I came upon someone who knew of her and her traffickers. They informed me that she was smuggled into another country and was probably dead. Once they are through with you, what else is there to do but die."

"What kept you going?" Zoe asked. She wanted to know everything. The more she knew and understood, the better it was for her to understand the call on her life.

"It was not hatred. It was the need to save someone from the same thing I couldn't save my sister from. So it was the need to be Batman, the Caped Crusader. In the end, just like you two, it was all in God's plan." Finishing up, he stared at them both and said, "Now that you know a little more about me, we need to finish this good food. Don't waste anything. We don't know when we will eat again." Pouring a glass of pineapple juice, he took a long sip of the ice-cold drink and then saluted the two women. They ate in silence for the remainder of the meal.

Chapter Sixteen

"Well, that was filling," belted Patty, breaking the silence from the solemn meal. She popped a coconut ball in her mouth, "Mmmm, I must say I like these Chuu Chuu balls." Laughing at her incorrect pronunciation of the food, she corrected herself, "I mean Shunka Shunka. I like the TPO rice, too. I must remember to make this dish for my parents when I get back to the States. The food tastes different here. What gives?" she asked, chewing the last bite of the tasty coconut pastry.

"It's fresher," said Zoe. "Our refrigeration system is not as high-tech as your country's. Although we have come a long way, and it has greatly improved, our meat shelf life is shorter. Also, we tend to buy our food daily from the local street markets and specialty grocery stores, which is why our food is so fresh. I remember the first time I tasted an American steak. It was quite different from the taste I'm accustomed to. I'm still getting used to the taste."

"Yup, I know what you mean," said Patty. "Food is cooked differently in every culture, but I do like TPO rice. It's light but very filling." Zoe, nodded her head agreeing with Patty, "Uh huh. In America, I like peanut butter and jelly sandwiches." Puzzled by her choice of food, they glared at her like she said something crazy. "Don't look at me like that. I'm not crazy!" laughed Zoe. "I know it sounds insane, but I like peanut butter and jelly sandwiches. I like how they taste together. While studying at night I would make two PB&J sandwiches and get a glass of milk. I would be in hog heaven," she laughed at the thought, wishing she had a PB&J sandwich now.

Patty laughed, "Zoe, you are weird!"

Kato watched the two. He was amazed at how they could go on and on about food. How innocent they are, especially Zoe, he thought. As they continued talking about their likes and dislikes of different cuisines, he wondered how they both got involved in the sex trafficking crusade. Did they fully understand what they were involved in or how dangerous this mission was? They sounded like two good friends, BFFs, sitting around the table for some girl talk, just shooting the breeze. He knew he had to get them back focused. Clearing his voice, he interrupted their conversation, "Uh, um! Girls!" They both gave him the evil eye. "I mean ladies. We have business to tend to. There is a note on the napkin." He opened the napkin and showed them the note. "Well, what does it say?" cried Zoe, wishing she and Patty could continue their conversation. It felt good for once not thinking about what they would do later that night.

"It says that the child is eight like Zoe said. She was abducted in the middle of the night. Her parents are still searching for her. They are offering a small reward. They believed it was an inside job within the village, possibly someone they knew. It's believed she isn't drugged, so she is aware of what's happening to her."

"How did they get her?" inquired Patty.

Annoyed by the question, Kato snapped at her. "Aren't you listening? Didn't you hear me say it was an inside job!"

Zoe, losing her patience with how Kato was treating them, scolded him, "Kato, you must stop being short with us! We're not children! She asked you a question! Don't forget we're in this together. We are a little frightened and concerned for the young girl and ourselves!"

Kato apologized. "Hey, you two, I'm sorry for getting so worked up. Please forgive me. When I think about grown men having sex with little children my anger rises. I think about my sister! As a man, I don't understand! These are innocent children!" Kato knew he was allowing his commitment to the mission to get to him and he was taking it out on them. He had to stay focused. Too much was at stake. Taking a deep breath to control his thoughts, he said, "It appears that I have been apologizing a lot for my behavior. I don't want to seem hard. It's not good for us to argue among ourselves. We can't get distracted. We must stay focused."

Zoe understood how he felt. The more she knew about the evils of sex trafficking, the more determined she was to help in the fight. No longer upset, she felt compassion for him. "Look, Kato," she calmly said, "we know you have been doing this longer than us. We get it! But don't keep hammering us. We're here, aren't we? We need each other if we are going to get the little girl. I didn't quit medical school to lose." Zoe then noticed how quiet Patty had become, and became concerned. "Patty, are you ok? What are you thinking about? You have become too quiet. Are you afraid? If you are, you can stay here, and no one will think less of you. I promise," she assured her friend.

Patty shrugged, "No, that's the funny thing. I'm not afraid. I don't know if that's a good or bad thing. When Kato told us about the little girl, a strange peace suddenly came over me. A peace I can't explain. Like no matter what, I'm... we're going to be ok. Smiling at her friend, Zoe replied, "That's the peace of God. His peace will keep you, and it will keep us." Remembering what the woman at the restaurant told her about telling Bible stories, Zoe laughed inwardly. It wasn't time for a Bible story, "Come on, Captain America, we must get ready. We have a little one to rescue."

Kato feeling guilty about his actions, apologized again. "Zoe is right. I'm sorry for my behavior. And Patty, I owe you a separate apology. It was I who became unglued, not you."

"It's okay, Kato, really," Patty reassured him. "I lost my best friend, but you lost your sister. As Zoe said, we're in this together. Let's get the girl and fuss later."

Finally, thought Zoe. She was glad they were getting along. "Kato, finish telling us what the note says." Nodding his head, Kato finished reading the note. "It says to wait outside by a reddish-brown building down the road from the club. They are going to put the young girl in the car. The locals know what's happening; they won't stop you but won't help you either." Kato paused from reading, "They are afraid. It's not only sex trafficking; it's probably big money. When the money is this big, you can be certain drugs and weapons are involved. Whoever is behind this must be powerful. Putting the napkin down, he looked up at them and said, "Anyway, the car will be open, and for a brief moment...ten to twelve minutes max, the little girl will be in the car alone."

"That doesn't sound right," said Patty. Zoe agreed. "I'm with Patty. It sounds too easy."

Trying not to lose his temper again, Kato ignored their remarks, "Look, I told you, the locals are afraid. They are afraid for their lives and the lives of their children. The men with the little girl know the locals won't touch her. Besides, someone within them is aiding us. Whoever that person is will make sure the girl is alone. He will have the excuse already played out. Again, these men are ruthless, not smart."

"What are we to do when we retrieve the girl?" Zoe asked.

"There's a safe house between the two buildings with a trap wall. We have to get the girl there. No one will say anything. They will act like they saw nothing."

"What happens then? Will the men look for the girl or cause terror on the locals?" Zoe inquired. Patty was wondering the same thing. It felt like something out of a James Bond movie, but this wasn't a movie. This was real.

"No," said Kato. "Most likely, the men will flee because whoever purchased this young girl will kill the men for losing her. The local police will get involved, and the person doesn't want his name associated with this. He would rather lose the money."

Engrossed in the whole spy thing, Patty asked, "Kato, do you think it's someone high up?"

"Yes," he replied. "I believe it is. That's why we must be careful. Like the waitress at the restaurant, Alana, said, don't trust anyone." He looked down as he said the woman's name.

At the sound of the woman's name, something jumped within Zoe. She couldn't recall telling him the woman's name. She looked at him and asked, "Kato, did I tell you her name? The lady at the restaurant, did I tell you her name? Kato stared at her as if she lost her mind, "Don't you remember?" Scratching her head, trying to remember, questioning herself, she said, "I must have…how else?" "Yes," he told her. Yawning, looking at his watch, he said, "Let's each take a breather. I'm exhausted." He got up from his chair and walked over to the bed. He took his shoes off and laid down on the bed. After a few moments, he was asleep, snoring lightly. Zoe watched him. Oblivious to what was going on, Patty excused herself to go to the bathroom to freshen up, leaving Zoe alone on the terrace to think.

"Lord, I don't recall telling Kato the woman's name. I must have told him between eating the ham sandwich. I must have forgotten that I did. Maybe it was because of the sandwich." Thinking of the sandwich made her want to throw up again. She took a sip of pineapple juice and looked at Kato sprawled on the bed. Listening to his light snores, "He goes to sleep fast when he's tired," she said under her breath.

Chapter Seventeen

Still pondering about Kato, Zoe turned around when she heard Patty's voice. "I could really go for a nice, long bubble bath. Calgon, take me away," sang Patty, mimicking the retro commercial from the nineties her mother often referred to when she needed a break from the kids and her father. Pulling up a chair across from Zoe, she saw from the woman's posture something was deeply troubling her. It showed all over her face. "Whoa, Zoe! What gives?" cried Patty. "You look spacey or lost. Like a zombie or something! What's up?" Where is the person telling us to get it together?"

Zoe closed her eyes and took a deep breath. She had to get herself together. That thing with Kato was messing with her mind. Opening her eyes, she saw the other woman staring at her. "Patty," she asked, "Do you recall me telling Kato the waitress' name at the restaurant? I don't remember me telling either of you. I don't even remember if she told me her name." Patty looked at Kato sleeping. Hearing his gentle snores, she said, "I don't know. Girl, I wasn't all there! Kato and I were arguing the entire time you were in the bathroom. I wasn't paying attention when you came back to the table in a daze, talking about how that man bumped into you. I was getting over Kato and me kissing to keep the two men who walked into the restaurant from being suspicious. But it does seem strange. So much has happened today. Nothing is real. I told you, it's like some low-budget spy movie."

Hearing that they were kissing bothered Zoe. She didn't know why she felt uneasy about them kissing; she shook it off, "Yeah, I guess you're right. The woman at the restaurant said I shouldn't trust anyone. She told me not to trust her either." Patty saw how Zoe reacted when she told her she and Kato kissed, but she played it off. "Surely you don't mean Kato? He was right there with us when Camille was briefing us. Don't forget Zoe, his sister was a victim of sex trafficking, and he has helped many victims of sex trafficking."

"I don't know?" said Zoe. "Sometimes, you can't rule from your heart. You have to rule from your mind."

"Zoe," Patty asked her, "I'm curious. Do you trust me? With me? Are you ruling from your mind or heart?"

"No. No. No! Not you, my friend! I trust you! It just seems something is not right in the midst of things. I've known you since that day at the meeting. Kato, we just met." "Well, don't get too bothered about things or him! He is a big pain in the rear! He's attractive, but he's so arrogant and full of himself. Besides, we need him, and he is good, Zoe. That much I can see. Hopefully, we won't see him again when this is over."

"Yeah, I suppose," said Zoe, even though something kept nagging her in the back of her mind.

Patty shrugged and reached for a banana from the fruit bowl. Peeling the fruit, she said, "I've always wondered why bananas stay fresh longer on the vine, and then the moment you take them off they go bad." "You take them out of their habitation, their environment," Zoe said without a second thought. Patty took a bite of the fruit, with her mouth full, "Yeah, I suppose, but I do love me some bananas. I always have to a fault. It was nice of the hotel to give us a fruit bowl with our order. I'm going to put a banana and some coconut balls in my pockets just in case I need a quick snack tonight."

Zoe watched Patty devour the banana. She was amazed at how much the woman could eat. She laughed and said, "If that's your fault," pointing to the fruit peelings, "consider yourself blessed or weird." Laughing along with her, Patty said, "No, too many bananas are not good for you…too much potassium…too much potassium…not good." Zoe burst into laughter, "You sound like an ad for a doctor or some medical research." Cracking up from the joke, Patty howled, "No, I sound like my grandmother when she tells me to stop eating too many bananas." Then changing the subject, she said soberly, "Zoe, Kato is okay."

"Huh?" said Zoe, baffled by Patty's sudden solemn tone.

"I didn't want you to get that weird look in your eyes again as if you were a million miles away. That's why people say it's something about your eyes. Your eyes take you to faraway places we can't see or go. When you get like this, you are in your own world. I had to break the ice to get you to refocus. We can't afford to have division in the team. Yes, Kato gets on my nerves, but I have to believe we can trust him. He seems straight so far."

"You're right, Captain America," she said with a grin. "It was getting tense. It's all coming to the top. It was easy when we were planning all of this. Now that we're about to execute the plan, it's something different altogether." "Uh huh," agreed Patty. Patty unhooked her locket from around her neck. Staring at it briefly she handed it to Zoe. Somberly, she said, "Here, Zoe, it's my best friend Lizzy's locket. I want you to take it. Please keep it as a keepsake in case I don't come back alive. You know, in case something goes wrong." Zoe looked at the locket. "Girl! Keep your locket! Put it back on to remember your friend. It will give you strength." She handed the locket back to Patty, "Nothing is going to happen to you. We are all coming out of this." Patty took the locket back, "Zoe, what if we don't?" she asked. Zoe could hear the fear in her friend's voice. "We will. We will, Patty," Zoe reassured her. Although she had doubts, she didn't want to alarm Patty. She boldly said, "We have God on our side. If He is for us, nothing and no one will be against us."

Drinking the last sip of pineapple juice, savoring the flavor and moment,

Zoe sighed, "Ahhh! This pineapple juice is so good and fresh. How I missed fresh pineapple juice when I was studying abroad."

"Yeah, it is fresh," said Patty, still thinking about the locket.

Changing the gloomy mood, Zoe grabbed her backpack. "Here, give me some bananas and the Chu Chu balls, as you call them. I'll put them in the backpack along with the other items. The journey is long, but we don't have to be hungry. The woman at the restaurant gave me some packets of dried nuts and fruit. I'll put them in my backpack, too." Patty raised her hand to give Zoe a high-five, "That's what I'm talking about, girlfriend! Amen!" Both girls burst into laughter. Handing her the items, Patty asked, "Speaking of backpacks, what did the woman at the restaurant give you? You never said anything about the meeting between the two of you." "Oh yes," squealed Zoe as she lifted her blouse to show the other woman. "She gave me these... a small knife and a gun she called Jesus."

"Jesus?" shrieked Patty. "Why?"

"She said Jesus would protect me."

"Well, then, if that's Jesus, give me the knife," said Patty. "I need something to protect me!"

Gently pulling the tape from her skin, Zoe handed the knife to Patty. Taking the knife from Zoe, Patty looked at it and said, "I'll call this my Guardian Angel. Now we have Jesus and our Guardian Angel protecting us." They both burst into laughter at the names they called their weapons. Patty grabbed the backpack and said, "I'm going to put some extra fruit in the backpack. I'll put enough for the both of us, but not Kato. Let him starve for being so mean." She put a couple of apples and two more bananas in the backpack but decided to take one banana out to eat. Taking a bite, grinning, she said, "Yup, you can't get enough bananas. Love them to a fault."

Zoe smiled at her friend.

Chapter Eighteen

Enjoying the peace and quiet on the terrance as Kato slept and Patty took a quick shower, finally alone, Zoe talked to God. Since she was a little girl, she loved to talk to God. It was her peace. Often, she would sit for hours, listening to His voice, meditating on His Word, or talking to Him about her fears, plans, and desires. As early as she could remember, her parents took her to church. When she got older and it was required for her to attend youth church, she defiantly stood her ground. "Father," she would say to her dad, "I don't want to attend youth church. I want to stay with you and Mother and listen to the preacher talk about God." It was a battle for her mother, who insisted she attend youth church. "You will not understand the things the minister will say, Zoe. You're too young. You'll understand if you go to youth church," her mother would always say, but it was in vain.

Pleading with her parents that she would understand, her father finally gave in to her pleas and told her that she could attend church in the main sanctuary for a month, and in the month's time, he would give her a test to see what she had learned. She would go to youth church if she didn't learn anything or didn't understand what the minister taught. Zoe agreed. When her parents gave her the test at the end of the month, they were astonished at how much she understood the messages. They marveled at her spiritual wisdom and knowledge of the messages but even more at her relationship with God. From then on, Zoe remained in the sanctuary with her parents. She would sometimes tell them about the messages.

In the past, her faith always provided the answers or guidance she needed. She always knew what to do after she prayed. Now, for the first time in her life, she didn't have an answer after she prayed. She didn't know what to do. Sitting on the terrace she prayed, "Father, I need to know if this is what you want me to do. Please, Lord, let me know. I'm afraid, and for some reason, Kato makes me suspicious of him." Tears streaming down her face, she continued to pray as she thought about the first time she discussed the mission with Camille, which now seems so long ago.

They had been at the camp a little over a week when Camille got word that a young girl was abducted from a village outside of the city's perimeter by human traffickers. The girl's family gave the agents a description of one of the men. It fitted the description of a man who worked for someone they were after for years. Knowing this could be the break they hoped for, the agents contacted Camille to see if she had a team in place. It was a dangerous mission. She needed someone to go along with Kato. If not, she would have to go. She didn't want to because of a conflict of interest and there was a busload of children arriving later in the week. She needed to be there when the children arrived. Overhearing the woman's dilemma as Camille and a counselor discussed the mission, Zoe volunteered to go.

"Zoe," said Camille, "I know you want to help, but it's too dangerous. I can't allow you to go. I don't know what I would do if you were hurt or, became a victim of sex trafficking yourself. That would be a fate worse than death." Not adhering to the woman's words, Zoe pleaded, "Camille, I'm not afraid." Listening to the young woman's pleas, Camille sighed, "You sound like an eager young schoolgirl. This is not school, Zoe. It's dangerous. You must realize this?" "I know it's dangerous, but I know this is what I came here for," cried Zoe. Staring at the pretty young woman's face, Camille, knowing she was losing a battle she never had a chance of winning, still needed to make the young woman understand what she was getting into. She continued trying to persuade her against the idea. "Zoe, there are many things you can do here to help. You can help provide medical care to the children." She had to give it one last push to attempt to change the young woman's mind. However, the more Camille tried to persuade Zoe, the more resilient Zoe became in her pleading. Determined, she didn't waiver.

Zoe boldly told the woman, "Camille, I understand the danger. I prayed and prayed. I know this is what I am supposed to do. I don't know why. One morning, I was in medical school in America. I went to that first meeting. The next thing I know, I'm here assisting in the fight against human trafficking and helping victims of sex trafficking. I didn't ask for this, nor did I ever think about this growing up. When you are called, and purpose has you, you don't ask why. You believe and do. Trust me! I need to do this."

"But Zoe…," Camille was about to say something but was interrupted by Zoe. "I know what you are going to say. I hear it in your voice like I heard it in my parents' voices…."

"Zoe, my dear heart, I am not saying you are not called to do this, but what if it's another way? What if it's not going in the field? What if I need you here with me? That's part of the calling, too. Not everyone called is the boss. You need workers to assist the boss."

Camille's words had no effect on Zoe. "Camille, my parents will tell you that there is something about me. Some may call it a stubborn streak, but it's something more that I can't fully explain. When I know in my mind it's right, my heart is set. It's no use trying to talk me out of it. Besides, at the meeting you said some of us were destined for this. It was our purpose like it's your purpose. Don't you remember?"

Knowing she lost the battle, Camille closed her eyes, inhaling before speaking. She loved the young woman's resilience. Opening her eyes, she smiled at the persistent young woman, "Zoe, I'm not trying to talk you out of this. I just wanted you to know this isn't America or where you are from. The people in this world don't care about your parents or how influential they are. These people are brutal. They are not only selling people for sex;

they are also trafficking and selling drugs and weapons. Zoe, it's organized crime! We don't want you to become a martyr."

Zoe gulped, "A martyr?"

"Yes, a martyr because they will kill you without mercy, that is after they rape you. And they will rape you, and sadly your body may never be found."

"Well," she replied confidently, quoting the scripture, "Absent from the body is to be present with the Lord."

Camille loved the young woman's tenacity. "Ughhhh, Zoe!" she cried out. "I am serious! You are not in Sunday school where the teacher tells you to quote the scriptures."

"I know I'm not! Camille, I'm serious too! I can't explain. It's bigger than me. I know it is!"

Weary of the conversation, in exasperation, Camille gave in. "Zoe, are you certain?"

"Yes, Camille!" I know this is what I'm supposed to do."

Camille sighed, "I know, Zoe. I know," She was tired of trying to persuade the young woman. "I needed to hear this from you. I needed you to say it. The moment I saw you, I knew. I don't want you to go; it's a dangerous mission. But I know you have to go. Your eyes say it all."

"My eyes?" asked Zoe.

"Yes, your eyes," answered Camille.

Relieved Camille was letting her go, Zoe said, "It's funny because that's what my father always said. He would tell me it's something about my eyes."

"Yes, Zoe, God is with you no matter what."

"Camille, do you know why my father named me Zoe? It's not an African name, per se, but he wanted me to be named Zoe. My mother protested in the beginning, but when he told her why, she immediately said yes, 'that is her name.'"

"I know what your name means. It means Life."

"It's more," Zoe informed her. "Zoe means Life in Greek. However, the biblical meaning of the word Zoe is eternal Life, never-ending Life, an abundant Life. Zoe is the God kind of Life! That is why I said absent from the body is to be present with God. You see, no matter what happens, I have eternal Life. So why should I fear? I have the God kind of Life."

Zoe was too busy telling Camille about the origins of her name she didn't see the tall, handsome man walk up. Even though he was supposed to stay in the house with her and Patty, she hadn't seen him but a few times since the airport ride. As he listened to the young woman give a history lesson about her name, he winked at Camille, putting his two fingers to his lips, signaling her to keep quiet. He was enchanted with the beautiful young woman and her beautiful brown eyes. Zoe, catching her breath, realizing they were no longer alone, blushed at the handsome man standing beside Camille. She hoped she didn't sound foolish or, worse, embarrassed herself. She had to learn to control herself when she was adamant about something. She would go on and on until she proved her point. I must pray about this, she thought.

Camille, seeing the young woman's blushed face, smiled within. There was definitely something about Zoe, she thought. "Zoe, let me introduce you again to Kato. Zoe, Kato. Kato, Zoe. You remember him from the airport, yes?"

Zoe shook her head, "Yes."

"So I heard. Life…ahhh, good! It's so lovely to meet you again, Zoe, or may I call you Life?" he grinned, hoping he would cause her to blush again. It made her look adorable. "By the way, I love your name. Such enthusiasm!

It fits you very well.

"Thank you," she replied. Never one to be lost for words, she found herself just that, a loss of words. She blushed again.

Camille, clearing her throat, "Uh, um, Kato has been with us for years. He has seen a lot, but it's getting worse." She turned to the man, "Isn't it, Kato?" She didn't give him a chance to comment or agree. "But on a positive note, worldwide, more people are becoming aware of Knowing she lost the battle, Camille closed her eyes, inhaling before speaking. She loved the young woman's resilience. Opening her eyes, she smiled at the persistent young woman, "Zoe, I'm not trying to talk you out of this. I just wanted you to know this isn't America or where you are from. The people in this world don't care about your parents or how influential they are. and sex trafficking. They are hearing about it more. It's becoming quite a trending topic in America and other Western countries. More Hollywood celebrities are talking about it. Unfortunately, people fail to realize that many rich and powerful men worldwide are involved in this business. It's a multi-billion-dollar business. Until we get new laws and punish the ones doing it, I'm afraid it will be another trend or hot topic until the next one comes along." Finishing her last statement, she turned to Kato. "Kato, do you have everything you need? Are you good on the pickup and round up information?"

Shaking his head, "I'm good," he told her.

"Camille, what is so special about this particular girl?" Zoe asked, finally gaining her composure. She didn't know why the man made her uncomfortable.

"There is nothing extraordinary special about this girl, Zoe. Nothing exceptional, that is, other than her parents are very destitute. She is at the bottom of the class structure and labeled 'a nobody' in the world. But this little girl is special to God. She represents all the little girls from all over the world, just like her, who have been sold or abducted. If we can save her, we have saved many. These children are special to God. Remember this always. She gave the young woman a motherly hug. Camille turned to Kato, "Kato, please take care of our girls. Bring them both back."

Puzzled, "Both?" he asked.

That's right! You heard me. Both! There is another one. Her name is Patty. You met her in the limousine, too. She will also be going. She's at the infirmary getting her final shots and checkup. She's American, around the same age as Zoe. They met at a meeting I was holding in Baltimore. They're two peas in a pod, like sisters." With a serious tone, she glared at him, "Kato, they are like daughters to me. Please bring them back safe and unharmed."

He winked and assured her, "I promise I will." "Good! We'll continue to meet to discuss everything. Kato, tomorrow we will meet up with our POCs." "POCs? What are POCs?" asked Zoe.

"Point of Contacts," answered Kato. "They are people who will guide us and provide us with the necessary information about the area and the situation."

"Yes," said Camille. "Once we meet with our POCs, they will inform us of everything they know. From there, it is all you three. It's been a couple of days since the young girl was abducted. We have to hurry. We have at most three days to get there and get her. Zoe, you'd better get plenty to eat and plenty of sleep. We have much planning to do. Come on, Kato. We need to make sure you have everything you need." They walked away, leaving Zoe in total adrenaline.

Relieved she and Patty could go, Zoe watched Camille and the handsome man walk towards the building in the center of the village, talking as if they had known each other for many years. There was an intimate familiarity between them. Zoe wondered why she noticed. Shrugging her shoulders, she went to find Patty. "I hope Patty is finished at the infirmary. There is so much I need to tell her."

Chapter Nineteen

Relaxing on the terrace, Zoe eventually dozed off to sleep. The cool breeze on her face woke her up. Stretching her arms to yawn, she saw that the sun had set and darkness was on the horizon. Glancing at her watch, she quickly jumped up when she saw the time. "Oh my goodness! Look at the time!" she cried. Although she was glad to have gotten some shuteye before the night's adventure, she didn't mean to sleep so long. Looking over at the two bodies sprawled on the bed, Patty at the bottom and Kato at the top, she was relieved to see they were still sleeping. She needed a moment to herself. Getting up to go to the bathroom, walking past the two, she noticed how Patty was curled up like a little child, whereas Kato's long, lean, muscular body took over most of the bed. "Humpff," she grunted, "He does seem to take over." Chuckling to herself, she watched him sleep. He was very handsome, she thought. Feeling the urge to use the restroom, she took one last look at the man before she went to do her business. Washing her hands afterward, looking into the mirror and seeing her reflection, she whispered, "Zoe, after tonight, I have a feeling that nothing will ever be the same." Opening the door, enjoying the quietness, she tiptoed to the terrace. She didn't want to awaken them. Not yet.

From the terrace, everything in the town looked tranquil. "It's beautiful," she gasped. Watching the handful of people walking about, she longed for her parents and brother. It was the first time she thought of them since their last goodbyes. The last time she saw her parents, she was walking out the door to return to the village. She hugged her father. He hugged her back so hard she couldn't breathe. He hugged her as if he would never see her again. Kissing his cheek, she promised he would see her again. "Father, I'll be back. I promise." She went to hug her mother to say goodbye, but her mother looked at her with a strange, sad look. She swiftly hugged her, giving her a peck on the cheek, and whispered in her ear, "I love you, Mommy. I promise I know what I'm doing." Her mother returned the kiss, "I love you too, Zoe. Please be careful."

Her mother, always composed and starched, looked like she was about to fall apart. She didn't. I'm glad, Zoe thought. If she had, I don't know if I would've been able to leave. Her mother was her hero, and even though Zoe never told her, Zoe was in awe of how her mother managed to remain cool and calm at all times. Yes, she had her moments, but like Zoe, everyone knew when she was passionate about something. "I am so much like my mother," said Zoe. "How I wish they were here right now, even Jaheem. I would give them all a big kiss and hug. I miss them dearly," she whispered, trying not to cry, but the soft tears trickled down her face. Grabbing a tissue from the table, she wiped the tears from her eyes. Suddenly thirsty, she tiptoed to the sink to get a glass of water. Turning the faucet on low so they wouldn't hear the water flowing, she filled the glass to the top. Drinking the lukewarm water, she gazed at the two as they slept. "They are still sleeping peacefully." Putting the empty glass down, she grabbed her backpack. Opening it up, she found what she needed: the infrared NV binoculars. Taking them out and discreetly hiding behind the curtain, she looked down the street at the area where the car was supposed to be. There it was! Excited, she screamed in a high-pitched voice. It was loud enough to wake up Patty and Kato.

"What? Huh?" screeched a startled Patty. Jumping up from her sleep, she rushed over to her friend. Concerned, she asked, "Are you okay? Is something wrong?" Wiping his eyes, Kato yelled, "Zoe, are you nuts? Do you want to wake up the entire place? What's wrong with you!" Trembling with excitement, Zoe cried, "I'm sorry for the outburst, but it's there! It's there!" She petitioned for him to come over to the curtain. "See! Look! The car is there! It's right where the note said it would be!"

Patty grabbed the binoculars out of Zoe's hands. Looking through its lens, "It does look like the car," she squealed. Kato got up and purposely strolled over to where the two were standing. Patty attempted to hand him the binoculars, but he ignored her and peeked through the curtains. Growing impatient, Zoe took the binoculars from Patty and shoved them in his hands. "Here, you can't see the car through the curtain. You need these! The infrared will allow you to see the blue marker on the hood. See!" Kato raised his eyes at her but didn't say a word. "The windows are tinted; you can't see," she said. "Yes, it appears to be the car," said Kato dryly. Waiting in the background to get another look, Patty cried, "How conspicuous are they?" Kato replied, "I told you they were brutal, not intelligent. Anyway, everyone knows who they are. I told you they were scared. But don't worry. No one will think that you two are capable of rescuing anyone." His tone was condescending. Zoe looked at him, but Patty, full of excitement, missed the undertone of his words. Seeing Zoe watching him, Kato glanced at his watch and said, "Ladies, it's time to go!" At that moment, Zoe had to go to the bathroom again. She knew it was because of the excitement. "Oh no!" she said under her breath so they couldn't hear. Knowing it was useless, the urge was pulling on her, "Wait a minute. I have to go to the bathroom. Also, I need to check on Jesus and pray."

Kato, losing patience with the two, groaned, "Pray! We already prayed! How many times do we have to pray?" Standing up for her friend, Patty said, "As many times as Zoe wants." Giving her a "girlfriend" smile, "Go ahead, Zoe. Do what you have to do." Thankful for her friend's intervention, Zoe smiled, "Thanks, Patty!" "Ughh! You two will either be the death of me or...," fumed Kato.

Rushing in the bathroom to avoid an accident, Zoe tried to go, but hardly anything came out. Finishing up, she flushed the toilet and washed her hands. "Okay, I'm ready!" she said coming out of the bathroom. "I have the gun. She, I mean Alana, called it Jesus. If I need to shoot it, well, that's praying." Laughing about her comments about the gun, she looked at Patty and asked, "You ready?"

"Ready as I'll ever be," said Patty excitedly.

"Are you ready?" Patty asked Kato. She knew he was in a sour mood but didn't care. She was too excited.

"Yes! Now let's go!" he growled. He knew he was short with them, but in his defense, they had to be on time. Timing was everything.

Zoe went over to Patty. Excited, she asked, "Ready, Captain America? It's time to take care of our business!"

Kato, now calmer, said, "The night is about to break into full darkness. It's still warm outside. You don't need a jacket; a sweater will do. You don't want to look conspicuous. And Zoe, make sure you keep Jesus well hidden." Zoe saluted, "Will do, Batman!" Patty laughed, "Look conspicuous, now that's funny. I can't help but look conspicuous. I'm white. I'm probably the only white woman here. People will know I'm not from here."

"No, there are more…see…well, not many!" said Zoe, realizing Patty was probably right about being the only white female in the town. Trying to appease the moment, Zoe assured her, "Well, you're sorta kinda represented. You're my sister from another mother. Anyway, now you know how I feel at a country music concert, and I love me some country music." Patty interjected, "Don't forget peanut butter and jelly sandwiches too!" They both laughed. "You are a strange person, Zoe. I love you, but you are still strange," said Patty, laughing at her friend's quirkiness. She stopped laughing when she saw Kato getting upset. "Okay, let's roll! I'm ready! By the way, Kato, I have a weapon, too." Patty pulled out her pocket knife to show Kato, "Meet Guardian Angel!" Dumbfounded at the woman's excitement over a small knife, "A pocket knife!" he scoffed, shaking his head. "Really!" "Yes, really!" said Patty, ignoring him. "It's like my shield. You know Captain America has a shield."

"Okay, okay," said Kato, becoming frustrated again. "Put it away! Sheesh! With Zoe's Jesus and your shield, I guess now we can take on the entire dark forces."

"Condescending, aren't we?" huffed Patty. She was tired of his uppity attitude. "Yes, aren't we?" echoed Zoe as she took one last look through the curtain with the binoculars. "Hey, they put something in the car's back seat," she squealed, making sure she didn't scream. "It looks like it's wrapped in a blanket. It's small." "Do you think it's the girl?" asked Patty, high on adrenaline. "Yes!" said Zoe still looking through the binoculars. "Kato, you don't think they knocked her out, do you?" she asked.

"No," said Kato. "They wouldn't harm her. The note said she was not drugged. They may have given her something light to sedate her, but nothing heavy. Whoever it is, he's paying good money for her. He doesn't want a badly beaten or drugged girl. He wants a virgin." He looked at his watch again. They had to leave now if they wanted to make it. "Shall we go?" he asked impatiently.

Zoe put the binoculars back in the backpack. "Let's do this!" she said. But feeling the need to go to the bathroom again, she sheepishly looked at them. "I'm sorry. I need to go again. I guess it's anxiety!" She put the backpack on the table. "Kato, can you grab the backpack for me? Not waiting for him to answer, she looked at him and said, "One last time, I promise," as she rushed to the bathroom. This time, nothing came out. It's just nerves, she thought. Taking a final look in the mirror, she rushed out to the waiting pair. "Okay, it must be my nerves. I'm ready."

"That's okay, Zoe," said Patty. "We're still on point. If you haven't noticed, I eat when I am nervous."

"Yes, you are Captain America," said Kato teasingly.

"Yes, and you are, Kato, Batman," Patty said with a mischievous grin.

"Don't look at me. I'm not Robin," laughed Zoe. Overcome by her laugh, with warmth in his eyes, Kato softly said, "No, you are not, Zoe. No, you are not."

Chapter Twenty

"Where is the little girl?"

"She's right where we left her."

"You didn't put her out cold, did you?"

"No, I'm no fool," growled Laos. "I know the instructions. Give her just enough to put her to sleep for the ride. She should be good for the four-hour drive." Still upset about the young girl's age, Laos started complaining again. "I can't believe we have stooped this far. It's a bad omen. I can feel it!" Tired of his friend's sour mood and complaints about their profession, Kosi angrily yelled, "Laos, are we going to go down that road again? Look, I'm tired and hungry, and I need a drink! I don't want to hear you complain about some poor little girl! It is what it is, so get over it! We've been in this business for twenty years. Don't forget you're Seian's number one man. So you'd better get it together! You don't want him to hear about how you feel. You know what he would do to you!"

Realizing he was getting on his friend's nerves, Laos apologized. "Hey Kosi, no, I'm cool. Sorry, man." I had a moment, that's all. It won't happen again." Kosi gently slapped him on the shoulder, "It's all good, my friend.

Remember, we are being paid to deliver a package, that's all! You have to focus on the package. It's not time to get a conscience. It's way too late for that anyway."

"Yeah, you're right, but I can't stop thinking about the girl being someone's daughter. She's a child! You know what they will do to her," he groaned as he cogitated on the fate of the young child.

"I don't focus on that," said Kosi. "The men who do this have to answer to a higher power. For me, it's all about the money."

"I hope they rot and the maggots eat their flesh," said Laos.

"Then we will rot with them, eh," replied Kosi. "Come on! Let's put her into the car then get a drink. You need one. Don't worry she will be safe. Who will touch her? The locals are afraid. We bring money into the town, and they allow us to do our business. It's a win-win for all."

"Some win-win," grumbled Laos. It's for everyone but the poor and defenseless. Yeah, man, I do need a drink—a stiff one!"

"Now you're talking, my friend."

The two men walked away leaving the car unattended. Not worried about the child in the car, they headed to the local tavern to get a couple of drinks. They knew nobody in their right mind would think about stealing anything from them. Who would be crazy enough to interfere with their boss? He was a man of great prominence and stature, yet equally brutal and vicious when double-crossed. He would kill his own family if they came between him, his money, or his business. He was very good to both men. Always gracious with the money. But even they knew not to double-cross their boss. They would vanish without a trace.

Not too far away, Zoe, Kato, and Patty silently entered the hotel's elevator. Laughing moments ago, neither said a word as the elevator took them to the lobby floor. Watching them from his peripheral view, Kato saw how quiet they had become. Grinning to himself, "Zoe and Captain America. What a lovely yet dangerous combination." With a soft sigh, he thought, There is no turning back from here. Not looking at the two, he asked them again. "Are you sure?" They simultaneously said yes, although they didn't portray the confidence they shown in the room.

As they entered the lobby from the elevator, Zoe scanned the area. That's strange, she thought. There was no one in the lobby. It was quiet. Too quiet. When they checked in earlier, there was a small bustle of people coming and going. Now, there was no one around. An eerie-like feeling came over her. She glimpsed at the front desk and saw the gentleman who checked them in earlier. He appeared to be staring at something, pretending to be busy. She took one last glimpse at him as they walked out into the cool night air. She thought she saw the gentleman making eye contact with Kato. She turned around and looked at Kato but said nothing. When they walked out the door, the guy at the desk reached for the phone and dialed a number. He waited for someone to answer. "All is well," he said upon hearing someone pick up. A click on the other end indicated the person had hung up. The man hung up and went back pretending to be busy.

Zoe's mind was consumed with thoughts of Kato. She pondered, "Did he and the man exchange glances?" She gazed upon him, and that's when she noticed the backpack was missing. Suppressing her urge to create a scene, seething with anger, "Kato!" she angrily whispered, "Where is the backpack? The cell phone, along with the number to call, and all the other items are in there. I specifically asked you to grab it! Where is it?" she said trying not to yell.

"I'm sorry, I forgot it," he said, his voice calm and steady.

Zoe, no longer able to contain her anger, screamed, "You what?"

Stunned by her anger and tone, Kato, in retaliation, yelled back at her, "Look, I'm sorry! Okay! In my haste, you going back and forth to the bathroom, and Patty playing Captain America, I forgot it! Give me a break. The bag is not here, okay! Get over it! We have to concentrate and focus. Don't forget, we are on holiday! We're supposed to be happy, young college students traveling, hanging out, and having fun. He took a deep breath to control his temper. He didn't like getting her upset, and he knew she was very upset. He pulled a candy bar from his pocket and handed it to her, "Here, Zoe." His voice calmer, "Have a piece of chocolate."

"Kato, I don't want any chocolate!" Still fuming, she shouted, "And why did you look at the man behind the counter, or was it my imagination again?"

Kato looked at her. "Zoe, what are you talking about? Are you getting all crazy on me? Is this how you respond to things? First, you go nonstop to the bathroom, and now you're all discombobulated!"

Irited by his words and insinuation that she was losing it, Zoe yelled, "Kato, DO NOT attempt to put this on me. I know what I saw. And you didn't forget the bag, did you? I'm beginning to think you left it back at the hotel on purpose!"

With a gleam in his eye, Kato winked and said, "Good! You're angry! A lover's quarrel! That's why I did it. I knew you would notice and respond the way you did." He smiled at her. "I called you, didn't I? Now come here, my love, and let's pretend to make up. We want people to think you are mad at me." He pulled her over to him, acting like he was trying to make up with her.

She pushed him away. "Hummpf! Mad is for dogs. And I'm no dog! Angry that he was smiling and making fun at her expense, she said, "Don't play games with me, Kato. I don't like mind games. And right now, I'm not feeling you!"

Kato, getting serious, said. "I'm not playing mind games with you, but see, we're almost at the car. You were too tense. Your mind was not where it should've been. I had to get you stirred up. It worked. I left the backpack in the room on purpose. But see, I have a banana for Patty and some caramel peanuts for you because I know you like peanut butter. The phone is in my pocket." He tapped his pocket. "I have the other information elsewhere on my body. You see, we have everything we need. Now, are you still angry at me, my love?"

"I'm not your love, and I don't like games!" she spat out, her anger seeping through her words.

In a stern voice, he replied, "And I don't want you killed! You were acting like you were on some top-secret mission. And Patty over here was acting like a beautiful dumb…."

Patty, quiet the entire time they were arguing, finally spoke up, "Hey, you better not say what I think you are going to say!" She snatched the banana from his hand and began peeling the fruit. "By the way, thank you. I do love bananas. But you're still full of yourself—butt hole!"

"You're filled with a lot of spite tonight, aren't you, Kato?" said Zoe, no longer angry at him, could see the reasoning behind his plan. However, she didn't like how he went about it.

"Well, if I am, I did what I set out to accomplish. I took your mind off the assignment. See, we are here. There's the car. It's beautiful tonight, isn't it?" He turned to the women, needing to see their faces in the moonlight. The moon's reflection against the black sky made them even more beautiful. Ebony and Ivory, he thought to himself.

"Yes, very beautiful and quiet. Serene, isn't it?" said Patty, mesmerized by the beauty and tranquility of the night. "I have never seen so many stars before. It's breathtaking!"

Zoe looked up in the sky, "Yes, it's a beautiful night. Though, it's a little too quiet." Where is everyone—the people? she asked, "There were a few on the streets. Now we are the only ones."

Kato answered her. "Zoe, no locals come this far down the road. They perceive us as mischievous tourists looking for adventure." He pointed to an area, "See over there, that's where the young hip people go. That is where they can, as they say in America, drink and act out. The locals think we are naughty young tourists going to the club, up to no good. It gives them something to talk about in church. We are heathens to them!" He laughed heartily at his words.

"Kato, that's too funny," laughed Patty. "We're heathens! I haven't heard that word in ages. My grandmother used to call me and my brother that!" She howled. Zoe laughed, too, "I've never been called a heathen." She smiled at the thought. Seeing them at ease, Kato said, "Ahhhh, see I made you laugh. Now Zoe, my love, give me a peck on the cheek as lovers do when they make up. Let's smooch."

Zoe giggled. She was no longer angry with him, "Kato, stop calling me my love, and no, we are not smooching! And who says smooching anyway?"

"Well, I tried," he shrugged, pretending to sound disappointed. "Anyway," pointing to the car, "we are here. My source says we have approximately twelve minutes to get the girl and take her into the abandoned building over there," he pointed to a brick wall. "Once inside, we'll wait for a vehicle to pick us up. It will not come until the other vehicle is long gone, which won't be long because the drivers will be running for their lives, trying to escape out of the country. They will not be here looking around, talking to the locals. No one will talk to them anyway." Glancing at his watch, he told them, "If my calculations are correct, we now have exactly eleven minutes. In American football, eleven minutes is a long time; in real life, eleven minutes isn't enough time."

"How do you know when the guys will come out," asked Patty.

Kato pointed to a window on the second floor at a building further down the dark street. "You see that?" They both looked up at the window. There was a small light coming from it. It looked more like a candle's glow than an actual light. "The light is still on. When the light goes out it means they are coming. We have to be quick when we approach the car. You got Jesus?" he asked Zoe. Adrenaline high, Zoe touched her blouse, "Yes, I got my gun

Jesus, and I have Jesus," she told him.

Kato nodded his head, "Good! Patty, wait here behind this building and be on the lookout. Zoe and I are going to the car to get the girl." Kato, now full of control with authority, said, "Everything is going as planned. Patty when you see me and Zoe with the young child, quickly run over to the car so we can all get into the building together. Run like your life depends on it. If something goes afoul, run back to the hotel for help." With urgency in his voice, he said as he began to move out, "Come on, Zoe, let's go get our package." Upon hearing her name, Zoe nodded her head and followed Kato to the abandoned car. "The young girl is small. Most likely she is sedated, so she will be deadweight. Our insider is supposed to make sure the car is unlocked. So it should be easy to grab her and run," he assured her.

Patty stood guard. She watched as they walked to the car. She noticed Kato walking slowly behind Zoe. Not giving it a second thought, she assumed he was being careful. Glancing up at the window, she saw the light go out. It was only a couple of minutes. They had at least eight minutes to go. She tried to warn them, "Kato, Zoe, please hurry! The light went out! The light went out!" she said in a high-pitched voice. They couldn't hear her. Still attempting to warn them about the light, she noticed the dark figure moving towards them. No longer caring who heard her, she screamed, "Zoe, look out! Someone is behind you. Run!" Patty, too busy trying to warn them didn't see the dark figure behind her. Opening her mouth to scream again, she felt a hand cover her mouth and something sharp go into her arm.

As they approached the car, Zoe could hear her heartbeat. It sounds like loud drums, she thought. "Kato," she softly called out his name. Looking around, she saw he was a few feet from the car. "Look in the car. Do you see anything?" he whispered. Barely hearing him, she answered. "Yes, I see a sack! She opened the unlocked door as Kato predicted it would be. "It must be the young girl," she thought and tried to pull the sack out. "Kato, you have to help me pull her out. She's too heavy for me by myself!" At that moment, Zoe thought she heard Patty scream. She looked up but didn't see her in the darkness of the night. Believing everything was going as planned, she went back to retrieve the young girl. "Kato, here she is! Looking around to see where he was, Zoe cried out, "Kato, where are you? Here she is, Kato! Let me pull the blanket open." Her heart beating loudly, with all her might, she pulled the sack out of the car and opened it. It was a rug rolled up. "What is this!!" She cried in horror. "This is a setup!" No longer trying to be quiet, she screamed." Kato, this is a setup. The girl is not here!" Frantically, she cried out, "We have to run! Lord, where is Jesus? Kato, we have to…." She saw the gun in his hand pointing at her.

"I'm sorry, little one. Alana told you not to trust anyone. Besides, the money is too good."

"Kato! Why? Why?" In haste, she looked across the street to search for Patty. Screaming as loud as she could, "Patty, run and get help! It's a setup! Run…" She never saw the blow to her stomach coming, knocking her out. Kato gently put her limp body into the car. "You pretty little fool!" Seeing the two men approaching the car, he asked, "Did you get the other girl?"

"Yes. We got her," one replied.

"Where is she?" Kato asked.

"Over here." He pointed to a lifeless Patty. "We knocked her out with a drug." Pointing to Zoe, he asked, "Do we need to do the same to this one?"

"Yes," said Kato. "Pretty, young, naive, foolish girls! Where is their God now? It's a shame we have to kill them. What were they thinking sending these two amateurs to fight an army? He looked at the two young women, "Leave the American one for me. I want her before she goes on the market. She has a mouth on her and needs to be taught a lesson."

Kosi pointed to Zoe, "How about that one? Do you want her, too?"

"No," said Kato. "We will see what Seian wants to do with her. She's a fighter. Shame too. She's definitely a looker. Pity she has to die. I'd heard her tell that crazy Camille that to be absent from the body is to be present with the Lord. I guess she will soon find out. Come on, it's a long trip ahead. We got four hours to go. We have to make it before daybreak. Do you have any food? I'm famished. Being with these two young idiots can make a person hungry." Kato turned around, looking in the back seat. He asked Laos, "Where is the young girl?"

"She's right here in the back seat, rolled up the blanket. In her haste, the woman didn't see the blanket. She took the decoy, the rug like you said she would do."

"Good," said Kato. "I purposely started a quarrel with them to get their minds off track. It worked. Put them all in the back with you, Laos. It will be tight, but they are all knocked out, so lean them on each other so you will fit comfortably. It's a good thing the car is big enough. When is the buyer coming for the girl?"

Kosi answered him as Laos took care of the three lifeless bodies. "The buyer is coming tomorrow. He wants the young girl right away, so we have to get moving. By the way, there's a sandwich in the glove compartment."

"What kind?" asked Kato.

"Club."

Grabbing the sandwich from the glove compartment, Kato looked hungrily at it. "Ahhhhh! What a masterpiece!" He took a big bite of it. With his mouth full of food, he turned to the two men and said, "It's all in a day's work."

From the back, Laos, peering into the passenger's side mirror, watched Kato devour the sandwich. He shook his head and muttered under his breath, "I'm getting too old for this!"

Chapter Twenty-One

Patty, waking up from the effects of the drug, touched her head, "Oh, my aching head! she moaned. "My worst hangover didn't make me feel this bad. I can't feel any lumps, so why do I feel like a truck ran over me?" Slightly dizzy, she fell backward on the lumpy mattress and glared up at the ceiling light. It was too bright for her eyes. Covering her eyes, she sat up. Still in a daze, she looked around the room. She was relieved to see Kato sitting in the chair beside the bed watching her. She let out a loud shriek. "Kato! I'm so happy to see you! Where am I? Where are we, and why are we in this strange place?" When he didn't answer, she asked him again, "Kato, didn't you hear me? What happened? Where are we? Where's Zoe? Is she safe?" Then she remembered what happened. "I saw the light turn off. We were supposed to have at least eight more minutes. I saw someone, a dark figure lurching in the back, moving towards you and Zoe. I tried to scream to warn you. I felt a hand around my mouth. That's all I remember. I don't recall anything after that." At that moment, she looked down and saw her feet. They were tied up. "Why are my feet tied? Why am I tied up?" she screamed. Alarmed and frightened, she tried to untie the rope around her feet. It was too tight. "Kato, what's going on? You better freaking tell me, or I'll...."

"Or you'll what?" he sneered. "You pretty young American fool! You now belong to me! Tsk, tsk, tsk! Why do you Americans think you can always save someone? Don't you know how big the sex trafficking business is? I'll tell you. It's bigger than you, me, and Zoe," he said, mocking her naiveté.

"What the ...! This is not real! You're part of this? Zoe was right! She said she didn't trust you! You bastard! I bet that story about your sister wasn't even true, was it? Where's Zoe? What have you done to her? I swear I will kill you if you hurt her!"

"You are a little feisty, aren't you? I knew you would be! As for Zoe, unfortunately, by now, she is probably dead, drugged, or worse, in someone's dirty bedroom being forced upon. It's a dirty and evil world. A world where money talks and everyone else looks the other way."

"Oh, no! Nooo!" Patty screamed, tears falling relentlessly from her eyes. "Kato, how could you betray us like this? We trusted you! You were right with us from the beginning. You were with us with Camille! How could you be so evil? Oh my God, not Zoe!" She wept for her friend.

Kato watched as she cried. Unfazed by her tears, he said, "Didn't the woman tell Zoe not to trust anyone? You don't pay much attention, do you? Although I can't fault you. I intentionally poked at you so you didn't see what you needed to see. Everything was there in front of you to see. My job was to keep you on the defense. You never had a chance. You were bent on being your friend's Marvel crusade partner. You only focused on that. You left Zoe to fend for herself as you did your friend Lizzy. You, as they say, was the weakest link." Laughing at her shocked face, he continued, "Oh yes, I did give you such a heartwarming story about my sister. I should receive an Oscar for my storytelling. I am from Sudan, but my family is long gone. Whether they are dead or alive, I don't know. We got lost when we fled the country during the civil war. I've never seen or heard from them again. Touching, isn't it? Sadly, that is my life. I knew I could get to your heart if I pulled on your emotional strings. It was downhill for you once I told you the story about my sister. I had you where I needed you to be. Zoe was harder. She kept picking up the vibes. I thought for sure she had figured something wasn't right with the backpack incident. In my quickness, I told her I purposely left it behind to keep you both on your toes. Surprisingly, it worked. You'd never noticed the guy in the background when you were on lookout. He was there all the time waiting on my signal. Some watch person!" he grunted.

"You scumbag!"

Mocking her, "Still don't cuss, do you?"

No longer afraid and feeling brave, she boldly asked, "What's going to happen to me? What are you going to do with me?" Smacking his lips, Kato undressed her with his eyes. "Well, for right now, you belong to me. To put it bluntly, you are my sex slave. After that, like your friend, you'll go to the next bidder. You see, sweetheart, this is your life from now on. You can either do it drugged or enjoy it without drugs, but you are no longer free. Oh, by the way, when I finish with you, you will cuss like a sailor."

"Kato," a woman's voice on the other side of the door called out, "She wants you now." At the door stood a young woman in her early twenties. The young woman, once a great beauty, now frail and lifeless, waited for him to answer. Annoyed that he was interrupted, Kato shouted at her, "Ok, tell her I have some unfinished business to take care of! I will be there in thirty minutes, give or take. I want this one to scream with passion first. Now leave me alone!" The young woman walked away. With lust in his eyes, he grabbed Patty and pushed her down on the mattress, "Get used to this my pretty young thing, because this is your new life."

With all the might she could muster, Patty thrust her tied legs into his groin. "I'll die first before I let you touch me!" Reaching for the pocket knife, she cut him deeply in his thigh. Screaming at the top of his lungs as he felt the pain in his leg, Kato looked down at the blood. In a rage, he smacked her hard across the face. Ripping her blouse open and getting on top of her, he covered her mouth. "You stupid fool! You don't know what you're doing! I will teach you to submit. You belong to me! Now let me whisper sweet nothings into your ear, Captain America!"

Chapter Twenty-Two

"What happened to you?" asked the woman.

Stumbling from the room, zipping up his pants, Kato answered her, "That little vixen stabbed me in my leg. I should have killed her. She doesn't know who she is messing with!"

Unmoved by his words, the woman threw him a towel, "Here. Wrap it around your leg. I'll get someone to look at it. Try not to get your blood all over it or anything else. By the way, how did she get the knife pass you all?"

"It's funny how I laughed when she told me about the knife. We all laughed. Who's laughing now?" he growled.

"How did she get the knife?" The woman was curious.

Annoyed with the questions and the pain in his leg, Kato angrily told her it was Zoe. "Our little Zoe gave her the knife...the knife you gave to her. She called it her Guardian Angel, her shield like in Captain America. You know, Captain America is a Marvel Comic hero- a good guy who fights bad guys." Seeing she was laughing at his demise, he stopped with the story.

"Never mind, besides, it's complicated. The two of them were complicated. The bottom line her shield stabbed me."

Now bored with the conversation, the woman asked, "What did you do to her?"

"What do you think?" he smirked, satisfied he got what he wanted, even though it cost him a scar. "I handled my business and, as you requested, I put her to sleep with a small drug. She will be out for a long time."

The thought of the young woman stabbing her attacker made the woman smile inwardly. Good for her, she thought. "Kato, I don't want her drugged. They have to see her. She's fair market. By the way, where is the little girl?"

"She is in the room."

"Is she still out?" She asked looking away. She didn't like that the child was so young. Although the money was too good to pass up, the girl's young age bothered her. Watching Kato as he tended his leg, sighing, she said, "I hope this will be the last young girl. Too much bother."

"Yes," answered Kato. "But the drugs will wear down eventually. She is still not eating. She's frightened. I don't blame her. I would be too. Looking at his leg again, he winced in pain, "It's a cruel world we live in."

The woman spoke in a British accent, quoting a passage from the book, 'A Tale of Two Cities,' "Yes! 'It was the best of times; it was the worst of times'. Yes, it tis, yes it tis.'"

Aggravated due to the throbbing of his leg, Kato angrily cried out, "Don't get melancholy on me, Alana! We have to finish the business. Do you have all the documents with the contact information? Those documents are very crucial to Seian's operations. If someone gets a hold of them, it could mean many deaths, ours included."

"I have it here." She showed him the envelope in her hand. "Where is

Zoe?" she asked.

"Zoe is still sleeping. The drug will wear off in a couple of hours. She will be okay. It's good for her to sleep. She doesn't need to know her fate just yet. It's a shame to do this to her because I like her."

The woman nodded, "I agree. There's something about her. It's her eyes. They had this strange impact on me. I believe it was her faith. She has a lot of faith." Sighing, "The business, it's getting bigger and bigger. More money is involved and more perverted sick men." Frustrated about everything and watching Kato still messing with his leg, Alana scolded him. "Go see about your leg, Kato! I will send someone to care for it and to make sure it's not infected. We'll talk later today. How about this evening? I'll look in on Zoe later." She walked away leaving him limping and grumbling about his leg. Once he wiped away the blood, he saw it wasn't as deep as he thought. It still caused him much pain, but he was thankful; it could have been worse.

"Stupid shield," he scowled as he limped away.

Chapter Twenty-Three

Kato was relieved there wasn't any infection in his leg. He had come too far in the business to be wiped out by a spitfire of a girl. Those foolish girls, he thought. They wanted to be superheroes. Well, look where it got them—locked up and waiting to be sold to the highest bidder. Mumbling under his breath, he patiently watched the young woman sent by Alana clean his wound. She poured something on the wound causing him to flinch. "She tried to hurt you, didn't she?" asked the young woman. Smiling smugly, he said, "Yes, but don't you worry. I took care of her." Then feeling a sharp pain in his leg, "Ow!" he screamed, jumping from the pain. Scowling at the young woman as she bandaged his leg, if he didn't know any better, he swore she pulled the bandage too tight on purpose. The young woman could sense his eyes watching her. She looked up at him and smiled. In broken English, she said, "I'm sorry, sir. Sometimes I don't know my strength. Anyhow, it's done. No need to worry. You'll be okay. The cut wasn't deep, but it will leave a scar. You can walk on it without problems."

Kato wondered how long she'd been at the house and why she wasn't sold like the others. Grateful the wound wasn't deep, he smiled and said, "Thank you for taking care of it." Giving him a tight-lipped smile, the young woman gathered her belongings and left. Confused by her smile,

Kato rose from his seat. Now was a good time to check on Zoe. She should be waking up from the drug.

Limping from the wound and now the tight bandage, Kato walked down the hall to see Zoe. Quietly opening the door where she was being held against her will, he stood in the entranceway watching her sleep. Such a vision of loveliness, he thought. Marveling at her beauty, he gasped, "My God, she's beautiful! Oh well," he sighed. "It's time to wake the beautiful princess up. She must know her fate." Going over to the bed, kneeling beside her, he gently tapped her shoulder, "Zoe. Zoe. Zoe, can you hear me? Can you hear me, Zoe? Wake up, my love. Wake up, Zoe." Feeling the gentle taps on her shoulder, Zoe opened her eyes. Still a little lightheaded from the drug, she asked, "Kato, where am I? Why do I feel like this?" Touching her head, now fully awake, she screeched, "Kato! Now I remember! You set us up! You no good piece of crap! You set us up! How could you? Where's Patty? What have you done to her?"

Folding his arms across his chest, he waited until she was finished. Then, clapping his hands condescendingly, he replied, "Bravo, my Zoe! Always the protector, aren't you? Think you are the savior, don't you? You thought you could save the world one child at a time. Well, my friend, tell me, who's going to save you? You're far away from home. No one knows where you are. Sadly, you'll never see your parents again. You should have done what your parents told you to do. You should have stayed in medical school and become a doctor. It's a shame you didn't. Now look at you. You are beautiful, educated, and refined. What a waste!" He said, shaking his head."Unfortunately, your life will be like so many others, a piece of property until they are finished with you."

"Where is Patty?" She angrily asked him.

"Patty gone!" he smirked.

"Gone! What have you done to her? You'd better tell me!" demanded Zoe. She was so concerned for her friend that she didn't realize that her life was in danger. Kato was in awe at how she worried about her friend and not herself. "The same thing that will happen to you, but first things first! Let's get you something to eat. That's the least I can do for you. After all, we did share some good times, didn't we?" "Kato, I've never wished bad on anyone, but today, if you touch me, that little girl, or Patty, your life will be one of evil and misery. No good will come of this." "Awww, such a sweet Christian woman. I must say, your parents raised you well, didn't they?"

"Kato, why? Why are you doing this?" "Is it money?" she asked.

"What else? Money! Something you never had to worry about. As for me, when you are poor and don't know where your next meal is coming from, morality goes out the door, and survival takes over. The money is very good, and there is plenty of demand. One day, I will have enough, and then I won't have to look back at this place. I can live how I want to, be comfortable and secure, and no longer worry about where I live or what to eat. I will live as you do, or did, eh, Zoe?" "You are wrong, Kato. No matter how hard you try to hide or forget this place. It will always be in your mind, along with all the people you have betrayed, hurt, and killed. You will never be able to forget, no matter how much money you have. You know money can't make you happy." "Said the little rich girl who never lacked anything in her pampered life." His voice was full of mockery. "It's easy for the rich to say these words. They actually believe this nonsense. The rich don't know what it's like to be poor and hungry." Zoe shook her head, "Kato, there are many poor people in this world, and they still don't do what you are doing. My parents worked hard for what they've achieved. Their parents were poor."

Becoming annoyed with her righteous attitude, he said, "Save your words for someone who cares. I didn't come here for a lecture, nor did I come here to stare into your beautiful brown eyes. I came here to feed you because your journey is about to begin and food will be scarce. You need to eat now because you don't know when the next time you'll eat a good meal again."

"Kato," she said his name so softly that he briefly forgot why he was there. Were there many others? Did you trap them like you did Patty and me? Is Camille part of this?" Caught off guard by the gentleness of her voice, Kato cleared his throat. In a deep, husky voice, he said, "Camille does not know, nor is she part of this. She is very trustworthy. Too trustworthy. She was so eager to have my help that she failed to do a proper background check on me. If she had, she would have known I wasn't who I said I was. As far as others, sadly, there were, but none as bright and beautiful as you. You are different. It's a shame you will not live to see your full potential. What did you say to Camille, absent from the body, present with the Lord? I hope you will remember your words when it comes time to say goodbye."

Zoe, shocked at the mention of being killed, asked, "You will kill me?"

"Yes, if we have to. You are a fighter! You will be no good to sell."

Fighting back her tears, she didn't want him to see her cry, "Where is Patty?"

"I told you Patty has already gone to her new owner. By now, she has probably had three. What do you want me to say? Lovers? It's a cruel world we live in, eh?"

"Kato, you're a scumbag! You're going to die if you keep this up!" she screamed.

"I won't, anyway, not right now." Touching her shoulder, he said, "I need you to eat. I will send the servant woman in with your meal. Please eat. We need you healthy." Getting up from kneeling, he limped towards the door. Looking back at the young woman on the bed, blowing a kiss in her direction, he whispered, "Good night, my Zoe. We will meet again to say goodbye." "Kato, wait. What happened to your leg?" she asked. With a wide grin, he answered her, "The knife you gave Patty, the 'Shield' as she called it. She stabbed me with it. The irony is, the shield did protect her a little, although I still got the last laugh." He walked out of the room closing the door behind him. At the sound of the door closing, Zoe put her hands over her eyes and burst into tears. "Father, I need you to show me. If it's my time, prepare me, but if it isn't, what are you doing?" She quietly sobbed as she remembered that day that changed her life forever.

Chapter Twenty-Four

It was the second meeting on human sex trafficking. Since it was close by and the sun was still bright, Zoe went alone. The females who went with her to the first meeting decided not to go. She understood. Their parents paid a great deal of money for them to attend the prestigious institution. They couldn't afford to waste their parent's money. They were empathetic when she told them she was still going and wished her well. Even though she asked them out of courtesy, she was relieved when they told her they weren't going. She wanted to attend the meeting without interruptions or be on a time schedule.

Like the first meeting, the room was crowded with women from all walks of life and ethnicities. However, unlike the last meeting, many were in their late teens or early twenties. A few middle-aged women were at the meeting, but fewer than the previous. There were a few men in attendance that came with their daughters. Zoe selected a table in the front of the room. She wanted to hear the speaker without interruptions of small talk or whispers from the back. It was quite a surprise to see the girl she met at the first meeting there. Patty came over and sat down next to Zoe. The two quickly became absorbed in small talk. Their conversation ceased when the speaker introduced the guest speakers. For the next three hours, no one said a word as they listened to the horror stories of victims of sex trafficking.

One by one, their stories, which seemed so surreal, portrayed the horror and brutality of the dark world of human sex trafficking. No one in the room wanted to believe it existed, especially in America. The women's stories brought this dark reality to light.

Camille, the beautiful African woman who spoke at the last meeting, came to the podium. "No one wants to say sex trafficking, the act of selling women, young girls and boys, exists in America. You believe yourselves as civilized, dignified, and decent people who protect their children. Your men are the crème of the crème as far as the world's and society's standards. They are morally upright. No matter what you want to believe, sex trafficking exists in America. America is the number one country in purchasing sex, including purchasing victims of sex trafficking. It's a big problem, and each year, it's becoming a bigger problem. Atlanta is one of the major hubs of human slave trafficking in America. It brings in millions of dollars each year. Caucasians, Blacks, Asians, Latinos, Mexicans, men of all ethnicities. They are your doctors, lawyers, bankers, teachers, professors, students, clergy, white-collar, blue-collar, middle class, upper class, politicians, entertainers, athletes, and professionals."

"I thought prostitution was a joint agreement with a woman and her pimp," said a woman in the audience.

"First of all, nothing is a joint agreement when it involves a girl and a pimp," said Camille. "Most likely, it's an abusive, manipulating, and controlling relationship. The man tells the young, vulnerable girl he loves her, and because he loves her, she should do anything for him, even sleep with other men. If she doesn't, he may force her into it by violet threats or harm to her body."

"It's the if you love me, you'll have sex with me ploy," said an older woman. The crowd murmured in agreement.

"No, it's more than that. It's rape, and it's a form of slavery. Many victims are left at the waste side after being used and abused. They want to get out but can't or don't know how. They can be killed or beaten if they try to run away. The victims are mentally and physically damaged, believing they have no other option but to continue this way of life. Brainwashed to believe they are nothing, their hope is depleted."

Like the last meeting, someone asked, "Why are we in this country just hearing about this?"

It's not new news. We've been talking about sex trafficking for some time, only now you are listening. But that's all you are doing; you are only listening. This happens every day in your very own suburban neighborhoods. We like to think that only the poor are affected. I'm here to inform you that everyone is affected regardless of background, ethnicity, or social status. I don't want to preach to you. I want to educate you and, hopefully, save one of your own. Sex trafficking is a form of slavery. It's the exploitation of women and children, and yes, some of the children are your sons, but the majority are women and young girls. The customary ages of girls abducted are between twelve and twenty-two. There have been cases, especially in lesser-developed countries, where they are abducting girls ten years of age or younger. They are not only forcing these individuals into sex trafficking but also exploiting them into pornography. Men who look at pornography don't care or have no idea that many girls are underage and are doing these lewd acts against their will. They call it entertainment; it's not. Every year, hundreds of thousands of people are trafficked globally in exchange for money and other goods."

"Why can't the governments of these countries stop these atrocities?" asked one of the men.

In some countries, women are considered subservient to men. These countries don't care about women's rights or equality for women. The women are there for them, the men. In some of these countries it's not surprising when you hear about a woman being killed by her husband if she refuses him or he is upset with her. He may not get jail time. It's their way of life, their culture. You are blessed in this country. You have rights. These women don't! That's why they are fighting for their rights! That's why the number of victims sold into human trafficking is staggering."

China and Russia traffic many girls. It's part of organized crime. *"Organized crime is largely responsible for the spread of international human trafficking. Sex trafficking—along with its correlative elements, kidnapping, rape, prostitution and physical abuse—is illegal in nearly every country in the world. However, widespread corruption and greed make it possible for sex trafficking to quickly and easily proliferate. Though national and international institutions may attempt to regulate and enforce anti-trafficking legislation, local governments and police forces may in fact be participating in sex trafficking rings."*[1]

Men go on vacation to purchase sex with these girls. It's not considered a crime in these countries; however, it is a crime when it's a young girl who has been abducted and forced into sexual servitude or slavery. One reason for the proliferation of sex trafficking is because in many parts of the world there is little to no perceived stigma in purchasing sexual favors for money, and prostitution is viewed as a victimless crime. Because women are culturally and socially devalued in so many societies, there is little conflict with the purchasing of women and girls for sexual services. Few realize the explicit connection between the commercial sex trade and the trafficking of women and girls and the illegal slave trade. In western society in particular, there is a commonly held perception that women choose to enter into the commercial sex trade. However, for the majority of women in the sex trade, and specifically in the case of trafficked women and girls who are coerced or forced into servitude, this is simply not the case."[2]

A hand went up. "What can we do?"

"We need your help spreading this information to your communities and on social media. With your help, we can save one girl at a time. I have a few ladies who would like to share their stories. They are very graphic and may make some of you uncomfortable, which is good. You need to be uncomfortable because what you are about to hear is not a Hollywood movie. It's not Lifetime television. Their stories are real. The first woman's name is Jenna. Jenna, please come and share your story." The audience

---

1   Sex Trafficking | Polaris https://polarisproject.org/human-trafficking/sex-trafficking

2   Sex Trafficking | Polaris https://polarisproject.org/human-trafficking/sex-trafficking

clapped as Jenna walked to the podium.

A young woman in her mid-twenties, dressed very chic came to the podium. Taking a deep breath, she began. "Hi. My name is Jenna. I'm twenty-six years old. You see me now with my stylish matching outfit, seemingly put together, but the truth is, my life hasn't always been this way. I've been all over the Middle East and some parts of Europe but have never seen their beautiful countryside. I have been to Paris but have never eaten at a café in Paris. I did get a glimpse of the Eiffel Tower as I was trafficked through the city on my way to another location. My abductor was a person who befriended me when I was alone and vulnerable. He said the right words and made me feel like I was somebody because all through my life I thought I was a nobody. The funny thing is, I was fourteen and didn't realize that many fourteen-year-olds felt this way. I come from a middle-class family. My parents worked hard to make a decent living, giving us the best they could. Our needs were always met, and some desires, too. Something happened to me at fourteen. I started feeling down on myself. I felt like an ugly duckling. The girls in my class were developing, but I was skinny and flat-chested with a crooked smile. I wasn't popular, and the friends I hung out with were in the same boat as me. I was insecure, lonely, and felt that nobody understood me. I didn't realize I was an easy target for a predator. I was what they looked for in a girl.

One day, walking out of a Dairy Queen, licking a vanilla ice cream cone, a young, handsome, brown-haired, brown-eyed guy approached me and called me pretty. I looked around and saw that he was talking to me because no one else was around but me. He said his name was Jonathon. I believed he was a good Christian young man because that's what he told me he was. He asked me all about myself. He offered to buy me another cone. I told him no and that I had to go. He asked if he could meet me again. He told me there was something special about me. I reminded him of his sister. She was beautiful and petite like me. He told me he liked small-framed girls. I was flattered. Here I was with this really cute guy and he said he liked me. I met him the next day, the next, and so on. I never told my mother or my friends about him, and my mother never asked why all of a sudden I was this happy-go-lucky teenager. She was happy that I was finally happy. I didn't realize then that he didn't care for me. He was only grooming me.

It went on for about a month before he asked me to have sex with him. Although he never asked me in those words. He was very clever. He said, 'I love you, Jenna. I want to take care of you. I want to protect you, my beautiful fawn.' He could take me to the moon and back with those words. I was his forever. He told me that to seal our love we needed to make love. I was fourteen and a virgin. He said he would be gentle with me, so we had sex. It hurt and I started to cry. When it was over, he wiped my tears and fears away. He said he would always be gentle and take care of me. I believed him. For the next couple of weeks, all we did was have beautiful sex. I started skipping school. He started buying me clothes. He said I look cute and sexy in the outfits he bought. They were a little skimpy, but I was so in love I didn't care. Well, a month after our first tryst, things started to change. He began to change. He was no longer sweet and kind. He was getting a little crude. I didn't notice in the beginning. After all, he loved me, and when we had sex, it was still good.

One day, while we were in his apartment, that should have told me that he was older, but I ignored the red flags; some guys came in. He told me that if I loved him, I would have sex with them because he owed them money. To keep us both from getting killed, he needed me to have sex with them. Here I was, fourteen years old, having sex with two grown men. They were not very gentle. They were rough. After they left, I told Jonathon I didn't want to do that anymore. He slapped me. I hit the floor hard. And then he left. I was through. I was getting my things to go, but he returned and apologized before I could gather all my belongings. He actually started crying. He asked for my forgiveness. He said it was hard for him to see me having sex with other men. Of course, I forgave him. I believed him and I loved him. I told him I forgave him and then we had sex. It was different, but again I loved him, so it was still nice. About a week later, my mother noticed me acting strange. She told my father, and they questioned me. At about that same time, the school called and informed them that I wasn't attending school. I had been away for over a month. My mother punished me and drove me to and from school every day. She watched me like a hawk and took away my cell phone, so I had no contact with Jonathon.

Even though he didn't treat me the best, I still missed and loved him.

A week or so went by. I was in between classes. I saw his car outside. During the class change, I walked out of school. I thought he was waiting for me. But when I walked up to the car, I saw him talking to another girl. I approached him after she walked away. Before I could say anything, he looked at me and said, 'I waited for you, but I didn't see you. I knew you would see the car.' I was thrilled and a little hurt he was talking with the other girl, but I was so glad to see him that I hugged him. He opened the door for me and told me to get in. I did. It would be ten years before I would see my parents again.

It started out innocent, or so I assumed. In the beginning, he would say to me, 'We are Romeo and Juliet. Instead of killing ourselves, we'll run away together.' That's every little girl's fancy...running away with their prince charming, right? We drove to Idaho. It was there I knew it wasn't love but something else. He started telling me that I had to pay my way. So I did. I started sleeping with three or four men a day. I'd just turned fifteen. That's when I found out he was twenty-five. I tried to escape. When he caught me, he beat me up. Gave me a black eye. He said I was his and I belonged to him. I had to do what he told me to do. I had sex in the backrooms of sleazy and classy bars and casinos of well-respected clubs. There were always men wanting to have sex with me. I soon saw that there were other girls like me. Some were Americans, but many foreigners, especially Asians. Sometimes there would be two girls to one man or three men to one girl. They like a lot of oral sex and freaky things.

One time a minister came in dressed in his clergy attire. I was happy because I thought surely he was there to rescue me. But he was there to have sex with me. He was quoting the Bible the entire time we were having sex. He prayed for me when he was finished. It was unreal. To get me through the day sometimes Jonathon would spike my coke. I never did drugs. I believe that's why I was able to come out better than some of the other girls. He brought a new girl to the house. She was now his favorite. He began treating me like dirt. He said he was through with me. That I was going on a trip. He raped me and then forced a drink down my throat.

When I woke up, I was on a plane heading somewhere. On the plane there were two men there to guard me. They both had their way with me. Yes! It's real! People don't want to believe it, but it's real. I was in some country in the Middle East passed around like a joint or some novelty. I learned to survive by making sure I knew how to do what they wanted me to do so they wouldn't drug me. The girls who fought back were often drugged. I didn't want to become a drug addict, so I pretended to enjoy it when deep down, I hated my life and wanted to die.

I can't recall how many men I have been with. I never saw money exchanged, but I know I've been purchased and sold numerous times. I've been with all kinds of men from various ethnicities. That was my life for ten years. I would still be there if it weren't for an American student who came to me one night. I thought he was just like the others, but he whispered to me to pretend like we were having sex. He informed me that he was there to help me. Two weeks later, I was back in the States, damaged, broken, and completely lost. I felt abused and used. I thought it was my fault that this happened to me. It took me about two weeks to call my parents. When I did, my mother answered the phone. I heard my father burst into tears in the background when he heard it was me. Both my parents aged a lot in those ten years. I finally told them what had happened and all about Jonathon.

The police tried to track him down but could never find him. They told me his real name probably wasn't Jonathon. It took a long time for my father to heal. I think he died a little knowing that his little girl went through so much. My mother was the strong one. Her faith kept her going. God promised her that He would bring me back to her, and she promised God that she would accept me back in whatever condition other than dead. She was the one who helped me the most. My mother got me to go to counseling, and we went to a support group together. She told me to tell my story, my testimony, so no other girl would go through what I went through. My father eventually came around. It's still hard for him. I don't think he will ever be the same. These men prey on girls like I was: insecure, vulnerable, and lonely."

Chapter Twenty-Five

Weeping silently, Zoe didn't hear the footsteps entering the room. Alana, seeing the young woman sitting cross-legged on the bed crying, not wanting to disturb her just yet, quietly watched her. She assumed she was praying as her lips moved without a sound. The tears on the young woman's face troubled her. "Zoe," she said softly. Zoe looked up. She couldn't believe her eyes. Standing before her was the woman who helped her at the restaurant. Groaning, she wailed, "Oh, No! God was everyone in on this? You, you!" she stuttered. "You betrayed the organization too?" The woman softly replied. "I told you, my dear, not to trust anyone. Not even me. And I was never in the organization, not your organization anyway. Oh, by the way, I see you met the other side of Kato?"

First Kato, now this woman, Zoe's faith was shattered. "How could you?" she cried.

"Oh, you sound so young, so juvenile! How could you?" Alana said, mocking the young woman's naiveté. "Such an innocent one, aren't you? Full of I'm going to save the world, aren't you? Well, who's going to save you? By now, Ms. Camille has informed your parents that you are missing. I wonder what is going through their intellectual minds now. Their little Zoe is lost for good. They won't ever see her eyes again. Such a waste and a shame, but I told you, this is a multi-billion-dollar industry. You are messing with the big boys. As my mama would say, 'You should've put on your big girl panties' because when you're messing with grown folk's business, it tends to be messy. No pun intended."

Zoe shook her head in disbelief at the woman's analogy. "How could you be in a business that sells women?" You're a woman! As a woman, you know what they are doing. Don't you care what happens to these little girls? Hitting a nerve, a truth, Alana, annoyed and frustrated with the whole ordeal, lashed out, "Stop with the melodrama, Zoe! Do you see this house, my servants, and my life? I stopped caring long ago. I have no feelings. Just like many of the girls in this business. In a couple of months…." She looked away. "In a couple of months, they become the walking dead, as you will too."

"Doesn't it matter to your conscience how God sees you? Don't you have a soul?" Zoe asked her.

"My soul? Silly little naïve child! Again, this is a big boy's game. It's the big league. There are no consciences or souls here! There is no compassion. Look around. What do you see? A dark, big, ugly world filled with lust, greed, ambition, and power. This world doesn't care about these individuals. It doesn't care about the wounded or damaged. It only cares about fulfilling a dirty, lustful need…one's desires, and if it means having sex with a young girl, as long as the need is fulfilled, everything else doesn't matter. You think these men who are having sex with these young girls are poor from poverty-stricken countries. No, these men are powerful, rich, and very influential. They don't care about these girls or how young they are. To them, these girls are yesterday's trash. Do you know what happens with trash? They throw the trash out when they are finished with it. Did you really think you could come here and stop a business that's been here since the age of dawn? Little girl, you are messing with people's money. You know what they say. People act funny when you start messing with their money, but in this business, people will kill you if you mess with their…." Alana paused. She didn't want to talk about the inevitable.

"You know Zoe, I thought surely you would have gotten the message when Kato slipped and said my name. He said he would, and he did. You should've listened to your inner spirit because you were correct. I never told you my name; therefore, you never told him my name. I had hoped you caught it to call it off, but you wanted to be the little girl's savior. Now, look where it has gotten you. Dead! Because no matter what happens Zoe, they will kill you!"

Zoe was shaken at the mention of the word killed. It was the third time she heard the word. First, her brother, then Kato, and now Alana. " Alana, how did all this go down? Why us?" she asked, trying to sound brave.

The woman looked at her, "We found out! Didn't you know we would?" she asked the young woman. "There was an informant in the village. Money can buy anything and anyone, eh? That's where Kato came into play. He knew Camille, your Camille. They go way back. He needed access. She was his access. She once liked him and probably still does. Love and money will ruin you every time. Women are foolish when they fancy someone. They think with their emotions and hearts, not their brains. By talking to Camille, Kato, an insider for Seian, learned about a task force assigned to get the child. He already knew about the abduction, but he had to remain quiet. He found out that you and the American were assigned to the mission. It was bad judgment on Camille's part. In the beginning, Seian didn't want either of you. The young girl was risky as it was, but Kato convinced Seian that he could get three for the price of one. Kato told him how young and beautiful you both were. It was a no-brainer. It was easy, too easy, I must say. But it's not that complicated when no one is paying close attention. Kato wasn't supposed to be the one to bring you here. The other guy who was supposed to transport you somehow got killed. Seian trusted Kato, so he was chosen. To make a long story short, that's how it all went down. Kato gained your trust, and now you are here!"

"What is going to happen to me?" Zoe asked.

"Don't worry, your life will not end as the others in sex trafficking, which is a slow death. I promise. You will be spared that life. I will not let them toss you from one man to another. They will kill you and dispose of your body. It will be quick and painless—one bullet to the head. You won't know what hit you. Consider this your last meal. You are extremely beautiful, Zoe. Not just outer beauty but more inner beauty. You're radiant and regal, like a Queen who sits on her throne. Your name means life?"

"Yes, my father named me." Thinking of her father brought tears to Zoe's eyes. Alana, seeing her tears, softly said, "Beautiful name. It fits you very well. Too bad your life will be short-lived. Ironically, your life will not live up to its name."

"Who said it won't or didn't?" Zoe boldly cried out.

Impressed with the young woman's open courage, Alana said, "My, aren't you the brave one, even when death is knocking on your door. You're not afraid to die?"

"If I say no, then I will be lying to you," said Zoe. "I'm very much afraid, but I trust my God. He will deliver me out of the lion's den, but if He doesn't, I trust Him!" Trying to control her tears, she continued, "I don't have any regrets, for I'm too young to have regrets. I wish I hugged my parents and brother harder the last time I saw them, particularly my mother. I wish I had tried to make my mother understand or that I understood her stance on this. I wish Patty hadn't gotten caught up in this looking for her friend. She would be here today. I wish I had made a difference for these girls who felt like no one cared about them and that they were nobody. I wish I could save that little girl and tell her that she is somebody, that God loves her, and that she is special to Him. I pray that when the time comes, God will give me strength and peace and that I will go with dignity as I take my last breath in this world, but to answer your question, yes, I'm very scared."

Alana looked strangely at the young woman. "Zoe, I must confess, you are an extraordinary creature."

"No, not extraordinary, just Zoe. Tell me something, Alana. I need to know. How did you get involved in this? This cruel, dark world of human sex trafficking?" She wondered how someone as intelligent and beautiful could end up in this world.

Alana knew the young woman had struck another nerve with her question. Lately, she often wondered herself. "Zoe, I was never like you. I came from a different class structure. I wasn't dirt poor, yet poor is poor when you don't have money for things. I wanted stuff. For me, it was ambition. I fell in love with a man who was a friend of a man of great influence in my village. He didn't tell me what he did or the other women he had. I didn't ask. I was thrilled when he took notice of me. I loved him, or I assumed it was love. It was love based on what I knew love was or is. I loved the jewelry, the traveling, the big house, the clothes, and the money. All the things that the world tells us we should love. When I found out what he was doing, it was too late. I walked in on one of his men molesting a thirteen-year-old girl. I walked out, but not before seeing the frightened girl's eyes. Nothing like yours. Her eyes were as big as saucer plates. I heard her cry out in pain. I heard her sob. I turned and walked out. It was less than a minute, but it seemed like an eternity. Seian knew I saw the girl being raped. I never said anything. He didn't either. I think he was waiting for me to say something. Something inside of me said to be quiet. I did! I don't know, but I believe now that he would've killed me on the spot if I had said something. The following week after the incident, he took me to Paris and brought me beautiful clothes and expensive jewelry. We made love like nothing happened. I think then he knew he could trust me.

After we were there for two weeks, it dawned on me that this was also a business trip. One day he drove to this dark alley. I can't recall the place, but it was dark. It was the middle of the day. The sun was shining brightly, but the alley was dark. He kissed me on the lips and told me to stay put. He got out of the car to meet two well-dressed men. Money was exchanged, a big bag, like something you would see in an American Hollywood movie. Yet, this wasn't Hollywood. This was real. I saw two young Asian girls around the ages of fifteen and fourteen. They may have been younger. I want to believe those were their ages. While all this was taking place, I glanced over at Seian. He saw my glance. When I noticed he saw me, I immediately looked away. The alley was dark, and yet we made eye contact.

It was a few, ten minutes tops, before he returned to the car and another car pulled up. I saw the two girls dragged into the other car. I could see one was kicking and screaming. A man got out of the car that pulled up and knocked her out. Literally, "BAM!" She fell out in the other man's arms. She was knocked out cold. Seian returned like nothing happened and calmly said, "Sorry that took so long. I had to take care of some business." He was watching how I would react. Nonchalantly, I said, "Ok, let's get something to eat. I'm starving. He started to laugh. That's when he knew he could trust me. Little by little, he would let me know what he was doing. I discovered that he is big in human and sex trafficking, like his father, a prominent doctor in their village. His father doesn't dabble in it anymore. He made enough money to live comfortably for the rest of his life. My friend, the man who has great influence in my village, is also a trafficker. He isn't as big in it as Seian.

Sometimes, I work with Seian to get the girls. Very rarely, but sometimes, he would ask me to assist him when the law was close to capturing him. They never could. Seian has a lot of corrupt police on his payroll. I already told you we found out there was a mole in the group, and they were trying to infiltrate some young girls to help catch us. He knew Kato through a friend. Kato was up and coming into the business. He was very astute, full of wisdom, very charismatic, and cocky but extremely wise. Seian trusted him. He doesn't trust many, but he trusts Kato. Probably because Kato is like him, brutal and takes what he wants, not caring about anyone's feelings. You saw that in him. That's why you believed him even when you were suspicious of him. Kato reconnected with Camille. They used to be lovers, on and off, in prior years. She had a thing for him, so she never did a background check on him. He came out of nowhere, and she let him in. That's how it all started. I've been with Seian for over five years. I've seen many girls, as young as twelve come and go...." She looked away, "However, never one as young as this one, the one you were trying to rescue.

Zoe, appalled, said, "Alana, you traded your soul and the souls of these precious little girls for jewelry, gowns, and clothes! "

Alana, exasperated, screamed, "Oh, Zoe! Everyone can't be perfect like you! I know where I'm going in eternity. I know the day when death comes to take me, the party will be over. Until then, I live my life full of champagne, caviar, and all the luxuries a girl could ever dream, crave, or desire."

Sad for the woman and her life choices with sincerity, Zoe, with compassion, told her, "I will pray for you, Alana."

Alana knew the woman's words about praying for her were sincere. They came from her heart. In deep sorrow, she said, "No, Zoe. I made my bed. I must lie in it. Pray for yourself. You will need it more than me. Goodbye, Zoe. I wanted to say goodbye because the next time we meet, there won't be a lot of words exchanged." She walked out, locking the door behind her.

Zoe walked over to the small table and chair and sat down. Soft tears began to trickle down her face. She began to pray, "Father, if I say I'm not afraid to die, you know I'm lying. I'm terrified. This is not what I thought my last days would be like. I wanted to be married, have children, to make a difference in the world. And yet, here I am in a strange place, a strange land with people who have lost all sense of humanity and compassion. Did I miss you, Lord? I'm not as brave as Daniel in the Lion's Den, nor as brave as the three Hebrew boys thrown in the fire. These stories now all seem like fairytales to me. Lord, my faith and hope are wavering."

Sobbing uncontrollably, with deep pain, she cried out, "I don't want to die…not now! I want to fulfill my purpose. This wasn't the purpose you had for me, was it? Was this your plan all along for me? Tell me, Lord! Speak to me, please, Father. Where are my angels encouraging me and telling me it's going to be okay? Please tell me that my life wasn't in vain. That my walk as a believer wasn't in vain. Help me to understand. I trust you, Lord, but please help me understand!"

Exhausted, Zoe walked over to the bed, falling face down on the mattress; she cried herself to sleep.

Chapter Twenty-Six

The Bible says, "'Choose this day whom you believe.' Who are you going to stand with, or what are you going to stand for? Honestly, I don't know who or what I will stand with or for anymore. It all happened so fast. Like it's still a dream, a nightmare that I can't wake up from no matter how hard I try. I didn't mean to get involved in human sex trafficking. I was a street-wise young, naïve woman from India who wanted to get out from under the poverty-stricken areas surrounding my family and friends. The stench of poverty, the hopelessness surrounding me, and the four corners of the wall that closed me in as a prisoner without the bars made me seek the life I wanted. The life I craved. The life that would take me out of the hell that was my everyday existence. There was no hope for me and the other girls where I come from. There was barely enough food for the families. What little food we did have only made our stomachs growl more intensively. It seems that our stomachs even knew we barely had enough to eat.

An older woman who looked worn out and tired asked, "I'm a mother with two teenage daughters. I'm concerned about them. They are wild, disrespectful, and don't obey the rules I have in place. I want to know how did it happened to you? How did you get to that place of no return?"

"How? I don't know how. I knew the why, especially in the beginning. When you have no hope, you are liable to do anything. My everyday life pictures were not beautiful; they were pictures of filth, ugliness, and desolation. We lived in survival mode every day. Every night when we laid ourselves to sleep, we thanked God above and breathed a sigh of relief that we survived to fight or exist another day. Funny, when we saw death, sometimes we felt envious because it appeared the pain on the deceased's face was replaced with a smile. How ludicrous does that sound, and yet it's the truth. In death, there is no more pain. There is only peace."

"When the men came to your village, what did they say? How did they lure you?"

"They lure you with stuff. Promises of stuff, which back then, meant a lot, but now don't mean a pot of beans. When they showed me a pearl, not a necklace, but one measly little pearl, it was the most beautiful thing I ever saw. There was a pretty young lady with them. She didn't say much, but she was dressed to the nines. She was the recruiter. She would teach us how to conduct ourselves for interviews. It was an international telemarketing firm in India recruiting young girls. The pay was not the best, but you could work your way up the ladder to a possible manager position. You would have to stay in a house with two other girls and share a bathroom. When they said I would have my own room and would only have to share the bath with two other people, it was a no brainer. I signed up immediately. They gave us each $100.00. No fooling! It was the most money I had ever seen in my life. I secretly gave half to my mother. If my father or any other men in the family knew about the money, they would have taken it from my mother. I kissed my mother goodbye and told her I would see her in three months because they told me I had to work at least three months before getting a vacation. They got me all dolled up in this pretty navy blue dress with a red, white, and blue scarf. It was very patriotic. I never felt so beautiful. We went in the car, me along with two other young women from my village. They took us to a fancy restaurant about forty or so miles out from our village. I didn't know the place existed. I ate the best meal I had ever eaten in my life. The next thing I knew, what started out like a fairytale turned into a nightmare."

"What happened?"

"They continued to let me and another girl eat while they took the other girl away. She was darker than both of us. I guess someone who had never been with a darker woman wanted her. That's what I think because we never saw her again. The restaurant was filled with men from various backgrounds and cultures. There were a few young women, but they just kept their heads down. They didn't say a word. At first, I didn't think anything of it. I kept eating because they let me have whatever I wanted. I didn't question it. Finally, the other girl asked what happened to the girl they took in the back. Before she could ask anything further, the man who was nice to us in the beginning slapped her so hard in the mouth she fell out of her seat and hit the floor. WHAM! That's when I knew I had made a mistake. It was too late. The next thing I knew, the same man reached over to me, picked me up from my seat, food still in my mouth, and covered my mouth so I wouldn't scream. The sad thing was no one in the restaurant said anything or came to my rescue. Everyone remained silent and continued to eat their meal.

He carried me to a room in the back filled with men. The light in the room was very dim. There must have been four men in the room. Each man had his turn with me. I guess I blacked out because the next thing I knew, the young girl, the recruiter, was there washing me up, trying to console me, telling me that I would get used to it and just give them what they wanted if I wanted to be safe and live. So here I was, each day back to what I was during…surviving to live another day. I had all kinds of men: fat, big, tall, skinny. Men who were so big they tore my inside up, and men who were so small, I had to laugh. I laughed at one man. He kicked me in my stomach so hard that I was out for two weeks. I never laughed out loud again. On the plus side, it was a relief. I got more sleep during those two weeks than I had in months. I had some who wanted me to tie them up. Others wanted me to urinate on them. I had two men at the same time… one on one, three on one. I must have been doing something right because I was one of the lucky ones. They kept me fed, and I got a day off every now and then. Men asked for me when they came. I didn't cry out to God, but now I know He kept me from losing my mind. There are some sick, perverted men out there, and they don't care. My body is so messed up. I can never have kids, and I don't want any. I don't ever want to get married." She looked down when she finished. Camille came back to the podium. "Thank you, Maya. The next speaker is Hannah." Everyone clapped.

A tall, medium-built, pretty blond-haired woman with beautiful hazel green eyes came to the podium. She took a long breath, and with tears in her eyes, she began to speak. "Hi, my name is Hannah, and I am from North Carolina. My uncle sold me into sex trafficking after he raped me. He told my father I ran away. How do I know? I was gagged in his closet when my father came in to inquire where I was. He said that I had run away, but the real truth was he sold me for some drugs. Can you believe that he sold me for some drugs? My family is very influential in our town. My uncle was, as you would say the outcast of the family, the wayward child. He owed some men money from drugs he was supposed to sell, but he blew the money and the drugs partying. It was a large amount of money, and the men were threatening to kill him if he didn't come up with their money. That's where I came in. He promised the men me for his life.

He brought one of the men to our house while we were having a family gathering. My parents were furious, especially my mother. While my parents were arguing with my uncle in the kitchen, my sister and I were in the family room with this strange man. It wasn't as if my parents had left us there alone in a room with a strange man. My grandparents were there in the living room with us. The man looked like dirt. He was clean, but he looked like a dirty old man. He kept staring at me. It was creepy. When my uncle came out of the room, he got his coat, and he and the man left. Before they walked out the door, the man looked at my uncle and said, 'Yes, she will do. This will pay off your debt.' I think I was the only one who heard him. My grandparents, my mother's parents, went into the kitchen to console my mother, who was still livid. My little sister had left the room. That's when I heard him say what he said. He looked at me with a crooked smile and said, 'See you later,' as he and my uncle walked out the door. I felt frightened, but I didn't tell my parents."

"What happened next?" asked someone.

"Two days later, my uncle came by our house. I was home alone watching TV. My sister was at her friend's house playing. Our school had a teacher's conference, so the kids were off on a training holiday. Everyone in town knew because it's a small town of primarily upper middle-class families. The majority of the kids in my neighborhood went to the same private school. So, my uncle knew this as well. My uncle knocked on the door. I looked through our peephole and saw him. I felt uneasy, but I let him in the house. I knew my mother would be home within the hour. He asked where my father was because he needed money. I said, "Dad is at his firm working." He knew my dad's work schedule. The next thing I knew, he shoved something into my arm. I immediately went limp. I do remember him dragging me out the door to his car. His flaw was that my neighbor down the street saw him driving away in his car with me slumped over in the front seat. She had seen him several times and knew he was my father's brother. She didn't think anything of it until they were searching for me. Then she came by and told the police what she saw. That's why my dad went over to my uncle's house. It was too late. He had already raped me twice. He kept telling me that I had to get used to it, and if only my dad had given him the money, this would have never happened. When my dad came in the house, I heard him yelling and swearing at his brother. I never heard my dad use words like that before. My uncle kept telling him he didn't know what he was talking about. He only gave me a ride to a friend's house like I asked him to. That was the last time he saw me. He said to my dad, 'Maybe she ran away.' My dad screamed some more obscenities and said he was calling the police on him. He left. I tried to scream, but I was so damaged and hurt I couldn't. I lost my voice." Tears streaming down her face, "He took away my virginity.

When my dad left, my uncle made a phone call. After the call, he came and got me. Looking at me, shaking his head, he cried, 'Oh my God! What have I done?' But it was too late. Before my dad could come back with the police, the man who came over to my house with my uncle walked in. He handed my uncle a bag that looked like drugs and took me away. He raped me the same night. Then he took me to a strange hotel, where two men, a white man and a black man, were waiting for me. They were high. They also took turns with me. I woke up two days later in Atlanta, sleeping with one man to the next. Mostly Americans, but there were a couple of foreigners. They like Asian girls, so thank God I wasn't in high demand like them. We all went against our will and traveled from one event to another. We were more like high-priced call girls without getting paid. To keep us in control, they threatened to kill us and our families. We were not concerned about ourselves. We were already dead inside. We were concerned about our families. These people were brutal. They would do it.

Our housing was reasonably pleasant. We did eat and dress well. But we couldn't go anywhere without an armed escort. A guy who knew my uncle told me that my uncle was shot dead over drugs. He didn't tell me because he was concerned. He just told me in passing on my way to another man after leaving one. I think I had seven men that day, so when he told me the news, I wasn't even upset. I was too numb to care. I lived this life for years until one day, the men who were trafficking me got busted. I was one of the lucky ones. I made it out ok. I have my family and friends who support me, and now I go around the country telling my story, hoping that I can stop something like what happened to me from happening to other women. Sadly, many girls don't have a happy ending." She abruptly stopped. Tears streaming down her face, she quietly said, "Thank you." She stood at the podium weeping until her mother came to get her and walked her back to her seat.

Camille returned to the podium. "Now we will have Tianna."

Tianna, a pretty African-American woman with mocha-brown skin and long, wavy black hair, began to speak. "People don't think this stuff happens and that our stories are cruel and vile. They want to believe that we make these stories up. They can't believe in this day and time sex trafficking is real. They go home to their perfect world, look at television, play on the computer, or get on social media when at night, young girls and boys are being raped and abused by the thousands. People fight causes they can visibly see, like saving the whales or dolphins or the planet. They are all good causes. And yet, no one is fighting for us or trying to save us. It's as if they are ashamed of our stories, our truths, and us. They can't look us in the eye. It's hard for them to comprehend our pain and our suffering. They are fighting causes for inanimate objects or animals. It makes them feel like they are doing something worthy so they can go to bed in peace."

"Why do you say this?" asked someone in the room.

"It's true! My mother's boyfriend raped me. My mother wanted a man so badly she didn't care what this man did to me when she wasn't around. She would go to work and ask this stranger to watch me. Crazy, right, and yet it happens every day to black girls, white girls, Latino girls, all girls; they are being raped or touched by someone they know. When I told my mother, she took his side and called me a liar. He lied and said I was coming onto him; I was too fast. I was getting fresh with him. Like I wanted a grown, ugly man who smelled like crap! I told my mother, 'What do I want and need with a man who is thirty years older than me?' She believed him over me. He kept doing it while she was at work. So I stopped telling her."

One of the few males in the room asked, "Why didn't you tell your other family members?"

"Shame, guilt, because if truth be told, I felt ashamed and dirty, because after a while, I started liking the feeling. But, when it was over, I cried like a baby as he got up, zipped up his pants, and went into the other room and watched TV. He didn't even wash up after himself. I couldn't tell my family. In the Black culture, we don't tell family business. My mother always said, 'What happens at home stays at home.' I really believe this is where the commercials got their slogan. It had gotten so bad I started running around with the wrong crowd. My father, who my mother divorced, tried to help me, but it was too late. Besides, I couldn't tell him. He would have killed that man. The thought of my father going to jail for the rest of his life for that piece of scumbag, I could never forgive myself, even though I was the victim."

"It would have been in self-defense," someone said from the middle of the room. Everyone mumbled in unison.

"I know," she said quietly. "But, I couldn't drag my family's name in my shame. So I left. It was easy finding a man to take care of you. There are a lot of older men from all facets of life who like PYTs."

"PYT? What is that?"

"Pretty Young Thing. They go wild over PYTs. They are not getting any at home, so they come out in the day like they are going to work and knock on your door, and for whatever price you ask, they give it to you just to be satisfied for about an hour or so. If you are lucky, you get regulars, and they always bring you some trinkets because they feel guilty."

"You were like a prostitute? That's how you got started? How did you get caught up in trafficking?"

"Messing with some white chick named Melissa, Mel for short. We were becoming friends on the avenue. By this time, my dad was really down my back. My mother was too, because she finally believed me. I told her that it was too late. What was done was done. I don't know if she ever forgave herself. Eventually, I forgave her. I didn't want to hate anymore. And I used to really hate her. Anyway, Mel and I went to a party. We hooked up with some 'Ballers'. They took us to Las Vegas for a couple of days. They went home but forgot about taking us with them. We were stranded in Las Vegas. Mel met up with some foreigners. They asked us if we wanted to go to Paris on their private plane. We both said yes! They gave us about two thousand apiece. Now, you would've thought we would take the money and use it to purchase a plane ticket home, which is what I wanted to do, but I let Mel talk me into going with the men. They promised to give us the money for our plane ride home. We went shopping with the money, purchased a few clothes, showered, got something to eat, and met up with the men. They were middle-aged, so we thought they were harmless. I was in my late teens. Mel was twenty-one. We thought we could take them if we had to. We got on the plane, and "BAM," the freaks came out of the men! They gagged us and did everything you could imagine to our bodies. We didn't have any passports, so there we were in some foreign country without passports where women are treated like servants. That's how I ended up in sex trafficking. Passed from one man to another."

"You don't sound bitter. Why?"

"I'm not bitter. However, I'm not the sweet, innocent girl I used to be. It's real. The only thing that kept me alive while going from one man to another was the hope that I would see my home, America, again. I had prayed to God, and He gave me that hope. Faith and hope were my food and water. They kept me going. Now, I am an advocate against human sex trafficking. I go around the country teaching and speaking to audiences about the realities of sex trafficking. I'm not saying this is my calling. I am only doing this so no other girl goes through what I did. I raised enough money to build a shelter for young girls to have a place to go to when a family member or friend molests them. Ladies, let me share this with you. Many women who have young daughters don't understand that their daughters have the same things they have. They allow strange men to come into their homes, and when the daughters get older and start maturing, these men start looking at their daughters in lust. Did you know there are many cases of young girls molested by their mother's boyfriends? Many times the mothers of these young girls believe the men over their daughters. They are so desperate for a man's love and attention that they turn their eyes from the truth."

Someone asked, "Whatever happened to your friend Mel?"

"I don't know," Tianna answered. "When we got off the plane, they separated us. I haven't seen her since. The world of sex trafficking is big."

Camille returned to the podium, "Thank you, Tianna, for your brutal honesty and raw truth. Thank you, Jenna, Maya, and Hannah, for your gut-wrenching stories, too. It's getting late. I know many of you have to leave. We are heading back to Kenya in a few days, but we will be here for another hour to answer any questions you may have for one of the speakers or myself. Please take a brochure, and please get involved! We need you to get involved and take care of each other. We are our sister's keepers."

Inspired by the meeting, Zoe wanted to speak with Camille, but she was surrounded by women. She waited until she was finally alone.

"Hi, Camille. My name is Zoe. I was at the last meeting. I wanted to speak with you then, but my friends who I came with had to leave." She didn't know why she was nervous talking to the woman. She was tall, beautiful, and from her continent Africa. It should've been easy to speak with her.

With a warm and inviting smile, Camille said, "Hello, Zoe. Life correct?"

"Huh?" said Zoe. She was caught off guard by the woman's acknowledgment of her name.

"Your name means life," she repeated.

Zoe suddenly felt shy, smiled back at the woman. "Yes!" she burst out. Realizing Zoe was nervous, Camille gently put her arm around the young woman's shoulder. Zoe was grateful for the woman's sensitivity. "My father named me Zoe. I'm from Nairobi, Kenya. I am here on a student visa, studying medicine at John Hopkins."

Oh, you are from Nairobi? We are heading to Nairobi in a couple of days. We have a village there, hidden away. We help victims of sex trafficking."

Zoe's interest was piqued upon hearing that the woman was traveling to her country. No longer nervous, she began to ramble, "Yes, my parents are both well-known surgeons in Nairobi, Western Europe and parts of Asia. I'm going into the family business as well."

"Oh, really," said Camille. "I'm from Johannesburg, South Africa. I travel all over the world speaking on human and sex trafficking. There are a few who do this regularly like me. Hopefully, after these meetings, we will get more volunteers. We need all the help we can get. Our goal is to have a safe house or two in every city where there is a need. We are making much progress. Some big name Hollywood celebrities are assisting us. This is always a plus because they have many followers and can help bring in more funds. I'm grateful for all the assistance we get."

Zoe was surprised at what came out of her mouth. "How can I help?" She didn't hear Tianna walk up.

"You can help by not just standing looking concerned but by being concerned enough that it brings out the passionate anger in you to do something. Fight a battle that's not yours per se, but as a woman, it's yours. Allow God to take you and teach you how to help another young girl so she won't be here telling her story. Instead, she's in high school or college telling her story on Instagram, or Tik Tok about a homecoming dance, a prom dress, a football game, or whatever young girls talk about these days. We need a voice!"

"Tianna!" cried Camille, trying to hold her temper, aware of the woman's insensitivity. She looked at Zoe and said, "Zoe, please excuse Tianna. She gets a little feisty to the point she can be aggressive at times. She doesn't mean to frighten you." Camille gently scolded the other woman, "Tianna, what did I tell you about coming off too hard? Be gentle," she smiled, letting the girl know she wasn't upset with her.

"Oh, she didn't frighten me," replied Zoe. "Trust me. My mother has the same mannerism." Turning to the other woman, she asked, "Are you saying I am that voice? That's crazy!"

Tianna began to speak in a gentler voice, "No, Zoe, not as an individual. A voice comes from many. A voice that is not afraid to hear our stories, our truth. Not afraid of making a difference, causing a change. To make governments aware that sex trafficking is real. It hurts. God is not asking you to be the 'Voice' of a movement. Whatever He is calling you to do, it's part of the many that make up one voice. His Voice. Do you see that young girl over there sitting quietly in the corner?"

"Yes," said Zoe, staring at the girl in the corner.

"She is only eighteen. Pretty young thing, isn't she?"

Zoe nodded her head, "Yes!"

"Her life is basically over. It will take God and God alone for a miracle. She was abducted at an amusement park. Being at the wrong place, doing the wrong thing. Should she be penalized for this? No! She's young and full of youth; when we are young and youthful, we do stupid things and trust more. No one, especially our parents, can tell us anything. We think we know it all. We have all the answers. What a waste youth is sometimes. When we finally get it right and learn from our mistakes, our youth has faded. You know why she sits in the corner?" She didn't wait for a response. "No, I am not looking for the answers, so don't try to guess. She sits in that corner because soon, her life will be over. She has full-blown AIDs. She got it from one of the men who repeatedly raped her. The sad part is that there were so many she doesn't know who. Do you think these men care? No! They are selfish and greedy. Her life will just be another one who passes this way. May God bless her soul." Tianna looked at Zoe and with compassion in her eyes, said, "Zoe, we don't need a shero or a superwoman. We need a voice. We need a voice of many for the many. Each year, there are an estimated 800,000 women and children who are trafficked across international borders. Wouldn't it be great if there were people who would speak for them?"

Zoe hung her head. There were so many thoughts going through her mind.

Seeing Tianna was overwhelming Zoe, Camille stepped in, "Thank you, Tianna. Come, Zoe. It's a lot to take in. That's why many people close their eyes. Let's go get something to eat."

Zoe looked at the two women, "Thank you both for the information. Camille, it was a lot, but I know what I must do. I want to help."

"I know," said Camille. "I can see it in your eyes. This meeting was very successful. First Patty, and now you, Zoe."

Zoe's eyes beamed with light upon hearing the other woman's name. "Patty!"

"Yes, Patty," said Camille.

Chapter Twenty-Seven

"JaMar, what did the police say? Did they have any news about Zoe? I don't know how long I can take this waiting!"

"Anna, please darling, we must believe! We must have faith!" JaMar was weary from a lack of sleep and worrying about his daughter's safety, yet he didn't dare tell his wife how he was doing or feeling. He kept it all within. He didn't want to frighten or upset her more than she already was. However, his face couldn't hide the strain of stress he felt. It had been days since they heard of Zoe's abduction.

Anxiously waiting for her husband's response, Anna frantically inquired again. "JaMar, you didn't answer me! Are the police still searching for Zoe? Is there any new information about Zoe's whereabouts? Did the police find anyone who knew anything? Please tell me, JaMar! I need to know. I need to know about my Zoe!" she sobbed. "I cannot fathom the thought that she is no longer here on this earth. I can't believe my little girl, my strong, infallible, beautiful daughter is gone! Please tell me, for I can't stand the silence anymore."

Becoming weary of his wife's endless questions, JaMar, trying to keep his patience, told her, "Anna, trust me! The police have nothing more than what they informed us of already. I spoke with the detective today. A woman in the town saw Zoe with a young Caucasian female and a tall African man who didn't look like he was from the area. She was leaving a bar when she saw them walking down the street towards the dark alley. She assumed they were heading to the club where all the young people and tourists go. The locals stay away from the club. She said they looked strained. They were joking, but the mood wasn't cheerful. It was heavy, like something was on their mind. The woman noticed this because although they were smiling, their smiles looked forced. She wondered why three beautiful faces looked so serious while pretending to smile. Even though it was dark, she noticed Zoe. She thought she was beautiful, in a queen-like stature."

"Yes, that is our Zoe," said Anna, whispering her daughter's name.

The woman took her eyes off them and started walking home from a long day of working at the bar. She heard a woman scream and became frightened. Hiding in one of the corners of a building, she saw a shadow of a person reaching out to one of the girls. She caught a glimpse of the other two. She saw someone hit Zoe and pushed her into the car. She became frightened because she knew that the girls were in trouble. She knew that many men came to that part of the town to pick up girls. The townies, as they are called, know what's happening but won't say anything. They are afraid for their lives. She watched as the black or dark blue car drove off, then she ran down the street. The next day, still frightened, she told one of the ministers in the community. He called the police. They kept her name anonymous to protect her. The local police confirmed that the woman's description was identical to the three young people who stayed briefly at the hotel that day. They were there for a few hours and left. The gentleman who checked them in remembered them well. He never saw them again after they left.

Anna went over to her husband. "JaMar, what are we going to do?" Her face showed the fear she was feeling inside.

JaMar, holding back the tears, said to his wife, "Like I already told you a thousand times, Anna, we must pray and believe God."

Frustrated with the waiting, Anna shrieked, "I'm tired of praying and believing! That's all I've been doing: praying and believing! JaMar, what if they raped our Zoe before …."

JaMar put his arms around his wife to console her, "Shh, shhh, my dear. She is okay. You must believe she wasn't raped, and she's not dead. You have to believe, Anna." Sobbing in his arms, she cried, "There are so many young girls who die and are never heard from again. Oh my God! I don't want this to happen to our Zoe!" She sobbed louder. Wiping his wife's tears with his hands, JaMar said, "Now, Anna, that's not our Zoe and you know it. She's resilient. She has the faith of a mighty lion. You must believe that God is with her. He has her. It's our only hope." Hugging his wife, he gently said, "I'm tired too, my love. I haven't slept well since we heard the news. I, too, have cried a thousand tears, but I must believe she's okay. It's a small ounce of faith, but it's enough to believe. That's all I have. Zoe will be fine."

"JaMar, I remember the last day we spoke. If I had known then, I would've been more sympathetic and compassionate."

JaMar's voice full of frustation, shouted, "Anna, stop it! Don't say it! She's okay!"

Anna, stunned by her husband's sharp tone, controlling her voice, softly murmured, "She was always different, so strong. I admired her so, and I must admit there were times I was furious, and yes, I was sometimes envious of her strength, zeal, and faith. When she came to me telling me she wanted to do this and take time off from medical school, I was so proud of her, but my stubbornness couldn't tell her at the time. I wanted to show her off as Dr. Armani, like the beautiful daughter she was."

JaMar corrected her, "IS Anna. Like the beautiful daughter, she IS!"

Anna, understanding his comment, quickly changed her words. "Oh yes, like the beautiful daughter, she IS. I wanted to show her off to my friends and colleagues as Dr. Zoe Armani. That day she came to us about wanting to get involved in sex trafficking, I knew then she was no longer my child. She belonged to Him, God. He was ordering her steps. From that day, I knew no matter what I said or how I said it, she would not have listened to me. I was not her source. I am just her mother," she sobbed again. "He is her God, her Savior. JaMar, how can you compete with Jesus?"

"You can't, Anna. He will always win," JaMar said softly, his voice filled with understanding and compassion.

"Yes, but right now, I feel I have lost my Zoe. I want my Zoe back! To have her fighting against me, standing up to me, with her beautiful, unwavering, strong-willed faith, like the lioness she …IS. I miss her so much! My heart aches for our daughter. Please, JaMar, even if you have to lie, just for this moment to ease my heart, tell me that she will be okay. Please tell me!" Anna said, crying uncontrollably.

Squeezing her tighter as he caressed her back, JaMar listened to her cry. He let her cry until she had no more tears left. Lifting her chin with his hand so she could see his eyes, he said, "Anna, listen to me. I don't have to lie. She will be okay. She's in God's hands. He will take care of her as He sees fit."

Hearing her husband's words, Anna wondered if Zoe would be okay on this side of glory or in the glory to come. She didn't tell her husband what she feared.

Chapter Twenty-Eight

Lying on the bed with tears-stained eyes, Zoe knew in her heart she had made the right decision. From the moment she went to the second meeting to telling Camille she wanted to get involved and arriving at the village, she believed she had heard from God. She remembered getting on the plane, heading back to her native land, rehearsing in her mind what she would tell her parents.

She was a little anxious as she boarded the plane from Baltimore-Washington International (BWI) Airport to fly to her native home, Nairobi, Kenya. She hoped the long flight would prepare her for the task before her, and that was telling her parents of her decision to leave the prestigious medical institution, Johns Hopkins University, to pursue what she felt in her heart was the right thing to do. She wasn't worried much about her father. It was her mother she was more concerned about. What could she tell her mother? "Mother, I'm leaving medical school so I can go and save the world." She could hear her mother's words, "You're WHAT? Zoe, don't be foolish! You are called to do no such thing! You are to be a doctor, join the family business, and one day take over the practice as planned."

She knew in her right mind her mother's words were logical, but she wasn't reasoning with her mind. She was reasoning with her heart. Something was tugging from within that said this was the right thing to do. Thankfully, when she informed her professors why she was leaving school, they all agreed she could take a year off. They were proud of her decision. One of her professors, who was a Christian, prayed with her. She could always share this information with her parents, giving them hope that she would finish school if this didn't work out. Yet, there were still so many unanswered questions. She prayed she was making the right decisions. Her heart said yes, but her mind was saying otherwise. It helped that Patty was with her on the plane. Her presence provided a much-needed anchor in Zoe's thoughts. Listening to Patty, who had a gift of gab, gave Zoe rest from her anxiety.

Patty had made her decision immediately at the first meeting that she wanted to help in the fight against sex trafficking. Her best friend since grade school was a victim of it, and she felt it was partially her fault. She never forgot how she, along with family, friends, and the local police, searched the Baltimore area looking for Lizzie. They posted her pictures on social media, hoping someone would provide information. The police said that it was probably the work of a human trafficker, and although they would continue to keep the file open and pursue Lizzie's whereabouts, it was probably a lost cause. In similar cases, once the victim was trafficked to another state or country, it was out of their jurisdiction; the FBI got involved. They informed her and Lizzie's parents that the possibility of them finding Lizzie was slim to none. Lizzie's parents were blue-collar, hardworking people. They took it very hard. They had three children, and although Lizzie gave them the most trouble, they loved her deeply. The thought of them never seeing their youngest child again took a toll on their already fractured lives. It was soon after the police report Lizzie's parents split up. It was then that Patty knew it was what she had to do.

Patty's parents were very supportive of her decision. They were also hardworking, blue-collar, working-class people, so the thought of their daughter doing something noble, such as helping to find her friend, was pleasing to them. Patty knew they didn't fully understand what she would be doing. Like so many others, sex trafficking was not part of their everyday existence. In Baltimore, the Orioles were winning and people focused on them making the playoffs. When she told her parents she was going to

Nairobi, Kenya, they told their family, friends, and church members. Her father gave her some pocket change, hugged her tightly, and told her he loved her and was proud she was his daughter. That was the extent of her telling her parents. She left the next day. For the first time in her life, she felt like she was making a difference.

After high school Patty tried community college, waitressing, and clerical work, but none of those panned out for her. But with this, in her heart, she knew it was the right thing to do. She was glad that Zoe, the beautiful African woman with the beautiful brown eyes, was there to share the experience. When she found out Zoe was going, she knew they would be more than friends.

Zoe and one of the girls from the university who came with her sat at the table where she was sitting at the first meeting. Patty took an instant dislike to the other girl with Zoe, but Zoe was different. She wasn't like the other girl. It was something about her. She was focused on what the speaker was saying. Patty knew Zoe was there for the same reason she was, and that was to make a difference. She saw how Zoe's eyes lit up and took in everything as if she was drinking from a river yet never filling up. Patty wasn't necessarily envious or intimidated by the students but felt uneasy around them. Even though she was an A/B student in high school, she didn't feel smart around them. At one time, she thought about going into the medical administrative field because she was very detailed-oriented and had excellent administrative skills. However, during the first year of community college, she knew this wasn't the route for her.

It was no surprise when she saw Zoe at the second meeting. She knew Zoe would see the big picture. She was right. At the first meeting, Patty informed Camille that she wanted to be part of the fight against sex trafficking. Camille was ecstatic. When Camille told her Zoe was joining the fight, Patty was overjoyed. Together, she believed they would make a difference. The more they talked on the plane only confirmed her initial observation.

The eighteen-plus-hour flight to Nairobi began to take its toll on the young women. After talking nonstop for four hours, Patty finally fell asleep after drinking two glasses of wine. Zoe attempted to do the same, dozing off for an hour or two but never fully getting any rest. Although she was used to traveling long distances on planes, the thought of her telling her parents of her decision wreaked havoc on her mind and prevented her from getting the rest she needed. She wished she could order drinks as Patty did and go to sleep. Gazing over at her friend, who was sleeping soundly with a smile on her face, she envied the sandy, blond-haired sleeping beauty. Not a care in the world, she thought. Zoe smiled within, feeling a strong bond between the two. It was great they would be together. Both were very different, yet they were of the same kindred spirit. She was relieved when the pilot announced over the speaker that they would be landing soon. She didn't want to think anymore about telling her parents what she had done. Looking out the window and seeing the vastness of her country's beauty she admired so much, took her mind off her parents. She never got tired of looking at the land. It was majestic and breathtaking. Thank God they were flying first class. Camille insisted, especially since they weren't getting much pay for what they were doing.

As the plane circled to prepare for landing, Zoe nudged Patty. "Wake up, Sleeping Beauty! It's time to get up. We're here. See!" Opening her eyes and feeling the effects of the drinks, Patty smacked her lips. "Ugghh! Now I know why I don't drink a lot!" she cried, "I need a mint!" Zoe smiled as she gave Patty a mint. "Now that you are up you can see my beautiful country. Look!" Zoe was eager for her friend to see the beautiful view of her country from above. Patty looked over Zoe's shoulder to see the view from the plane's window. They both marveled at the scenery from below. From the plane, Patty could see some parts of the savanna. Her face lit up. "Oh, there are some giraffes," she squealed with delight. "And is that a hippo I see?" Zoe laughed. It always amazed her how people reacted to seeing the wild animals in the national park. She was used to seeing the animals. There were many different species, all majestic and regal, and many very dangerous, yet seeing them still fascinated her.

As the plane descended, Zoe and Patty could see the view of Nairobi, Kenya, Zoe's home. "Wow! It is beautiful! I never realized how very modern it is. It looks like an American city." Once again, Zoe smiled. She didn't take offense to her friend's ignorance of her country. "Oh yes! We even have a McDonald's," she laughed. Patty blushed, "My bad!" Westerners huh? We really got to travel more," she grinned.

Going through customs and retrieving their baggage was a breeze. Thanks to Camille's connections, they received preferential treatment and were escorted through the terminal as VIPs. Once outside the terminal, Patty, overcome by the heat and humidity, cried out, "Where is the car to pick us up? Seriously, I'm dying here!" "Come on," said Zoe. "You'll get used to the heat. Besides, you have to." "Neevverrr!" shrieked Patty. Zoe smiled. She had grown very fond of Patty. Her sudden outbursts always made her laugh.

Seeing the car ahead, Zoe tugged Patty's shirt. "Patty, there's the car. See the sign, Ms. Zoe and Ms. Patricia. Come on, let's get you out of this heat before you melt." "No need to tell me twice," Patty cried. As they approached the car, the driver asked for their identification. Seeing it was them, he helped them with their bags and opened the door to the air-conditioned inside. Sighing, Patty said, "Ahhh, now I can get used to this luxury." Zoe felt the same way. The air-conditioned vehicle was a blessing from the heat. "Where are we going?" Zoe asked the driver. Before he could answer, the door opened, and Camille entered with a handsome man getting in beside her.

Zoe always thought Camille was beautiful and regal, but today, she had a special glow on her face. She wondered if it was the handsome man's doing. "Patty, Zoe, this is Kato." "Sweet!" said Patty under her breath. Zoe didn't say anything. Suddenly, she felt very uncomfortable in the presence of the man. They rode in silence for the majority of the ride. Breaking the silence, Patty asked, "Where are we going?" Camille answered the young woman's question. "Well, tonight we're staying at a hotel. For the rest of the time, we will stay outside the city limits in the village. It's about fifty miles out. It's a secluded area where we house the victims of sex trafficking before they're sent to safe places. We have to keep a low profile in our business. We don't always know who is with us."

Patty, not liking the bit of not staying in an air-conditioned facility, said, "What? Where are we staying?" Speaking up for the first time since getting into the limousine, knowing that fifty miles wasn't safari country, Zoe teasingly said, "Basically, Patty, we are staying in the jungle with the lions and tigers, but no bears! Oh, my!" With that last remark, Zoe burst out laughing. She didn't see the man staring at her. "Camille!" Patty cried, "You can turn this vehicle around and send me back home to the sweet U.S.A. where the AC flows freely! I'm not staying with any animals that can eat me in one sitting!" Zoe, still laughing, said, "Patty, don't worry, you'll get used to the heat and the humidity. Your body will get acclimated." Patty rolled her eyes at her friend, "Zoe, this is not funny. Ain't nobody got time to live in the jungle!" Seeing the young woman was upset, Camille softly said, "Patty, I promise you, if you are not okay, we will send you back. I promise." Patty shook her head. The remainder of the ride and the entire night she didn't say anything to anyone.

A few days later, not only did Patty become acclimated to the heat, but she became a regular trooper. She immediately got involved in helping the children and assisting the medical team with generic first aid. She wore a bandana around her head and neck to offset the heat. As they were eating in the commissary one day, she told Zoe, "You know, the heat is not as bad as I first perceived, although you have to wear a lot of deodorant. I kid you not! I smell as bad as some of the animals." They both laughed. "Who would have thought that me, Patty from the streets of Baltimore, would one day be in Kenya...the continent of Africa, helping a cause such as this? When we first got here and saw the children so traumatized and damaged, my heart ripped apart. I didn't know humans could be so cruel to such little ones. I almost broke down when we saw that twelve-year-old girl give birth to a baby. She was raped. Now she has a child to remind her of this for the rest of her life. I can't imagine what is going through her young mind. I know now this is what I was searching for." Zoe nodded her head. She felt the same way. "Yes, it's heartbreaking to see these children. They are babies, yet many of them have had experiences twice and three times their ages." "Zoe looked at the children playing nearby, "I didn't know man's lust could be so cruel."

Finishing up their meal, Zoe said, "Come on, there is someone I want you to meet. He's the cutest little boy. He was trafficked for work, but he ran away. Someone found him and brought him here." Patty, taking the last sip of her drink, gathered her plate. As they walked toward the trashcan, Patty turned to Zoe. "Zoe, you know you still have to tell your parents about quitting school and doing this. You can't keep this kind of thing from them." "I know. I know," said Zoe. "But the timing is not right. I know what I'm doing is right, but you don't know my mother. She can be adamant when she believes she knows what is right."

"Like you?" replied Patty with a smirk.

Zoe shook her head, "No, how about me to the fifth power." They both laughed.

"You know," said Patty, "The only hangup here is that there are no dudes to joke around with. It's bad enough we can only use our phones during special times of the day, but we can't even get on social media! Other than that Kato dude, who always stares at us like we are some zombies when he comes around, the rest are doctors or caseworkers," said Patty. "What about the security guys? Zoe asked her. "They seem ok. Although I'm only casual with them." Zoe made sure she always kept boundaries with the males in the camp. "Nah! Too intense!" said Patty. "I had a guy back home in Baltimore. His name was Bryan. We were just 'Smashing it' if you know what I mean. Nothing serious, but I sure miss him right now."

"'Smashing it'? What's that?" asked Zoe. Patty stopped, "Zoe, girl, don't tell me you don't know what 'Smashing it' means. You're not that green, are you?" Zoe blushed, finally understanding the meaning of the word. "Oh, sex. You mean sex! And no, I'm not green. But I don't smash it if you get my drift." What? Never?" cried Patty. "Never," said Zoe. "Don't get me wrong. I'm no saint. I just decided to wait until my wedding day. I promised God I would. Besides, look at us. We're too busy to get serious with anyone."

"Yeah," Patty agreed.

Changing the subject, Zoe said, "Anyway, let me introduce you to my little friend. He's adorable. Wait until you meet him. I promise you'll find him adorable, too."

The women were so absorbed in their conversation that they didn't realize how loud they were talking. Thinking they were among themselves, they didn't see Kato walking behind them. He overheard their conversation. "Hmmm," he thought, "interesting."

"Kato! Kato! Didn't you hear me calling you?" Kato turned and saw Camille running up to him. "Camille, my dear, what is it? You sound intense. What is it?" Rushing to his side, breathless, she watched as his eyes remained fixed on the two young women. She saw how his eyes were more focused on Zoe. She shook it off. This was more important. "They have the girl. She is young. We have to act quickly!" she told him.

"How long do we have?" he inquired. "We have to move out tomorrow evening after dusk. Everything is in place," she told him. Pointing to Zoe and Patty, he asked, "Are they ready?" Sighing, Camille said, "We'll see, but if not, then it's you and me. Let's go tell them."

They found the two women playing with the little boy Micah, the name he told them. "Zoe, Patty," Camille said, "We are ready! Are you ready?" "Yes," they replied. "Good," replied Camille. "We will meet tonight and talk about everything."

Zoe knew that it was time to do the inevitable. "Camille, I need a vehicle and a driver. I have to go home." Camille looked into Zoe's eyes, "OK! They will be ready for you within the hour. But Zoe, if you're not back by dusk tomorrow, we will go without you."

"I understand. I will be back by then. I promise," Zoe reassured her.

Zoe walked away, leaving them standing, watching her as she went to gather her things for the long ride. She was ready to tell her parents.

Chapter Twenty-Nine

Abaeze quietly tiptoed onto the patio in search of Anna. He found her with her eyes closed and assumed she was sleeping. He knew this was rare and didn't want to disturb her, but duty called. "Excuse me, Madam, there are some visitors at the door. They said it's urgent and wish to speak with you and Sir!" Startled upon hearing the urgency in the man's voice, Anna jumped up from her seat. She was on the patio trying to rest, but like always, she would think of Zoe, and rest would never come. Getting up from the chair and adjusting her clothing, she asked her servant, "Visitors? Did they say what they wanted?" "No, Ma'am," he answered. "They only said it was urgent and needed to speak with you and Sir." Wondering who would want to speak to them, "Where is Sir?" she asked. "He's in his study reading a book. But I know he is praying just by the way he is reading. His eyes are closed tight." Anna smiled, "Ahhh, I know what you mean. I bet he is reading and his brows are making those lines that look like roads with many turns on his forehead." She began chuckling, reminiscing of happier times. Sighing, she said to the servant, "Ok, please let them in the parlor. I will go tell Sir. Hopefully, it's about Zoe. It seems so long ago." Remembering their last conversation, "If I could just go back and hug her one last...." She stopped in the middle of the sentence. Tightly closing her eyes, determined not to cry, she said "Never mind, Abaeze, please inform Sir we have visitors in the parlor. I'll go to them instead." "Very well, Madam. Do you need me to pour tea or get them any refreshments?" he asked. Anna smiled at the loyal butler. "Not so subtle, are you, Abaeze? I know you and the other servants are family and want to know if they are here about Zoe, too. Normally, yes, but this time, if they are here for what I think they are, I don't feel in the mood to entertain. I'd rather have my Zoe back."

The servant nodded his head. "Yes, Ma'am. I understand. We pray for her safety every day. We're family, ma'am. We have watched Zoe and the little Sir grow up to be beautiful children and now grand citizens of our country. You are very wise. I did want to know, not for gossip, but we, the staff, are very concerned."

"Thank you, Abaeze. I know you're all concerned. And yes, we are family. Now, please go get JaMar so we can find out what our visitors want."

"Yes, Ma'am."

"Oh, Abaeze," she called out to him.

"Yes, Ma'am."

"Thank you for your prayers. We are very grateful for the staff's prayers and patience during this trying time. Please let them know."

"Yes, Ma'am. Will do."

Walking down the hallway, Anna stopped at the partially closed parlor door. Hearing voices inside, she paused and took a deep breath before entering the room. "Lord, please let it be good news," she said under her breath. Opening the door wide, she bravely walked into the room and saw the detective with three unfamiliar faces with him. The detective stretched out his hand to greet her as she entered the room. He could tell by the strains on her face that she hadn't been sleeping well. In a soothing voice, he said, "Dr. Armani, my apologies. Forgive me, us, for disturbing you and your husband, the other Dr. Armani. We have some news about the situation and possibly Zoe's whereabouts. Is your husband home? I prefer to speak with both of you."

Taking the detective's stretched hand, Anna graciously welcomed him, letting him know it was okay to interrupt them. "Detective, it's kind of you to come, and I say that sincerely. Any news is good news. It's the not knowing that keeps our minds uneasy. But yes, my husband is here. He should be joining us any minute. I sent our butler to get him. He was in his study reading. He reads all the time now; it calms his mind. As for me, I stare into the sky watching it turn from blue to dark. That is what calms me." The detective nodded. With heartfelt sympathy, he said, "Yes, Ma'am. I do understand. I pray that this information will give you an ounce of hope. In the end, all we have is our hope."

At that moment JaMar walked in, "That is so true detective. Our hope and faith in Christ keep us from losing our minds. Hello my dear, detective, and guests whom I do not know." Kissing his wife on the cheek, he whispered in her ear, "I was reading." Smiling at her husband, Anna said, "I know. I can see your lines. I pray that it has calmed you." "Always, my dear. Always." Turning to his guest, JaMar shook the detective's hand, "Now, detective, to what do we owe this pleasure?"

"Excuse me for the interruption," said the detective as he shook JaMar's hand, "Let me introduce you to Detectives Chi and Dembe and Ms. Camille. They are here with some information that you will want to hear."

"Ahhh," said JaMar, shaking the two men's hands, "Personal Guardian Angel and Peace. It seems God did hear my prayers. He brought us an angel and peace." Gently mocking his wife, he said, "See honey, and you only thought I was reading. Ms. Camille, the pleasure is ours to meet you as well."

"Forgive me detectives and Ms. Camille," said Anna. "It's an inside humor. My husband studies African names. He is quite a scholar when it comes to our heritage. He studies the origin of names, particularly the names of our people. Turning to the two men, she said, "I assume your names mean peace and angel. Is he correct?"

Detective Chi spoke up, "Yes, Ma'am, he is."

Winking at his wife, JaMar grinned, "See, Anna, and you always think I am sleeping when my eyes are closed." He smiled at the guests, "It's good to smile again, even if it is for just a brief moment, eh detective? Because I fear that once you share your news, whether good or bad, it will take away my smile. Am I correct?

"I'm afraid that depends on you, Dr. Armani. There is hope," replied the detective.

JaMar gestured for them to sit. "Please sit. We have stood too long. Now it's beginning to be awkward. Would you care for tea or refreshments of sorts, cookies or cake? Me, I have a sweet tooth. I love cake, don't I, my dear?' JaMar knew he was rambling, but in his defense, he didn't know if he was ready to hear the detective's news.

The four guests sat down in the spacious room. JaMar continued to stand.

The detective said, "No, sir. We don't want to be here longer than necessary. It's not a social call."

"Then do start," said JaMar. "We've wasted enough time. I can see the anxiousness on my wife's beautiful face."

Clearing his throat, the detective informed them of the current situation. "We do have some news about Zoe. We have a source in the organization but can't contact the person. We don't know if that person is working for us or against us. Perhaps Ms. Camille can further explain."

Camille, a little nervous, let out a slight cough. "Uhmmm…before I start, please know that I'm very sorry for what you are going through. I blame myself. I knew she was too young. They both were. But Zoe kept pleading with me, telling me she was called to do this. I looked at her and believed her. I still do. It was her eyes. They were so determined, unafraid, full of courage, and such force. I've never encountered someone quite like Zoe, so very persuasive and full of conviction."

Struggling to hold back tears as the woman spoke of her daughter with such affection, Anna said, "Yes, you've captured the spirit of our Zoe very well. Ms. Camille, please don't be so hard on yourself. We don't hold you responsible. We know our Zoe. Once she sets her mind to something, it's nearly impossible to dissuade her. Her convictions are as unyielding as a steel wall. And if she believes God is on her side, nothing can deter her. There's no need for apologies," Anna reassured the woman. "Please, continue."

"It was supposed to be an easy mission. We had all the background, the information, and the intelligence. There was a young girl; we now know her age—eight, very young even for this organization. They kidnapped her from her village. It was a relative who sold her to the traffickers. We got word of who did it and where they were taking her before the hand-off. Someone doubled-crossed us, or our channels got blotched. Either way, all three were captured."

No longer able to hold back the tears, Anna let out a small moan as water filled her eyes. "Oh my God! What could a grown man do with a child so young?" Thinking of Zoe, she cried, "Oh my God, our Zoe!" JaMar went over to console her.

The detective empathizing with the woman's pain, said, "I know it sounds horrible. The world of sex trafficking is ugly! It's a billion-dollar business. There are some very powerful people involved. The man who abducted Zoe is one of the most notorious in the country and on the continent of Africa. I know it's not a plus, but it's far worse in other countries, such as China and Russia. I pray that she isn't transported to one of those countries!"

"Detective!" JaMar scowled, "If you and Ms. Camille are here to bring hope, I must dare say that you are not succeeding!"

The detective apologized for his insensitivity. "Please forgive me, Sir, Ma'am. I didn't mean to cause you more concern than you already have, but there is hope. We found out that Zoe is still with her abductor and is unharmed. Our inside source says it is harder to transport the young girl because the people who wanted her are no longer alive. Some younger men who just got into the trade killed them. They are not interested in younger girls. They want females twelve and older."

Anna, shocked, gasped.

The detective looked down at the floor, "I know twelve is still young. The good news is the man who has them now doesn't want the young girl. They are trying to find a buyer for the girl. It's buying us some time. This new group of traffickers is not necessarily into trafficking the girls per se. They get the girls to sell to potential buyers. Unfortunately, they make a pretty penny in human trafficking, particularly sex trafficking." JaMar, upset and filled with righteous anger, asked, "Detectives, why can't something be done about this? It's inhuman! Pure demonic!"

"Dr. Armani, Sir, we are angry too. We are doing everything we can and we are making great breakthroughs. It's better, but we still have ways to go. As I stated, it's big business. And the money is plentiful. Many people's lives depend on the money it brings in. It's their livelihood. To mess with them is like taking their money. They can get extremely violent when you mess with their money. People are scared, especially the poor. In this country, the poor are targeted. We don't look at the poor like we look at the well-to-do, the rich. If Zoe was not affected, would you even care about the young girls trafficked into sex slavery?" Offended by his remarks, Anna fumed with anger. "We didn't know this existed at this magnitude! How could we do something about it if we didn't know? Don't judge us, detective! We understand lack and poverty!"

Knowing he upset the woman with his comment, the detective assured her, "No, Ma'am, I'm not judging you. However, when life is pleasantly good and all your needs and desires are met, it is human nature not to pay attention to those outside that daily existence. I thank God for Ms.

Camille and your daughter, Zoe. I do feel awful that she was captured. Dr. Armani, you must believe we are trying everything possible to free your daughter and the others. It's the wait that is the hardest."

"What happened to the other female who was with Zoe? Where is she?' asked Anna.

"We don't know. The two women were separated. Most likely, they sold her since they couldn't sell the young girl. She is an American and can't be traced. She may be in another country by now."

JaMar anxiously turned to Camille, "Ms. Camille, what about the young man with them? Do you know him?"

Hanging her head low, Camille sighed, "I thought I did," she answered. "Now I realize I didn't know him. We were once in a relationship, but that was long ago." Camille knew she would always love Kato even if the feelings weren't reciprocated. Regaining her composure, with a brave smile, she continued, "Listen, we have to stay focused. No, I'm not you, and my love for Zoe is not as strong as yours, but I love Zoe and Patty. I love all those young girls. They come to us broken, abused, physically and mentally damaged like they are a piece of wood, discarded when the wood gets warped. They are hurt and rejected; they feel abandoned by people because some of their friends and family sold them into sex trafficking. All I am saying is that for such a time as this, all I have is hope. I hope and believe I'm making a small contribution, a dent into this ugly world of sex trafficking. I believe this is what I'm to do. What I'm created to do. And that's what I saw in Zoe's eyes. A call to help."

Weary from all the news, Anna asked the woman, "Camille, give it to me straight. I have my big girl's bloomers on. Do you think Zoe will be okay?" Camille looked into the other woman's eyes, "Ma'am, I don't know. It doesn't look good in the natural, but God is much bigger than us. We need to continue to pray. I have to believe and hope He will come through. Please know that if this is it for Zoe, she fulfilled the call."

Fed up with the conversation and where it was going, JaMar abruptly ended the meeting. "That's enough for today!" he growled. Taking the hint, the detective rose from his seat. The others followed. "We must go." Turning to JaMar, he said, "Doesn't seem like much hope, does it…but a mustard seed can grow into a large plant. Regardless, I will get on my post and call you if anything happens." JaMar, appreciating the man's commitment, thanked them, "Thank you, detectives, and thank you, Ms. Camille. Also, thank you for bringing us an angel and peace…," he said, smiling at the two detectives. "You are welcome, Sir," echoed the three.

Anna rose from her chair, using the excuse of needing to freshen up. She thanked her guests and excused herself, but before she could leave the room, she burst into tears. JaMar, feeling a sense of helplessness, watched his wife leave the room in tears. The others felt the weight of the moment, and hung their heads in sorrow. Clearing his throat, JaMar turned to them, "Let me show you to the door." Walking them to the door, he noticed Abaeze, his loyal servant, casually dusting the paintings in the foyer. JaMar smiled. He knew he was eavesdropping to let the other servants know what he had heard. He didn't care. They loved Zoe just as much and were praying for her safety. Beckoning Abaeze, he said to the man, "Abaeze, please let our guest out. Please excuse me, detectives, Ms. Camille, I must tend to my wife. Have a good day." With that, JaMar went to find Anna. "Good day to you as well, Sir," said the detective.

JaMar found Anna weeping on the hallway stairs. "JaMar!" Anna rushed into her husband's arms. "Did they think they were bringing us good news? If that is good news, I fear the bad news. JaMar, I've never imagined not seeing Zoe again until now. I don't think I could go on. With all my degrees and my position, nothing matters anymore. I would give it all up to have Zoe back. I want my Zoe back! Oh, JaMar! How can God be so cruel?" "Shhh, my darling, shhhh. Let us not lose hope." JaMar gently held her until she became calm. Once he saw that she was finally calm, he kissed her on the top of her head and said, "I am going to read, my love." "Yes, you go on," she said, wiping her tear-stained face. "Dusk is coming. I think I'll go out on the patio and look at the sky." They both walked away in pain as Abaeze watched from afar.

Chapter Thirty

"What do you mean you don't want the girl now? We had a deal! That's not my problem! It's yours! Do you know that one of my men was almost killed in the process of getting this girl? If you don't pay up, it will be very bad for you, my friend! Very bad!" roared Seian. Listening to the other end of the phone conversation, full of rage, he shouted, "I don't care who was caught or killed. I did my part of the bargain! It doesn't matter what happened, we had a…hello? Hello? Hello!" Seian looked at the phone, "Incredible! Just plain incredible! I can't believe they hung up. They hung up on me! Do they know who I am? Do they know I don't play, especially with my money? Alana! Laos! Kato!" screamed Seian.

Laos rushed into the room upon hearing Seian's screams. Out of breath, he asked nervously, "What is it, boss? What has happened?" Seian, seeing that Laos was the first to arrive, shouted at the man, "Laos, go get the arsenal. There is going to be bloodshed! An all-out war!"

Alana rushed into the room, barely catching her breath. She heard Seian's words about a war and became frightened. Sensing his anger, she cautiously asked, "Seian, what happened? I heard you screaming. What has happened, my dear? What has made you so upset? Please tell me?"

Seian, full of rage, answered her. "He hung up on me! Can you imagine him hanging up on me? In all the years I have been in this business, no one has ever hung up on me or not paid me my money! What is this crazy madness?" He looked at Laos and yelled, "Laos, go do what I told you to do!" Alana, fully understanding what was happening, went over to Seian; in a calm voice, she said, "Seian, do you know what you're doing? Do you know if you do this, it will be bloodshed, and no one will survive? Trying to talk him out of it, she said, "These men are dangerous! I fear them myself! Please tell me what has happened, my dear. Tell me! We can work it out?"Seian pushed her away. "Woman, you sound like a fool!" Seian saw that Laos was still in the room. Getting impatient with them both, he yelled again, "Laos, go do as you're told! Now!" Not wanting to further anger the man, Laos rushed out of the room.

"No, my dear," Alana said softly. She knew when he was like this, the only way to make him hear was to speak calmly. "I sound like a wise woman who is still alive. Now, tell me what has happened to make you sound like a madman? Who has hung up on you, my dear?" At that moment, Kato entered the room. "What's all the commotion? I heard it throughout the house. Everyone did!" he asked. "Kato," Alana rushed over to his side, "Thank God you are here! Please find out what is wrong with him!" Pointing to Seian, "He is talking about a war. He sounds like a madman!" Alana, distressed, pleaded with Kato to find out what caused Seian to become furious. Discerning his surroundings, Kato gazed at Seian. He whispered to Alana, "I don't know him like the rest. He may kill me." Desperate, Alana raised her voice at the man, "No, he won't. He trusts you! Now go! Please find out!"

Kato slowly walked over to where Seian was standing. He could tell by his demeanor that Seian was extremely upset; carefully choosing his words, he asked, "My friend, what has happened? We ought to know if we are going into bloodshed the reason behind the war. I'm not afraid to die, but please, my friend, you have everyone upset and on edge. Tell me what's wrong!" Seian, now calmer, began to speak, "The Klan that was supposed to purchase the young girl, their leader, was arrested and possibly killed. It was a setup. No one knows what happened or how it happened. The guards were not in place. It appeared they had surveillance on him. He was getting too sloppy. I told him, but he laughed and said, 'Who would dare go against me?' Does he not know what lengths I went through to get the young girl? How much we paid the uncle? Kato, my friend, I don't like to get the young girls, but the pay is very good!" He paused and became angry again, "I will kill all of them!" With a soothing voice, Kato told him, "My friend, their Klan is more dangerous than ours. I know of them. I have seen them when someone double-crosses them. They have deep connections in China and Russia. You will be fighting a war where there will be no survivors. Is this what you want?" Seian growled, "It has nothing to do with death! It's about my honor! My reputation! They will not pay me! I have lost money!"

Relieved that Kato finally calmed Seian, Alana carefully approached him. In a soothing voice, she said softly, "My dear, they will pay you. This was no fault of theirs. I guarantee there is already bloodshed. I'm afraid innocent people in that village are paying the price for his capture or possible death. He is or was a very vicious and evil man. No heart or soul, so all are paying." Realizing they still had the girl, she asked, "What do we do with the young girl? Surely, she cannot stay here. It's too dangerous now, especially since the leader was caught and most likely killed. We still have the other girl, the Zoe girl, to deal with too. We must get rid of them both quickly before the authorities come looking for us." With a wicked grin, Seian said, "Yes, I know what you are saying is true. You have good sense. You know how to calm me well, don't you? Indeed, it is a dangerous lifestyle we live, but it's even more dangerous when you have a child as young as the girl. We have to get rid of her at once! We must get rid of them both! There is only one way," he said. "We must kill them both. The Zoe girl, too, as you call her. It's such a waste for her life to end this way. From what you say about her, she appears to come from a well-to-do, educated family. Shame she has to die. The young girl, on the other hand, comes from poverty. Her world was bound to come to this place, or worse, she would have starved to death. The poor, no one really cares about the poor. They are nuisances."

Kato knew from experience when Seian's mind was made up, it was the end of the discussion. He didn't come this far to get nothing for the two girls.

He, along with the others risked their lives. To see them both killed would be a waste of his time and efforts. "Seian," he asked in a low, cautious voice, "Why don't we continue with the plan and sell them? The young girl and the Zoe girl. I know it's a silent code that influential families are not to be touched. But she is here now," he said, hoping Seian would figure out what he was implying. "Anyway, her family has probably realized by now she is dead or sold into sex trafficking. Why not just do what they believe? It's been more than a couple of days since they were kidnapped. We can get a good deal for both. Two beautiful African virgins! Think of how many people would be willing to purchase such creatures. There is a high market price for both, and a girl of Zoe's caliber, you should get a pretty penny."

Alarmed that Kato would even think about such a plan of selling Zoe, forgetting that Seian was in the room watching her, Alana rushed over to Kato and lashed out at him, "Kato, are you crazy?" We can sell the young girl, but we can't sell Zoe!" Seian eyed the woman carefully. "What is it, my dear? Have you a fondness for the girl? Are you the mole?" Realizing that she made a grave mistake in showing sympathy in front of Seian, Alana quickly stepped back and looked at him. She knew he was watching her. Careful with her words, she replied, "Don't be silly! I'm in this too deep to have any feelings. It's just that in all the times we trafficked, we have never had a woman like Zoe. With her background! We can't sell her. Don't forget, there's a code," she said, hoping he would see that she was only speaking the truth and not getting sympathetic on him. Seian could handle anything but someone being disloyal to him. Alana saw how he dealt with disloyal people. She took a big gulp and waited for his response.

"What do you suppose we do with them? Let them walk out the door? No, my dear Alana, we cannot do that at all," he said, pressing his lips tightly. He then winked at her letting her know he wasn't upset about her outcry. Turning to Kato, with a shrewd smirk, he said, "Kato, my friend, I do like the way you think. You think like me. The money! After all, that is why we do this, eh? For the money!" At that moment, Laos came into the room with weapons in his hands. Walking over to Seian, he said, "The men are all armed and ready."

Seian, seeing his loyal servant in full arsenal gear, slapped him on the back. "Put the arsenal back, Laos. There will be no bloodshed today!" He walked over to Kato and Alana. "Thank you, my dear and my friend for talking sense into me. It was wise of both of you to stop this madman," he paused briefly and looked at Alana, "as you called me, my dear. Laos, no one will die today. I must go now and make some calls. I know of someone who may be interested in both of them. He is a successful doctor from South Africa. He has a wife and two children. He will take care of the Zoe girl and will only use her for himself until he is tired of her. But he will treat her accordingly. He likes older girls anyway. As for the little girl, he will keep her safe until she is ready to take her place in his world. Yes, he will pay good money for them both."

Relieved that the crisis was over, Laos, holding up the two machine guns, said, "I guess we don't need these, do we? I'll tell the others." He left the room, muttering to himself, "I'm getting too old for this!"

Alana watched him leave. Once he was out of earshot, hoping to get on Seian's good side again because of her earlier outburst, she meekly said, "Seian, the man sounds wealthy." Seian, aware of what she was doing, answered, "Yes, my dear, he is very wealthy. The wealthy ones are some of our best customers. They do not bother their wives. The wives shop and dine while they get their sexual pleasures from the girls. Tis a cruel, cruel world we live in, my dear."

After watching the two interact in polite conversation, Kato knew it was a good time to ask Seian something. "Excuse me for interrupting Seian, but I want to ask something of you."

"Go ahead, my friend," Seian replied.

"A man such as this caliber, will he mind if she is a virgin? I'm referring to the Zoe girl or woman."

Seian pondered the question, "Hmmm…I never really thought of that." His kind doesn't prefer virgins. They are like the clergy who come here looking for young girls, but not the virgins. The thought of them taking a girl's virginity will play havoc on their self-righteous minds." Sighing, he said, "It appears I have to search elsewhere."

"Can I make a request?" Kato asked, aware of the consequences of what he was asking.

"What is it?"

"Can I be the one to take Zoe's virginity? I have no scruples, and I do like virgins."

Seian laughed heartily, "Ahhhhh, so the Zoe girl has put a spark in your eyes, too. She must be special. What if I care, eh? She will be sold soon, so do what you will. It may be better if you take her. That way, when she meets her new owner, she will not be a tigress when penetrated. Seian, finished with the conversation and satisfied with the outcome, walked to the door. "Very well, my friend, go to your Zoe." He turned to Alana and said, "Alana, I need a drink. Are you coming, my dear?"

Alana knew it was not wise to keep Seian waiting, but she didn't care. "Just a moment," she said. "I will be with you shortly. Let me collect my nerves. It has been a day. I thought for sure that it would not end so well. But you always make the right choices, my dear. Thank you, for I am very much relieved." Looking at her strangely, with a devious grin, Seian said, "As you wish, but don't be too long. I feel like, well, you know, the stress." Alana nervously smiled back at him, hoping he didn't see her uneasiness. He smiled at the two as he walked out of the room. She waited a few minutes to make sure he was gone before she spoke. Seeing it was clear, she spun around to Kato in rage, "Kato, how could you ask Seian of such a thing? How could you even bring yourself to do this to Zoe? You know she is better than this!"

Kato retorted, "Better than what, or who? Because she is rich that makes her better than the poor girls. If you asked me, they are all the same. She is just another girl to me," he snorted. Anyway, what is it to you?" Staring at her, he inquired, "Are you sure you're not the mole? Shaking his head, he continued, "You know it was either this or death. Besides, it's time someone breaks our little Zoe. She is too uppity for her own good."

Exasperated about the whole thing and being called a mole, Alana put her hand on her forehead and groaned loudly. Scoffing at his words, she said, "Me a mole? Don't be absurd! You know I'm not a mole! I would be dead! And Zoe is not uppity. It's something else." Frightened for Zoe's safety, she pleaded with him. "Kato, you can have the young girl or other girls, but not Zoe! She's not like the others. I beg of you, don't do this. I would rather see her shot and killed than raped by you. She will have to endure this when the doctor comes. Allow her some peace before he comes."

"I don't want the others. I want Zoe," he said. He cautioned her, "Alana, be careful. You don't want Seian to get any wrong ideas about you. You know how he can be."

"Don't be foolish!" she cried. "Seian knows he can trust me. I have proven this to him. He has nothing to worry about." She didn't let him know that she was worried. She had seen how Seian looked at her. She knew she had to make it up to him to prove her loyalty. It has been nothing but trouble since we got that little girl! she thought. She went over to the window to admire the view of the beautiful landscape outside. "It's such a beautiful day. Beautiful outside, but ugly inside," she said aloud for him to hear.

Kato, not caring, replied, "I must go. My work is never completed. However, this time, I think I will thoroughly enjoy this task. Who knows? I may even have lunch, dinner, and dessert. Ahhh, yes, I'm looking forward to fulfilling my appetite. You'd better get going yourself. You don't want to keep Seian waiting," he warned her as he left the room.

"You Bastard!" she cried out after him.

"I have been called worse," he yelled back at her.

Chapter Thirty-One

Kato found Zoe sleeping peacefully on her back. He walked over to the bed. Her face radiant, her breathing gentle; she looked more beautiful than the last time he had seen her. The calm before the storm, he thought. She looked lovely enough to kiss. It reminded him of the fairytale 'Sleeping Beauty.' He was the prince who would sweep her away. Laughing inwardly at what the fairytale portrayed, he chuckled. "No, this is not a fairytale and I'm not the prince. I'm the big, bad wolf ready to eat little Zoe."

Sitting down on the bed beside her, he continued watching her sleep. He could watch her for an eternity. Although he hated disturbing her, he knew he had a job to do—and what a job it was. Sighing, "Now is as good time as any," he said. Tapping her gently on the shoulder, he softly called her name, "Zoe…Zoe…Zoe…Zoe. Wake up, sleepy head. Wake up."

"Huh? What?" Opening her eyes, forgetting where she was, Zoe glanced around the room. It quickly came back to her when she saw Kato sitting on the bed staring at her. "Oh, it's you!" she frowned. "To what do I owe the pleasure? Have you come to bring me more bad news? Or have you come to tell me my time is up?"

Ignoring the woman's frowns, Kato whispered, "Ahhh, my Zoe, yes, your time is up. That is, your time of innocence. After today, you will know what it is like to be touched as a woman by a man."

Annoyed, she said, "You are full of games, aren't you? What are you talking about?" Curious of his stares and feeling uneasy, she grabbed the thin blanket to cover her body. "And why are you looking at me like that?" she asked.

With a smirk, Kato replied, "I have good news and not so good news for you. I will tell you the good news first."

Hoping she sounded brave, Zoe said, "Well, you don't have to play games. I don't trust you, and I am trying in my heart to forgive you! I asked God and prayed for you and for me so I don't have any unforgiveness toward you when I meet Him. I don't want this to be the last thing…." Unable to finish her sentence, she began to cry.

"I'm touched," he said, trying not to be overtaken by her tears. He didn't know why her tears moved him. He quickly caught himself. He came to do what he had to do; his emotions could not take over. He would make sure he wouldn't hurt her. Mesmerized by her beauty, he turned away before he lost his nerve. She was breathtakingly beautiful. More beautiful than any woman he had ever met. "Oh well," he shrugged, regaining his composure, "Tis a cruel world we live in," he said, mimicking Seian, "A man gotta do what a man gotta do."

Taking her hand, looking into her eyes, his voice hoarse, he gently said, "Zoe, the young girl is safe, for now anyway." Upon hearing the news, Zoe let out a small cry of joy. Closing her eyes," she thanked the Lord. Kato watched as her lips moved. He smiled. She's praying even though her life is in danger. "Amazing," he said in a low whisper, "she is extraordinary!"

Opening her eyes, Zoe realized he was still holding her hand. Pushing his hand away, the brief joy she had was now gone. She knew there was more to why he was there by his crooked smile. "What happened? Where is she?" she scowled.

Very astute, aren't you?" he replied. "If you must know, the authorities have caught the man who was to purchase the little girl. Whether dead or alive, he is no longer a threat to any other girls." Although Zoe was relieved to hear the news, she couldn't help but feel sad. "Yes, but he is only one out of many."

"Well, as I said, the young girl is safe for now," Kato told her.

"Where is she?" Zoe asked.

"She is somewhere in this house. They are keeping her under lock and key. By the way, I thought you might want to know that she is eating now. Normally, we don't take advantage of young girls. Our boss mainly deals with girls twelve to eighteen, sometimes older. This is a rare exception. The money was too good to pass up."

"Oh my God, what kind of animals are you people? They are still children!" she cried.

"Correction," he said, "They are no longer children when they can bear children. Anyhow, what is it to you? They are poor, and as I heard you say, they are nuisances. You said it yourself that your parents didn't want you to help them. Your parents discarded them as irrelevant, didn't they?" He knew he was egging her on. For some reason, he liked it when she got fired up. It brought out the best in her. She was going to need it where she was going.

Angrily, she yelled, "I never said that! DO NOT put your dirty words in my mouth! Anyway, it doesn't matter what they or others say. I know they are as important as anyone else and so are their lives. The Lord said, 'The poor we will always have with us.' He never looked at them in any way but love. He said for us to take care of the poor."

Kato laughed, "Silly girl! Your idiotic ideology is going to be the death of you. In your innocence, you fail to see the truth. The poor are discarded and barely tolerated. They embarrass us. Look at the young girls you see here. Do you think they are relevant? Do you think they have the same privileges as you? Do you really believe their lives matter? Do you see how Western countries treat their poor? The majority of the girls sold into sex trafficking are from impoverished backgrounds. Many of their relatives sell them to the traffickers. You see, my Zoe, even they know that being poor is not a good life. You're fighting a losing battle. It's a battle that will never be won. Yes, we will always have the poor with us, for they are to be used, misused, and then discarded because they don't have a voice. It's like a silent code no one likes to discuss, but everyone knows."

"I never knew anyone with so much potential could be so cruel or talk about God's people like you do. God loves all His people. You call me silly, but you are a fool! Just because you were handed a raw deal in life doesn't mean you should make others miserable. I trusted you! I believed in you! How could you?" Her voice became angry, "Kato, I wish you would…" she stopped before she regretted her words.

"Die? Is this what you were going to say?" He acted shocked.

"I never said that!" she yelled. "Again, don't put your dirty words in my mouth!" Frustrated and losing her patience, she asked, "What do you want anyway? What is your other news?"

"Ahhh, yes, let's get back to why I am here. I almost forgot. Forgive me. The girl is safe, but she will be sold to another, a wealthy gentleman. He will take care of her as his house servant until she comes of age, and then she will be sold. It is her destiny unless the wealthy man takes her for himself."

Zoe was still angry over the situation but relieved the young girl would not be sold right away, "That is still not comforting to know, but at least there is still hope. She will have time to be rescued," she said.

"There is more," he said slyly.

"More?" Her eyes widen. What else could happen, she wondered.

"Yes, more," he nodded. "The little girl will be sold with another girl."

"Patty! Is she here? I thought you said she was gone! Where is she?" she demanded. No longer able to contain her anger, Zoe rushes to hit him, but he stops her in motion, grabbing her hands and swinging her across the room, causing her to hit her arm on the only wooden chair in the room. She yelled out in pain, "Ouch!" Seeing blood from the scratch, she yelled again, "See what you made me do!" Kato, not caring if she hurt herself, said, "You did that to yourself. By the way, Patty is gone. I didn't lie to you. She left the same day after she tried to stab me with that little knife of hers, or the shield as she called it. But I got the last word, or should I say, feel." He went over to her to help her up. She refused his help. Getting up on her own, holding her scratched arm, she walked over to the bed. As she walked past him, Kato could still smell the amber vanilla body lotion she had put on days ago. She even smells beautiful, he thought.

Sitting on the bed, rubbing her arm, she asked, "Then who is left?" It was then she knew he was talking about her. She was the other girl to be sold. His look confirmed her fears. Realizing he was referring to her, she let out a loud sob, "No! Please, God, noooo! Please tell me that you are not referring to me. Please kill me. I will kill myself first! Oh, God, please help me," now sobbing uncontrollably. Seeing her tears, Kato reached over to touch her cheeks. Feeling their wetness, he said, "It is as you say, your destiny. But I'm afraid there is more that I have to tell you, my Zoe."

"I am not your Zoe, so don't call me that! Do not insult me further. Do not make me hate you any more than I already do," she said as she pushed his hand away.

Kato's lips curled inward, and with a mischievous look, he said, "You will hate me, but you will hate me as you cry out in joy and pain."

Zoe weary of the conversation, and the man, asked, "What are you getting at? And why are you still here? Please go away while I wait for my fate. Just go away! Leave me with the last ounce of dignity I have left!"

Captivated by the woman, taking a deep breath, in a raspy voice, he said, "I can't, for you see the man purchasing you will take very good care of you. You will be his sex slave. You will not be tossed to and fro. In a couple of years, he may even release you, that is, if you promise you won't tell the authorities. If you do, well, two things, you decide which is worse: death or being tossed out into the hands of many men. But there is one thing I have to tell you about the man." He paused, watching her closely, waiting to see her reaction. He saw that her eyes were full of fear. He continued, "The wealthy man, it appears, has a conscience, a self-righteous one, but it's still there. It seems he doesn't like virgins. Lucky for me, eh? The thought of him taking something as precious as one's virginity away from a girl appalls him. Ironic, isn't it? If it weren't so pathetic, I would laugh myself. You see, the perverted scum has two young daughters. He thinks of their virginity. And so, this is where I come in." He moved closer to Zoe, resting his hand near her thigh.

Frightened, Zoe looked for a place to run. Trapped, she asked, "What are you saying? Are you saying what I think you are saying?"

"Zoe, you have never been with a man." Eyeing her intently, "You said so yourself at the village. You were casually talking to Patty about sex. Girl talk. I was close by pretending I wasn't listening. You told Patty that you are waiting to be married. It was expected of you. Your perfect world expected this of you. But if you want to survive where you are going, I must do what I need to do. Zoe, I'm a man. I must do this. It's for your good. If not, they will sell you to another who will treat you worse than dirt. He will not be as kind as the doctor. He will toss you away when he's finished with you. Then you will be tossed from one to the next. You will be like the girls we saw in the videos. You don't want that do you, Zoe?"

Tears streaming down her face, sobbing uncontrollably, Zoe pleaded with him, "Please, please, please do not do this to me. Please, I beg you for mercy, for the love of God, for my love of God, please do not. Please! I promised God I would wait. Please do not break my vow. Do not do this to me! I will not cry when they take me to this man, but please do not do this to me! You have already taken enough from me, please, I beg of you!"

"It's too late!" said Kato, with desire in his eyes, "I'm aroused! In this world of sex trafficking, once a man is aroused, you can't stop him. If you try, he becomes a savage beast. A lesson you will soon learn." He slapped her in the face, knocking her to the floor. Hitting her again, he grabbed her off the floor and threw her on the bed. "This is what is going to happen to you if you get them aroused and you start acting uppity," he said, ripping her blouse, exposing her bra. Grabbing her breast hard, he unzipped his pants.

Knowing she was about to be raped, Zoe cried out, "No, please, not like this! I've never been…please, I beg of you! I have never been with a man!" Kato laid on top of her and opened her legs. With all her strength, she fought to keep her legs closed. She tried to break away from his tight hold, but his grip was too much for her. Putting his tongue on her neck, Zoe let out a loud scream as she felt a pain in her stomach. Succumbing to the rape, she passed out, but not before her screams could be heard in the hallways and nearby in the room where Alana and Seian were sitting.

Seian smiled as he heard the young woman's screams. "Good!" he said, "The deed is done." Alana, hearing the screams, turned away from him. She felt for Zoe. It wasn't supposed to end like this. Deeply remorseful and sorrowful, she wept silently, hoping Seian wouldn't notice. Seian, pretending to check his emails on his smartphone, watched her closely but didn't say a word.

Chapter Thirty-Two

"Kato, you didn't have to do what you did to Zoe!" cried Alana, lashing out at the man. "She's going to die no matter what! You didn't have to be the one to take her virginity! What has happened to you? You have turned into an animal like the rest of them! Is it the money? Don't you realize that with all the money in the world, it still can't buy happiness? Look around me! Look! What do you see?" Alana threw up her hands to let him know how unhappy she was despite all the luxuries surrounding her. "Do you see happiness among the expensive jewels, the furs, the designer clothes, and bags? No," she cried. "All you see is death, filth, and rot. Did you get caught up in the game of fresh meat? I thought you were different, Kato. I thought you cared. When Seian inquired about you, I thought you were okay. I told him so. Kosi said you were okay, too. He worked with you before and considered you loyal and fair. You fooled us all, didn't you? You played us like a fool, and now you are part of us!" Throwing her hands up in frustration, she cried, "To do this! Oh, what price you have paid! You have sold your soul like the rest of us." Walking over to the window, shaking her head, tired and weary, she whispered under her breath, "What a price we all have paid."

Kato's voice low and filled with anger, yelled back at her. "You sound foolish!" He was tired of her scolding him about Zoe. He did what he had to do and felt no remorse, but the woman's words still stung. "Laos, Kosi, and Seian knew about me. They knew where I came from. It was and still is all about the money." Lowering his voice, in a dangerous tone he said, "You better be careful. The man at the store said there was a mole. Luckily for me, I know that ain't you, is it? I know you aren't the one because you wouldn't be worried about Zoe. You wouldn't have to worry at all. You'd be dead and your body would never be found." He made sure she understood his warning.

Deeply regretting all she had done, Alana said, "You are correct. I'm no insider. I'm not a mole! I told you I'm in too deep to get out. I didn't know it would get this far. I didn't know I would be in so deep, and now, I can't get out even if I wanted to. No, I will die in this filthy, rotten place surrounded by jewels, furs, and other luxuries that people think they need." She stepped back and looked around the room. "It's a beautiful house, isn't it? Funny, that's all I saw or wanted to see when I first came here: a beautiful house filled with stuff. I didn't care. I didn't think it would get this far. I didn't know about the young girl. You have to believe me," she pleaded, hoping he would see her truth. "I didn't realize Seian would stoop so low for money that he would become so cruel, so evil. No, I'm not the one. I will rot like the rest of you when my time comes."

Kato, taunting her sudden remorsefulness, said, "Then you better see Zoe before it's too late. She will pray for you." Shrugging his shoulders, he grinned, "Shame it has to end this way for her. She's such a good kid with beautiful brown eyes. Hmmph, under other circumstances, I would have tried a different approach to getting to know her. We would have been great friends, and maybe she would have given herself to me of her own free will. Now, her life, like the lives of so many others, is over. That wealthy doctor will only keep her for a year or two. He likes fresh new meat. Men like that want to be in power. They like being in control. They like submissiveness to the degree of slavery, manipulating their victims into surrendering their will to them. He thinks he is in control when he gets a new young girl. It's a power trip for him. He craves it. He likes to have control and domination over helpless females and males, too, because sometimes he wants the tender bodies of a young male. Although he dare not say; he is anything but a virile man." Thinking about Zoe, he mumbled in an audible range that Alana could barely hear. "Zoe will fight back; he won't like that in her. She will eventually lose the physical battle but she will never submit spiritually. No, she only submits to her God. Her will is strong in her faith. Her faith you cannot break. He will not kill her, but he will sell her, but only after he uses her like a wooden spoon. He won't break her spirit, but he will break her soul!"

Upon hearing his words about Zoe's future, Alana in a loud voice, spewed out, "Men like that disgust me!"

No longer caring how loud he was, Kato shouted, "Men like who? Like me? You have some nerve, Alana!" With disgust in his eyes, he continued, "Look at you! You're no better than the doctor, Seian, or me. You are worse! You're a woman! Now, suddenly, you are getting a conscience. Now you are getting remorseful and having regrets! You're like the madam who knowingly pimps the young girls. She knows they are too vulnerable to comprehend what's going on. She pretends to mother them, to nurture them, and all along, she is pimping them to the highest bidder for money. Like her, you don't care about these girls. As long as it doesn't happen to you, as long as it doesn't interfere with your lifestyle, as long as it doesn't interfere with your expensive clothes, fine dining, and exotic trips, you couldn't care less. Men like that disgust you! You disgust me, Alana!" He spat out. "You know why? You have a man like the ones who disgust you. It didn't bother you then, so why now? Don't look at me with your pretentious hurt eyes. You know I am telling the truth! The truth hurts, doesn't it?"

"You don't know nothing about me…," cried Alana.

Looking into her eyes, he said, "Ahhh! Now I see. Now I understand. You do see the truth! Do you think you're Seian's only one? You are the main one, but you're not his only one. He keeps you because you're his front. With you, he can portray himself as a great citizen of the land. People will admire him; children will look up to him, and all will adore him.

You are like those wealthy Westerners who commit crimes. What do they call it? Oh, yeah, white-collar crimes. They are the ones who sell drugs, launder money, drive fancy cars, live in huge mansions, write the laws, and enforce the laws while they break the law. They are the ones who tell the court systems to put the low-life, petty thug criminal in jail for stealing a piece of candy while they are the real criminals." He laughed. "Such irony if I say so myself. Their money makes them envied, adored, and worshipped while they keep doing what they do. You, like them, are hypocrites to the first power. So don't talk about the Seian or me like you are innocent. You only like Zoe because that's who YOU want to be. You want to be Zoe! You want to live her lifestyle. You want her life! You want to go to school at a prestigious university. You wouldn't care anything about her if she were poor and uneducated. You didn't care about the rest, but now that you have met Zoe, you start to care. There are thousands of girls trafficked as sex slaves every year, so please don't get high and mighty, or worse, self-righteous all of a sudden. At least you know who I am and what I am about. I'm about the same thing you are about. I'm about the money, and if I can get a little action with a beautiful, young, sweet thing, so be it. That's fine with me because it's all in a day's work. Besides, those are the perks that come with the job. After all, soon, Zoe and the little girl will be gone, and it's the start of a new day and new girls. Nothing will change."

"You have become an animal!" Alana roared.

Satisfied with her response, Kato grinned widely, showing his beautiful white teeth. "No, my sweet dear, I am becoming you. That is what you see. You! Ugly, isn't it? No matter how you dress it up, it's still ugly. Before you talk about me, look at you. Look in the mirror and see the same thing you called me, an animal! We are all animals. The only difference is some of us are more violent than others. Our kind, Alana, is called predators."

Hitting a nerve, Alana softly said, "What you say is the truth per se, but you must understand. I didn't know this was going to take place. It happened."

"Yeah," replied Kato sarcastically, "and the nice piece of jewelry around your neck Seian brought you just made it easier for you to be purchased. It made it easier for you to swallow, to accept. You, Alana, my dear, were also purchased by the highest bidder. So, there is no need to try and convince me, beg, or plead. It's over. It is what it is. Since the beginning of humanity, men have sold themselves for trinkets. I think the Bible says something like this, 'Judas sold Jesus out for a few coins.' Well, that's what you did, too."

Alana, exhausted and fed up with the conversation, said, "I don't want to talk about it anymore. You shouldn't have done that to Zoe."

Nonchalantly shrugging his shoulders, Kato told her, "It was going to happen to her no matter what. I just was the first one who did it.'

"I know, but it wasn't supposed to happen like this...." She suddenly stopped in mid-sentence. Kato looked at her curiously, wondering what she was about to say. She shook her head and stared at the door. "Shhhh!" she whispered. "Seian is coming. I don't want him to get suspicious and start asking questions. You know he can tell when I'm nervous and not telling him the truth."

As Alana predicted, Seian entered the room moments later. Glancing at the two, he could tell they were discussing something and abruptly stopped when he entered. Suspicious of what they were discussing but not saying a word, he walked over to Alana and gave her a small peck on the lips, and said, "Ahhh, there you are, my love. The doctor is on his way for the little girl and the Zoe girl. I spoke to his person. He will be here in a couple of days. It's been almost a week. I will be glad when they are gone; then it will be back to business as usual. He is excited to have them both, although I believe he will sell the little girl to a man in the Middle East. I don't care as long as I get my money. That little girl almost cost me one of my best men. What a bother to get them so young." Turning around, pretending to see Kato for the first time, he greeted the man. "Kato, I see you are here too!" He looked at Alana, "Was I interrupting something?" Aware of the man's deception, Kato played along with the lie, "No, my good man, you weren't. We were talking of nothing of importance. Talking while waiting, which seemed like an eternity. I was telling Alana about the Western culture and their perception of the poor."

Seian knew there was more to the man's story but went along with the charade. He nodded and said, "Yes, a very interesting group. They are very self-righteous. They are trying to save the world and won't even save the people in their own backyard. And yet, we find them most interesting, in an admiring sort of way. But enough of that. I heard the screams of the Zoe girl, or now I guess we can say the Zoe woman. I take it the young virgin's screams were not those of passion?" Seian grinned as he imagined the scene in his mind. "It's nothing like the screams of a young virgin going under the knife for the first time. Deafening, if you ask me. That's why I like Alana. She was not, how you say, fresh meat." He laughed heartily.

Rolling her eyes at his remark, Alana replied, "You make me sound like a dead piece of meat rotting in the streets."

"No, my love. You have me all wrong. You are like a fine wine, just right. Always is and always will be," he assured her. Alana smiled at his compliment. "Thank you," she replied.

Walking over to the wet bar, Seian poured himself a drink. Filling the glass to the top, he took a long sip, "Ahhh, sweet!" Turning to Kato, he said, "Kato, I don't think I will ever get used to the screams of the young girls. Those screams can be haunting." Alana stared at him, watching him drink, "Don't stare at me that way, my love, with those accusing eyes." Raising the drink to his mouth again, "Yes, I have a conscience if that is what you wish to call it, but my conscience doesn't pay the bills or keep you in a lap of luxury because you do like the finer things in life, don't you, my love?" Not waiting for an answer, he asked Kato, "By the way, Kato, how was the Zoe girl?" Kato laughed, "She was what you say, very unwilling. As you can see she clawed like a tiger and scratched me on my arm." Kato showed them his arm with the scratch marks. "I don't think she liked it at all, but after a while, who knows, because she passed out. It wasn't good for my ego or reputation, but it wasn't all in vain if you know what I mean?" Seian laughed at Kato's last comments, "Yes, I do! I see you didn't go back for more, and it has been a couple of days. What is going on with the Zoe woman?"

"No, once is enough for me," Kato told him. "I like my women to be willing; it's good for my ego." Kato's wide grin made the other man laugh again. Kato told them about Zoe. "She is not saying much; she is eating sparsely. I had Alana's girl servant put drugs in her meal, so she's pretty much drugged up until they come for her. The little girl, too." Concerned, Seian said, "I hope not too drugged. We don't want them too drugged for the doctor. He can do whatever he wants once they are in his care." "No, no, no," Kato assured him. "She is using very little. It's only enough to keep them both sleeping. I checked on them. They are ok." Seian took another sip of his drink and said, "Great! Thanks for taking care of them. They are nuisances, but the money is great." Turning to Alana, he said, "My love, when this deal is over, how about we take a trip to Paris?" Alana, relieved that the conversation ended, smiled, "Do you have another run?" "Yes, but this time, it's the usual run. It's one of my regular clients," he told her.

"Speaking of clients, who is this doctor that purchased Zoe and the little girl?" asked Kato. "Seian took another sip and placed the drink on the table. "He is a very well-renowned and well-sought-after surgeon. I believe he is a cardiologist."

"Seian, aren't you afraid that Zoe's parents may know of him?" inquired Alana.

"No, he is not from this part of the continent. He is from further south, and he travels intensively to America. He is primarily known there. He should be here within a couple of days." Seian turned to Alana, "My love, go and get your girl servant, Selah, to assist you in getting Zoe cleaned up. Fortunately, she doesn't have to be checked to see if she is a virgin. Kato took care of that. Thank you, my friend." Seian bowed to Kato, expressing his thanks. Kato returned the gesture. "I want to get rid of those two as quickly as possible. Besides, I want to speak with Kato about going to Paris with us. He has never been on a trip with me. I want to brief him on what to expect. I'm giving Laos a break this time around. He almost got himself killed on the last trip."

Happy to leave the two, Alana walked over to Seian, pecking him on the cheek, whispering in his ear, "You are sweet to me. I can't wait to go to

Paris. The scenery will do me good." Seian returned the gesture, "Yes, run along, my love. I will get with you later. Now leave us." He brushed the woman away. Alana smiled once more at Seian before she left the room. Seian watched her go. When he knew she was no longer in earshot, raising his eyebrows, he frowned and asked Kato, "What were you and Alana talking about before I came in and interrupted you? The atmosphere was intense. It appears that she was upset. Surely, you couldn't be talking about the Westerners with such intensity?" Kato shrugged his shoulders and said, "Nothing really. She was very upset about what I did to Zoe. She seems to have taken a liking to the young woman. I told her it was going to happen, so why not make it sooner than later. I laughed at her rebuke. In response to my laughter, she scolded me and called me an animal." Kato scoffed at the last words.

Seian listened to the man and replied, "Yes, I saw she was upset. I saw her facial expressions; her eyes gave it away. I can always tell when she is trying to hide something from me. In my line of work, you must be very observant. If not, you can get killed. What a pity, she's becoming so soft that she could become a bother to me." Taking another sip of his drink, he said, "She has changed. Her mood has changed since they arrived, especially the Zoe woman. I don't like them in my house and will be glad to get rid of them both. There have been nothing but bad vibes since they got here. I want them out! That's why the doctor is not coming to get them."

Curious, Kato asked, "What do you mean?"

"I didn't want to say anything in front of Alana. I'm becoming suspicious of her. The doctor can't come to get them. It would raise suspicion about him being here, particularly with him being who he is. His servant is coming. His servant is African. The surgeon is a white Afrikaner. Unfortunately for Zoe, the assistant will rape her before he gives her to the doctor. The doctor will not care. He loves African women. It's a good thing that you did what you did. Another would've been brutal and wouldn't understand how delicate virgins are." He paused and said, "If you know what I mean?"

"Yes, I do," Kato replied. "Is this what you wanted to speak to me about?" he asked.

"That is one thing, but there is another matter. I trust you, and for this reason, you must come to Paris with us. I need you to get rid of something."

"What is your something?" Kato's curiosity was piqued.

Seian took sip of his drink and put the glass on the table. "I need you to get rid of Alana."

Kato's eyes widened in shock, "Alana?"

"Yes! Her behavior is causing me some concern. I don't trust her. You know how this business is? You don't trust anyone."

"What is it that you want me to do with her? Find someone to buy her? I believe she is still a good package. There may be an older guy willing to buy used goods."

"No, she's too old. I want you to get rid of her permanently," he said cold-heartedly.

"Ahhh!" said Kato, fully understanding what the man was asking him to do, "That is why so much amour and affection, calling her my love. I was wondering what that was all about." Shaking his head at Alana's fate, he said, "It is a cruel world we live in, isn't it?"

"It is not cruel per se; it's just business, and business is still business. Out with the old and in with the new. Besides, my new love is waiting to move in. Seian showed Kato a picture of his new woman. It was the woman at the compound that got the girls ready.

"Sweet!" whistled Kato.

Seian poured another drink. "Come, let me pour you a drink. We'll drink and talk! He poured Kato a drink and handed it to him." Kato took the glass from Seian's hand, "Yes, let us drink to business." They raised their glasses, "To business!"

Chapter Thirty-Three

Alana was relieved to leave the men. The sight of them was beginning to make her nauseous. In all her time knowing Seian, she never knew him to be so cruel and heartless. Sadly, this was her life and the bed she made. There was nothing else to do but wait and see how things would pan out. She knew Seian enough to know that he wouldn't think twice about getting rid of someone he didn't trust. She would attempt to hide her emotions better. Her disgust for him and his world, the world she allowed herself to be pulled into made her lose sight of how dangerous Seian was. She had to be extremely careful from now on. Realizing her life was in danger, she planned her next step. "I will put it all behind me when we get to Paris. When he touches me, I will respond. Even though the thought of him touching me disgusts me, I will pretend, and hopefully, he will not see behind my pretense." Satified with the plan she went to find the servant girl, Selah.

She found Selah sitting quietly on the patio stairs looking up at the sky. She was once a beautiful girl, but the brutalities of human sex trafficking took its ugly toll on her. At eighteen, she was violently assaulted by one of her suitors. In a drunken stupor, he kicked her in her pelvis after he finished his business. She lay bleeding on the bed for hours before someone came to help. Not knowing why she felt compassion for the poor, wounded girl, she took her in and got her the medical help she needed. The doctor had to perform an emergency hysterectomy to save her. It would take three months before Selah could walk again. She wasn't good for anyone after that. Alana pleaded with Seian to keep the girl as a servant. He finally said yes. Looking at the girl sitting there, Alana often wondered why she was still alive. Before the assault, she was sold and sexually abused by many men; it's no wonder she wasn't dead from all that. "She's a fighter, resilient to the end, but her soul is dead," Alana said under her breath. "That will be Zoe, dead in her soul but not in spirit." She cringed at the thought. "Selah," Alana called the young girl, "Come, we need to get the girls ready. They will be leaving soon. We have to make sure they are cleaned." The girl quickly got up, like a dead person waiting to die, she responded, "Yes, ma'am."

It had been a couple of days since Kato violated Zoe. Not knowing what to expect, Alana and Selah entered the room and saw Zoe sleeping. She stared at the young woman. Despite everything that had happened to her, she was still regal and beautiful. Alana envied her. Was Kato right? "Do I want to be like Zoe?" she asked herself. She knew her choices would never allow her to have the life she desired. If only she could go back in time, her choices would be different. But it was all to no avail; she couldn't go back in time. With that realization, she focused on the job she had to do. She saw the bloodstains on the sheet. They were no longer red but brown. She turned to Selah, "We must wash her up, but please be careful. She is a delicate flower." Selah nodded.

Patting her gently on her face, Alana said softly, "Zoe. Zoe. Zoeeee! It's time to wake up. Zoe, wake up! The time has come. He is almost here for you. We've come to clean you up. Wake up, Zoe." Feeling the touch of the woman's hand on her face, Zoe quickly jumped up from her slumber. Upon seeing Alana, anger filled her heart at the sight of the woman who betrayed her. What are you doing here?" she shouted. Alana, hurt by the young woman's angry stance towards her, ignored Zoe's piercing gaze. Looking down to avoid the young woman's eyes, she saw the blood on Zoe's upper thighs and realized Zoe was a virgin! She gasped.

"Zoe, I'm so sorry! "There's blood down there between your thighs. Here, let me wash it off. Let me clean you up." Zoe looked down at the blood-stained sheet and her blood-stained upper thighs. Seeing everything for the first time, she cried out in agony. "Oh, Lord! What has happened? What did I get myself into? I trusted you, Lord! I trusted you!" Sobbing great big sobs, clutching her stomach, she winced over in pain at the realization of what had taken place. Rape! Her innocence stripped from her. Not only was she going to die, she was no longer a virgin.

Alana, deeply moved by the tears, said, "Let me wash you up." She gently attempted to wash the stained blood from Zoe's inner thighs. Zoe roughly pushed her away. "Leave me alone! Haven't you done enough!" she snapped. Ashamed and embarrassed by her sudden outburst of anger, Zoe lowered her head; with tears in her eyes, she calmly said, "Alana, please leave me alone." Noticing her torn blouse exposing her bra, she tried to cover her shame.

To make matters worse, she began to feel the pain between her legs and stomach; the stomach pain was more intense. Holding her stomach, she began to cry again. She didn't want to look down between her legs, not in front of the two women. She didn't want them to see any more than they already have. Even though it wasn't her fault, she was ashamed of being raped and losing her virginity. And although she wasn't familiar with the pain associated with losing one's virginity, she didn't want them to know she didn't know. She had some dignity left. Books could tell you one thing, but the reality of it happening was another story.

Feeling her stomach again, she felt something sharp on her far right side. It was Jesus, the weapon. With all that had happened, she forgot that she had the weapon on her. She smiled inwardly. In Kato's haste, he didn't frisk her. If he had, he would've found the gun on her. "He forgot!" She said under her breath. Alana and Selah attempted to clean Zoe up again. Alana knew they had to get her cleaned and ready. They had to move quickly. She didn't want Seian to come in at any time to find out that the young woman wasn't ready to go. She didn't want to upset him further. She feared for her life.

Clutching her stomach again, Zoe bent over in pain. Selah, seeing she was in pain, tried to wipe her stomach. Zoe pushed her away with such a sharp thrust it caused the girl to fall hard on the floor. She wasn't angry at the girl; she didn't want her to find the weapon. Zoe took the wet rag and started wiping her legs and stomach, "I can do it myself!" she yelled. They watched her as she cleaned the blood between her legs. I wonder why he didn't find the weapon. She didn't want to say the word rape. It's such a dirty word. She couldn't bring herself to think about being raped, even though she knew she was. Touching Jesus again, she felt a little overjoyed. "If I must die, I will not die alone. Maybe I'm supposed to take someone with me." But in her sane mind, she knew this wasn't the case, but still, the thought of having Jesus next to her gave her new strength and hope. She still couldn't understand how Kato didn't see the gun. "Maybe he was in too much passion to notice anything." She smiled at the thought of how Jesus kept it hidden. Remembering where she was, she stopped smiling. She didn't want them to become suspicious or wonder what caused her to smile. Still wondering why the gun wasn't found, she didn't hear Alana's questions.

"Huh? What did you say?"

"Does it hurt Zoe? Did he hurt you?" Alana asked. Compassion showed on her face.

"I don't know," said Zoe in a low, audible voice, "It was my first. The thought of losing her virginity was almost as bad as the rape. Her first time was to be with her husband on her wedding night. She made a promise to God. "I don't know, but my face and stomach hurt."

"Your face and stomach?" Alana looked at her with curiosity. She'd never heard of a woman's stomach hurting after sex.

"Kato slapped me, and I guess you know why my stomach hurts. He must have shoved me in my stomach when he was trying to force himself on me. Apparently, he did some job. I don't remember anything else. I blacked out, or at least I think I did. I don't remember. I guess the Lord kept me from remembering." Suddenly remembering who she was talking to, the enemy, she abruptly stopped talking like they were old friends. "You're not my friend!" she roared. "Why are you so concerned about me or any of the girls? All you care about is you and your lavished lifestyle! You didn't care about these girls before. Why now?" Cocking her head to the side, she asked accusingly, "Surely you don't have a conscience? Is that it? All of a sudden your conscience is bothering you? Well, you picked a fine time for it to bother you!" Now annoyed, she cried, "Please go! Leave me alone the both of you! I can wash up by myself!"

"Ok, Zoe, we will go, but please know it wasn't supposed to be like this," Alana said apologetically.

"What wasn't?" Zoe asked. Even though she was in pain, her curiosity won her over. She wanted to know what had happened to the beautiful woman that caused her to make destructive choices.

"My life!" Alana said regretfully. "I had dreams, too. I didn't think my need for material things would lead me down this path of destruction. I was a good girl, poor, but still a good girl. My father and mother did everything possible to care for my siblings and me. We were one of the few in my village with two working parents. The people in the village didn't think highly of my father. When you are poor, people don't value you. To us, he was a king. He was a man of integrity, honest, and good. I saw how the people looked at him. People like you and your parents. They despised his poverty, his lack, and his insufficiency. He didn't care what they thought of him. He didn't care about their stares or their hurtful words." She quietly wept as she remembered her father. "He didn't care how they treated him. He would be the first in the stores. Other people of influence would come in, and the shopkeeper would walk away from him and wait on them. He just waited and smiled. We couldn't afford the medicine when he became sick with the cough. No one would help us. They just continued to stare at our worn out clothes and shoes. Mindful, we were clean. My mother didn't play that. She would say, 'This is where you are now, not where you will always be. You may not have the finest clothes, but as long as you have a creek to wash in, you and your clothes will be cleaned.' We never smelled, and though our clothes were worn, they were cleaned.

When my father died, our King died, and our life was never the same. There was hardly anyone at his funeral. Before he died, he blessed all of us and hugged my mother. She was with him in our neat, tiny two-bedroom apartment." Tears flowed softly down Alana's face as she remembered her mother. "She wasn't the same when he died. She left us when he died. She lost part of herself when he died. She lost her strength to overcome the stares and the talk. She became angry with people. She was angry at her poverty. It was poverty that kept my father from getting the medical help he needed.

No one knows what it is like to be poor, not American poor, but really poor. We live in a world of haves and have-nots. That is what divides us, not our ethnicities, religion, or culture. The have-nots continue to fight among themselves. They are the ones that are taken advantage of, and the haves don't care. Let them kill each other for all the have's care. Let's take their little girls and boys, for they are not worth anything anyway. It's a game to them. When the game is over, they go home to their opulence lifestyles. Do you think they will hurt one of their very own? No! To them, it's a new sport. As long as it's not messing up their neat and precious little world, they don't see it as wrong. They don't see it as evil. They are privileged. It's their right. Money is no option. They can buy anything for the right price. Everything has a price; even an innocent young girl has a price." Looking into Zoe's eyes, she asked, "Do you know who purchased you? A well-renowned surgeon like your parents! He saves many lives: the lives of the ones who can pay for his services. It's ironic that this doctor who is called to save lives, takes the lives of so many innocent girls. Pretty sad, isn't it? He doesn't see anything wrong with what he is doing." Alana got up and started walking to the door. "I will leave you, Zoe," Alana said sadly. "You can clean up yourself, but please know this wasn't the life that I wanted. No, this was the life dealt to me. And when I saw a chance to get out, I got out. I did, but now what a price I paid." Remorsefully, she shakes her head back and forth. "What a price I paid!"

Zoe, filled with compassion for the woman, said, "Alana, It's never too late. God still has a plan for your life."

Alana smiled. "Zoe, do you know why I liked you from the first time I met you? I saw you and immediately liked you, which is rare for me. But I knew there was something different about you. Your eyes are unique. Your eyes make you. Your eyes are you. When you walked into the restaurant that day, I knew you were the one. You reigned and walked so regal even now when your life is possibly on the brink of death—because you will die before they take you; you will not submit. I know this of you. You are royalty. Not because of your parents, it's because of whom you belong to. You are God's daughter. His face and glory are all over you. I always looked at you and never understood what set you apart. I couldn't understand. Now I do. Now I know it is His Glory that is upon you. You walk with God. It's evident that His hand is on you." Alana gently said, "Zoe trust Him even in death. Selah, come, let's go." She called the young servant girl. "We will be back one last time to get you, and then, Zoe, we will say goodbye forever."

"Alana, whatever happened to your mother and your siblings?" Zoe asked. She needed to know why the woman felt she had no other way out.

"My mother died a couple of years after my father. I believe it was five, but now it seems so long ago. She died a very bitter and broken woman. Life had dealt her a cruel blow. My siblings and I were scattered when she died. Relatives we had never met came out of nowhere and took us away. My brother is in America. He's a taxicab driver last I heard. But they are all dead to me now, and I am dead to them. We are like dogs; we go from pack to pack."

"I am sorry to hear about your life. Truly, I am. I will pray for you. It's not over until God says it's over," Zoe assured her.

Admiring the woman's sincerity, Alana said, "Kato said you would pray for me…even with all you were going through. He wasn't joking. Zoe, he was good. Kato. I mean, he started out good. But like all of us, the money eventually got to him.

Zoe looked away, trying not to cry at the mention of Kato's name. She wanted to believe he had some good in him, but it was hard, especially after what he did to her.

"Selah, let's go," Alana whispered to the servant girl. She glanced one last time at Zoe and quietly closed the door behind her.

Hearing the gentle click of the door closing, alone and frightened, with sadness in her voice, Zoe uttered under her breath, "Lord, I don't know what you are doing, but please let me know I haven't missed you. I'm not afraid to die. I know I will see you face to face. But I am scared of this unknown. If this is your will, please tell me, let me know that I didn't miss you. That this wasn't in vain. I know that you work all things out together for the good of those you call and love. I know you love me, Lord, and see the big picture. I need to see the little picture because right now, I don't see it. I don't understand why you brought me here to this place to die. Help me to understand. Why are you prolonging this? It's hard and my faith has left me." At that moment, she touched her stomach and felt the weapon. Realizing she still had it. She knew God didn't forsake her. In tears, she cried out, "Thank you for Jesus!"

She cried until her tears were no longer wet. The pain was unbearable, but she knew the Lord had her. "I trust you," she whispered, wiping her tears. Although hungry, she didn't touch the food. She knew they had put drugs in the food. She learned through fasting how to stay strong and endure, but it was getting harder to stay focused. Fear of the unknown mixed with hunger caused her great pain within. Weary from crying, she closed her eyes and went to sleep.

Chapter Thirty-Four

Zoe sat staring at the wall. It had been two days since Alana and the young servant girl Selah checked on her. Remembering the woman's last words brought an unknown fear to her, a fear she never encountered. Mustering up enough strength and trying not to focus on her fate and the possibility of death, she focused on her life, her parents, and her brother Jaheem. She had a blessed life. It was full of love, warmth, and many blessings: family holidays to exotic places, attending prestigious conferences with her parents, a beautiful home with servants, and a host of family and friends who loved her. She never knew what it was like to be without, yet she never took her life for granted nor looked down on others. She wasn't ignorant. She knew that many weren't as fortunate as she. However, she couldn't imagine her life in any way except for what she knew. It was hard to conceive that the life she had always known would never be again. She would rather die than live without hope or a dream. She saw what happened to the other victims of sex trafficking.

Even though she hadn't been at the village long, the time she was there, she saw how the young girls looked lifeless when they first came from being rescued. Their souls were gone. They were the walking dead waiting to die. The horrific crimes against their bodies and minds portrayed the ugly truth about the dark world of sex trafficking. Many cried at night, still consumed with the horrors of what they had been through. When a male doctor or counselor approached them, they hovered with fear. To ease their fear, a female always had to be present when they received medical care. Zoe listened to their stories. She watched Camille hold and nurture them like they were toddlers instead of children or young women. Their eyes told the story of their rapes, abuse, and misuse. Their eyes depicted their torture and shame of being passed from one man to another. She didn't want that to happen to her, and now there was a possibility this would be her life. Feeling sad and hopeless, she looked around the room and sighed. As tears trickled down her face, she noticed the plate of food on the table. Someone had replaced the untouched meal with a new plate of food while she was asleep. No matter how hungry she was, she wouldn't give them the satisfaction of eating. Quietly meditating about her life, she heard a knock at the door. Without waiting for a response, the door opened. Alana and the young servant girl, Selah, walked in. "Zoe, it is time. He is here for you," said Alana.

Zoe silently prayed for strength. Mustering enough courage, she said under her breath, "I will not give them the satisfaction of seeing my tears. I will wait until I see my Jesus and shower Him with my tears." She walked past the two women without looking at their faces. Alana marveled at the young woman's posture of tranquility. "The Lord is with you, Zoe," she said softly. Zoe didn't bother to comment. Taking a deep breath, she walked into her unknown fate, knowing that no matter the outcome, she would be okay.

Zoe, Alana, and Selah entered a room where two men were waiting. The way Alana nervously looked at one of the men, Zoe assumed he was the mastermind of the entire organization. He was the man in charge. Her assumption was correct when the other man beside him anxiously asked, "Is this the girl you were talking about, the Zoe girl?" Seian stared at Zoe as she entered the room. It was the first time he had seen her. Raking her from top to bottom with his eyes, Seian replied with a lustful tone, "Yes, she is the one. Quite a beauty, isn't she? She is worth her price! No wonder Kato wanted her." With his eyes on Zoe, Seian didn't hear the other man's question. "Are you sure she is the one? I don't want any mistakes when I take her to my man. He will kill me if she is an imposter."

Insulted by the man's insinuation of deceit, Seian hotly replied, "You insult me! "Why don't you trust me? I don't care about her one way or another. To me, it's all about the money." Seeing Seian's anger rise, the man quickly changed his tone. He knew he was dealing with a very dangerous man. Laughing nervously, attempting to soothe things, he said, "I trust you as far as I can see!" Seian's brow rose. "What?" The man smirked, "I don't trust anyone in this field. We're all backstabbers, wouldn't you agree?" No longer angry, Seian laughed at the man's remarks. "I must agree with you on that, my friend." He pointed to Alana and said, "I was only telling Alana that the other day." Still ogling Zoe, he whistled, "But she is a beauty, as you would say. It's a pity what's going to happen to her. Come from good blood, too. Her parents are renowned doctors. What a waste and shame they will never see their daughter again." Both men stared admirably at the beautiful woman. Zoe listened as the two men ogled and talked about her as if she was not there.

"She is a real African regal queen, beautiful inside and out and in a womanly way if you know what I mean?" said Seian, "What? Has she been touched?" The other man asked angrily. "I thought you said she is a virgin!" Eyeing the man suspiciously, Seian replied in a low, calm voice that Alana was very familiar with when he was careful with his words. When Seian spoke in this tone, Alana knew he meant business and that business was suspicion, which often resulted in death. "What is it to you, and why are you so angry with her being touched? I was told the doctor doesn't care about virgins. He doesn't like them. He says they are too squeamish and frightened. He doesn't like breaking them in." Carefully monitoring the man's body posture, he asked again, this time his voice was even lower and more reserved, "So why are you concerned? You should know this about your client. Especially since you are his man about business." He then scanned the room. "Alana, where is Kato?" he asked, his voice depicting his concealed anger. Yelling for his protégé, "Kato! Kato!" Alana knew he was upset. She quickly answered him. "Kato went to get the child. He had to wake her up. It appears she has become feisty all of a sudden."

The other man, sensing the atmosphere in the room changing into a possible conflict, retracted his stance. His earlier abrasive tone changed into a calmer, humbled voice. He didn't want to offend the powerful man. "Easy, man! No offense. I know my client very well, too well. He doesn't like virgins, but I do. She was promised to me. I would break her in, especially when I heard how beautiful she was when you described her to my client. It's nothing, just part of the business I get to enjoy. You can say the perks of the business, eh? I don't like them once they've been passed around from one man to another. I like them young and pure if you know what I mean."

Seian, still cautious of the other man, said, "No offense taken. I was a little apprehensive at first, but all is well now. I understand. You can't trust anyone. What did you say earlier? We're all backstabbers in this business. Let bygones be bygones. Besides my friend, she has only been touched once, so she's still new if you get my drift. She's still fresh." The other man grinned. Seian, growing impatient, still cautious of the other man, yelled, "Alana, go see where Kato is and what's taking him so long!" Alana jumped at the mention of her name and fled the room to find Kato. She took Selah with her. Seian, becoming frustrated, watched as they quickly left the room. "Sheesh! She's just a little girl! I will be glad when that little thing is out of this house! She and this Zoe girl or woman have been nothing but trouble since the first day they arrived!" Shaking his head and swearing, he said, "If the money wasn't good I would get out of this business." With those last words, Seian let out a loud chuckle. "What am I saying? I won't," he grinned. "You and I know there is an increase in perverted men wanting little girls." Shaking his head, he replied," We are sick, aren't we? I include myself."

"You have never been with a child?" asked the man.

"No!" Seian said, offended by the man's question, "What can a little child do for me? Trust me! I am in it for the money and money only. I don't care either way as long as I get paid. And get paid this time I will. But I tell you what, I won't be doing little girls anymore. Too dangerous! I'll stick with the Asian girls. They are easier to smuggle." Zoe gasped at his words. Seian spun around in anger and said, "Don't look at me like that, Zoe girl! I don't have a heart, I know and I don't care! When it is my time to die, I know where I am going, and you do too. The only difference is you'll get there before I do."

Zoe watched as the men talked back and forth with each other. Suddenly, she wasn't afraid. She knew she had Jesus, the Son, and Jesus, the weapon. She felt a sense of peace. She boldly said, "I don't condemn or judge you. I feel sad for you and the life you choose to lead. It's a life filled with evil, perverted acts, hatred, and filth. You don't…." Alana walked into the room in time to hear Zoe's comments. She rushed over to Zoe and cried, "Zoe, be quiet! Don't make it harder on yourself. You can get killed right now!" Seian, caught off guard by the young woman's sharp tongue of criticism of him, clapped his hands in mockery. "Oh, now I see why they call you the Zoe girl. You are a queen. A strong one, aren't you? Be careful with your words, Zoe girl, or you'll be a strong, dead queen." He pointed to Alana, "Do you think you are better than her or the other girls? To me, you and the rest are nothing but a paycheck. You better watch yourself. I don't have a problem killing a person. Do I, Alana?"

Alana, trembling with fear, pleaded with the girl, "Zoe, please be quiet!" Seian, astounded at how Alana protected the younger woman, became furious. "Alana!" he roared, "Where are your manners? Pour our guest a drink." His voice dripping with anger, he said to the man, "Forgive me for not offering you a drink. It appears that the help is no longer helpful." Alana, frightened, went to pour the man a drink. Her hands violently shaking as she gave him the drink. He put it down on the table without taking a sip. "I'll drink when the deal is finished," he said.

Zoe didn't care anymore. No longer afraid to die, she cried out. "Why should I be quiet? My end is my end! Regardless if I go to the doctor, my body has already been ravished and raped! Why should I be quiet? For you!" She pointed at Seian. "For him…for dirt…he is not worth it!" No longer holding back her tears, she said, "I came because I thought I was making a difference. And yet, here we are, being sold as sex slaves. It doesn't matter if I come from wealth and the young girl comes from poverty. We are both sold to the highest bidder. Alana, did you think I would go without a fight?" Tears streaming down her eyes, she said, "I'm not worried about me anymore. I worry about the many girls I can't help who will never see their freedom again. The girls who are used and then

thrown away like, as you said, yesterday's trash! I don't care! You are a...."
Seian, full of rage at her outburst, went over and slapped her, knocking her
off her feet. The other man quickly went to the fallen girl and tried to stop
him from hitting her again. "Stop!" he yelled. "She doesn't belong to you.
She belongs to the doctor. If you hurt her, he will kill you. She is not worth
it. She is just another piece of...."

Watching Zoe get knocked on the floor, without thinking, Alana rushed
over to Seian's side, hitting him on his back. Crying, she shouted, "Stop,
please! Stop, please! Haven't you had enough? Aren't you tired? Leave Zoe
alone. Her fate is already worse than death. You know that…just leave her
alone," she sobbed. Alana knew that by protecting Zoe she had crossed
the line of no return. Taken aback by what just happened, Seian scowled
at Alana and the man, then turning to Zoe, he inquired, "What is this?
Something is indeed strange. I have been in this business for many years,
and I have never had anyone protect a girl like they protect you. What is it
about you, Zoe girl? What is it about your eyes and your skin that makes
people want to touch you? He looked around. Getting irritated, he yelled,
Kato! Where is Kato? He's always here when I need him. It doesn't take
long to retrieve a small girl." Pulling his gun from the holster on his hip,
he began tapping the handle. "Hmmm, let me figure this out because it's
getting complicated, or is it? You know, my good man, I've been thinking.
I never told the good doctor how beautiful Zoe was. We only talked money.
That's all money—two for the price of one. In fact…," he stopped mid-
sentence as Kato entered the room. "Kato, where have you been?" asked
Seian. Kato, observing the room, noticed how everyone seemed uneasy. He
saw Zoe bent over on the floor but didn't say a word. "I was getting the
little girl. She was fighting back with a vengeance as if she knew. I'm sorry,
but I had to smack her. Selah eventually helped me get her back up. Such a
strong-willed little girl! She's going to be quite a handful for the doctor. He
may not keep her if she continues to…." Seian hollered at the man, "Stop
babbling! Where is she now?" He was still angry over what had just taken
place. "Selah is getting her ready," Kato answered. "She should be here any
moment." Looking over at Zoe hunched over on the floor, "What have I
missed? Is she hurt?" he asked. "No!" growled Seian. "She was running off
at the mouth. Kato, go get the girl. I want them both out of my face!" Kato

nodded and quickly left the room. Seian swore, "No one is competent these days! Where is the money?" he angrily asked the man. "Right here." He gave Seian a white envelope full of large bills.

Seian counted the money. Satisfied, "All there," he said to the man. "When the girl comes, you take them both and go!" The other man nodded. Seian was about to say something else but paused. With a sly grin, he said to the man, "You know, there is something very strange going on around here. I can sense it. Alana knows I'm rarely wrong when I sense something is amiss, don't you, my love?" Alana shook her head in agreement. "Alana, come here, my sweet." Frightened, Alana went over to him and stood by his side. She was terrified. She saw firsthand what he did to people who went against him. She nervously asked, "What is it, Seian, my love?" Pulling her closer, he said, "All my love," in a soothing and caressing voice. "You were pretty amazing moments ago, weren't you? Fighting for Zoe and all. In all the time we've been together, I've never seen you do this for any other girls. You've never fought for me! You even yelled at me, didn't you?" He smiled at her. Alana, trying to sound brave, "Seian, darling, you are foolish. I didn't yell at you," she assured him. "I didn't want to see Zoe hit anymore. Is that wrong, my love? I'm tired, or as you say, it's been a long week. It feels like forever since we got that little girl. I want her and Zoe gone." Wearily, she added, "I need some rest. Paris looks so good to me. I can't wait to go." Seian kissed her on her lips, "Oh my darling." Pulling her towards him, grabbing her around the waist, he smiled down at her again. "You are so right. You do look tired. I was going to take you to Paris and take care of some business there, but you do need to rest, so my dear love, rest peacefully." Hugging her tightly, he shot her twice in the stomach. Feeling the bullets pierce into her skin with great force, Alana looked at him, then turned to look at Zoe. Taking a final breath, she fell dead to the floor. Seian brushed her lifeless body to the side, turning to the man, he said, "Well, that is that. Now, you and I, my friend, have some unfinished business, don't we? You see, I'm no fool. It took me some time to grasp everything." Staring at the dead body, he told the man, "Don't be alarmed. I was going to kill her in Paris before I had one last rendezvous, but oh well. It was time. I couldn't trust her anymore. Going over to Zoe, who was still on the floor, he said, "When she took up for you, Zoe girl, I knew she would never be the same again. Her loyalty to me was gone. Shame too. She was a good woman. I really liked her, but what do you say? It's over. It's time for some new meat. But first things first, Zoe woman. I think I will have my way with you before you leave with the good man. I want to know why everyone wants to be with you," he said, caressing her cheeks. The man rushed over to him, "Fool! What are you doing? Don't you know she belongs to the good doctor?"

"Yes, I know," Seian growled, "but he won't mind. After all, she is no virgin, is she Kato?" Seian glanced over at Kato, who just walked into the room. Kato, seeing Alana's body sprawled out on the floor, chuckled at the man's comments, "No, she isn't. I took care of that little problem. When you get finished, I think I'll go another round." "That's why I like you, Kato," said Seian, "but you, my good man," Seian moved towards the other man, pointing his gun at him, "There is something about you that I can't fathom. I can't figure it out. You are not who you say you are, are you?" Observing the gun pointing in his direction, the man nervously replied, "What are you saying? You talk like a fool! Get the young girl so we can go. I'll definitely tell the good doctor about you. Either he will have you killed, or he and his friends will never do business with you again." "I don't care!" shouted Seian. "Kato, go tell Selah to hold off bringing the little girl here right now. You see, I do have a conscious, a small one," he laughed. "I don't want her to see her future. Go at once," he demanded. Kato glanced at Zoe before he left the room in a hurry.

Seian, folding his arms with the gun still pointing at the man, said, "As for you, if you are the doctor's man, then have your way with her right now. If you don't, I will, and Kato will. He's like me. We don't care. It's all about the money to us. But if you don't, you will watch me, and then I will kill you. You see, I noticed how upset you were when I informed you that Zoe was touched, or should I say, no longer a virgin. You were a different upset. Not in a lustful way that I've seen too often. And then you said the doctor told you how I informed him how beautiful Zoe was. I never spoke with the doctor. I spoke with his assistant to conduct the business. So he couldn't have personally told you about Zoe because I never told him. I've never met the doctor. Do you think he would directly talk to me? He is too wise for that." Seian eyes moved to the dead body on the floor and then to the man, and with a wicked look in his eyes, said, "Let's say that this is your last meal, too." Not believing what she was hearing, Zoe asked, "What are you saying? You want him to rape me in front of you?"

"Oh, Zoe," mocked Seian, "He won't do it. But I will." Seian walked over to her, grabbing her from off the floor; he threw her on the couch while still aiming his gun at the man. "He is going to watch me, and when Kato returns, Kato will have his way with you again. When we are both finished, I will kill him. Then I will kill you." Ripping her already tattered clothes, partially exposing her left breast, he kissed her on her neck. "Believe me, Zoe woman, Kato is younger than I am and much more handsome, but I will make you cry out both in joy and pain. You will have enjoyed your last meal too when I finish." He asked the other man, "Now, what's it going to be? Shall you or shall I? Either way, she will be filled up."

"You are a fool! A dead fool! A sick, dead fool! You have no idea who you are tangling with," the man screamed, "You have no idea!"

At that moment, Kato walked into the room. Seian, unzipped his pants and laid his gun down, "No, you have no idea who you are dealing with!" he growled angrily at the man. "Kato, my good man! Watch him as I have a little pleasure with the Zoe woman."

Zoe screamed, "No, please don't! Please kill me first, but don't…!" Remembering she had Jesus, her weapon, she pulled it out from her torn clothes and pointed it at Seian. "No one is going to touch me! You touch me and we will both die today!" Amused, Seian laughed and said, "You are true to your name, one of a kind. You make me want you more. Poor Zoe! We knew you had the weapon. The gun Alana gave you. Go ahead and shoot. There are no bullets," His eyes widened, full of mockery, shaking his head, "No bullets…. We emptied the gun when we drugged you. I am going to enjoy myself, Zoe girl." With lust in his eyes, aroused, he pounced on her. Zoe screamed. She heard the gunshots go off. Looking down at her clothes and seeing the blood, her world went dark and she left her body.

Chapter Thirty-Five

"Is she still sleeping?"

"Yes, Anna. If she doesn't wake up soon I'll call the doctor," JaMar promised his wife.

Wearily, Anna replied, "What can he do? She has been through the wringer. There is no medicine to cure her. You should know this. We are physicians! Have you not forgotten how they brought her to us? All beat up with her clothes ripped and torn, exposing her body." Anna sobbed, "JaMar, the authorities said she was raped. Oh my God! They raped our precious Zoe. How can they be so cruel? What kind of world do we live in when young girls are sold as sex slaves?"

JaMar, just as weary and distressed, went over to comfort his wife. Holding her close, he softly said, "Shhh, Anna, dear, it will be okay. We must remember that Zoe is safe at home with us now. We can thank God for this miracle; it could have been worse. We will work things out as time passes." He kissed his wife gently on the nose. "We have been through much, but nothing like our Zoe. If she needs to sleep, let her sleep as long as she needs to."

"JaMar, the thought of her being there gives me nightmares," cried Anna. "I still wake up in a sweat. I don't know what to do or say to her. I was the one who told her not to go. I was the one who told her it wasn't her responsibility. How will she look at me now? Will she look at me with shame, remembering that she was raped? JaMar, I can't handle it if she hates me. I can't!" she sobbed louder.

Moved by his wife's tears, JaMar held her tighter. They've been through a lot in the past few days. "Anna, please don't get distraught. She will not hate you. She will love you just as much as she always has. She is just like you, a firecracker. We will all get through this together one day at a time." JaMar reassured his wife as he continued holding her in his arms. However, in his mind, he didn't know if they could survive this. He only told his wife so she wouldn't get hysterical again like she did at the hospital when they brought Zoe in to examine her. He would never forget the sight of his beautiful daughter's body lying lifeless on the examination bed. Spread out, he could see the bruises on her body, the blood stains, the torn clothes, but most of all, he could see the bruises between her thighs. This was a father's worst nightmare. His only daughter had been raped. If the person who raped her wasn't already killed, he would've gone looking for him.

The doctor informed them he had given Zoe a sedative, that's why she looked lifeless. After watching her for a while, they left to speak with the detective who was waiting for them in the hallway. The detective informed them that it was a miracle that Zoe and the little girl were alive. Miraculously, the little girl wasn't touched. They were able to get her out of the house before anything happened. Seian had become suspicious of the man who claimed the doctor sent him. His suspicion was correct. The authorities had apprehended the doctor trying to escape to America. He was going there to get another girl. He was very cooperative with them. He had no choice. He knew his sentencing would be less harsh if he told them about his man going to pick up Zoe and the little girl. He was a well-renowned physician. Now, the only place he would practice medicine would be in prison. The doctor's man of business scheduled to get the two girls tried to run, but the authorities caught up with him, too. Like the doctor, he was on his way behind bars.

The detective had an insider but couldn't get to the person. By a stroke of luck, they apprehended the doctor's man. That's when they decided to take the chance and pretend one of their own was the doctor's point of contact. The undercover detective was furious when he heard that Zoe was compromised. The last report the police heard was she was unharmed. The task was to get Zoe and the little girl out unharmed. Unfortunately, they sold the American woman. They were still looking for her. So far, their attempts were futile. Being the wise man that he was, Seian told the undercover detective to rape Zoe. When he refused, Seian knew he was an imposter. Seian informed him that he would rape Zoe and then he would kill them both. They had to act fast. The detective had already watched him kill the woman, his lover, in cold blood. He couldn't intervene because it would have exposed the entire operation. They wanted Seian. They had been trying to get him for years, but he was too quick and wise. He always had an alibi and was respected and admired in the city where he lived. They knew he had officials on his payroll but didn't know who. Thankfully, once the doctor was caught, he exposed everyone. It was sad when one of the top public officials was Seian's accomplice.

When Zoe took out her gun, that was the detective's chance. Seian was focused on Zoe; he didn't see the other gun pointing at him. He shot Seian in the back. Zoe screamed, and they both fell hard off the sofa. Seian's body toppled on hers. When the detective rushed over to view the bodies, he was relieved to find Zoe okay. Other than being covered with Seian's blood and a bruise on her head from the fall, she was fine. Seian, on the other hand, was dead.

JaMar, hearing the harrowing details of what his daughter went through, slumped to the floor and sobbed. The tears he held in for so long finally rushed out. The reality of his daughter almost dying was too much for him to bear. With his hands on his head, he moaned in agony between sobs. Upon hearing the news, Anna burst into tears. She wailed so loud that they had to give her a sedative. Jaheem, watching his parents in pain, remained calm. Clenching his teeth to fight the tears, he knew he had to be strong for them. He assured the detective they would be okay. "Thank you. I will take it from here. I'll make sure they get home safely," he told the man.

It would be a couple of days before Zoe could go home. The doctor warned Anna and JaMar to let her rest. "I have given her some light sedatives; she needs to rest her body and mind," he told them. He was not only their doctor but also a friend and colleague, so it was personal to him. He knew they would eventually be fine, but the healing journey would take time. "Give her time," he said.

When Zoe finally came home she slept for two days straight. Anna watched over her night and day. She slept in the oversized chair beside Zoe's bed, never leaving her daughter's side. Other than bathing and using the bathroom, she was with Zoe. When the servants brought her meals up to her, they saw she barely touched her food when they picked up the trays. JaMar knowing his wife needed to be with Zoe, spent the nights restless in his study. What used to be his haven now turned into a place of emptiness and sadness. In hurt and anger, he cried out in agony to God. "Why did you allow this to happen to my daughter?"

Chapter Thirty-Six

Waking up from days of deep sleep, Zoe looked around the room. Blinking twice to see if she was dreaming, she opened her eyes wide like a kid on Christmas morning. It wasn't a dream. She was home. The pictures on the wall, the beautiful full-length mirror made of ivory, the four-corner poster bed, and the photos of friends and family on the nightstand were all there like she'd left them. She looked at the crème colored walls that always brought her peace and comfort; letting out a quiet sigh, she silently thanked God as the gentle tears trickled down her beautiful cocoa-brown face. She was home. Home in her bed. She was safe.

She felt the softness of her covers. Her torn clothes were replaced with her favorite UGG pajamas. She loved them because they were soft and made her feel warm and snuggly inside, especially during the cool nights. She pulled the covers off her and put her feet on the floor feeling for her slippers. They were always there by her bed. Miraculously, they were still there. She slipped into them. Never had they felt so soft. Walking over to the mirror, she hesitated. It took a moment before she could gaze at the reflection staring back at her. She saw the bruises on her face from the slaps and burst into tears. Her life would never be the same. It had changed. She was changed. Looking down at her breast, she then moved to her inner thighs, remembering what had happened. Sorrowfully, she would no longer be able to give her husband the precious gift she cherished: her body. Touching her inner thighs and at the thought of someone violating her there, remembering everything: Patty, the little girl, Camille, Kato, even Alana, she sobbed uncontrollably. Her sobs were so loud the upstairs maid heard them and rushed to tell her parents.

Naiijad, bursting into the room, out of breath from running, found them in the breakfast room drinking their morning coffee. Unable to speak, she held her hand up, signaling she had something to say. Anna, fearing it was about Zoe, cried, "What is it? Is Zoe okay? I just left her sleeping," Taking a deep breath, Naiijad shouted, "Zoe is up, and she's crying!" JaMar quickly jumped out of his chair and rushed to the door, almost knocking over the short-stout woman. Looking at his wife still in her seat with her head hung low, he asked, "Anna, are you coming? Our daughter is up. She needs us!" "No, JaMar," a teary-eyed Anna replied. "Not now. I can't! You go! It was okay when she was sleeping, but now I cannot bear it if she doesn't want to see me. I love her too much to cause her any more pain than I already have. She has suffered enough." Not understanding his wife's reasoning, he gently glanced at her one last time before quickly leaving the room.

Seeing her employee's pain, Naiijad reached over to her with comforting words, "It's alright, Ma'am. Zoe isn't that kind of person. She loves everyone, and she loves you and Sir very much. Everything will be fine." Anna looked at her with a gentle smile, "I hope you're right, Naiijad." Sighing, sipping her now lukewarm coffee, she looked exhausted. "It seems that I have aged these past weeks." "No, ma'am," the maid assured her, "You are still a regal queen." Anna smiled at her and said, "Don't worry about the dishes. I'll get them. I need to do something. Tell my husband I'm in the kitchen if he is looking for me." A wide-eyed Naiijad shook her head in shock. "Yes, Ma'am!" Naiijad realized Anna must be deeply distressed. She rarely did housework or cooked. Her work kept her very busy. If it hadn't been such a solemn time, Naiijad would've passed out on the floor at the thought of seeing her mistress doing the dishes.

Rushing to reach Zoe, JaMar took three steps at a time up the stairs. Reaching the top step, he took a moment to catch his breath. Inhaling then exhaling to calm himself, he walked slowly down the hallway to his daughter's room. He paused at the slightly opened door. Anna insisted it stayed ajar in case Zoe woke up. Peeking in, he saw his beautiful daughter standing in front of the mirror staring at her reflection, crying. He smiled, affectionally remembering the argument with Anna for purchasing the mirror for Zoe. "You spoil her too much, JaMar," Anna told him. And yet, he still got the very expensive mirror. He couldn't say no after she begged and pleaded until he could no longer resist. He went against his wife's wishes. Anna was upset with him for a couple of days. But it was worth it. Now, seeing his daughter in front of the mirror caused his heart to ache with pain just thinking about all she had gone through. He gently knocked on the door. Before she could say come in, he opened the door and rushed to her. As tears started pouring out of his eyes down his cheeks, he grabbed and held her tightly. He didn't care. She was home. She was safe! His beautiful Zoe, with her beautiful brown eyes, was home. Feeling the embrace of her father's gentle yet strong arms around her, Zoe cried in his arms.

"Oh, my darling daughter, I thought I had lost you," cried JaMar. Kissing her on the top of her head. I thank God, He brought you safely home to your mother and me."

"Oh, Father, I just…," Zoe couldn't speak. "Thank God! I didn't think I would see you or Mother again. I was prepared to die, but Father, I wasn't ready to die. And then what they did. What he did! I trusted him!" She started crying harder in her father's arms. JaMar, holding her tighter, soothed her with his hands. Still embracing her, he grabbed some tissue from the dresser and handed them to her. "Here." As she wiped her eyes, he stared at the photos on the dresser of Zoe and her friends laughing and acting silly. If only they could turn back the time, he thought. "It's okay," he said soothingly, "You're safe now. The Lord has brought you home like He promised. As long as you are safe, my precious one, we will get through everything else." Zoe, feeling somewhat better, looked up at her father,

"What happened to the little girl?" she asked.

JaMar smiled. He was very proud of his daughter. It was just like her to put other people's concerns over hers. "She's fine. She wasn't harmed. She is on her way to an orphanage until her parents come to get her. In the meantime, she's taken care of. We made sure of that."

"Oh, Father! She was so young. They are all so young. I thought I could make a difference," she said, stammering over her words.

Her father lifted her chin, staring into her eyes, he gently said, "Zoe, you did. The little girl will be fine thanks to you, Camille, and Patty. You all made a difference. God used you to save her from sex trafficking. Always remember, you take a city, one building at a time. That's what you did."

"The last thing I remember was Seian trying to…." She couldn't say the words. Her father comforted her, "It's okay. You don't have to say anything." She was quiet for a moment. Slightly smiling, she said, "I pulled out Jesus." Shaking her head, she said soberly, "Father, if it weren't so serious, I would be laughing like crazy right now. Here I was with Jesus, and I didn't realize they took the bullets out." Curious, JaMar asked, "Who is Jesus?" Zoe told him, "Jesus was the gun Alana gave me at the restaurant. Alana named it that. They didn't take it from me. I figured if I had to die, someone was going with me." Remembering Alana and feeling sad for the woman, in a low whisper, she said, "Seian killed Alana. Father, I believe she wanted to change. I believe she wanted to stop living that life. I believe she did. The last thing I remember was Seian coming towards me. I pointed Jesus at him, he laughed and tried to attack me, and then shots were fired. That's all I remember."

"You see, little one," her father said, "Jesus was loaded but not in the gun."

"I'll never forget this experience," Zoe told him.

"You are not supposed to. God allowed you to have this experience to do something. To make a difference."

Pondering her father's words, Zoe walked over to her bed and sat on it. Her father sat down beside her. They sat in silence until she looked up at him and asked, "Where is Mother? Why didn't she come up with you?" In a quiet voice, she asked him, "Is she angry at me?"

"No, but she thinks you are upset with her. She is very upset about what happened to you. She loves you very much. When you came home from the hospital, she washed you, put your pajamas on, and watched you all night in your room. She fears you will not forgive her because she fought hard for you not to go. She feels guilty and blames herself. She's hurting Zoe, and she is hurting for you. Your mother loves you very much."

"Yes, I know she does," said Zoe. "I must go to her and let her know I'm fine!" She looked at her father once more. He looked tired, but she knew he would be okay. Blowing him a kiss, she rushed out of the room to search for her mother. Running down the stairs to find her mother, she almost tumbled over Naiijad. "Naiijad, where's my mother?" she asked the woman. Naiijad wanted to rush over and hug her, but she didn't. She knew it wasn't time yet. With a wink and a sly smile, she replied, "She is in the kitchen washing the dishes."

"What? The kitchen?" Zoe was shocked at the thought of her mother in the kitchen. "Really?" "Really," the maid replied with a shrug. "Well, that's a new one," laughed Zoe. Naiijad laughed, too. "It feels good to laugh again," she said under her breath as she watched Zoe walking swiftly towards the kitchen, searching for her mother.

"Mommy! Mommy! Where are you?" Zoe burst through the door to find her mother in the last place she ever thought she would be, in the kitchen at the counter making of all things, peanut butter and jelly sandwiches.

With a gentle smile, Anna looked at her daughter and said, "I thought you might be hungry. I'm making your favorite."

"I am," replied Zoe. Getting the milk from the refrigerator and two glasses from the cupboard, Zoe sat at the kitchen counter and watched her mother make peanut butter and jelly sandwiches.

Chapter Thirty-Seven

Several weeks had passed since Zoe came home. Other than a few close friends and family members, no one knew what had happened to her. Everyone in the house attempted to adjust back to their previous routine before the incident. That's what they called it. But what they once considered normal would never be normal again. This was their new normal, and in this normal, the silent code was to never talk about what happened to Zoe.

Zoe could see the love and warmth in the eyes of her beloved servants when they approached her. She knew they knew she was raped. She was uncomfortable to be around them or anyone, even her parents. Even though it wasn't her fault, she was embarrassed and ashamed. Knowing that everyone knew only made the shame worse. It was something she had to live with for the rest of her life, the reminder that her innocence was brutally taken. She didn't cry as much as she did the first week home. However, in the stillness of the night, alone in her bed, she thought of Patty, Camille, the little girl, Alana, and even Kato. She would remember the details of that terrible time when she was imprisoned like an animal. The thought kept playing in her mind: if she hadn't been rescued, she would have been sold like a piece of jewelry as someone's sex slave. The almost reality caused her to burst into tears. She was lucky, or in her case, blessed. There were so many others who were not as fortunate. Their lives were ruined all because of someone's evil lust.

JaMar and Anna tried their best to make her comfortable. It was hard for them as well. The thought of their only daughter being vulnerable and they couldn't do anything about it made them feel helpless. They couldn't rescue her or fix it like they had done so many times in the past. No, this time, they had to trust God and walk out the process while enduring the hurt, pain, and unanswered questions. They were thankful to God for bringing her home. They knew many young girls were not as fortunate.

Feeling helpless for not being able to help his daughter when she needed him, JaMar made sure he was at her beck and call. He hadn't had a good night's sleep since her return. He would often stay up at night just in case she called his name. She rarely did, but when she did, he was always there. One night he heard her cries from her bedroom. He rushed to her side and held her as she wept in his arms. He couldn't cry with her. It wasn't the time. He needed to be strong for his daughter. But when he went back to his room, full of anger, he wept bitterly as Anna embraced him as he did for her on many occasions. Taking him into her arms, she soothed him as he cried openly for their daughter.

Anna and Zoe became closer than ever. Anna even took time off from her practice to be with Zoe. Like her husband, she was close by if Zoe needed anything. JaMar didn't want to know everything that happened. It would've made him angrier. Anna was the opposite. She wanted to know everything that her daughter went through. She didn't pry but waited patiently until Zoe was ready to talk. In the waiting, they talked about school, America, social media, and clothes, comparing the fashions of the two countries. Every so often, Zoe smiled or laughed. To Anna, it was beautiful to see her daughter smile and laugh again. They were few and far between, so it was a special joy when they did occur. Anna asked Zoe about her plans to return to America to finish her medical degree at John Hopkins.

Zoe looked at her mother, her eyes a beautiful, haunting glow, and calmly said, "I don't know what I am supposed to do, Mommy. I do know it's not time for me to go back to school, not yet anyway, or for that matter, possibly never. I know what happened to me wasn't in vain, and though I can't comprehend all that took place. I am waiting to hear from God. He is quiet, so I am quiet." There was a sense of tranquility in her words. Although this was not what Anna wanted to hear, she sighed and gently said to her daughter, "Then I will wait in silence with you." They continued their small talk about fashion and how well she and JaMar's practices were doing.

The following day JaMar and Anna were in their bedroom discussing Zoe. Anna cried out in frustration, "I believe Zoe needs to return to school! She must return to the States and finish her medical education." Not wanting to get into an argument with his wife, JaMar listened. Waiting for him to comment, when he didn't, Anna continued her rant, "I know she has been through so much! My God! The thought of our precious little one in the arms of a stranger! I still can't even say the word. But she needs to go on. She can't dwell in this place for long. She may never bounce back from this place!" Slightly irritated but not wanting to argue, JaMar dryly replied to his wife's words, "Now dear, when have you known Zoe not to bounce back from something?" Exasperated she was not getting the response she wanted, Anna rolled her eyes. "Yes, in the past, she would, but so much has happened now. She is different. We are different. Our lives will never be the same." "Yes, we are different," JaMar said softly. He was used to his wife's passionate rants. "We have to take it one day at a time, Anna. I promise time will heal us all. Our hope is in God. He will heal us in His time. You cannot rush this process."

Anna was about to say something, but JaMar quickly interrupted. "Shhhh! I want to go back to the way things were, too. But we can't. We have to wait and trust God. Anna, Zoe will be fine." Closing her eyes, deep in thought, she asked, "Will she, JaMar?" "Yes, she will," he answered back. "It will take time. You were never one for patience," he said, "Must you always have to fix things."

Hurt by his words, Anna told him, "This is different, JaMar. It is not about what I want, nor is it about me. I don't want Zoe to allow what happened to her to destroy her spirit. I'm afraid she will sit there forever if she continues to sit in the garden. She went through something that many never recover from. I'm concerned and scared, that's all." She starts to tear up. Looking at JaMar, she groaned, "And, yes! I do want to fix it! I want to see her smile again. I want to hear her laughing again. I never thought I would say this, but I miss her arguing with me. She is my daughter, dear God, and I can't fix this. I can't kiss the boo-boo and make her feel better. That's what mothers are supposed to do, and this time I can't." Wiping the tears from her eyes, she said, "It seems all I do is cry!"

JaMar understood how she felt; he moaned in agony, "Me either, Anna! I'm her father! How do you think this whole thing makes me feel? I'm supposed to protect her. I'm supposed to watch out for the bad guys and scare them away. Yet this time, I can't be her protector. I can't be her knight in shining armor. It hurts me very much, too, my dear. Very much! I am trying not to be angry with God. I have to trust Him. It's hard. But we both must!" Anna nodded her head, agreeing, "It is hard," she told him.

"Yes, it is," said JaMar.

Observing the weariness on her husband's face, she said, "JaMar, do you know what Zoe told me when I asked her about school?"

"No. What did she say?" he asked.

"She looked at me with her beautiful eyes and said, 'Now is not the time to think about school.' She told me she is waiting to hear from God before she does anything. She said He is quiet; therefore, she has to be quiet." Anna smiled and said, "Where did we ever get a child like Zoe? Where did she come from? Where did she get that much wisdom? You know I couldn't say anything. I told her I would wait quietly with her."

JaMar looked at his wife. "Well, Anna, we will wait quietly together. The Lord has this, and He has Zoe."

Getting frustrated again, Anna huffed, "Where is Jaheem? I thought he would be here by now. We haven't seen him since the hospital. I know his business is confidential, but he can allow at least one day to visit his sister. That son of mine is so unthoughtful?"

JaMar laughed, "Ahhhhhh. It's good to see you back, my dear."

A sudden knock on the bedroom door interrupted their conversation. "Yes!" They cried simultaneously. It was Naiijad. "I am sorry to bother you both, but a visitor is downstairs waiting to see you. He says it's urgent and that he must see you right away." "Who is he?" asked Anna. "I'm sorry, Ma'am, but he promised me not to say. He has someone with him. Another man." "Ok," replied JaMar. "Please tell the gentlemen we will be there shortly." Looking at his wife, he said, "It's probably the detectives wanting to follow up with some things. Let's freshen up before we go down, eh? You have mascara running down your face, and I need to wash my face with some cold water." Walking towards the bathroom to wash his face, JaMar wondered, "When will this ordeal stop?"

Naiijad closed the door and smiled. She was thankful that this time, the visit would not be like the last visit, full of doom and gloom when the detectives and the beautiful woman with them came to talk about Zoe. This visit will be a pleasant surprise. It's what the family needed. She went downstairs to inform the guest.

"They will be down shortly," she told one of the men. He was tall, with a cocoa chocolate complexion, and very handsome. With a wink, he grinned at her, "Did you tell them who it was?" Blushing, she smiled. He always had a way of making her smile, as if she was the most beautiful woman in all of Nairobi. "No, sir, I didn't," she said, grinning with her new teeth from the dentist. The man took notice and commented, "Looking good, Naja! I love your smile." Hearing the man use his pet name for her, she blushed again. "Thank you, sir!' She turned around and left the room, leaving the two men alone. She was happy that joy had come to the house.

The other man watched but didn't say a word. Looking around the room, he saw how exquisitely decorated it was. Even though the house was borderline massive, it had a homey feeling of charm and serenity. You could feel the love and warmth. He let out a small whistle, and turning to the man, he asked, "Will they be ok?" With a wink, the other man said, "Yes. No worries, my friend. I got this!" "Yes, but the last time you said I got this, I almost died," he said sarcastically. The man was about to reply but couldn't because of Anna's loud squeals as she and JaMar entered the room.

"Oh, my God! Son, you are home!" Anna screamed with delight as she rushed to hug her son. Moved with manly tears, JaMar waited until Anna had stopped hugging their son before he hugged him. Slapping Jaheem on the back with a father's manly hug, JaMar grabbed his son and hugged him with such a firm embrace that Jaheem almost started choking. JaMar was happy that his son was home at last. Trying not to cry, especially in front of the stranger, he silently thanked God for bringing his family home safely.

"When did you get home?" Anna asked, forgetting how only a few minutes ago she was upset with him for not calling or coming to see Zoe. Jaheem, glad to see his parents, replied, "I got in late last night. Where is Zoe?" he asked. "I can't wait to see her. I know she went through so much. Is she okay?" He knew he was rambling. The thought of his precious little sister going through such a traumatic ordeal made him almost burst into tears, but he didn't, no matter how much he wanted to. He was on business. He would cry later when everything was fine, but he had to take care of business first. He didn't want his sister to see anything else but the business side of him. He knew what he needed from her would be a lot. He needed to know if Zoe was too fragile to do what was needed of her. That's why he waited two weeks before he came home. He wanted to make sure she would have enough time to get some understanding. He knew how his little sister processed things. He had to wait until she could process everything that happened to her.

"Anna, knowing her son very well, knew he was rambling. She looked at him intuitively and said, "Zoe is well. She has good and bad days, but she is doing much better. She will be so happy to see you. It will make her smile, for they are far in between." Hugging him once again. After what they had been through, she didn't want her children to leave the house ever again.

Silent tears fell from her eyes as she hugged him harder. If only I could keep them both safe, thought Anna.

"Anna, don't suffocate the boy! He can't breathe!" cried JaMar. However, his voice was cheerful. Breaking the tension, everyone chuckled at the thought that the small but mighty woman could suffocate the tall, powerful man.

"Son, Zoe is fine!" JaMar reassured his son. "She is resilient. It will take time, but this will pass. I'm so glad and thankful you are here. With everything that has happened, it's good to see you home. We are one big happy family, regardless of what took place…" he looked away. "Regardless."

"Zoe is in the garden," said Anna. She sits there every day. Come on, we will go to her! She will be ecstatic to see you!" She then noticed the stranger standing patiently next to Jaheem. "Jaheem! Where are your manners? You have not introduced us to your friend."

Clearing his throat, Jaheem introduced the man to his parents, "Ahem, Dad, Mom, I'm not exactly here on holiday. I'm here on business. This is one of my partners. We need to talk to Zoe. I know you both wanted me to be here sooner. I waited until Zoe had time to grasp everything she went through. I know two weeks may not be enough time, but we must talk to her."

Raising his brows, "We?' asked JaMar.

"Yes, my partner and I, Dad. I can't give you his name yet. It's confidential. So, is it okay to talk with Zoe?"

"Will the nightmare end?" sighing, JaMar said under his breath, but everyone heard.

"Dad, Mom, it will be okay. I promise!"

Frustrated with the secrecy, Anna shrieked, "Jaheem, I thought you were here to visit your sister. Not on business. She needs you…." Knowing his wife was about to go on another rant, JaMar held out his hand, "Anna, let the boy do what he needs to do." Turning to his son, his eyes pleading, he asked "Son, is it alright if we sit in on this? She is our daughter. I don't want her to be troubled. She's been through enough."

Jaheem knew he couldn't say no by the looks on his parent's faces. Hoping he wouldn't regret his decision, he sighed, "Yes, it's okay, Father." He turned to his mother, "Mom, you have to promise you will be quiet and let me do what I need to do. Let me do all the talking. No matter what unfolds, the tears, the cries, you must let me speak to Zoe without interruptions or interference. I'm on important business! If you can't promise me you won't interrupt, then no, you can't be there when I speak to Zoe."

"We promise," JaMar said, his voice stern, glaring at his wife, "Don't we?"

Anna knew her husband meant business when he talked in that tone, "Yes, we promise not to say a word," she said.

"Good!" Jaheem replied, his voice filled with optimism, "Let's find Zoe. Where is she again?"

"In the garden! They both cried out.

"Ahhh, yes, brain freeze." Turning to the other man, "Are you ready?"

"Yes," he replied. He didn't know how things would unfold. He clung to a small ounce of hope everything would end well.

Chapter Thirty-Eight

The gentle breeze of the wind and the warmth of the sun's heat saturated Zoe's body as she sat meditating on the patio. She looked lovely in her white off the shoulder blouse and fashionably ripped blue jeans. Her mid-length hair flowed softly on her cocoa brown shoulders. She was a vision of beauty, wrapped in the tranquility of the garden, surrounded by an array of beautiful colors and aromas from the many flowers and plants. Gazing up into the blue sky, she looked like the Zoe from the past, a schoolgirl on holiday without a care in the world. She exhaled as she noticed a cloud covering the sun—one lonesome white cloud encompassed by the blueness of the sky as the sun's rays gleamed through it. Marveling at its beauty, she whispered, "Today is a good day. I won't cry today."

Since the day she came home, she thought a lot about the call to help in the fight against human sex trafficking. She thought of the rape, or incident as they called it. She thought about Patty, Alana, the little girl, and all the other girls she couldn't help, but Patty and the incident were constant on her mind. No matter how hard she tried to forget, they haunted her day and night. It helped that Camille called several times to check on her. Their conversation was soothing to her spirit. She never told Camille about the incident. She didn't want the woman to feel it was her fault. They mostly talked about Patty and the children at the village compound. They were praying for Patty, but so far, there was no word of her whereabouts.

Taking a sip of the ice-cold lemonade Isabella, their cook, put out for her, she heard her brother's voice from behind. Excited to see her big brother, with a smile, she quickly turned around. Stopping dead in her tracks, she gasped out loud. In front of her, standing next to her brother and parents, was the person who betrayed her and Patty. Kato! "You! You! What are you doing here? I thought you were dead! I will never forget that you raped me!" she screamed. Tears rushing from her eyes down her face, and just like that, the once beautiful day turned ugly. With accusing eyes, she turned to her brother, "Jaheem! How could you bring him here? He raped me!"

Jaheem moved quickly to his sister's side. "Zoe, please let me explain! You don't understand!" JaMar, stunned by his daughter's remarks, looked at the stranger with venom. His body flinched. Balling up his fist, he was ready to harm the man who hurt his daughter. Anna shrieked so loud that the servants came rushing out to the garden to see what had caused their mistress to scream as she did. Naiijad had hoped Jaheem's visit would be a pleasant surprise for the family, but upon viewing everyone's faces and seeing Zoe's eyes filled with tears, she knew that his visit would be anything but pleasant.

With Zoe's outburst, Anna's scream, and the servants running out as if someone had died, Jaheem turned to his parents; taking control, he sternly said, "Dad! Mom! You promised you would not interfere!" He addressed the servants in the same tone. "Naiijad, Isabella, Albeaze, we're fine! Zoe was shocked to see me. Everything is fine. Now, if you would please leave us! We are in the middle of something important!" The hurt in their eyes from his sternness and abrasive manner toward them was evident. They nodded, understanding that this was a family matter. Jaheem, sensing their hurt, quickly apologized. In a calmer voice, he said, "Please forgive me for being so abrupt. Everything's fine. Before they could ask if they wanted refreshments, he added, "Oh yes, please bring us some more cold lemonade and ice water. Thank you." He hadn't meant to be so stern with them, but he was on important business. He would explain to them later, but for now, he had to deal with Zoe.

Jaheem gently embraced his sister, giving her a big brotherly hug. Zoe, still infused with anger, clenched her fist. She didn't trust her brother; he brought the enemy into their home. Jaheem whispered into her ears, "I promise you, I will never allow anyone to hurt you. I love you 'Pumpkin Girl.'" Zoe eventually succumbed to his embrace. She knew when Jaheem used this term of endearment, he only meant it in love. "Do you trust me?" he asked her. No longer angry, she slowly nodded her head up and down, "Yes," she said softly.

"Good," replied Jaheem. "Here they come with the refreshments. We will talk when they leave."

Naiijad and Albeaze could feel the tension in the air. Curious about why everyone looked tensed, they took their time putting down the glasses and pitchers of cold lemonade and water. Albeaze inquired if they needed anything else. Jaheem nodded, "That will be all. Please close the door behind you." Seeing the love and concern in their eyes, he realized that they were part of their family. They loved them like family, and the feelings were mutual. With compassion, he said, "Thank you both. I promise all is well." Albeaze nodded and pulled Naiijad's sleeve; she was the nosy one. "Come on," he whispered. They went into the house and softly closed the door. When Jaheem heard the door close, he turned to the group, "Anyone for a cold drink? You may need it," he said as he poured himself a cold glass of water and refilled Zoe's glass with lemonade. "Sit," he told everyone. JaMar, Anna, and Kato sat down as instructed. Once everyone was seated, Jaheem sat down next to Zoe. "Well, where do we begin?" he asked.

"At the beginning," cried Anna. JaMar, taking his wife's hand, firmly squeezed it without making a sound. He shook his head letting his son know, "I trust you, and I have your mother under control."

Jaheem cleared his throat. "Yes, let's start at the beginning. But first, let me introduce you to one of our agents, Agent Braxton, or as you know him Zoe as Kato. Agent Braxton is from the South Africa Consul. We were working together on this project. It was an international undercover operation to expose and capture some of the most dangerous drug-human trafficking leaders in our country and the world. They were some of the most notorious people, and with the aid of you and others, Zoe, we captured and killed some of the leaders. We still have some prominent ones left, but the ones captured, we believe they will talk, exposing many more in the ring. You see, my dear sister, you did play a major role in helping fight the war against human trafficking."

Hearing that Jaheem knew how dangerous these men were, Zoe's heart filled with anger again. She couldn't believe her brother had jeopardized her life to capture someone. She shouted, "You set me up knowing I could've been killed! And now Patty may be dead! All because you wanted to get Seian! How could you, Jaheem?"

Hurt by his sister's accusation, Jaheem replied, "No, Zoe. Please let me explain. We did not set you up. Trust me! It was quite a surprise when I found out you were selected and not Camille. I immediately tried to get you off the mission, but I couldn't. We had invested so much time, effort, and money that a slight change would've made them suspicious. When I saw you at the store, I had hoped I could persuade you to go back home; you know how that went."

Agent Braxton looked at Zoe with a solemn smile, "It was supposed to be Camille, not you. In the end, we realized that Camille wasn't the best candidate. When you came along, persistent and strong-willed, the authorities thought you would be the perfect candidate. Something about your eyes that said 'pick me,' so we did. I didn't find out until we were at the store that you were Jaheem's little sister. By then, it was too late. The plan was in action, and the pickup was for that night. Jaheem and two other men were watching from the back of the store. When he saw you, he was extremely upset. He sent a note to the storekeeper to give to me. The storekeeper put the note in the bag. In the note Jaheem begged me to take care of you and do whatever had to be done to protect you. When he came out that day, he came from the back of the store. Also, I was looking at him when you saw me looking back in the hotel. He was there in the back watching. I nodded, promising him I would, even if it meant slapping you around a bit. I didn't enjoy that part of the job, but I had to keep my cover.

I apologize for hitting you. I'm sorry."

"Was Camille in on this too?" Zoe asked. "I trusted her."

"No," said Jaheem. "Camille still doesn't know the true nature of Agent Braxton. Before working in this field, she and Kato, as she knows him, were once romantically involved, so we decided it wouldn't be good for them to work together. She liked him more than he did her.

Not sure why he was defending himself, Agent Braxton clearing his throat blurted out, "But in my defense Zoe, we had a summer fling years ago." Still not trusting him, Zoe felt somewhat relieved by his comments about his relationship with Camille, but she didn't know why. "Oh, ok, she replied," still trying to process everything. Sitting across from her was the man whom she had first trusted, now somewhat despised because, in the end, he had to rape her to ensure their survival.

"Zoe," Agent Braxton said, "Camille knew little about the plan. Believe me, if she knew your life was going to be in such danger, she would not have let you or Patty go with me."

"Patty, I almost forgot! What about Patty? Zoe asked?"

"Patty is alright. She a little banged up, but she's okay," said Jaheem. "We were able to get her from the person who purchased her. He was one of the leader's right hand men. Unfortunately, he was killed in the struggle." Zoe could feel her temper rising again. "Do you mean to tell me you both put us in danger with one of the top ring leaders? What if they had killed us? "No, Zoe, no!" Jaheem reassured her, "We had you covered at all times. One of Seian's top men turned against him. He was the mole. That's how we finally infiltrated the organization and got in with Seian. The mole's conscience was getting the best of him. We connected him to Kato or Agent Braxton. He recommended Agent Braxton to Alana, who informed Seian about him. Seian trusted the mole, so we had to wait until everything was perfect for Seian to accept Agent Braxton. It took some time because Seian did his homework. Our international team turned Kato, umm, Agent

Braxton into a true villain."

"Yes," Agent Braxton added, "We were a real life James Bond movie. Once Seian said yes, we were in. The little girl was the perfect opportunity to get him. We knew Seian was only in the business for the money. He didn't partake in the raping of the girls…if I may be so, ummm forward. He was known for his brutality but not for ….ummm you know what I mean." He didn't want to spell it out for her in front of her parents. After all, she was still…, he didn't finish his thought due to Zoe's loud interruption.

"But he was going to rape me!"

"Yes! That's why I had to shoot him," said Agent Braxton.

Shocked, Zoe asked, "You were the one who shot him?"

"Yes," he said, gazing into her eyes. "It was to my surprise when I had come back from securing the little girl that Seian was about to harm you. That wasn't his norm. It took a while to secure the girl because she was frightened and didn't trust anyone. I didn't lie when I told Seian I had to sedate her to keep her from screaming. The young servant girl, Selah, assisted me when she found out who I was. They are both free now. Seian had already killed Alana, so I had to act fast. I knew he didn't have a problem with killing anyone who posed a threat. I promised your brother that I wouldn't let anything happen to you. I didn't want to face him if something did. When I got back and saw Seian was suspicious of Agent Thomas, I knew I had to move quickly. Agent Thomas wasn't prepared to shoot anyone. His job was to get you safely out of there. Like I said, Seian is, or was, a smart man. He knew something was amiss; luckily for me, you pulled out your gun, causing his attention to focus on you instead of Agent Thomas. It gave me enough time to sneak up behind and shoot him while he was on the couch with you. You didn't see me because you were going to shoot him. What were your words, 'If I am to die, I'm taking someone with me.'" Grinning, he said, "If the situation weren't so dire, I would've burst into laughter. My little Zoe was fighting to the end. Not afraid and ready to take someone with her. You were brave, dear one, very brave." Catching himself for getting too personal, he cleared his voice.

JaMar, watching the man's posture with his daughter, mumbled, "Hmmm. There is something here," he thought. "But no matter if he saved his daughter, he was the one who took from her.

Zoe, remembering everything, said, "I was frightened. I prayed, and then I had a peace. Then, lowering her head, she whispered, "Tell me something, please..."

"Yes," replied her brother, "Anything."

"Was Alana an agent too?" She said it so low they could hardly hear her words.

Zoe's eyes portrayed the sadness she felt toward the woman. Understanding his sister's compassion for the slain woman, Jaheem attempted to comfort her. Carefully watching his words, he gently told her, "No. Alana was not. If Seian hadn't killed her, she would've been in jail for the rest of her life. Alana knew everything Seian was doing. She was an accomplice. She made a choice, and that choice killed her."

"I believe," interrupted Agent Braxton, "She was changing or wanted to change. When she met you and saw how good and compassionate you were, I believe she wanted to change her life. Also, the little girl didn't help. She assisted him with many girls in the past, but this was different. The child's age made her see the harsh reality of what they were doing. She came to herself and didn't want to do it anymore. Like your brother said, sadly, other than jail, death was her only way out. Seian would've killed her eventually. She wasn't his first, and if he hadn't died, she wouldn't be the last to succumb to death under him. He was a cruel man."

"Yes," Zoe said quietly, taking everything in. She knew now it was a good time to ask about the incident, and she had to ask in front of her family. Although things were different than perceived. She understood why Kato did what he did, but she still had to ask him the dreaded question despite everything he told her. With boldness and courage from within, looking directly into his eyes, she asked the man she knew as Kato, not Agent Braxton, "Why did you have to rape me?" With that, the once dried tears started flowing down her face.

Staring into her eyes, Agent Braxton hesitated before answering her. *It's her eyes! There's something about Zoe's eyes. Her eyes saw truth.* He knew from the beginning when he'd first met her, her eyes pierced into places, deep places that few could see. She had a special discernment to see things clearly. *The things God showed her. She was God's child, and her eyes brought forth that truth.* Agent Braxton cleared his throat, carefully considering what he was about to say. He knew he was in the presence of her father and brother. "Zoe," he said tenderly, "I didn't rape you. I never touched you. Not as a man would a woman. I didn't rape or touch Patty either. I had to rip your blouse and bruise your inner thighs to make them believe that I touched you."

Shocked and relieved she wasn't raped, Zoe was still puzzled. No longer caring who was in the midst, it was as if she and Kato, not Agent Braxton, were the only two on the patio, "What about the pain in my stomach and the blood between my thighs?" she asked him.

"Zoe," he said with compassion in his eyes, "I had to knee you in your stomach hard enough to knock the wind out of you but not hard enough to do damage. When you were knocked out, I cut my arm to pretend that you scratched me and placed my blood between your thighs. Gross, I know! But at that moment, I did what I had to do. The blood on the sheets was the blood from your arm when you fell off the chair when I slapped you. I didn't know if Alana was okay with not exposing me to Seian. I could see she was starting to change, but she was still terrified of him. The young girl, Selah, who was assigned to wash you up, was also frightened. I couldn't trust her at all. When they saw the blood, the bruises, and your torn shirt, it validated my story and affirmed to Seian I was on his side."

Anna inwardly gasped at the realization that Zoe didn't realize she wasn't raped. *Zoe doesn't know a man intimately,* she thought. *She always* assumed Zoe knew. They had talked somewhat about the subject but not as much as they should have. Grateful that her daughter was still pure, she knew she had to sit down and talk with her about the facts of life, and very soon! Coming to grips with her daughter's innocence in the ways between a man and woman, under her breath, she thanked God for keeping her daughter from the cruelties of sex trafficking.

Embarrassed at her lack of knowledge on the subject, Zoe blushed. "That is why Alana looked at me funny when I said my stomach ached. When she looked between my legs and saw the bruises and blood on my inner thighs, I quess she believed I was raped because she left me alone. She began to weep, "All this time I just assumed."

Knowing it was his fault she had gone through so much pain, Agent Braxton wanted to comfort her but decided against it. He saw her father giving him a strange, stern look. "How would you know Zoe?" he said to her. "It's nothing to be ashamed or embarrassed about." Watching the two intermingle, JaMar was relieved his daughter wasn't raped but still didn't trust Agent Braxton. The young man appeared to be fond of his daughter. JaMar wasn't ready to release her yet. He just got her back.

"I feel so foolish," she whispered.

Jaheem, impatient with Agent Braxton and Zoe's small talk, cried out, "Zoe, no, you were not raped, but please listen! We have something important to ask of you. We hope you don't say no, but if you say yes, you must tell your story. And it won't be to a few."

"What is it?" she asked.

"We need your voice." He told her. "We need you to tell your story to the United Nations Council. Tell them about the evils of human sex trafficking; tell them what happened to you. Many world leaders will be there to hear your story. They need to know how brutal and cruel human and sex trafficking is. We are fighting a battle, but we are losing because many don't believe what horrible situations these innocent young victims are trapped in. Many believe these victims choose this life of sexual promiscuity because of their poverty or because they want to. They don't believe they're violently forced into this world. We are gaining ground, but there is much more ground to cover. We need you, baby sister. There will be others; you won't be alone, but we need you, too!"

Troubled by her brother's request of what he was asking her to do, Zoe cried, "You are asking me to tell all these strangers about what happened to me and what I saw! What they did to me. Jaheem, I can't! I just can't! It's too painful. They treated me worse than a dog! I was nothing but a piece of fresh meat to them—less of a human, a commodity. I know now I wasn't raped, but the thought of being raped! You have no idea what I've been going through! I can't share this! How could you ask this of me, Jaheem?"

Agent Braxton interrupted, "Zoe, it is needed of you! Think of Alana, Patty, the little girl, and the others. Yes, they treated you like you were less than a human, and you could've been raped. But you weren't raped. You are free. You are safe, home in your parent's beautiful house, sipping ice-cold lemonade on the patio. Think of the many that are not. We saved you, Patty, and the little girl, but think of the many we can't save. We need your voice! It's your destiny, your call! I know you were studying abroad at John Hopkins, but look at it this way. No school, regardless of its prestige, could prepare you for this. Only God can! Zoe, this is your destiny!"

"You sound like Mordecai!" Zoe shrieked.

Agent Braxton looked puzzled, "Who? What? Mordecai! Who is Mordecai?" he asked.

Jaheem, with a heavy groan, dryly informed his partner, "Mordecai, my friend, is in the book of Esther in the Bible. When Mordecai, Ether's uncle, told her that she was the one called by God to tell the King what Haman was trying to do to the Jews, he told her that if she didn't, God would raise up another, but she would die." Jaheem, slightly irritated, said, "Zoe, we are not Mordecai, and you are not Esther, but we do need your voice. I know you well enough to know that you know what you went through was not in vain. You know in your heart there is more for you to do."

Zoe inhaled. She was torn between doing the right thing and the fear trying to overtake her. Letting out a loud exhale, she looked at her parents, then her brother, and finally at the man she knew as Kato, not Agent Braxton. Shaking her head in total surrender, she said, "I know! I know! I was sitting in the garden meditating. I couldn't hear His Voice, so I waited patiently and quietly. But I've never been so frightened. You want me to speak about sex trafficking? It sounds so surreal! I don't know what to say or do."

"Yes, you can, Zoe!" Anna, no longer able to be quiet, spoke up. "You have to answer the call and speak for the ones who do not have a voice. You are the voice in the wilderness." Jaheem didn't say a word about his mother's outburst. For once, he was thankful for her butting in. Zoe looked at her mother, "Mother, do you realize what you are saying? What about medical school?"

"Yes, I do," said Anna. "This is more important than medical school." Anna used the same analogy Zoe used on her about dropping out of medical school, "And look at it this way, you will be saving lives."

"Zoe," her father said, "Remember how you capture a city? You take one building at a time. You are about to capture a city."

Still a little hesitant about speaking in front of so many world leaders, Zoe finally agreed to their request. "I'll go. I'll speak. But, Jaheem, you must tell me what I must do and you both must be there with me."

"We will on both accounts," Kato and Jaheem said simultaneously, their voices filled with relief and excitement. Relieved, both men sat back in their chairs, looked at each other and grinned. "I'm so happy you said yes, Zoe," said Jaheem. She winked at her brother, "Did I have a choice?" He winked back, "Nope! You didn't. Although I was worried you would say no. I know you've been through a lot. Even though what you thought happened didn't, the reality is what it did to you will help others understand." Slapping his hands on his lap, Jaheem, grateful everything went as planned, hugged his sister. "We will let you rest, my sister. Next week we will start preparing you for the biggest audience you will ever have to speak to. And they will hear you, Zoe!" Agent Braxton nodded his head, agreeing with Jaheem, his voice filled with genuine admiration, he said, "Your eyes will tell the story."

Zoe blushed.

JaMar saw how his daughter reacted to the man's words. "Well, wonders do exist. Our daughter blushes." He still didn't trust the agent.

Jaheem was elated the outcome was positive, and they could soon start preparing Zoe. He asked his parents, "Father, Mother, do you have any questions? "They both said no. "Good! I'm starved!" said Jaheem. "Shall we go and get something to eat?" Satisfied, they rose from their seats and walked toward the door. Agent Braxton called out to them as they were about to open the door, "I will be with you in a moment. I want to speak with Zoe privately." Noticing JaMar's stare, he quickly said, "I promise, sir, I would not do anything to hurt her. I want to apologize to her in private."

"Ok," said JaMar in a stern voice, "Don't take too long. The sun is about to get hotter." That was his cue to the agent that he was still in charge. Agent Braxton understood what JaMar implied. "Yes, Sir," he replied.

Watching them leave, closing the door behind them, Zoe felt uncomfortable with the man she knew as Kato. She wondered what he wanted to say to her that he couldn't say in front of her family. Watching him through her lashes, she studied him. Agent Braxton seemed more poised and confident than Kato. Not wanting to stay in his company too long, she asked, "What would you like to say to me? I believe we said everything we needed to say." Agent Braxton, hoping his words convey his true feelings and apologies for what he did, cleared his voice and began to speak. "Zoe, I'm sorry you had to go through what you did. Trust me, had I foreseen Seian hurting you in any manner, I would've never left you alone with him. It was out of his character. I wish you hadn't gone through any of it, especially seeing Alana shot and killed. It was unfortunate that you had to witness the brutality of the world of sex trafficking."

"Yes," said Zoe, her voice low, remembering everything that had happened. "As far as Alana, I prayed for her. Two days before they came to get me we had a long talk. Kato, I mean Agent Braxton, I believe she wanted to change. She wasn't proud of her choices or life up to that point. By the way, thank you for not raping me,"she mumbled. She was relieved she kept her vow but was embarrassed that she didn't know she wasn't raped. Feeling uncomfortable, she looked down at her feet. Agent Braxton knowing it was uncomfortable for her to talk about the topic, gently said, "Always know, Zoe, when a woman is touched in her most sacred place, as I like to call it to keep you from blushing, she will know. Whether it was intentionally or unintentionally, she would know. Trust me. When it is your time," he spoke in a low, husky voice, "That man will be very, very fortunate and blessed." Blushing, Zoe shyly said, "Thank you! Thank you for everything. The slaps hurt, but as you said, you were doing your job."

"Yes, but I also feared your brother's wrath," he laughed. "Come on, we better go join the rest of them before your father comes out and kills me with his stares."

"You are funny," she laughed. "My father would not hurt a fly."

"Maybe not a fly, but anyone who hurts his daughter, trust me, he will."

He rose from the chair and helped her from hers. They walked to the door slowly, each not saying a word. Kato could smell the amber vanilla scent coming from her body. "Ummm!" he smiled.

Zoe, feeling the closeness of his presence, knew she was safe. They have been through a lot in a short time. She was ready for the future and what God was preparing for her.

Chapter Thirty-Nine

Zoe waited patiently for the Council to call her in to speak about her role in the fight against sex trafficking. As she waited, the hallow, partially empty hallway was her solace. Thinking she had several months to prepare, she was caught off guard when Jaheem notified her that the Council wanted to hear from her sooner. The Council was eager to hear from individuals directly involved in the fight against sex trafficking, so they pushed it up by a month. As the day approached, the thought of speaking to world leaders and telling them her story was overwhelming. Lacking confidence, she tried several times to back out. On the day she was to go to Vienna, Austria, she became nauseous as her parents drove her to the airport. Anna saw that Zoe was apprehensive about speaking to the Council. She put her arm around her daughter and gently said, "Speak the truth, Zoe. Speak what's in your heart. God will take care of the rest."

For Zoe, it wasn't that easy. Although she didn't experience the physical trauma so many had, emotionally, she still dealt with the aftermath of seeing Alana killed and the almost reality of being raped and trafficked. Nothing prepared her nerves on the day she was scheduled to speak to the Council. It was more challenging than perceived, and she wished she hadn't agreed to tell her story. Rarely unglued under pressure and not easily lost for words; when she went over her notes she couldn't comprehend the words on the paper.

Agent Braxton, or Kato, as she found out was his real name, made sure she was comfortable. Even though he was there on business for the South African Consul, he sat with her until it was time for him to leave. He got her a cup of coffee and a sweet bun to ease her mind. Neither was in the mood for serious conversation. To occupy time, they talked about Vienna's beautiful countryside. Zoe was fortunate. She was familiar with some of the city's landmarks. She had traveled to the country with her parents several times when they had to speak at global medical conferences. In the past, when she attended the conferences, she would spend time at the hotel, relaxing by the pool reading a book. This time she was the speaker, not her parents. And although everyone agreed it was best for JaMar and Anna to stay home, Zoe wished they were with her now. She needed her parents for comfort and strength. Taking a deep breath, attempting to calm her nerves, she could feel the sweat seeping through her blouse. It didn't help that it was hot and stuffy. She doubled doused with deodorant but now wondered if it was enough. Deep in thought, she didn't hear Agent Braxton telling her he was leaving to go and sit in the area designated for his country.

"Zoe, are you listening? I must leave now, but I will be with you when you speak. I'm proud of you?"

"Huh?" she stammered, struggling to comprehend what he was saying.

"I have to leave," he said again.

"Must you?" She didn't want to be alone. "I could use a friend while I wait. My nerves are shot, and I must confess, I am not as confident as I appear to be," she smiled, hoping he didn't see the anxiety in her eyes.

"You will be fine," he assured her. "Once you get started, you will be okay. They will be drawn to you. Your eyes will tell your story." He kissed her gently on the cheek and got up. From a distance, Camille watched the two. She saw the way Kato looked at the young woman and how he stayed at her side. She knew he would never look at her the way he did Zoe. With a heavy sigh, she went inside the room. She was also there to speak on her organization's role in the war against human trafficking and sex trafficking.

Now alone, Zoe sat staring into the abyss, her mind a battleground of nerves and determination. Her thoughts were on the man who just kissed her. His gentle kiss moved her more than she wanted to admit. Shaking her head back and forth to regain composure, she said, "I must focus. I'm here to speak of something of the utmost importance." Looking down at her white blouse and tailored black skirt suit, she blurted out, "Ughhh! It's too hot to wear black and definitely too hot for stockings." She would have preferred to wear one of her more colorful or pastel suits. They were more appropriate for the warm weather, but the dress protocol was necessary when addressing the Council. She looked down again. Taking the napkin she used to put her half-eaten sweet bun in, she brushed the imaginary wrinkles off her skirt with a determined flick of her wrist. She was busy brushing her skirt, she didn't see the figure standing before her. Seeing her view blocked, she quickly looked up and let out a small squeal.

"Patty! Oh, my God! You're here! Look at you! You are safe and here!"

Zoe, excited at seeing her friend safe and standing before her, started crying tears of joy. Patty grinned and sat down beside her. The two hugged for what seemed an eternity. Finally letting go, Zoe spoke first. "What? How? When?" Seeing her friend again and thinking about all they had been through, she cried, "Oh, Patty, I thought I had lost you forever. Especially when they told me you were sold. There is so much to tell you!" She knew she was rambling but didn't care. Patty laughed. "Slow down, Zoe! Slow down! It's so good to see you! Girl, who would've thought we were part of a sting operation! Like a James Bond movie for real." Zoe smiled, wiping her nose. It was just like Patty, she thought, so American and so full of dramatics. She was glad her friend was safe.

"Zoe, I thought our paths would never meet again!"

"Patty, the last I heard you were gone. Agent…I mean, Kato's words were Patty gone. I could've punched him right then and there, hard, too! Now I know he was on our side all the while."

"I know!" shrieked Patty. "Never would've imagined that he was one of the good guys all along! I thought he raped me. I found out later that he only drugged me to keep his cover. Too bad I had to stab him!"

"Oh yes, I do recall him telling me you stabbed him. Well, it was good you did! Served him right! At the time, I thought he went to the other side, the dark force." At her choice of words describing Kato, they began to giggle like two little schoolgirls. The guard glanced over at them with a stern look, and like two naughty kids getting caught with their hands in the cookie jar, they quieted down.

"What happened," Zoe asked.

"Well, they did attempt to sell me to some guy from the Middle East, but they intercepted him and his men, and bam, the last thing I knew, he was killed and I was rescued. I tell you something, he wouldn't been able to do anything for a while. I still had my shield, so I stabbed him in the groin," she burst into laughter again.

"Patty, you didn't?" Zoe howled, bursting into laughter. No longer concerned with the guard's stern stares, the thought of Patty stabbing her kidnapper in his private parts made them laugh even harder. "Zoe, I was banged up a little. At one time I thought I was a goner. They blacked my eye. I fought back. They broke my wrist, see?" She showed Zoe her wrist. It was still in a small cast. Seeing the cast, Zoe, moved with compassion of hearing about her friend's unfortunate events, asked, "Does it still hurt?" Patty moved her wrist around to let Zoe see it was much better. "Not as much now. It hurt so much in the beginning I almost cursed like a sailor."

Zoe smiled, remembering how Patty hated swearing.

"Zoe," she said solemnly, "Lizzie is dead. She OD." Patty looked away.

"Oh, Patty, I am sad to hear the news of your friend."

They had been through so much. Each had a different story, yet their stories were the same. "Yes," she replied. "The good news is that the authorities were able to track her down. Can you believe it? She was finally located in some country in South America. Although decomposed, her body was sent back to her parents for a decent burial and closure." Patty turned away. "Zoe, we did all we could do for Lizzie. I know this now. I no longer feel guilty about leaving her alone with that guy. I have peace. I'm just thankful we could save the little girl and, hopefully, others like her. This is our destiny, our crusade. We are like the Avengers!" Zoe smiled. It was so good to have Patty back. She was still the same ole' Patty. Despite all that she suffered, she didn't lose her zeal or spontaneous personality.

"Zoe, I am going to speak to the council, too. We are both going to share our stories and make a difference. I am going to tell them about Lizzie and even how I stabbed a man." She grinned. "We are fortunate that we are making a difference."

Zoe looked into her friend's eyes and said, "I was nervous, even frightened. I didn't know if I had the confidence to do this. With you here, now I know I can. We can. You are right, Patty. For such a time as this, we are chosen by God. I'm no longer afraid because I know this is what I am supposed to do. With you at my side, and me at your side, we are not Batman or Robin; we are Zoe and Patty, ebony and ivory, a force to be reckoned with…."

"Umm hmm," coughed Jaheem, letting her know he was there. "Zoe, the Council is ready for you. They will hear your voice now." He put his hand out for her. Zoe graciously accepted his hand. She winked at Patty as she got up, "It is time, Captain Patty!"

Patricia Rose Miller," Jaheem called Patty by her full name, "They are ready for you, too." Patty didn't wait for Jaheem's hand. She immediately rose from her seat. "Let's do this!" she cried out. The three of them walked toward the massive door. The guard who had moments ago reprimanded them with a stern look now bowed down at the three as he opened the door for them. Walking into the room, they saw rows of people from many walks of life and nationalities staring at them. From her peripheral view, she saw Agent Braxton nodding his head. Taking a deep breath, Zoe looked up at the ceiling and whispered, "Thank you, Father."

The Council representative greeted them and directed Zoe to the podium. She was the first to speak. Zoe walked to the podium, no longer anxious. She knew her confidence didn't come from her. It came from within. She looked at the crowd. They looked eagerly at her, waiting to hear her words. She noticed everyone wore black or dark blue suits. She smiled. Her eyes locked on the audience. "Good morning, distinguished men and women of the U.N. Council. My name is Zoe Zakiya Armani. Here is my story."

Behind the staircase, shielded from everyone's view, a man watched the entire scene. Hidden in the far corner, he saw the young woman and the man sitting on the bench. As the man comforted the woman, he knew the man was in love with the woman. He saw the other woman looking from a distance, watching the two before entering the guarded room. He watched the two young women reconnect like old friends, laughing like silly schoolchildren. He grinned as the guard frowned at them. "Let them laugh," he said softly under his breath. "They had been through so much it was time for them to laugh." He saw the other man come to get the two. He watched the three walk through the door as the guard, who frowned at the two women, now bowed before closing the door after them. His job was done. He was tired. He could finally get some much needed rest for the first time in a long time. Everyone he knew who could prevent his rest was either dead or behind bars for the rest of their lives.

For Kosi, it was the price to pay for being a mole. He could tell his friend Laos it was time to go to the beach and enjoy life.

From the Author

I wasn't aware of the magnitude of human sex trafficking before writing this book. Like many, I was oblivious to the truth or statistics on human sex trafficking. I had heard about it on the news. I saw some celebrities talking about it, and some endorsed the cause, but that was the extent of my knowledge. It didn't hit home because it didn't affect my world. All that changed in the Spring of 2017 when the Lord woke me up from my slumber and gave me the story "Zoe's Eyes." In the beginning, I wanted to call it the "Long Journey Home," yet as the story evolved, I knew it was about one woman's destiny to assist in the fight against human sex trafficking.

As for the storyline, it has redundancies. I did this intentionally, particularly when discussing the horrors of human sex trafficking and how we view the poor and underserved. I wanted these things embedded in your thoughts so you won't look at this as another good story but view it as what the book depicts: the evil brutalities of this ugly, dark world of human sex trafficking. Hopefully, you will partner with us in the fight and also intercede in prayer for the victims and for it to end.

Even though there may have been a hint of a possible love connection, "Zoe's Eyes" is not a love story. The book is about sex trafficking. There is nothing glamorous about sex trafficking, but I added some what-ifs to make it less sorrowful. Also, the book doesn't read from chapter to chapter. It reads in a series of events because everyone is affected when a person is trafficked. I wanted to convey this message and make people see this reality. Finally, someone asked me about the little girl and why I didn't give her a name. She has a name. Every person trafficked is her name. Also, why did I select Baltimore and Nairobi as my backdrop places? I am from Baltimore, Maryland, and I love my city. As for Kenya, after much research, and believe me, I did a lot of research, I decided to make the storyline coming from Kenya. I have been to Nairobi, Kenya. It's a beautiful country with beautiful people. Yet, in all its beauty, human sex trafficking exists.

The Lord doesn't use one voice. He uses many voices. Mine is a voice in print to speak to many who, like me, never realized the depths and harsh realities of sex trafficking. With my voice and your voice, we can make a difference. Our prayers and support can cause many to be saved from the snares of trafficking. My mother always said, "If you don't stand for something, you'll fall for anything." She also said, which I live by, "If you are not part of the solution, you are part of the problem." How do these two relate? Get involved and let someone know you care. I am paraphrasing this, but the message is the same: Am I my sister's keeper? Yes, I am.

For every book sold, I will donate thirty percent (30%) of that sale to fight against human sex trafficking.

****

Sex trafficking or slavery is the exploitation of women and children, within national or across international borders, for the purposes of forced sex work. Commercial sexual exploitation includes pornography, prostitution, and sex trafficking of women and girls, and is characterized by the exploitation of a human being in exchange for goods or money. Each year, an estimated 800,000 women and children are trafficked across international borders—though additional numbers of women and girls are trafficked within countries.

There is no official estimate of the total number of human trafficking victims in the U.S. Polaris estimates that the total number of victims nationally reaches into the hundreds of thousands when estimates of both adults and minors and sex trafficking and labor trafficking are aggregated.

https://polarisproject.org/human-trafficking/facts
https://polarisproject.org/human-trafficking/sex-trafficking

#Get InvolvedStop HumanTrafficking

National Human Trafficking Hotline 1 (1888) 373-7888